THE PROTE

Jenna Lincoln

ENDLESS CARNAGE. ENDLESS QUESTIONS.

Mara is a 17-year-old soldier who's spent years fighting a war that's lasted generations. Wide-eyed children, some just turned thirteen, rarely survive their first fights, despite her best efforts to train and lead them. What she thinks she wants is to uncover the root causes of the war between the Protectors and the masked Gaishan, maybe find a way to end it. But what she really wants is a future—for herself and the others—beyond the battlefield.

Then she's injured in combat, and when an enemy fighter not only heals her wounds but reveals his face, she sees the promise of all she desires. This cunning teen Gaishan has answers to her questions, but first she must commit treason and travel beyond the boundaries of her world. She must brave a place where everything rests on the point of a blade: her loyalties, her friends, her heart.

THE PROTECTOR PROJECT

Jenna Lincoln

www.BOROUGHSPUBLISHINGGROUP.com

THE PROTECTOR PROJECT
Copyright © 2015 Jennifer Gottschalk

ISBN 978-1942886-50-1

This book is dedicated to all the strong and beautiful women in my life: mothers, daughters, aunts, sisters, and friends.

CONTENTS

THE PROTECTOR PROJECT

Chapter 1

Mara stared down the line of her fellow Protectors. Only the youngest faces looked back at her. Anyone over fifteen watched the trees.

"Helmets," she called. The Gaishan would emerge soon, silent as the first evening shadows.

Nudging her horse through the ranks to the newest fighters, she wondered how many would be lost tonight. At seventeen, she wasn't the oldest fighter in her cohort, but she'd earned the right to lead and she meant to do it well. She stopped in front of a brother and sister from her level-one combat class. Both clutched long staffs. Both faces were blotchy with fear.

"Trust your training," Mara said. When the two children just stared at her with wide amber eyes, she leaned out of the saddle. "Keep your staff between you and the enemy. If they hit you with powder, if you're cut or touched with a weapon, run for the edge of the fight and don't let anyone near, not even family, until a healer clears you."

The small girl cast a worried look at her brother. "Yes, ma'am."

Mara made her way back to the center aisle and stood up on the stirrups. This, plus her own nearly two meters in height, provided a view of the entire cohort. "Check stripes!"

Crystalline energy shields bloomed and encased each fighter. Green stripes lit up along both shoulders of every person's uniform, one stripe for each year fighting.

"There're six hundred Protectors out here tonight. And a hundred fifty is us, the Greens," she yelled.

Someone in the middle rows whooped. A few laughed.

"We got a lot of new fighters with us. First fight," Mara continued.

The standing soldiers shuffled like rows of plants in the wind. "First fight" repeated along the lines.

"And after, when they're testing and checking and counting, I want one hundred and fifty Greens back at camp. Are we clear?"

"Ma'am" and "yes, ma'am" echoed through the ranks.

Mara stared at her soldiers for a moment before nodding and turning to view the rest of the troops spread out to the north and south of their position. The scrubby field easily held their full force with room to maneuver. Rough with dirt clods and clumps of grass, it wasn't great for footing, but their shields worked better in the clear than in the trees. This part of the Protected Territory had been designated for crops, but the explosive growth of the native plant life and the never-ending Gaishan raids prevented farming.

She'd seen the maps, had the boundaries and disputed territory explained, but it was hard to fight for land that would never be used. None of it made sense, not the battles, not the enemy's behavior, and certainly not the ongoing losses. A phantom itch between her shoulder blades, right where the latest whip marks were fading, was a clear reminder of the last time she'd voiced doubts. Her best option was to lead well and save as many as she could.

"Stand tall!" she yelled, venting frustration with the battle cry.

"Stand fast!" the group responded.

"Like you mean it, Greens!" Mara jabbed at the sky with her sword. "Protectors!"

"Stand tall!"

"Protectors!" she shouted alone.

"Stand fast!" The final yell rang fierce and resolute.

Along the battlefield, the other cohorts—Blue, Yellow, and Red—shouted with their leaders. Shoulder stripes glowed faintly with the corresponding colors.

As if answering the calls, masked fighters scuttled from the woods, moving into a horizontal formation at least two or three deep and stretching as far along the battlefield as the small force of teenagers.

"Steady!" Mara raised her sword high, swallowing the all-too-familiar battle dread. The Greens had the center of the line tonight, so the "go" signal was hers to give.

The enemy crept forward.

They always started slowly.

As soon as she could distinguish the gruesome features of a single Gaishan mask, Mara dropped her arm and yelled, "Protect the settlements!"

Urging her horse into a gallop, she used the momentum to kick and strike the first wave of Gaishan, until she was a living wedge splitting the shallow formation. Mara whirled on her horse, delivering overhead strikes, uppercuts, and side strikes, felling or disabling every enemy within reach. The cold field rang with the sounds of metal crashing against metal, against wood, against flesh. The sounds echoed, slamming into the memories of the last skirmish and the ones before that.

"Mara!"

The notes of terror in the scream brought instant focus.

Just south of their original position, a group of the tall, humanoid enemy surrounded a handful of the smallest Greens.

"Hold your shields!" Icy fear wrapped around her chest. She willed the trapped children to obey. "Protectors to me!"

She fought toward the cluster of outnumbered soldiers. One of the youngest fighters fell, shrieking and clutching his eyes. Then another doubled over retching, only to be bludgeoned on the back of her head. Their weak shields slowed the blows but didn't stop them completely. Several experienced Green fighters joined her as she charged away from the ground they had been ordered to hold.

Mara drove her horse the last few meters to the circle trapping her soldiers, slashing at enemy necks, torsos, and hands with her short sword as she went. She kicked from the saddle screaming in rage and cut her way into the Gaishan circle, planting herself and her shield in front of the fallen children. Other Protectors took on the Gaishan in pairs, some fighting from horseback with swords or staffs, most fighting on the ground, until the rest of the attackers scattered back into the battle.

"Take these two to the rear," Mara ordered the nearest soldier, trying to ignore the flinch from one fourteen-year-old and the panicked sobs of another. "Go!"

She remounted and rode out a few lengths, trying to get a sense of the larger fight. In the near dark, the dull red leather of the Protector uniforms blurred against the Gaishan black and gray. Mara shook her head and swore. Almost half the Green cohort was out of position. She put one hand to her mouth, attempting the two-note whistle that would remind the troops to check formation.

A mounted Gaishan burst around her flank, swinging its sword in a broad arc. Mara and her horse couldn't change direction quickly enough and the end of the blow bit deep into her thigh.

Stunned by the burning pain of the open wound, Mara dropped heavily onto the other stirrup. Her mare, interpreting the physical shift as a command, galloped toward the southern fringe of the battle.

Vision blurring, she twisted in the saddle, trying to assess the fight, and nearly fell into a tree as her horse steered them through a row of saplings and into the woods.

Agony disrupted Mara's ability to maintain her energy shield. Dizzy and nauseated, she pulled off her helmet and tried not to vomit. With one hand, she soothed her horse; with her other hand, she pressed hard on the gash. Hot blood trickled into her boot.

A Gaishan stepped out from the trees. Its hand came down next to hers, brushing Mara's fingers and the wound.

"Don't touch me!" she yelled.

The figure pulled off the Gaishan mask to reveal a human face, young and male. His smile was grim. "Mara, you were out of position."

Mara's breath stopped. She stared into the Gaishan's silver-gray eyes, felt the tremor of magic cross from his fingers into the torn flesh of her leg. The air shimmered and shrank, enclosing them. He was light haired and tall, not much older than any of the Protectors. The pain eased and the burning tapered to a mild sting.

"Your questions have answers. But you're asking the wrong people," he said.

She threw a punch at his mask-less face, but the Gaishan blocked it, trapping her hand.

His smile relaxed into a grin and he leaned closer. "One of the answers is, this isn't your fight." He slapped her horse on the rear, propelling them back to the field.

As several Protectors rushed toward her, Mara held out her still-tingling palm and shouted, "Did you see the Gaishan? I've been touched! Stay away!" Though the worst of the pain was gone, now that she'd been exposed to possible contagion, she couldn't risk anyone on the field, even fighting at a distance. With one last glance at the fight, she turned toward the healers' tent.

#

Hours later, Mara's horse clattered into the dimly lit stone courtyard of Northwest Protector House, kicking up the small dusting of snow. A sleepy groom stumbled out to take the reins. Mara dismounted and mumbled thanks, gritting her teeth against both the sharp pain of her wounded thigh and the dull pain of other injuries acquired during the past ten days of intermittent fighting.

Mara straightened her posture and her filthy uniform. She ran two smoothing hands across her hair, took a slow breath, and stepped through the archway. Shamed by the injury, she used short steps to disguise the worst of her limp. The two Protectors on duty in the guard shelter waved her through without challenge.

Her solitary footsteps stuttered along the hard floor of the outer hall. Purpose kept her moving, one hand brushing along the thickly whitewashed wall for balance until she reached her own door.

Inside, she bypassed the makings of a fire laid in the hearth and went straight to the small, tiered shelf under the window. She lit a white candle and a yellow candle, kneeling stiffly to recite prayers for peace and healing. The ritual complete, she added her own jumbled words of gratitude and supplication. Every time Mara returned safely from the lines, the candle ritual grounded her, returning light to the Light.

She wobbled over to her fireplace and just as the first flames went up from the kindling, a soft knock sounded on the only other door to her room.

"Come in, Annelise," she sighed.

A short girl nudged the door open with her foot and carried in a steaming bowl of water along with fresh strips of linen. "Let's have a look at you now."

Annelise helped Mara shed her battle uniform, taking extra care with the scratches along her arms and the bruises across her back and ribs. Mara shivered as the shredded pants joined the pile on the floor.

Her assigned partner and friend clucked softly and lifted a tunic from a hook on the back of the door. "Put this on, but hold it above your waist while I unwrap the bandage." Reddish-gold curls lay flat over one ear and stood out in tufts on the other side of Annelise's head. Her too-large night tunic hung down over soft leggings.

"It can wait until morning, A'lise. You should go back to bed." Mara was scarcely able to shape the words.

"You would do the same for me. Just a few minutes more." She helped Mara to a cushion near the fire and began to unwind the thin strip of fabric.

The older girl bit back a groan. The cut tingled at the surface and ached underneath. She should tell her partner about talking to a

Gaishan, about being touched. If anyone reported her, she would be severely disciplined—whipped, maybe worse. Sometimes those who had even incidental contact with the Gaishan disappeared for good.

"I was touched in battle. After I was cut," she croaked.

Annelise recoiled with a gasp. "You were not!"

"A Gaishan…it…he showed his face to me. He touched the wound, I think took the poison from it." She couldn't say more. Better if her partner didn't know that he'd spoken to her, smiled as though they were friends.

"This happened tonight?" Annelise let the last of the wrapping fall to the floor. Blue eyes wide, she stretched out a finger as though to touch the long length of dark-pink scar. "Are you sure you didn't bring the fog with you? That's the healing of weeks, if not months." She glanced at the door.

"Wait." Protocol demanded a partner run for healers if contagion was suspected. "I got cleared before they sent me back. It was open and bleeding before but…the healers used the binding glue, maybe it's some new something…" She rubbed her eyes.

Annelise nodded, her expression troubled. "Could the contagion do this?"

"No." She was certain. "The Gaishan…no. I'll report everything again tomorrow. Get checked by the healers again. I promise."

Chapter 2

She'd been dreaming of the Gaishan. The handsome enemy's information was urgent and her head ached from trying to understand. Disgusted with herself, Mara threw on a robe and limped through the cold, nearly deserted stone hallways toward the main washroom. Dawn was the best time to shower without company anyway.

In one of the partially enclosed stalls, she washed her hair, patiently working a comb through the long, dark mass. She cleaned her newest scar with extra vigor, just in case any taint lingered on the skin. She grimaced at the bruised feeling inside the muscle. It felt as though the injury had only healed on the surface, the tissue disturbingly loose and painful underneath.

Holding the rough towel with one hand, Mara used the mirror behind the sink to survey her other injuries. Pink welts streaked down her back. A bruise mottled one cheekbone and the red in her eyes made the blue irises bright and wild. Defensive marks discolored the length of her forearms, wrist to elbow. But in the growing light of day, the worst by far was the long scar running diagonally across her thigh.

Mara didn't linger in the washroom. She wanted to choose the moment to make her report rather than be surprised into giving it while wearing a robe in the hall. Off duty and out-of-uniform were irrelevant to the senior Protectors. A soldier should always be ready. Preparation was the key to success.

In her three and a half years of service, Mara had learned the rule of preparation through drills, surprise inspections, and impromptu fights. After the death of her second partner, they ordered her to the front line with nothing but the uniform on her back. In response to Mara's stricken protest, the senior Protector cited the rule of preparation and sent her out the gate. On that cold ride, she had dared to question the Protector cause for the first time. Dared to wonder why their lives seemed to mean so little and why no one spoke of ending the war. The questions had taken root, pushing tendrils of doubt into every aspect of her life as a soldier.

Back in her room, Mara changed into a canvas house uniform and stepped gingerly into battered work boots. Rather than think about the previous night, she opened the connecting door to see if her partner had been summoned yet to the lines.

Annelise turned and smiled. "There you are," she said. "I didn't hear you head out to the washroom. You could've called me and I would've went along in case you needed help."

"I got seventeen years that say I don't need help." Mara tried for bravado and missed.

Annelise didn't laugh or tease as she usually did. Instead she moved closer to look up at the taller girl's face. "Not feeling fogged this morning?" she asked.

"No."

"No dreams?" Annelise pressed.

"Just the nightmare of you going to the front lines," Mara said.

Annelise stuck out her tongue and turned in a slow circle to show her battle uniform. "I'm a proper soldier and I won't embarrass you. See?" She had survived her first year of skirmishes and battles but it was hard not to worry about the cheerful fifteen-year-old. "Besides, if they'd wanted me immediately, a runner would've come last night," the girl pointed out.

"True," Mara said. "In that case, let's eat. Don't want to be hungry while I'm giving my report five times in a row."

They walked through Mara's room and out into the Green corridor, following it into one of the main halls that formed one side of the square compound building.

"Well, if you stopped putting yourself in the middle of the action, you'd only have to tell it to the clerk one time. No one's ever asked me to give additional reports," Annelise said.

"Look, I'm going to get checked right after I give my report. And—" The doubts and questions had never bloomed into outright lies before. "And I'll say that I was exhausted, just passed out before you—"

"I looked you over, followed all the steps for an *assessment*, and I decided that you weren't at risk or risking me." She shrugged. "You'll get cleared in no time."

#

The duty station smelled like it looked, dusty and unpleasant. When the clerk behind the lone desk signaled, Mara recited her report. She detailed the battle: the number of Gaishan, weapons used, formations and tactics, and her own role in the action. She concluded with an abridged version of her injury and subsequent ride home.

Next she performed the standard memory task, matching pictures on sixteen different cards while the clerk timed her. She was then given twenty objects to sort. A few were new this time and Mara had no idea what they were. She created three sorts, one by material, one by size, one by purpose, as she usually did with this test. The sort by purpose was the hardest since some of the objects looked more like the symbols from the card matching than any type of tool or fastener or weapon. The memory and sorting tests started about four years ago, right around the time classes on reading and mathematics had been cut for all but a few. And usually Mara liked the challenge, but today she was too tired and worried to do her best.

The clerk recorded her answers in his book and gestured for Mara to sit on one of the few battered benches. She sighed. If the clerk thought a senior Protector needed the information, the soldier waited and gave his or her report as many times as required.

She'd left the Gaishan completely out of her report. An image of his face, slightly upturned eyes, and full mouth welled up in her mind. "Your questions have answers," he'd said.

He... Mara stopped the direction of her thoughts. Gaishan were not human. Thinking of the Gaishan as a person, as a boy, was treason. Several months before, a family of settlers who tried to befriend the Gaishan had been stripped naked, whipped in the main square, and banished from the Protected Territory with nothing. No clothes, no food, no livestock—everything forfeited to the settlement council.

"Mara? My office."

She scowled at the floor before flattening her expression to neutral. Haranu, the senior Protector in charge of magic, thought she deliberately ignored her magical potential to focus on combat technique. Of all the senior Protectors, Haranu could be the most exacting in taking reports. Just her luck.

The stern senior officer sat behind a wooden table and rifled through a stack of pages. Glancing up, she said, "Stand as you give your report, soldier, or does your injury prevent that?" Haranu's short, black hair gleamed nearly blue under the single overhead light.

"No, ma'am," Mara replied, steeling herself not to respond to the condescension. She gave her report word-for-word as she had told it to the clerk. Especially the lies. Haranu would pounce on any inconsistency.

"You say you dropped your shields at the edge of the battle," Haranu interrupted.

"Yes, ma'am," Mara said, eyes fixed on the woman's precise, perfect hair.

"And then you went to the healers' tent. Is that correct?"

"Yes, ma'am."

"And now?" she asked, raising one eyebrow.

Mara hesitated, her instinct to deflect attention from anyone else. "Not a hundred percent, ma'am. They got the cut to bleed less and it's mended a bit at the skin level, but the muscles and tissue aren't right."

Haranu shook her head. "Which soldiers were leading with you?"

"Fatima and Alonzo, ma'am. But they're in different cohorts. The Red and Blue groups held our left and right. It was the center, the Greens, who broke." Mara hated admitting that, especially to this woman.

"Whose fault was that?"

Mara stared straight into the woman's black eyes. "Mine."

"Senior Protector Twyla will determine the consequences for your failure," Haranu said. "You're dismissed to go directly to the healers. You've passed the first round of fog testing here and it's clear you're lucid, no amnesia. Nor do you have any visible skin lesions. But I'm sending orders that they take you through at least the next round." She scribbled on a piece of paper and handed it over.

"Yes, ma'am," Mara said once more, and turning on her right foot, strode from the room as smoothly as she could manage.

She concentrated on her stride and her posture as she walked back through the narrow hall, past the clerk, and out through the main doors into the courtyard. The light dusting of snow from the evening had long since melted, but a damp chill lingered. Mara paused to rest and secure Haranu's note in a pocket, disguising her purpose by scanning the light clouds above. White storms this early in the season were rare, but not unheard of.

The Gaishan only engaged the Protectors in clear weather, since their mind-fogging powders and contagions were far less effective in wet conditions. Maybe that was why Annelise hadn't been called yet?

The stables were situated directly between the duty station and the healing area of the compound. Haranu could not fault her for the route, as it was more efficient to check her horse on the way. It was something a soldier who wished to be prepared would do. Just inside the large door, the earthy smells of horse and straw brought back happy memories of a less structured life, of her first assignment as a groom and stable hand. Mara walked slowly, noting almost every stall was full. The cohorts were back.

When Mara stopped in front of Rowan, the mare whickered and reached her nose out above the stall door, sniffing for treats. Mara pulled a lumpy breakfast bar out of one of her pockets. Rowan chewed while her mistress checked her eyes and ears for signs of illness or irritation.

"You're all right then?" Mara murmured as she stroked the soft nose. In response, Rowan pricked her ears forward and blew out air. "Of course," the girl said. "I had to see for myself and thank you for getting us home." The mare stamped one foot and butted her nose into Mara's shoulder. She showed the horse her empty hands. "I'll bring another bar next time." She gave Rowan one last scratch behind the ears and then continued her measured walk toward the other end of the big structure.

Each of the four sides of the compound had a brightly colored door: blue on the north, red on the south, yellow on the east, and green on the west. Once inside the north door, it was only a few steps for Mara to the large group of rooms used by the healers in the main Blue corridor. The room for those with confirmed contagion was separate from the rest of the healers' suite. At least two of her soldiers were likely in there now. Mara touched the heavy wooden doorframe, stomach churning with fresh worry and guilt over the outcome of the fight.

Inside the main healing space, windows let in the mid-morning sun and soft blue and white hangings decorated the walls. Mara looked around, finding a few faces from her own cohort as well as a few from the Red and Yellow.

"Mara," a small soldier patted the empty stretch of corner bench next to her.

Mara dropped down next to Haleen, glad for a friendly face.

"When no one could find you in the retreat last night, we were in such a panic," Haleen whispered. "What happened? Are you hurt bad?"

Mara dropped her eyes to her leg and shook her head. "Not too bad. I got a bit of healing done last night. You?"

Haleen shifted closer to speak directly in Mara's ear. "I think I might have a bit of contagion in me." She was barely audible now. "I can't hardly keep food in my belly and sometimes I'm dizzy. I just noticed it these past few weeks at the front."

Carrying contagion was sensitive news. Mara bit her bottom lip and looked away. What if she herself was carrying some new form of contagion? If she'd exposed Annelise? The most recent cases of fogging caused open, oozing skin sores that spread from person to person with the slightest contact.

She shifted her weight back so she could see Haleen better. Freckles stood out against her friend's pale face and there were dark smudges under her light-blue eyes. Reddish brown hair frizzed out from under her house uniform cap. Haleen and Annelise were from the same settlement but sometimes they looked like sisters.

"Annelise hasn't been summoned to the front yet. Has Gunder?"

Haleen shook her head. "No, and I'm thankful for it. He was up with me in the night and I'd hate for him to ride out with so little rest."

"Annelise was up with me, too." Mara began to chew her bottom lip and stopped. It would be far worse for both she and Annelise than a lost night's sleep if she were caught lying about interaction with the Gaishan. But if he knew how the war started, knew a way to end it…

"Yes, but that's why we have them, isn't it?" Haleen chattered on. "A soldier fights better with someone to care for them. They was always goin' on about it in training and I didn't much pay attention. But now, when I get back from fighting, I'm so grateful I have Gunder to care for me, even if it's just for a few hours before he's off to fight. And I'm glad to care for him when he returns."

Most of the assigned partnerships were people of the same gender, but occasionally the senior Protectors arranged male/female pairs. Haleen and Gunder were a solid team, like brother and sister. Mara took a breath to ask Haleen about the new fighters in their cohort, if all the rest made it back, but a healing assistant beckoned.

"Stand tall, Haleen," she said instead, watching her friend trail after the healing assistant.

"Stand fast, Mara," Haleen replied over her shoulder.

Chapter 3

Much later, a blue-clad assistant escorted Mara to the door of one of the senior healers on duty. A man with russet hair and a pointed nose smiled at her and gestured to a padded chair.

"One moment while I finish these notes," he said.

Mara looked around the room, remembering the barred but large window with the gauze curtain, the candles in each corner and in position at each of the cardinal directions, the cluster of chairs, and the low, narrow bed.

Last season when sparring against another cohort, a less-experienced soldier had tried to throw her and ended up dislocating Mara's shoulder instead. She had been taken directly to this healer, Treyton, and he had repaired the shoulder in moments. Afterward, Treyton gave her medicinal tea to ease the pain and left her to rest and recover. It was an uncommon kindness Mara had not forgotten.

"Tell me about your injury please," Treyton now said.

Mara took a breath, the smell of the specially laundered sheets bringing the fear and vulnerability of that shoulder injury freshly to her mind, as it was the first time she'd been truly incapacitated. Bruises, cuts that needed stitches were routine, compared to that shoulder injury and now this anomaly with her leg. If the Gaishan had harmed her magically, if she carried contagion, Treyton would know.

"I was slashed in the leg," she said. "I don't think the blade was poisoned and I show no signs of contagion." She outlined the rest quickly.

"Why don't I take a look?" Treyton suggested, his patient hazel eyes crinkling at the corners.

"Of course, I—" She hesitated. "It's not entirely healed and I'd be grateful for your help." Mara unfastened her uniform pants and slipped them down to her ankles. Her linen undershorts ended just above the beginning of the sword wound.

"Would you stretch out your leg and tighten the muscles for me?" Treyton asked. Neither his face nor his voice betrayed any dismay at the sight of the now red and bunched scar running nearly from her hip to her knee. Treyton bent down and placed his palm over the center of the scar, generating a slight tingle of magical energy.

After a few moments of silent concentration, he asked, "The healers did this?"

"Yes," Mara said.

"Binding and sealing?"

She nodded, unable to stop herself from picturing the Gaishan who helped her.

"Last night?" His voice had clear notes of frustration now and his face showed it as well.

"Treyton, sir"—she stiffened—"I think…maybe I asked for the wrong thing. I just wanted the bleeding to stop so I could get home."

"There is power in this healing but it went wrong. Someone has more potential than they know how to use, clearly."

Mara opened her mouth to protest, to protect the battlefield healers, but he held up his hand.

"In order to allow this to truly heal, I need to open the scar at the surface, mend the interior, and then close it again. If the muscles and connective tissue are not repaired properly, you'll lose both strength and flexibility in this leg."

She swallowed. "I understand."

"Mara," the healer said, "when were you last tested for magical potential?"

"Three years ago, right before I was assigned to Green cohort."

"I can look up the details of your test later, but I'd like to hear what the assessment was." Treyton stood and began moving around the room, collecting items onto a tray. "We're going to do this right now. Partly because it's urgent and partly because I know you wouldn't stay in bed and rest until we could schedule a major healing for your leg. What I can see is that the wound was cleanly cut with no contagion. The magic did stop the bleeding, but this goes deep into the muscle. Trace elements of something else are in there, something I haven't seen before. Could be remnants of what was on the battlefield."

Treyton helped her to sit on the bed and bent down to pull off her boots and pants. "Go ahead and take off your uniform jacket. It won't be comfortable for the length of time you'll be lying down." As Mara undid the clasps, he asked, "What was the decision about your skill in healing with magic?"

She flexed her fingers. "They said my skill was strong but unpredictable. My focus was not sufficient to be trained in the healing arts." At the time, the assessment hurt, but looking back, she was glad it happened. Mara had loved the challenge of learning to fight too much to regret her assignment.

"How old were you, fourteen? Focus can be taught," he said as another man entered the room. "Jules, was it three years ago that we were so short-handed on the healing instructional staff? Or was it longer ago than that?"

"Three years sounds about right," the man said. "Hello, Mara." The newcomer gave her a warm smile. "I don't think we've met before. I'm Jules."

She shook her head. "No, I don't come to the healers much."

Jules was about the same age as Treyton, but with a more muscular build and dark olive skin. "This wound," he said, approaching the bed, "this makes up for several years of careful living. It happened at the front last night?"

Before she could answer, the senior healer tapped him on the arm. "Let's get the rest of our materials and I'll explain on the way." To Mara, he said, "Stay there; we'll be back in a moment."

As soon as the two senior healers left, she fished the note from Haranu out of her jacket pocket. The bed fit neatly inside a faint circle on the floor. On a nearby table lay bandages; linen cloths of varying size; a set of small, sharp knives; and a needle and thread.

If Annelise were here, she would be talking away about the details of her morning and how handsome Jules was or something else entirely to distract Mara from worrying. Even at fifteen, Annelise seemed to know how and when to offer support, though Mara could never ask, could hardly recognize the need inside herself.

Both healers bustled back into the room. "Please relax and drink this, Mara," Treyton said as he handed her a warm cup. "We're going to prepare your leg and then the circle. When you wake, the worst will be over. Any questions?"

Mara held out the note before she accepted the cup. "Order for additional testing."

The scent of familiar herbs like chamomile, *skara*, and mint in the liquid masked most of the bitter ingredients. She took a deep breath and swallowed half the contents. After a quick breath, she finished the drink.

She looked at the window to avoid seeing the tray of knives. Her stomach rolled, partly in protest to the potion she'd just consumed and partly in fear. "Did any of the youngest Greens come in last night or this morning? A brother and sister?"

"No, only two other Greens in here, plus the two in containment," Treyton said. "Everyone's going to make it."

Mara's heart stuttered and her shoulders sagged with relief. *Thank the Light.* "How long will I be here?"

"We'll work fairly quickly," Jules answered. "But we may need a bit more time to examine the magical traces in the wound and check for any other indications of fog."

It was suddenly harder to breathe. And when Jules pushed her shoulders toward the bed, she didn't have the strength to resist. But she was determined to block any thoughts about the Gaishan, just in case. Her brain slowed, the colors and smells fading away until the only input she processed was the steady beat of her heart.

Chapter 4

The sun warmed Mara's face and brought out the scent of the evergreen trees ringing the small clearing. Roughly fifty paces away, a figure emerged. His hands were empty but a sword hung from a belt slung low across his hips. Mara raised her energy shield, unsheathed her sword, and strode forward to meet the Gaishan.

As before, he wore the plain black and gray uniform that emphasized his trim, muscular form. His even features and light eyes looked human. Put him in a red uniform and he could be another Protector, someone she hadn't met from the North or East compound. Trainees were drilled and drilled: Mask equals monster; face equals friend.

"Mara of the Light, I'm glad you seek answers," he said.

A bark of laughter escaped before Mara could stop herself. It wasn't enough to commit treason in real life; she needed to continue the violation in her dreams? No one talked openly about hallucinations in the compound, but over the past few years, soldiers had reported wild stories while under the influence of Gaishan powders.

She jabbed him in the chest with her free hand. "This is a dream."

He blocked the next jab. "No, this is distance rapport."

Mara could sense him fumbling for words, searching her head for ways to explain. The intimacy of the thought connection, of being touched in her mind, was unbearable. She took two steps backward, gripping her sword until her knuckles went white.

"This is me getting a message to you without sending a runner," he said. "I can bring it to you myself, mind to mind."

"I don't want your message, Gaishan." The words were a lie, but this forced interaction was too much.

"I was trying to get information to you last night. But when your position changed, I was too far away to prevent one of…of the Gaishan from striking." He gestured toward her leg. "How are you?"

"I had to go to the healers." She hesitated, thinking. "I'm with the healers now, while I hallucinate that I'm talking to the enemy." She tilted her chin up, anger fading, replaced by worry. "I didn't tell anyone you tried to help me. They said it was necessary to reopen the scar, repair the internal damage, and then close it all back up again. Can they tell?" She gestured to him and back to herself. "Can they hear or detect rapport when I'm asleep?"

The Gaishan furrowed his brow. "No. Your body looks asleep because it is. Just your mind is here. I apologize for your injury. In my rush to help you, I didn't...I didn't think clearly. May I look?"

Something about his expression, the way he leaned down, coupled with the odd name he'd called her, connected with a hazy memory. "What's your name?"

"I'm Dalin."

Mara sheathed her sword and released her shield. Through her pants she felt his fingers brush along the raised ridge of scar tissue. Her heart began to hammer. "How old are you, Dalin? How long have you been fighting?"

"Nineteen. I've been a part of this for a while." He inhaled a long breath and let it out. "Your healer did good work. The cut is mending from within now."

She swallowed the relief, not sure she could trust this was anything but a product of her own imagination. "How do you know my name?"

"I've been watching you on the battlefield." He broke eye contact, pressed his lips together.

"Why would you and another Gaishan have different objectives?"

"Good question," he said. "The short answer is that a truce is coming. Some of us knew; some didn't. The long answer is complicated. When we meet we can speak of it further."

Mara raised her eyebrows. "A truce?"

"Yes."

"And where are we meeting?" It was hard to keep the laughter out of her voice. Never in five lifetimes would she consider sneaking away from Protector House to meet with the enemy.

Dalin leaned forward, his tone more urgent. "The true answers are beyond the protected boundaries. There's so much you need to know. It's critical that you leave the compound and come with me."

Steeling herself, Mara asked the hardest question. "Am I fogged in some special way the healers can't detect?"

"No," he began. "Well, yes, but it doesn't affect your health or cognition—"

"What?" Her voice rose in fear and she almost reached for her sword again, wanting the security of her trusted weapon in her hand.

"When I healed you, when I tried to heal you," he amended, "part of the magic or energy was distinctly ours, Gaishan."

"You contaminated me?"

"No," Dalin said. "No, but you are connected to us now and in danger because of it."

"Danger from my senior officers you mean, for lying. For talking to you and when they find out—"

"Please, you should ride out of the compound right now. At the very least, leave tonight when the healers' potions wear off. Promise me. I can reach your mind. I can guide you with words, give you a map."

Dalin moved closer, his dark grey jacket carrying the faint scent of something like sandalwood. He touched her hand and before Mara could pull away she saw Northwest Protector House from above, as if she were a bird.

"Go to the edge of the plateau and turn west." The view followed his words, gliding to the edge of the valley and turning toward the setting sun. "Head south and west until you reach the corner of the forest. A path and a creek run alongside each other." The view swooped along, showing the landscape as he described it. "Follow the creek into the forest. This place is a day's ride from the outermost trees."

Back in the clearing again, Mara blinked to reorient herself, realized she was holding Dalin's hand, and snatched her fingers away.

"I want to know what started the war. Why the Gaishan only attack the settlements and never the compounds. Why you disappear every winter. I want to know why the Gaishan fight in masks, especially if you look like this." She gestured from his polished leather boots to his close-cropped hair. "And if a truce is really coming, what will it take to make a lasting peace?" She stared hard, willing him to answer.

Dalin stared back, his expression assessing. Slowly he leaned forward and whispered, "Time to go."

The clearing faded, sunlight darkening to shadow as Dalin executed a perfect martial turn and walked away. Mara kicked at the ground, trying to ignore the warmth where his breath had touched her cheek and her genuine disappointment. "You're not even real."

"If you stay until they announce the truce, you'll know different." His voice carried in the stillness.

In the history of the long conflict, truces didn't last long. Getting answers would be the real fight. She took a deep breath and called, "*If* they announce a truce!" She watched him for a moment longer and then said, much more quietly, "Sure, when darkness takes over the world."

#

Mara's eyes flew open. Disoriented, she sat up too quickly, pulse pounding. A wave of nausea swept through her and she tumbled off the bed, landing hard on the floor. The sting of her palms and knees hitting the cold stone made her eyes water. Mara swiped at her face with a shaking hand.

Her house uniform and boots warmed by the fire. A pot of tea and some toast resting on her dresser confirmed Annelise's presence.

Mara pulled herself back onto the bed. She yanked the blanket up and curled into a ball. What had Dalin done?

She forced herself to breathe slowly until the room stopped spinning. When she uncurled, she sat up and swung herself around so that both feet touched the floor. Neat black stitches ran the length of the cut. She gingerly rubbed the area in the center of her thigh muscle and exhaled in relief to feel it whole, without any of the distressing looseness of the day before.

Mara stood first on her right leg and carefully shifted some weight to the ball of her left foot.

"Look at you up and about," Annelise said, bustling through their connecting door. She stopped directly in front of her partner, hands on hips. "The next time you have major healing, I expect to be called. How do you think I felt when those healers wheeled you in here last night? Do you doubt me?" Her voice rose with indignation.

Mara shook her head slowly, blinking away yellow spots in her vision. "You might have been called to fight," she said. "You needed to be ready."

Annelise huffed and stomped over to grab a stick from the hearth, poking it at the fire. "I was worried," she said, still turned toward the hearth. "I didn't even know where you were until I saw Haleen at dinner. And by then it was too late."

Mara hobbled over to pour two mugs of tea, fine tremors causing the liquid to slosh, and reached one out to her partner as a peace offering.

Annelise blew on her tea, bad mood lifting with the steam. "We'll see the whole compound this morning," she said. "There's to be a 'nouncement." To Mara's questioning frown, she responded, "In the main hall after breakfast. I don't know what it's about. But those folk have been arriving for two days now. So it's probably got to do with Roland and his"—she made a grand gesture with one hand—"business."

None of them knew what the senior communications deputy really did. But they had all been warned to treat him and his comrades with the same respect accorded to senior Protectors. Once, Mara had overhead the entire group referred to as the Military Science Corps, but for lack of an official title, the soldiers traveling with Roland were referred to as the Browns. Roland would appear with an escort of anywhere between two and twelve soldiers, be seen in the company of various senior Protectors, and then disappear again. Some of the fourth- and fifth-year Protectors disappeared when the Browns left, too. Mara suspected he was conducting messages between Northwest Protector house and other Protector compounds across the settled territory, as well as recruiting fighting talent for the Browns.

"And," Annelise continued, eyes alight with her best news, "all cohorts is returned in from the front."

"What?" Mara exclaimed, nearly knocking her tea into the fire. "No one is fighting? Is prepared to fight?"

"Well, I am," the small girl said with pride. "I got all my gear, weapons, and uniforms in top order. But now the quartermaster's saying he don't have room for all the returned folk's gear at once and to just keep it in our rooms until we hear otherwise."

Mara stared at her partner. These revelations were stranger than sitting with a Gaishan and having a chat. All the Protectors in from the lines—that did give some credence to the Gaishan's story of a truce.

"So I got all your stuff cleaned yesterday and it's piled up over there." Annelise pointed to the corner space between the wardrobe and the wall. "I did it as neat as I could. Rasar sent a runner with new leather uniform pants. Your others couldn't be repaired."

Mara craned to look and could just see her gear wedged precariously into the corner. Everything she needed if she decided to believe Dalin. If the assembly *was* about a truce, she would have proof of the unmasked Gaishan's honesty, about this anyway.

Chapter 5

After a trip to the showers, Mara walked with less pain. She braided her wet hair sitting down and awkwardly shuffled into her other house uniform. Through the connecting door she saw Annelise trying to make her loose, reddish gold curls lie smoothly.

Mara's gaze fell on the shelf beneath her window. Although spiritual observance was not promoted in the Protector compound, Mara had always found comfort in having a place to focus her prayers. She went to her small altar, lit just the white candle, and closed her eyes, murmuring words of gratitude for her healing. On a gray stone just to the left of the altar, she traced a finger over fifty-three scratched lines, one for each dead or missing fighter from their cohort since her partner died two years ago. If Dalin had information that could end the war permanently—

"You ready?" Annelise called from her room.

Mara blew out the candle. "Always."

"I wish I had your hair," Annelise said as they joined other fighting pairs from the Green cohort walking toward the main hall. Daylight streamed from the high windows in the open-beamed ceiling and patterned the bare stone floors with squares of yellow and white.

"You really don't," Mara answered absently, tugging on her braid. "It won't be dry for hours."

Around the final corner, dozens of soldiers streamed in the giant double doors to the Great Hall, which served as a central location for meals and gatherings. Only a few steps from the entrance, a senior Protector with silvering blond hair stood stiffly in her formal uniform.

"Mara," she rasped, "why aren't you with the healers? I saw you take a bad hit."

Mara bit her lip and turned to face the older woman. Senior Protector Twyla was head of the Green cohort, a great fighter and teacher.

"No, I mean, yes, Mistress Twyla. I was hurt but not so bad as to take overmuch of the healers' time." Mara held the woman's sharp, dark gaze for a moment and then dropped her eyes. Did Twyla know she had initiated contact with a Gaishan?

"The healers dumped her in her bunk late last night," Annelise offered. "She's loads better now."

"When I saw you half out of your saddle, I"—the grim-faced woman shook her head—"I couldn't reach you across the fighting. Our lines were a mess."

Mara swallowed and nodded, her eyes of their own volition tracing the jagged white scar that crossed Twyla's right cheek from ear to jaw.

"I got patched and cleared by the healers before I made for the compound," Mara said. She paused as a dozen or more senior Protectors walking into the hall diverted Twyla's attention. "It's all in my report."

Twyla frowned. She pulled Mara close and spoke directly in her ear. "Our cohort will follow you anywhere. But you act on impulse. You don't think through to the consequences. We're lucky our hit list was light." She released her hold and fixed both girls with a meaningful glare. "We will talk on this further," she said and strode over to join her peers.

Mara and Annelise quickly found seats at a table in the rear of the enormous room. They were sitting with a mixed group of latecomers from other cohorts so the conversation was limited to requests for the oatmeal and passing of berries from one end to the other. Annelise tried to get a game of guess-what-the-announcement-will-be going, but only got a few half-hearted guesses.

Mara filled her bowl twice, grateful for the fruit that added color and texture to her food. The milk in the pitcher was still cold and tasted wonderful. She eyed the oatmeal, considering a third bowl, before she saw the look on her partner's face.

"Not everyone's got seconds yet," Annelise murmured. "The compound's a bit short on supplies what with all the soldiers bein' here at once, plus the Browns."

Mara sat up straighter and looked around the room. She had been too distracted by seeing Twyla and by her own hunger to notice how loud and crowded the room was. The Great Hall of Northwest Protector house hadn't been this full since the last truce ended, nearly six years ago. Several tables of Green cohort soldiers lined part of the left side of the hall, and on the right, Yellow and Blue cohort soldiers clustered together. House uniforms were all the same, but cohort membership was displayed through patches on both the front of the uniform jacket and on the left shoulder. Protector lore ascribed different characteristics to each group. The Blue cohort was quiet and helpful; the Green cohort, the most serious about fighting technique. Yellow cohort was fun-loving and creative, and Red cohort was the fiercest and loudest.

"Hey, partner," Annelise spoke in her ear again. "You're staring around the Great Hall like you've never seen it. Don't want people to think you're foggy."

Mara stood and gathered serving bowls and pitchers. Annelise jumped up and asked the table to pass down empties. The partners walked everything over to the kitchen window and handed the dishes to the kitchen workers inside. Aside from the two rows of empty benches at the very front of the hall, most of the tables were nearly clean and cleared of dishes. Conversation hummed and began to get louder as the contained excitement in the air increased.

A commotion by the door caused the whole hall to turn and look. The senior Protectors in their full-dress scarlet uniforms marched two by two down the center of the hall. As both rows of front benches filled, Roland entered through the same door and strode purposefully to a small raised platform at the end of the room. He too wore a dress uniform, but in a deep shade of brown, nearly the same color as his skin. Roland's chest puffed out as he walked and both feet turned in slightly. It was hard to imagine him swinging a sword without losing his balance. Other soldiers in the Brown uniforms lined the walls. In contrast to the senior communications deputy, they were fit and alert, with weapons ready.

Roland stopped in the center and surveyed the crowd. With a small smile, he made a flourish toward the ceiling and a large ball of golden energy appeared overhead. The soldiers watched, many mouths hanging open, as the energy changed shape and became a golden knot with a lioness at the center.

"This is the emblem of your Queen," Roland shouted. "She sends both greetings and congratulations on this latest Protector victory."

The senior Protectors clapped politely. The regular Protectors shifted and whispered amongst themselves. Everyone knew they didn't have a queen. Mara's anticipation of a truce announcement dimmed a little.

The story children learned was that long ago a king from another planet had sent people to establish settlements. When the native life on the planet had proved less than amenable to civilization, further development was cancelled. The settlers stayed, but because of the Gaishan, they needed a fighting force. Each family gave up one teenager to the cause of protecting everyone else. After so many generations, the settlements and the Protector compounds were established fact while the idea of a monarch who ruled over so much had become more myth than history.

"And I bring you tidings of victories by other Protector compounds. Your fellow soldiers in the North and Northeast have triumphed over the Gaishan as well." This produced a much more boisterous round of cheering. He raised his hands for silence. The lioness in the knot emblem shimmered and turned her head.

"Yes, victory," Roland continued, "and hard won. But we can rejoice knowing our brothers and sisters who fell gave their lives to bring Protectors and settlers this first day of peace."

The clapping and cheering began anew, growing louder and louder. Soldiers stomped their feet and whistled.

Annelise poked her in the ribs. "What're you going to do in peacetime, Mara? You don't know nothing but fighting."

"Yes, I do," she said and gave Annelise a gentle shove.

Energy rippled as Roland raised his hands. The lioness and the knot emblem changed into a giant map. None of the senior Protectors had this kind of magic. Where did Roland come by his skills? Or was he the one controlling the images? Haranu might be able to pull off something like this, maybe.

"In the end, we won even more new territory and the Gaishan have been forced to retreat here." He pointed at the hovering map and a gray region in the south became darker and more pronounced. "Our resources have increased along with our territory. Those of you who have map-making skills and the courage to explore will be called upon to help us better understand and utilize our prizes. In particular, this river and this forest." As he gestured, first the river and then the forest became darker and more distinct on the magical map.

Roland brought his palms together and the map disappeared. He spoke about bravery in battle and courage in leadership. One at a time, the senior Protectors from the front benches stood and went forward to receive some sort of medal.

The audience shifted in their seats. Clearly, this was going to take a while.

Why did Roland call this a victory and Dalin call it a truce? The Gaishan hadn't mentioned a retreat either.

After all the senior Protectors had been praised and decorated, Twyla stepped forward. "Tonight we celebrate with a feast and dancing," she announced. The assembled soldiers cheered. She gestured for silence. "I know many of you will not feel easy in a celebration with plans for the future unsettled. To that end, the senior Protectors will provide each fighting pair with initial peacetime assignments. And," she went on, "you will all be granted five days' leave, effective tomorrow morning."

At this, many of the soldiers leapt from their benches, yelling, hugging each other, and laughing. Mara pasted a smile on her face and stood. Could she leave the compound as well? Even without a family or a settlement to visit?

"Mara!" Annelise was shaking her shoulder. "Real leave, with nobody at the front. Can you imagine it?" she grinned, her blue eyes dancing.

"Yes, it's exciting," Mara said, knowing she wasn't putting the right emotion into her face and voice. Her fellow Protectors were clustered in groups, gesturing and talking loudly. A few looked as surprised as she felt or worried. And a few looked mad, deprived of the chance to fight more of the hated Gaishan, at least for a while.

Twyla stepped onto the platform to survey the room. She turned to Zam and nodded, and together they maneuvered a table to fit at the top of the long aisle that ran the length of the room. They were as mismatched a pair as any of the Protector duos: Twyla tall and lean with silvering hair, Zam blocky and medium height with pink cheeks and a dark curly beard. She handed him a ledger and then carried over two chairs. A man in a heavily decorated Brown uniform joined them.

Before she sat down, Twyla made a gesture for silence and cleared her throat. "Protectors, let's keep this simple. Approach us, one pair at a time. Keep about three paces between each pair. Once you have your assignment, you are considered off duty for the next five days." A small burst of applause erupted in the back of the room.

Twyla held up her hand and glared. The sound stopped as abruptly as it had begun. "Please stay for the celebration tonight and plan to depart in the morning."

At first, no one approached the table. Then, as if a signal had been given, so many people stood at once that the room darkened, the light from the morning sun temporarily obscured.

"Hey. Lian and I are going to get in line before all the good assignments get taken," their friend Jahella whispered loudly. Jahella was a tall girl with dark olive skin, long black hair, and nearly black eyes. She was one of the few girls who always managed to look female in her uniform. "Gunder and Haleen are lining up. We're all going to meet in the east courtyard after and compare."

As the two standing at the table were dismissed, the next twosome in line moved forward while those at the front of the line waited a respectful distance back. Mara watched Zam mark in the ledger and wondered if the assignments had been determined ahead of time after all. Contingency plans were certainly part of Protector training. Perhaps the head Protectors had chosen job assignments as part of a contingency plan for peace?

They watched Lian and Jahella approach the table and stand at attention. Twyla spoke and both young women nodded. The pair exited down the south side of the hall, faces blank, eyes straight ahead.

Annelise murmured, "I wonder what they got? Are they assignin' folks as pairs? I didn't think of that."

Mara swallowed hard. She hadn't thought of pair assignments either. Could she leave knowing Annelise was depending on her to return?

"Don't make such a face, Mara," Annelise teased. "Let's just wait and find out." Another pair went by and then Haleen and Gunder. Haleen's face was still pale, but the healers must have cleared up her contagion concerns. Everything was proceeding quickly and quietly. The partners in front of them turned and marched away. Annelise nudged Mara toward the table.

"Female pair, Green cohort," Twyla said. The man in the Brown uniform looked down his nose at Mara, his upper lip curled back over yellowing teeth. She snuck a glance at Zam, but his eyes were glued to the ledger.

"Annelise," Twyla said, "your new assignment is in compound design and renewal. Report to Protector Baud when you return from leave." Annelise opened her mouth but Twyla motioned for silence. "Mara, your assignment is assistant combat instructor. You will report to Zam."

"Is this the one who was so gravely injured at the end of the last skirmish?" asked the man, thin fingers playing with one of the ribbons on his lapel. Mara looked to Twyla, not sure about answering to one of Roland's people.

"Yes, Garot," Twyla replied. "Mara reported an injury to her leg at the end of the fight."

"You seem to be fully recovered," Garot said.

Mara shifted her weight, straightening to her full height. Twyla nodded, giving her permission to speak. "Yes, sir," Mara said, anxiety bubbling up. Her breath caught and she cleared her throat. "I went to the healers."

Garot tapped a finger on his chin. "You—"

Twyla said quietly, "Dismissed, Protectors. A calm, orderly exit. Get some rest before the celebration." Mara and Annelise bent in a formal half-bow, and marched away from the table of leaders.

Mara kept her face and body under control. What did that man care about her injury? Would her report have gone to any of the Browns? She'd heard dark rumors about how Brown soldiers were disciplined. Time in the stocks, whipping, and facing the gauntlet were a few of the choice options. She followed Annelise down the corridor, through a narrow passageway, and out into the rear courtyard, stumbling when the shorter girl stopped.

Gunder hurried over like a big, awkward puppy and threw an arm over Annelise's shoulders. "What's your sentence, lass?" he asked.

Annelise pressed against Gunder's side for a moment. "I'm in for compound design and repair. And you, sir?" She reached up and brushed shaggy, dark hair from his forehead.

"I'll be part of supplies and acquisition," he said as the group formed a circle.

"I'm to help train the new horses," Jahella announced.

"And I'm to be explorer support," Haleen said, and then held up her hand as Mara exclaimed with jealousy. "Explorer support means tents, bandages, food, and water," she clarified.

Annelise gave her partner's hand a quick squeeze and asked
Gunder a more specific question about acquisitions. Mara only half
listened as they continued talking about peacetime and working
around the compound.

Jahella said, "Those of us who just finished the fighting for you
need rest. Look at Mara here. She's barely human." The group
chuckled as Jahella took Mara's arm and began steering her toward
the Green hallway. "And you, Haleen," the bossy soldier called over
her shoulder, "you need rest as well. Gunder, quit clinging to
Annelise and attend to your partner!"

Mara marveled at how her friend always said exactly what she
thought. "Are you a natural-born commander, Jahella?"

"Naturally," she replied, fluttering her lashes. She leaned in to
whisper in Mara's ear. "But we were being observed. What if
someone made a joke considered worthy of punishment?"

Mara stiffened and glanced around as they walked, the back of
her neck prickling under her still-damp braid.

Jahella nodded at Mara's reaction. "In the corner window I saw
a Brown. And I mean to wear your prettiest dress tonight," she added
in a much louder voice. They paused at Mara's door and she stepped
to the side. Even though it wasn't a major concern for members of
the same cohort to be in each other's rooms, technically only
partners were allowed free access.

"I want something bright," Jahella called. "Grab anything for
me to walk away with, in case someone is still listening," she
whispered, checking both ways down the hall.

Mara inhaled sharply. Her room had been searched. The pile in
the corner was in the wrong order and the bed covers weren't tight.
She jerked a red dress with a full skirt from her wardrobe but turned
too quickly and landed hard on her left foot. She let out a small gasp
and caught herself against the wall.

Jahella peered in. "Is it your leg?"

Mara took two, much-smaller limping steps toward the door.
"I'm all right," she said. "I just forgot and stepped wrong."

Jahella winced in sympathy. She reached out a hand to stroke
the crimson wool. "This is lovely. And the right length. My dresses
come from my older sister and she's not as tall as you."

"Help yourself." Mara forced a smile. "I have two other dresses that Elias's wife made for me. Just wish I had your shape to fill out the curves."

Jahella laughed and tossed her long black hair over one shoulder. "Perhaps the Browns prefer their women as straight as sticks and you'll be the most sought after dance partner."

Mara began to close the door in the girl's face. "Be gone, wench," she said in a fair imitation of Twyla's voice.

Before she could rest, she had to check her gear. Someone, a stranger, had touched her packs, her spare boots, her stove. Everything was still there. So what had they been looking for? She stared at the plain stone walls, worrying her lower lip between her teeth.

"Keep the clearing in your mind. Use it as a focal point rather than my voice."

"Dalin?" she said aloud.

"Hold your focus and we can talk in the clearing again."

"How…?" She squeezed her eyes closed and reached with her mind.

"Relax now," Dalin said. "You did it. You're here."

She looked around. It wasn't just her memory—she was there. She could smell the spicy musk of the evergreen tree sap and hear birdcalls. Excitement replaced some of the frustration she had from her previous conversation with the Gaishan.

Dalin smiled across the clearing. He wore the same plain gray uniform. "Good job," he said. "We hoped you might have the skills for distance rapport." His expression sobered. "I had to talk to you about Roland's mages. They look like soldiers but one of them is very powerful. He's the one to avoid."

"Do you know which one?" Mara asked.

"Not his name, but he was supposed to supervise assignments this morning."

Mara's confusion was plain. "Garot. You're saying he's a mage? How do you know?"

"We have a source in the communication deputy's entourage."

Mara frowned and let her gaze drift around the clearing. The tall trees created deep shadows at the edge of the forest, but here in the center she could still feel the sun. She studied Dalin for a long moment, comparing what she saw with the creatures she'd met in battle. He looked completely human. Which made him, according to her training, an ally. And if the answers he promised meant she'd never have to add to the tally of dead and missing soldiers, Light help her, she was tempted.

"Can you leave tonight?" he took a step closer.

"If I don't attend the celebration and dance."

"Do you like to dance?"

"I do," she said, her lips twitching into a small smile. "But I rarely have a partner who can look over my shoulder, let alone over my head."

"As you can see, our people grow quite tall," Dalin responded, gesturing to himself. "We will dance to celebrate the success of your quest, Mara of the Light. I promise."

She flushed. "I won't have time for dancing or much else when I arrive here," she said. "I only have five days of leave. It will be hard riding but—"

"You may need to stay longer," Dalin countered.

"I can't," Mara said. "Zam, my new"—she huffed out a breath—"the combat instructor I'm assigned to for peacetime, he'll get in just as much trouble if I report in late."

Dalin inclined his head, considering. "If you head out just past sundown and ride as hard as you and your horse can manage, you'll arrive in this clearing at midday on the third day."

She felt a gentle push and opened her eyes to see the dark wooden beams in the ceiling of her room. Dalin's presence was fading from her mind. *I will guide you as I can.*

Mara blinked and let her eyes rest on the window. Her stomach fluttered and the glass panes swam out of focus. How long until dark?

Chapter 6

Mara found Annelise in the midst of the decorating, straining to lift a swath of greenery higher. "May I offer my assistance?" she asked her partner, bowing.

Annelise huffed, "Yes, please." She pushed a hand through the curls on her forehead and blew out a breath. She pointed to where she wanted the garland fastened. Mara moved to comply. "I've got your assignment figured out, Mara," Annelise said. "They didn't pick you because Zam likes you or because you're a good fighter. They picked you because you're as tall as a Gaishan and we all need to practice on you."

Mara froze for a moment before turning to look over her shoulder at her friend. She saw no malice in Annelise's face; rather, her partner was chewing on a ragged fingernail and surveying the progress around her.

"Annelise, you know I couldn't help being born tall. Probably the Gaishan are born that way, too."

"Born? Like people?" Annelise scoffed. Many of the settlers held beliefs that the Gaishan were conjured, part dark spirit and part animal.

"Entirely like people. Just people who go to war in masks," Mara said, keeping her tone light.

Annelise narrowed her eyes. "I think I might even miss your foggy ways during leave."

Mara looked around as she moved closer to her partner and lowered her voice. "About leave, I-I want to take some time out of the compound, too. But did you hear Twyla say, 'those with families'? If you wouldn't mind, could I use visiting your family as a reason in case anyone asks why I'm riding out?"

Annelise's blue eyes blinked wide. "Truly, Mara? You would visit my family?"

Mara looked into her partner's hopeful face. "I would love to meet them. But first, I need to see something." She scanned the Great Hall for Brown uniforms. "I need to go back to the battlefield. Walk over it and try to understand what happened. After that, I'll come to your house."

Understanding dawned on Annelise's face. "But you'll have to say you're coming with me or Twyla might make you stay."

Mara shrugged and picked up another garland. "You know how the senior Protectors are." She handed one end to Annelise and walked toward the next empty space on the wall. "In fact"—Mara kept her voice casual—"I thought I might head out tonight during the festivities to avoid having that conversation."

"Won't you get reprimanded? For leaving early?" Annelise asked.

Mara tugged on the garland and Annelise walked over so that Mara could reach up and fasten her end. "I might get a reprimand, but it would be worth a few days on restricted rations to sort this out. Besides," she continued, "we'll be out of uniform. You'll be there. Jahella will be there, wearing my dress. Most everyone will believe they saw me."

Annelise bit her lower lip and put her hands on her hips. She scanned the hall, transformed into the scene of a harvest festival. "You want to miss all this?" she asked, gesturing at both the decorations and their fellow Protectors. The late afternoon sun picked out bits of dust and straw sparkling in the air.

"I don't," Mara replied and turned to gather boxes that had been emptied of decorative gourds and bundles of dried corn. "I don't want to miss seeing you dance with Gunder or any of it. But I need to slip away without fuss."

"You'll come for the opening? And the food?" Annelise pressed.

"If I can," Mara said.

"Do you know how to find my settlement?" Annelise asked, grabbing a broom and swiping at some debris in the corner. Mara took the nearby dirt catcher and knelt for her friend to sweep into it.

"I do," Mara assured her. "When I worked in the stables, we went there to trade for bridles, harnesses, and such."

"I know it's a truce and all, but might there be Gaishan about?" Annelise asked.

Mara stood and carried the full dirt catcher to a compost bucket. "Seems unlikely. Besides, I'll be careful and"—she paused, staring down into the mess—"I just need to see for myself how the injury happened."

Annelise gathered the stacked boxes. "Did you consult the weather watchers? Last I heard, they were predicting an early storm.

Not like that sprinkle we had the other night, but a real snowstorm. Some of us think that's why we're gettin' leave so early into the peacetime, so we'll come back before Protector House is snowed in for the season."

#

When the others went back to the Green corridor, Mara headed for the map room instead. The tightness in her throat and chest loosened in the cold, fresh air of the outer courtyard. She was too restless, too nervous to confine herself in any small space.

The map room was on the other side of the compound, adjacent to the library. It had four large tables each holding rows of shelves and drawers underneath. Mara was not surprised to be the only occupant on this particular afternoon. She walked directly to the materials detailing the regions south of Northwest Protector compound and laid out the maps, tracing the route Dalin had given her. Here was the meadow; here was the forest and the stream.

Her gaze skipped to the next map. The forest was larger than she had imagined. And the route looked longer than a three-day ride. She sighed and retraced the route, looking for landmarks and committing the whole thing to memory.

"Not satisfied with your assignment, Protector? Do you wish you had been assigned to the surveying corps?"

Mara spun on her right foot, hands up in fists. Garot stood at the next table, his pale eyes fixed on her, one eyebrow raised.

"No, sir," Mara answered, shifting into the required upright reporting posture, face hot with surprise. She fixed her gaze on his left shoulder. "I wanted to get a clearer picture in my mind of where the new truce lines fall relative to the last few skirmishes to the south. Sir," she finished. Her fingers itched to restack the maps and hide them from Garot's measuring stare. The man was thin and not quite her height but he radiated a cold power that crept across her skin.

He stepped around Mara to look at the maps. "Hmm," he said, "thinking of battle and not about the dance? Maybe Twyla was right about you."

She didn't respond, but a tingling of unease ran up her spine. Even without Dalin's warning, every hard-earned minute on the battlefield told her to retreat.

"Do you want to know what Twyla said about you…Mara?" As he drew out her name, Garot circled back around the table, his clicking boots impossibly loud in the silent map room.

"Up to your discretion, sir," Mara said.

"Twyla said you think like a general and that you have a gift for strategy." Garot paused. "But I think you have a questioning mind. And in the Queen's Army we do not tolerate questions. Is that clear?"

"Yes, sir," Mara said, striving for an even tone. This stranger in a Brown uniform had no right to treat her like a new soldier fresh out of training. "I was unaware Protectors were part of a larger organization." At Garot's expression, she added, "Sir."

"Where do you think Protectors came from?" Garot sneered. "Your training? Your weapons? All far more advanced than what's produced on this backward little pl— In these pitiful settlements."

She swallowed her shock and said, "Yes, sir."

"Tidy this mess, take yourself to the Green hallway, and stay there. This lax discipline is going to change. Can't have soldiers wandering into secure areas." His eyes drifted to the lone window. Knots of Protectors swept the courtyard and carried stacks of wood. Some just stood talking. Mara waited a beat to see if the Brown officer was finished speaking, then gathered the maps into their original stack on the table and left.

She took a slow breath and then another, once again glad for the bracing wind. Away from the sight lines of the library and map room, she changed course and headed toward the stables.

Chapter 7

"Rowan," Mara asked her horse after a few minutes of searching, "why are you in a new stall?"

Rowan stamped a front hoof and shook her mane. Mara fished a chunk of bread from her pocket and gave it to her horse. Then she eased into the stall and checked the mare's legs, hooves, and shoes.

"Want to go for a ride, girl?" she whispered. At the word *ride*, Rowan's ears pricked forward.

The sound of whistling carried down the row of stalls. Elias, the stable master, bobbed into view. He was one of the few in the compound who didn't wear a uniform. Instead he wore a buttoned-up vest with a long-sleeved shirt underneath, faded trousers, and ancient leather boots.

"How'd you get yourself so many horses?" Mara dusted her hands and leaned on Rowan's open door.

Elias grinned, his brown, weathered face creasing more deeply. "Hey, Mara girl." He caught her in a bear hug. "What are you doin' here with me and all my guests? Isn't there a dance or some such?"

"You know me. I'd just as soon be helping you." She smiled at the person who had been more kind to her than any other adult in the compound. If anyone could dispel the shadow of Garot's dark presence, it was Elias.

The stable master shoved his hands into the vest pockets. "Them Brown uniforms insist on the best of everythin'. The kids and I had to move the horses all around. Could have used you, truth be told."

Mara made a sour face. From her years working in the stable, she knew how much trouble a big shuffle could be. "I thought you might at least get the night off."

"Humph. We get to have our own bit of feast. But that head Brown, he's sending out at least two patrols every night. I can't go far. Someone's got to be here when they bring those poor horses back. And it s'posed to storm. Did you hear that?"

"No," she lied. Rowan stuck her head over the stall door and nuzzled her mistress's shoulder. Mara reached up to stroke the velvety nose. "I meant to seek out the weather watchers today, but I'm running out of time." She leaned forward and said in a low voice,

"Rowan and I were thinking about going out for a few days during leave."

"You should, girl," he said. "Just 'cause you got no family don't mean you can't get a few days away from this place. 'Course my missus would love to see you again if you want to come home with me sometime."

The unexpected offer prompted a pang of regret. Elias and his wife had taken her in before she was old enough to stay in the children's quarters and, later, home with them for holidays when it was permitted.

"Elias." Mara stepped forward and clasped him in an awkward hug. "Thank you. I wish I could."

The older man looked disappointed. "Well, as long as the compound keeps getting children to train, the missus and I will always have some about. But she would love to see you, in particular. Don't forget now."

"Of course," Mara said. She lowered her voice to a whisper. "If I was to head out early, say tonight, to beat the morning rush, I would probably need to avoid the patrols also?"

Elias pulled her into the stall and crouched down to check Rowan's shoes. "If someone needed a horse tonight, and 'course I don't know nothing about that, the first patrol will go out and back during the evening meal. That'd be a bad time to get going. Don't know when the second patrol will go though. It's been a touch unpredictable."

She rolled her lips together, considering. "They taking the usual routes?"

"Far as I know, but I wouldn't bet my stake on it," Elias answered, his dark eyes bright and sharp. "Them Browns don't say much, but I heard they might be looking for someone. Tell you what, I've still got a few horses in tight spots. You'd be doin' me a favor taking Rowan out for a stretch. I could move things around a bit and put that space to good use." He winked at Mara. "Besides the saddlebags you already brought out, is there any other gear you need to keep out here? Makes a bit more sense to take care of certain particulars now."

Elias whistled and a tiny stablehand came running.

"Yes, sir?" he piped.

"Cole, you go with this soldier. She'll be givin' you gear from her room to bring back to me. Got it?"

The groom bounced on his toes, clearly happy for the novelty of the assignment. "Yes, sir. Got it, sir."

Mara looked at her oldest friend, lifted her arms part way, and then let them drop. "Thank you."

He winked and walked back down the long aisle of stalls.

"Come on, Cole," she said. "Do you know where the Green corridor is?"

He bobbed his head, light-brown hair sticking up at the crown. "Everyone says the Greens is the best fighters."

"Is that so?"

He bobbed his head again and grinned, showing a gap between his front teeth.

"We fight to protect all the settlers," Mara said.

"Right an' that's why my family sent me here, as part of the tax from our settlement. I get to work and pretty soon become a soldier like you." They walked toward the main building. "You musta been a tax child, too, since you worked for Elias?" he asked.

"No," Mara said, and pulled open the heavy door for the groom. "No, my parents went missing. The Protectors brought me to Elias when I was five."

The interior hallway was quiet as they walked. Cole appeared to be thinking over her story.

At her door, he said, "But you still became a great Protector. Tax children or no, we can grow up to fight." He drew himself up.

She nodded gravely, heart clenching at the thought of this small boy going into battle. Even if his family only valued him as a tax payment, that didn't mean he deserved to become another slash mark on her floor.

After the groom left, Mara turned slowly, hands on hips, searching for any details she might have missed. Her fire had gone out again and the room was cooling. Her bed was made, her altar clean, tiny window closed. She ran her eyes over the chair, stool, and cushion near the hearth—all fine.

Judging by the fading sun, it was time to change for the celebration. Surprised that Annelise had not barged in to bother her about hair or clothes, Mara knocked on her partner's door.

"Annelise?"

"Come in," Annelise murmured.

Mara stepped through the doorway, appreciating, as she always did, Annelise's knack for creating a sense of warmth and cheer. Plump, handmade cushions were stacked neatly on either side of the hearth, a soft green blanket was draped over the chair, and matching curtains hung over the window. Annelise stood in front of her mirror, eyebrows drawn together in a small frown.

"Is that a new dress?" Mara asked.

"Yes. Well, yes and no." She pulled at the seam on one of her sleeves. "I bought the fabric last summer and I've been sewing on it in bits since then." She continued fussing with seams, first on the other sleeve, then the neckline.

Uncertain how to comment on sewing or style, Mara said, "That color is perfect for you."

The dusty lilac shade of the gently shaped dress brightened her partner's blue eyes and complimented the glow in her cheeks. Annelise had even tamed her hair into loose, orderly curls.

"Thank you," she replied, meeting Mara's eyes in the mirror. "I haven't really looked at myself out of uniform for a long while." She ran her hands down her sides and over her hips. "I look different than I did when I got here."

"Yes, but thank goodness for the truce," Mara said. "More time on the battlefield might have marked up that pretty face of yours."

A frantic knocking sounded on Annelise's door. It burst open and Jahella stuck her head through. "Mara, they're looking for you!"

Mara swallowed hard. "What?"

"Did you talk to a Gaishan?"

"I—" Mara began.

"Of course not, is what I told them. No one talks to the enemy, too busy fighting." Jahella folded her arms and nodded.

Annelise took a few running steps into the hall and crashed into Gunder.

"There's a group of Browns coming," he said. "They've been searching rooms and going door to door asking about any soldier who initiated contact with a Gaishan during battle."

Annelise dragged him into her room. "Do they think Mara did something? I don't want her to disappear!"

"You keep to yourself. Sometimes you just hang out in the stables or the map room. Everybody knows it," Jahella said, nodding at Mara. "Wouldn't be any special reason you aren't in your room when they come. Maybe you're taking a last-minute shower to be fresh for the dance."

Mara grabbed her cloak. "I should go. If the reports don't match or if the healers found something after all—"

"Won't matter what happened. They'll just take you," Annelise said.

Jahella clasped Mara's forearm. "See you at the next fight."

"Next fight," she agreed.

The tall girl opened the door and looked both ways down the hall. At the far corner, soldiers in Brown uniforms stood clustered outside two rooms. Mara walked the opposite direction, toward the Blue hall and the exit near the healers. It was hard to walk slowly, hard not to limp.

Pausing at the set of heavy doors, she wrapped and pinned her winter cloak around her shoulders. She knew she wasn't about to commit treason, even if it looked that way. Feeling suddenly light-headed, she took a few deep breaths and stepped out into the dark.

Chapter 8

The first moon to rise, Drasil, crested over the trees as a tiny sliver. Bodhi, the second moon, soon followed, slightly larger and brighter. They shed enough light for Mara's purposes, but left enough shadows to hide from patrols.

The battleground still bore the marks of recent fighting, churned earth full of boot and hoof prints, plants bent and broken. As she rode the perimeter, Mara noted lash marks on tree trunks from fighting staffs and swords. She slowed Rowan to a stop, creating a mental picture of the Protector stations and assignments arrayed across the cold ground.

They had been stationed along this piece of border for just a few days, the encampment prompted by reports of Gaishan activity. She never knew how the fighting ground was chosen—those questions were always rebuffed by senior Protectors. Something felt wrong as she looked over the otherwise unremarkable field of what had once been wild grasses. Did the Gaishan manipulate Protector forces into certain areas? And if so, why? Mara filled her lungs with frosty air and exhaled white mist.

"This battle," she said out loud, nudging her horse toward the western tree line. "Where was I? How did Dalin get to me?" Finding the tiny clearing where the Gaishan had revealed his face, she could now see how far away the center of the fight had been.

She lingered a few minutes more, fingers tracing the raised edges of the new scar through her pants, but the fighting ground didn't yield any new revelations. Dalin didn't appear. A vision didn't suddenly take hold.

Her soldier's senses opened to the cold, quiet night. The wind rattled the tall grass and nearly bare tree branches. Night birds called, long keening notes. One last time, she cast her eyes over the terrain, forcing herself to remember, to see the battle between teenagers and the tall, masked invaders. But a large cloud drifted across both moons, casting everything into momentary darkness.

#

For several hours, the girl and her horse followed a south, southwesterly path. Mara kept alert and awake listening for pursuit as well as any sounds of potential game. It would be important to try and hunt tomorrow. Scenes from the battlefield replayed in her mind, but sometimes she would change the ending and imagine herself punching Dalin in the jaw. Or maybe the eye. Without trickery, in daylight, she could hold her own against him.

The ripple of running water increased to a babble as the tired pair approached the stream, their first landmark. Rowan pushed through the undergrowth to the muddy bank and lowered her nose for a drink. Mara dismounted and unhooked her canteen from the saddle. When her canteen hand dipped into the icy water, she shivered. The full intensity of the white-storm season would be here soon. Judging by the moons' positions through the scudding clouds, half the night had already passed. She left her horse drinking and grazing to investigate the nearby tree line for a camping spot.

Within a few minutes, she found a flat enough area inside four trees about twenty paces from the edge of the woods. The press of fatigue goaded Mara to move quickly as she led her horse to the campsite and undid the mare's saddle, saddlebags, and miscellaneous gear. She rubbed down Rowan with the saddle blanket and folded it to lay out feed. Mercifully, the tent was a one-person set up. After stringing a quick tether, she draped two blankets over the mare's back. And with a last quick look around, she flopped into the tiny canvas shelter, rolled herself in the blankets, and fell into a deep sleep.

A few minutes or hours later, a voice said, *"Where are you?"*

"Shut up, Dalin," she grumbled. "'m sleeping."

"Mara," his voice came again. *"Can you picture your location for me?"*

She tucked the blankets under one side and turned over. "Not my senior Protector." But she opened her mind and filled it with an image of the stream and her tent inside the trees.

"Are you near where you first saw the stream? Or did you follow it for a while?"

"First sight. Rowan thirsty. Tired." The pull of healing magic in her system dragged Mara's mind toward deeper sleep once again.

"A shadow is moving toward you. You must travel as quickly as you can manage. You're in danger." Dalin's dream voice changed. *"Wake at first light."*

#

When the first fingers of sun brushed her tent, Mara woke as ordered. The memory of her dream conversation filtered into her conscious mind and she sat up, fumbling for her canteen. She shoved her feet into her boots, pulled on her jacket, and took the first two saddlebags with her as she crawled from the tent.

A soft glow painted the horizon, barely visible inside the trees. Rowan stood nearby, munching on forest plants. The horse flicked her ears and blew out a breath when she saw her rider.

"Ready for a big day, girl?" Mara asked.

The mare stepped forward and snorted in response.

"Don't worry—Elias packed you a nice breakfast." She pulled out the special bag of mixed grain, untied one of the tent flaps, and detached it from the rest of the structure. Folded, the tent flap served as a makeshift trough for Rowan's morning meal.

While her horse ate, Mara rewrapped and pinned her winter cloak at the shoulder. Not only was the cloak warm, it covered most of the brilliant red of her uniform. Leaving Rowan at the stream for a drink, she hurried back to the campsite to erase the traces of their overnight stay, removing bent twigs and crushed leaves from where the tent and the horse had rested. She poured water to soften the hoof impressions, then kicked dirt and leaves over the deepest prints. The same technique worked on the stream bank, softening and smudging boot and hoof prints. Standing in the grass, Mara buckled the saddle and checked every strap. She mounted her horse, pleased to see it was not full dawn.

Dalin had said a shadow was coming? It must be the Browns. Or other Gaishan? Not part of Dalin's team, group, squadron…there was an unsettling thought. She didn't even know how the Gaishan were grouped or deployed. Yet. It underscored the depth of her trust in a near stranger and former enemy.

On Roland's map, the region where she now traveled had been originally marked as neutral. Part of the new Protector Territory, it was where the mapmakers would soon begin their work. To be so uncertain was new to Mara. She felt vulnerable and that fear easily percolated into anger.

She tightened her knees, encouraging the horse into a smooth canter. From a pocket, she pulled out leftover pastry and dried meat. "Nothing like breakfast in the saddle," she growled.

The sound of her own voice, so angry and serious, made Mara laugh. The sun was rising, casting a warm glow across the grassy plain. Rowan was moving with grace and speed. Best of all, Mara was as free and unaccountable as she had ever been. She laughed again, anger dissolving. "Come and get me, shadow!" she yelled and shifted into a distance-eating run.

#

Neither the terrain nor the clouds changed in a sudden manner over the course of the long afternoon ride. But the bite and strength of the wind increased as clouds built in fortress formation, storm formation, in the north. Now that she and Rowan were on the final stretch for the day, Mara felt both tired and exhilarated. She leaned forward in the saddle and spoke in the horse's ear. "This is as far away as we have been. Ever."

Staying low over Rowan's neck, she looked ahead and caught a glimpse of something not tree or grass or bird. They slowed to a walk. Might as well look for a place to camp while searching for whatever had caught her eye. Nothing seemed amiss at the tree line. The ground looked inviting, a carpet of small leaves eddying in the light breeze. Mara stopped and leaned toward the trees. She smelled fire and something cooking.

It had to be a Gaishan. The Protector expedition wouldn't depart until all the soldiers had returned from leave. She knew they weren't, technically, in Gaishan Territory. But neither were they within the fully protected boundaries. Mara eased her sword out of its sheath. The smells drifted from around the next curve in the tree line.

Mara led her horse as close as she dared, dismounted, and quickly attached a short picket rope. She draped a blanket over Rowan and attached it to the saddle.

The wind came in bursts through the trees and rattled the underbrush. Fixing the direction of the campfire in her mind, she moved farther into the woods, partly to test the wind's reach and partly to avoid her cloak being blown into the branches and snagging open. It was imperative to keep her sword hand free and her body ready. Mara sent a little energy to her arms and legs to counteract the stiffness of the past days' riding and sleeping on the ground.

A few minutes later, she found the campsite. Her hand tightened on the leather grip of the sword. She could see a tent and a single warhorse, the fire, but no people. A single horse could mean a single rider. Or it could mean the camp master or mistress was here and a platoon of Gaishan would be along at the end of their patrol. In which case Rowan would give away her presence to anyone heading north along the trees. The thought made Mara want to run back, but she forced the impulse down. She took one step back and to the right, intending to circle around the camp.

Her second step took her directly into a person. Yelling, she whirled and swung her sword at the target's midsection.

Chapter 9

"Hello Mara," Dalin said, turning to the side and parrying her blow with a stick.

She yanked her sword from the notch in his makeshift staff. Hot anger burst to life across her skin. "You! What?" was all she could spit out. She desperately wanted to attack until the fury dissipated. Knuckles white from the effort, she checked her second swing and brought her sword back down to her side.

Watching her carefully, the Gaishan took two steps backward. "My apologies for startling you, Mara of the Light," he began, right hand resting on his sword hilt, staff in his left.

She growled, kicking at the dry leaves eddying in the wind.

"Mara," he amended, "I'm here, closer than our meeting point, because of the storm."

Wanting to glance at the sky for confirmation, wanting to look anywhere but up into his strange silver-gray eyes, she held onto her tattered calm. His sudden appearance had triggered every fighting instinct, if only he would make a move.

"The clouds are building to the northwest," Mara said through clenched teeth. "You think the white storm will hit here as well?"

"We have people with great skill in tracking the patterns of air and moisture." He stood very still, stick at his side. "The white storm will spread far south this time. Farther south than our meeting place."

She shifted her stance, anger changing to annoyance as her heart slowed. "Whoever heard of a white storm so large? How do you know these"—she gestured with her free hand and flipped back her hood—"ideas will be correct?"

Shifting his stance as well, the Gaishan looked just as he had on the battlefield and in the dream communication. Tall, light hair, dark clothes, relaxed but ready for action. "In our recorded history they, our 'weather watchers,' you would call them, have rarely been wrong when it comes to a big event like this. I thought…" Dalin paused. "The elders encouraged me to ride out farther to get to you before nightfall. To help you."

"I've been out in white storms before," Mara replied. She reached over her head and slid her sword into the sheath between her shoulder blades.

He inclined his head. "But you didn't need magical protection in those instances. Is that correct?" His face remained serious, without a hint of teasing.

"Yes," she admitted.

Dalin's expression relaxed into a smile. "Well, I have good news for you," he said. "The first part of the preparation for using this particular magic is to eat."

As the wind quieted for a moment, Mara's traitorous stomach rumbled.

He politely ignored the sound, relaxing his hands and jamming them into the pockets of his jacket. "Were you on your way back to your horse?"

"No," Mara said, feeling guilty. "I knew she was exposed but I was trying to determine how many were camped here."

"I was coming along the tree line to intercept you and saw you slip into the woods."

"You could have called out or given some kind of signal." She tossed her braid over her shoulder and began retracing her steps through the trees and underbrush. The Gaishan followed.

"With your hood over your face, I couldn't be certain it was you. As you know, the Browns have been scouting to the south."

Mara's step faltered for a moment. Glancing over her shoulder, she said, "I thought you could sense me with your mind." She pushed aside a low branch and held it. He didn't answer right away.

"For now, that's only possible in dreams. And even that much mental contact takes a lot of effort."

Together they emerged from the trees a few paces from her horse. He walked around to Rowan's nose to reintroduce himself while Mara quickly pulled the spike from the ground and coiled the picket rope. Only then did she spare a look at the sky. Thick, dark-gray clouds boiled overhead, and the wind outside the trees blew with considerable force.

"Do you know, did your weather watchers tell you when the worst of the snow will arrive?"

He followed Mara's gaze upward. "An hour or two. Our protections need to be in place before we sleep."

The Gaishan walked ahead, leading them along a different route back into the forest. As she fell into step, Mara shook her head, causing her braid to whip around and back again.

"Why am I so calm?" she murmured to her horse. A few minutes ago, she had been surprised and furious. Now she was walking back to an enemy's campsite as though he were just another Protector and this were a routine mission.

Dalin moved with smooth purpose, exuding an air of calm authority, like that of a senior Protector. But he wasn't just anyone; he was Gaishan. And his build was a good reminder since all Gaishan were tall and thin. But height and weight aside, he could easily be a soldier or a settler from the northwest.

In a tiny corner of her mind, she admitted his competence was attractive, as was the rest of him. But she tucked that thought away and decided to search the stranger for signs of hidden weapons instead. Dalin didn't wear a cloak but rather a heavy-looking, padded jacket. No sword or other long knife was visible outside the jacket, but certainly small weapons would be easy to conceal under all that fabric.

Mara smelled the cook fire and what had to be stew or soup as they broke through a thick stand of underbrush and into the clearing. Rowan whuffed and flared her nostrils.

The Gaishan added a log to the fire and turned to help with gear. With two sets of hands, it was the work of a moment to place her packed tent, blankets, and bags on the forest floor next to his. While she rubbed down her horse, Dalin produced a measure of mixed grain, similar to what the stable master used. Rowan ate from the makeshift trough, but the other horse, tall and broad with a golden mane and tail, remained a polite distance away.

Mara, too, remained at a polite distance. Even with a fellow Protector, she didn't talk much at camp. She shook out her tent to begin pitching it.

"Before you do that, let's eat," Dalin said. "I want to brief you on how the storm protection works so we can get started."

Training dictated horse, shelter, then food. But she was so hungry and the storm was getting closer. It was hard to trust this boy, but it was equally hard to imagine how this could be a trap. Gaishan were just as vulnerable to storms as the Protectors.

Dalin was spooning a delicious-smelling stew into both bowls and smiling. When she sat down on the cold ground, he handed her a bowl and began rummaging around in a pack. Mara lowered her nose into the steam. The warmth felt good on her face. The Gaishan handed her a spoon and a small loaf of bread.

"For dipping," he said, gray eyes crinkling at the corners. "We like to dip bread in our stew." He took a slow bite of bread and stew together, chewed, and swallowed. "It's not poisoned, in case you were wondering."

"You've already had several chances to kill me and I'm really hungry," she said. Taking her first bite, she groaned in pleasure. The creamy gravy and tender bits of vegetables were delicious and a welcome change from her fare the past two days.

When he tore off a hunk of bread and dunked it in his bowl, Mara followed suit. The bread was coarse with a hint of sweetness. Even though hunger heightened her appreciation, she was certain the flavors and textures complimented each other very well.

Mara tried to eat slowly, to show at least a soldier's version of manners. But the stew was so tasty, she found her bowl empty and her bread half gone in no time.

"More?" the Gaishan asked. He set his nearly empty bowl down, filled hers and his own.

As her belly warmed, Mara paused to glance around the darkening clearing. It was just large enough for the fire, two horses, and two tents. Trees formed a roughly circular shape and both needles and leaves covered the mostly level ground.

After a few more bites, Dalin asked, "How much do you know about magical shields?"

At the same moment, she started to ask, "How much time left before snow fall?" She made a "you first" gesture.

The other soldier looked straight up, then around the clearing. "We have less than an hour until the first flakes, maybe two hours until the full storm hits."

"Has the compound been impacted by this storm already?"

He dipped a bit of bread in his stew and looked at Mara over his bowl.

"I don't have the weather skills myself," he said. "Last night I received an update that the storm was moving faster and covering a larger area than first anticipated." He chewed his bite, thinking.

She watched his face, not expecting a lie, but sensing he was holding back. "And?" she prompted.

"And, I'll learn more while we sleep."

Mara lowered her eyes, concern for her friends taking momentary precedence over her own situation. Not that she could do anything from here. She hoped Annelise and the others had been able to get out from under the Browns and go home to enjoy leave.

"My question now," he said. "Magical shields?"

She answered carefully, sketching out in a few sentences the teaching about shields for battle.

"Can you shield yourself and your horse at the same time?" Dalin pressed.

"I don't know," Mara answered, surprised by the question. "We were told Gaishan"—she paused—"you wouldn't attack horses."

He pushed his lips out and blew, expression thoughtful. "I wonder how that information got to the Protectors," he said. "Even though it is true, it's both tactically unwise for us to allow you to know that and for Protectors not to know how to shield their horses."

Mara had thought as much herself.

The Gaishan stood and reached out a hand to help her up. She ignored him and pushed herself off the ground. "Do you have enough in your belly to manipulate magical energy?"

"Yes, thank you." She wanted to add, *It was delicious.* But having received so few compliments, she found giving words of praise difficult and awkward. Instead she turned to brush leaves off the back of her cloak.

"When we teach magical skills, we try to contain the work in a safe environment. You don't have the luxury of learning that way." Dalin paused.

Mara shrugged.

"What we're going to do will keep us dry and relatively warm for the duration of the snowstorm, but it takes energy and concentration."

Again she shrugged and nodded. She wondered what magical effort didn't require energy and concentration. He watched her in silence, waiting for a response.

Mara sighed. "First, shields are protective in nature, so don't worry you'll teach me something I can use against your people. Second, please don't confuse me with someone who is new to magical energy and its uses. I'm aware of the risks." She ruined the effect of her confident statements by shivering as wind whipped under the cloak and up her spine.

It was the Gaishan's turn to nod. He walked a few paces past the horses, held out a hand. "Walk the perimeter of the circle with me. It'll help us visualize the boundaries of our shield." He stepped out, slowly pacing along the tree line.

Mara took a slow breath and followed. Her injured leg was stiff with muscle fatigue and cold, and the stew in her stomach churned with tension. She'd never heard of a shield the size of a campsite.

"This is how we begin," he said, continuing his slow walk. "Pacing out the edges of the shield lays down a trace of our energy. When we stand in the center and push the shield walls out, they'll catch and hold onto these traces. Repeating the walking strengthens the traces. So"—he turned to look over his shoulder—"I usually walk it three times. Plus, my old granny told me the number three has energy of its own."

Before she could stop herself, Mara blurted, "You have a granny?"

"I did," he answered after several more steps.

Snowflakes puffed and swirled through the trees, causing the fire to flicker. As she walked behind Dalin, his strides even longer than her own, Mara was glad his urgency now matched hers. If the storm came before they were ready, they could lose the horses and potentially their own lives.

On the third time around, she concentrated on protection and safety. She shaped and held a mental image of waiting out a white storm in Northwest Protector House, snug and safe. Third circuit completed, the Gaishan walked to the center of the clearing, near the fire. He motioned for her to join him.

"When you use personal shields in battle, where does the energy come from?"

She hesitated, not certain what he wanted for an answer. "From me," she said. She tapped her chest and her head.

"All right," he said. "And how do you maintain your shields so they can last for hours if necessary?"

Another gust sent a heavy curtain of snowflakes over the horses and gear. The fire dimmed for a moment.

"I picture a place in my mind where the shield connects. I leave that place in charge of maintaining the shield while I fight." He nodded encouragement, reminding her of Zam in that instant. "It always worked until I met you," she added. "This is my first real battle wound." She pointed to her leg. "But I know my shield was still up when I—"

Dalin caught her hand. "I'll always be sorry I wasn't there to prevent your injury." He took a breath, looked around the clearing, and let it out. "My questions are to pinpoint how you were taught to source your shields. Personal sourcing works, but will exhaust the individual relatively quickly." He laced his fingers with Mara's as she took a breath to speak. "Usually this is months-long learning, but we have to hurry.

"For a shield this large, we source it in the earth, connect it to the living energy of the trees and creatures nearby. We'll bear some of the energy drain, but only a part."

"Understood," she said, which was partly true. The freezing wind numbed her cheeks and one eye watered at the corner.

"The way you tied the shield to a location in your mind? We're going to do that, but twofold. First here in the center of the circle we traced, second in our minds." He raised their joined fingers and reached for her free hand. "Skin contact will connect both of us to the source and lend me your energy."

The moment their other palms touched, Mara gasped as energy dumped through her body like a bucket of warm water. A low hum vibrated through her bones and her heart beat loudly in her ears.

Dalin closed his eyes, bending his head in concentration. She took deep breaths, despite her racing pulse, and brought back the image of the safe compound, thick walls protecting from the wind. After several long moments, the Gaishan opened his eyes.

"We did it," he said, relief in his voice.

"But the energy is still flowing," Mara said, raising their linked hands.

"I anchored it, so it should flow out to the shields in a moment. Feel that?" Dalin looked up. No wind and only a few flakes were drifting down to where they stood.

Outside the circle, the snow fell heavily. The shield wasn't like a flat ceiling where leaves or snow might collect. Instead, everything just slid over. The magical barrier also buffered the ferocity, if not the chill, of the storm.

The two soldiers locked eyes for a moment and, in unspoken agreement, let go of each other's hands. Mara immediately wrapped her arms around herself and walked to her small, neat stack of gear. Her horse seemed comfortable, but she shook out a second blanket and laid it across the mare's back. She bent to pull out the stake for Rowan's picket.

"I think—" Her voice emerged rough and husky. Mara cleared her throat and swiped a hand across her nose. "I think I should shift Rowan's rope so she's closer to the fire. That way she won't accidentally break the barrier."

The Gaishan looked up from feeding wood to the fire. "You can," he said, "but the shield feels like an invisible wall to animals. They won't try to go through."

"So you'll leave your horse where he is?" Mara asked.

Dalin, intent on the woodpile, barely glanced at his mount. "My only concern is that he be near Rowan so they can keep each other warm. If you move Rowan, I'll move Herald."

Mara swallowed. "That will be true for us as well," she said with reluctance. She bent and re-anchored the picket stake. The big warhorse snuffed and stepped closer. She moved her cloak aside to dig in a pocket for a few crumbled bits of treat. The horse nibbled from her palm while she scratched his ears. "You said his name was Herald?"

"Yes." The Gaishan relaxed near the fire, his long frame curved in a semicircle, head propped on one hand. "He was the firstborn of a new line of horse stock, the herald of good things to come."

Herald sniffed her empty hand. "Maybe more later, boy," Mara murmured. She wiped her hand on her pants and went to the fire.

"The ground is cold but the fire feels great," Dalin said, indicating the space opposite him. "We should get warm and eat again before sleeping."

Her eyes flicked to the small tent. It was one thing to trust the Gaishan as a fellow soldier, another to work magic together, but sleeping in the same tent?

She imagined Annelise scolding her. *Mara, would ya rather freeze to death? And anyway, you can still have your own blankets. We've all had worse-lookin' tentmates, that's for sure!*

She coughed to disguise the involuntary laugh that bubbled up. Her partner would snuggle right up to Dalin, Gaishan or not. He was friendly, resourceful, a skilled soldier, and admittedly, not hard on the eyes.

She shoved a lock of hair behind her ear, only then noticing the wind had pulled most of it out of the braid. With a quick twist, she released the leather tie and shook her unruly hair free. She looked up into the Gaishan's speculative gaze.

"Do you often camp in snowstorms?"

He looked past her to the snowfall accumulating in the woods. "No. Protectors tend to avoid skirmishes once the bad weather comes. If not running boundary patterns, there's no need to be this far north, especially during the coldest season. My home is much farther south," he added.

"This is the farthest south I've ever been," Mara admitted.

"That you remember."

"You're fogged," she snapped.

Dalin flicked his free hand. "Yes and no," he said. He leaned forward and poked the fire with a stick. For a moment, wood smoke billowed into a thick cloud, then thinned and drifted up to meet the falling snow.

Following the path of the smoke, she took in a surprised breath. It was as though they were enclosed in a small, glass shelter. The occasional burst of wind barreled through and the heat of the fire didn't stay contained as it would in a room, but in the center they were relatively comfortable.

She didn't want to talk about what she did or didn't remember, nor did she want to talk about being fogged. She wanted to pretend she and Dalin were a male/female fighting pair like Haleen and Gunder. Those two slept in the same tent during training exercises, the only time fighting pairs were out together.

"Do you have a plan for the second evening meal?" she asked, choosing what she hoped was an easy topic of conversation. Even though they had eaten a short while ago, Mara felt as hollow as she had earlier in the day.

Dalin pushed himself to a sitting position. "Let me show you the supplies and you can help me decide," he said. He stood and rubbed his hands together. Handing over two bulging saddlebags, he pointed to four wrapped bundles. "I thought we might roast two rabbits tonight and save two for tomorrow. I have the ingredients for bread, spices for stew, and some dried fruit."

"When you say two rabbits for tomorrow, do you mean tomorrow night?" She really wanted to ask how to make bread over a fire, but stuck with the more immediate concern.

"If the weather models were correct, this part of the storm will end sometime in the middle of the night. We should be able to head out midday, if it doesn't drop too much snow. Farther south, even a few hours farther, we should find game."

Mara dropped the saddlebags, a twin surge of panic and anger racing through her. "I can't go farther south," she said. "I chose to meet you to learn answers, to understand..." She stumbled over words that even as she spoke them sounded untrue. "I'll return to the compound when you head south."

Dalin placed the rabbits on two flat stones before turning to face her. "Mara of— Mara, whatever snow lands here will be at least double around and within your compound, maybe triple. Your comrades on leave won't be able to return until the end of winter."

She took a step backward and stumbled over a tent rope as the reality of the situation hit her full force. Dalin caught her arm and steadied her.

"You were in danger at the compound."

"But I'm safe with you?" The pitch of her voice rose.

"Yes."

"And I'll be safe farther south as well? Deeper in Gaishan Territory?"

"It'll be easier if you don't walk around in your uniform," he said, clearly striving to keep calm. "But overall, yes." With a sharp look into the trees, he asked, "Were you able to depart in secret?"

"I'm not sure. The Browns were doing door-to-door checks for people who had interacted with Gaishan. I left before they got to my room. But..." She hesitated, feeling sick about the possibility that any of her friends caught trouble in her stead. "It depends on how the questions went in the Green corridor."

"How many people know you left?"

"Only my partner. The rest of our group thought I was going to the stables to lie low. Why?"

"The Browns, as you call them, are very intent on the accuracy of their data and they don't like loose ends. If they're not tracking you already, they will be soon."

"The 'shadow' you saw." Mara took a few steps toward the horses, wanting more space between herself and her enemy. Rowan whickered softly. She was committing treason and it wasn't because she was worried about her own safety. It was about the tally marks carved into her floor and the lost lives they represented.

"My intention was to meet you and learn more about…about the war, how to end it, I mean. You said my questions have answers." She put her hands on her hips and glared. The fire glowed against the red of her uniform jacket and the sheen of her boots. "Your intention—or was it your mission—was to make contact and bring me back to your settlement?" The angry words captured the heart of her fear, that she'd been a fool and committed treason, true treason, for nothing.

Dalin glared back, eyes flinty, jaw set. "I came to take you to your aunt."

Chapter 10

The world stopped. All sound, all sensation gone. Mara choked on a breath and clenched her hands into fists. "Say that again," she demanded.

"I came to take you to your aunt. Your parents are dead but your aunt lives in my settlement." The Gaishan held perfectly still, watching her as a hunter might watch a wounded, dangerous animal.

She wanted to feel elation, wanted to weep or find some other way to express the flood of feelings cascading through her body. After being alone for nearly all her life, to learn she had an aunt. "Whose sister?" Mara rasped.

He blinked. "Your mother's. You look like her, your aunt, Elana."

"Elana," she repeated. "My mother's sister, a Gaishan."

Her hand flashed to the sword at her back as she launched herself at the tall soldier. She knocked him to the ground, straddled his torso, and pressed the sword blade to his throat. Every instinct screamed to kill, to end him and his lies. Her mind furnished a war mask over Dalin's face so that she saw not another human, but the mask of an enemy. All the intensity of fighting such a bizarre, terrifying adversary for nearly four years condensed into an intense need to punish this one individual. Mara leaned just a fraction closer and felt a cool knifepoint pressing into the skin above her heart. Shock and awareness tightened her already taut nerves.

She put her hand between her blade and Dalin's throat. With exaggerated slowness, she sat back and slid the sword into its sheath. When she stood, she offered a hand. The dagger had already disappeared back into the Gaishan's jacket, so he accepted the hand and stood. Mara mumbled an apology and turned away.

Dalin tugged her shoulder toward him. "Hey," he said. "You just taught me a lesson."

Feeling sick for losing her temper and betraying her training, she wrapped her arms around her chest and stood sideways to Dalin, not able to face him.

"My father is always telling me I need to control myself and my reactions. I'm a 'deadly weapon,' he says. 'People are uncomfortable around you.' When you laid me out just then, I got it." He grinned.

Mara knew he was trying to help her feel better despite her appalling reaction, but his words didn't ease the ache in her chest. "I don't," she began. "I've never..." She trailed off. "Lashing out at you like that, I shame myself and my teachers." She bowed from the waist, eyes on the ground. "Please forgive me."

"I accept your apology," Dalin said. "And I would appreciate it if you kept it to yourself that you got the drop on me." He held out his hand for Mara to shake. "Fair?" he asked.

"Fair," Mara answered, wanting to smile back.

"We're heading south together?"

She nodded. "South."

#

One of the things that made Mara a good soldier was her lack of hesitation when it came to questions of risk for potential gain. The Green cohort trusted her instincts above most when it came to determining the need for attack or retreat. While the safety of her cohort was paramount, she had a good eye for a potential advantage and where to apply pressure. She was also able to judge losing scenarios quickly and pull her comrades to safety. It was her cunning and skill that had largely earned the Greens their reputation as the best fighters in the compound.

Though she could not articulate her reasoning, instinct told Mara most Gaishan would not pose a threat. She was as deadly as Dalin and had just proved it. If the greatest risk going south was harm from the few Gaishan who would attack her as they would any Protector, so be it. To have family, even a single living relative, was well worth any potential danger. Better yet if she was able to gather information about the war along the way.

"I can cook the rabbits if you make the bread," Mara said, ready to return to dinner as the main topic of discussion. She clapped her chilled hands together. "Are your spices in one of those saddlebags?"

Dalin handed over his spice kit, the rabbits, and two metal spits. It took Mara an extra moment to assemble the interlocking tubes made of lightweight metal. Her head was still spinning from his revelation and her intense response. They worked in silence as he prepared the bread mixture and she rubbed salt and herbs into the rabbits before setting them to roast.

The bread pan rested on a metal frame over the fire. Its long handle made turning the bread possible so that both halves of the circular loaf could cook evenly. The spits connected to the metal frame as well, one on each side of the bread, so the rabbit drippings only hit the fire. Soon the food began to give off a delicious smell. Mara's stomach growled audibly.

Dalin looked over at her and grinned. "Me too," he said, patting his stomach.

"I didn't realize how hungry I was," she admitted.

"We used a lot of energy to set the shield and are each giving it a bit of energy now as well. It was worth the effort, though," he said, nodding at the sky. Thick snow poured from the clouds and slid around their shield. "It doesn't work quite so well in a stiff wind. We're lucky this is a relatively sheltered spot."

"The snow makes everything so quiet," Mara said. "These would be terrible conditions for stalking or tracking or an ambush."

"Don't forget the footprints, trails of broken snow, and soaking-wet gear."

"Is that why we stop fighting during white-storm season?"

Dalin was still watching the sky. "In part."

The rabbits were nearly cooked, as was the bread. And while the noisy eating hall of the compound seemed worlds away, Mara's sense of connection to her friends held strong. The Browns couldn't do much once everyone departed for leave. Annelise, Gunder, all of them had to be safely in their settlements by now. Smoke wafted in her direction, causing her eyes to sting and signaling that the meat was probably finished.

Gingerly touching the first metal spit, she found it hot, but not burning. She loosened it from the frame and laid the crispy rabbit on one of the flat stones warming by the fire.

From an open saddlebag, Dalin produced two plates made of the same metal as his other cooking gear. Lifting the bread pan from its rack, he tapped it once on a rock. Mara watched as he plucked a knife from a hidden front pocket and used it to loosen the edges of the bread, then cut the round loaf in half. He presented one half with a flourish.

Mara met his eyes in the firelight. "Thank you."

As they ate, neither soldier felt the need to make conversation. The afternoon had been too eventful and emotional for casual chat. Mara could sense her connection to the shield—the traces of energy, as the Gaishan had called their circular path.

"We take the shield down when we leave?" she asked.

Dalin paused with a piece of bread halfway to his mouth. He looked very comfortable, long legs stretched out, reclining on one elbow again. "We do," he said. "Opening the shield is much easier than closing it." He popped the bite of bread in his mouth. From inside his coat, he produced a slim bottle, took a sip, and offered it to Mara.

The contents of the light, metal container smelled of berry juice and something sharper. "What is it?" she asked.

"Honey wine," Dalin said. "It's mild but makes a good finish to a camp dinner."

When Mara took an experimental sip, the honey wine burst across her tongue with bright sweetness. A larger swallow ran warm and smooth down her throat. "That's delicious," she said with total sincerity. "Do you make it in your settlement?"

"No, we trade for it," he said. "You have had a...difficult day. Take another sip." Mara took one more drink and handed the bottle back. The Gaishan took a final pull, screwed in the stopper, and tucked the bottle back into his jacket.

Despite the physical and emotional stresses of the past days, she felt a sense of contentment. If she kept her mind in the moment only, the warm fire, the protecting shield, a full belly, and, oddly, Dalin's presence made her feel safe and relaxed.

"You're smiling," he murmured. He reached out as though to touch her face, but when Mara's expression faltered, dropped his hand. "I like it." He smiled and pointed at his own face. "See?"

"If I were with another Protector right now," she said, ignoring the overture, "we would've already cleaned up and gone to sleep."

"Really?" He sat up and stretched slowly, reaching toward his feet and then up to the sky. "If one of my fellow soldiers were here, we would tell stories and drink honey wine into the night."

"On a mission?" Mara scoffed.

"Depends on the mission." Dalin stretched again and stood. He took two steps around the fire and offered a hand.

She took it and stood, her cold, injured leg protesting.

"If you check on the horses, I'll clean the dishes and fill our water containers," he offered.

Her still-healing thigh muscle had stiffened up, forcing a slight limp back into her stride. Both horses stood with their blankets on. Mara tossed her canteen to Dalin before offering first Rowan and then Herald some leftover bits of bread.

During winter training, even just in cold weather, most Protectors shared tents in twos and sometimes threes. Gender didn't matter. A soldier is a soldier, went the thinking. But she lingered a bit longer than necessary with the horses. Dalin was cleaning the last plate with heated water and some type of gritty powder when she limped back to the crackling blaze.

"Do you want to bank the fire?" she asked. "Or put it all the way out?"

"Bank it," he said. "I scanned the perimeter to be certain we're entirely alone. No one from either of our"—he paused—"*groups* is anywhere near enough to come investigate a tiny trace of smoke."

She stooped to pick up the warming rocks and moved them closer to the coals.

"I'll take care of it," Dalin said. "You go ahead and get your gear settled in the tent."

She hesitated, the habit of doing at least equal, if not more, work than her fellow soldiers keeping her still a moment longer. She huffed out a breath. "Fine. I'll take cleanup tomorrow." *And some answers about the war*, she silently added.

"If you like." The Gaishan turned back to his chores.

Mara grabbed her blanket roll and her small pack of personal items, and knelt to crawl into the tent. Inside, she felt something soft under her hands and knees, a thick tent pad that would insulate against the cold ground. She sat up and knocked against something swinging from the tent roof. When her fingers touched the object, it lit. Turning the tiny lantern, the size of four sugar cubes stacked together, she looked for the energy source. But the brief skin contact put the light out again.

"The light is touch-sensitive," Dalin called. "Two taps for on, one tap for off."

Mara tapped the lantern twice. The little light, hanging from a short cord tied to the top tent pole, cast a soft glow around the tent. It was impressive how tidy and organized the space was. She laid out her blankets next to what looked like a big sack made from the same material as Dalin's coat, and arranged her gear down where her feet would soon be. Digging around in her small pack, she fished out a bag of cut-up sponge squares dipped in tooth powder. Not ideal for teeth cleaning, but better than nothing. She selected a square from the bag and began rubbing it over her teeth.

"Need anything from out here?" he asked, poking his head and shoulders into the tent.

"No. All set."

Dalin crawled the rest of the way in, making the tent seem suddenly much smaller. While Mara sat cross-legged facing the center, Dalin dropped to face the foot of the tent and pull off his boots. He shrugged out of his jacket, wrapping it into a ball for a pillow, and revealing a very thin and fitted shirt. When he bent to unfasten the ankle closings of his pants, she turned lengthwise and kept her eyes on the frozen laces of her boots. She managed to loosen them enough to wiggle her feet out.

The ongoing togetherness of Protector life prevented much self-consciousness, but Mara didn't know Gaishan customs. She didn't want to offend the other soldier more than she already had by knocking him down and putting a sword to his throat. When she heard Dalin slide into his sleep sack, she quickly stripped down to her undertunic and leggings. She rolled herself in her blankets, resting her head on her folded cloak.

Dalin lay on his back, hands behind his head, eyes closed. "Ready for lights-out?"

"Yes," Mara replied.

Reaching up, he tapped the little light once. In the sudden darkness, the events of the day began to repeat in her mind, chasing away the small sense of peace she had gained at the end of dinner. She curled into herself, trying to breathe calmly and shut out the images of soldiers in Brown uniforms harassing the Green cohort. In her distress and fatigue, Mara found herself missing Annelise even more. She swallowed hard. When would she see Annelise or Elias again? She swallowed again, tasting tears.

"You all right?"

"Fine," she croaked. "I'm fine."

"Here." Dalin dangled a small white square of fabric near her face. She took it and blew her nose, coughing several times.

"Wake me if you're cold in the night. Or you can just scoot over here," he said. "Either way."

Mara choked, nearly laughing in spite of herself. "What?"

"You know sharing body heat makes sense in a storm situation," he added.

She recognized teasing in his tone. "As I said, I'm fine." The wave of homesickness vanished as quickly as it came. She rolled onto her back and rearranged her blankets. "You'll have to fog me to get me over there."

"Duly noted."

Chapter 11

Mara dreamed of both battle and people she knew, had known, all jumbled into a mixed crowd of faces. Every three weeks rotating on and off the front lines, years of fighting, all melded into an ongoing struggle.

The quality of the dream changed and she found herself sitting at a table with two adults and a child. The woman was pale with blue eyes and long, dark hair; the man was darker-skinned with black hair and eyes. The little girl, resembling more the mother than the father, sat on several cushions atop a chair. All three were laughing. The man stood and began to clear small bowls and a platter from the table.

The woman looked up at him and smiled. "Ah, thank you, Esteban.

"Of course, *cariño*. You did most of the cooking."

In an explosion of sound and movement, a Protector in full red-leather battle uniform and red helmet, visor closed, crashed through the door. The soldier stormed across the room, knocked the mother out of her chair, and snatched the little girl. Both adults surged forward, screaming for their child, only to be shoved down and kicked viciously. The terrified girl called and reached for her parents as she was carried across the splintered door and into the night.

#

Waking at dawn, Mara shuddered with lingering horror. Her mind would not relinquish the last dream image of those desperate parents. They weren't dressed as soldiers, and neither adult moved like a fighter. They were afraid of the Protector and the Protector took their child. *Why would a Protector take a child?*

She sat up, felt the cold air rush into her blankets, and immediately lay back down. A few deep breaths did little to slow her heart. The interior of the tent smelled surprisingly comforting, like trees or maybe incense. Tree-sap incense.

"Hey, you're still here." Dalin opened one eye and looked at her. She made a face. "Where would I go? You have the food."

"True." He sat up with his sleeping bag around his torso and rubbed a hand through his hair, adding to its spiky chaos.

"Is this made of the same materials as your jacket?" She pointed at the sleeping bag.

Dalin looked down, puzzled by the question. Then he looked at Mara's rumpled blankets and his face cleared. "Yes, it is. Why? Did you get cold in the night after all?"

She ignored the teasing. "Does it cost quite a bit in trade?"

"You could say that."

Before she could ask any more questions, Dalin slid into the pants from the bottom of his sleeping bag and flipped forward to look out of the tent flap. "Clouds are gone," he reported. "Snow doesn't look too deep from here."

Slipping into her uniform jacket and trousers was easy, but the cold wet boots presented a challenge. "Do you want to take care of the horses or breakfast?" she asked as she rolled her blankets.

"I can organize a small breakfast, but I hoped we might eat in the saddle."

"I'm used to eating in the saddle," Mara said. "That will give us a strong start this morning." Since the tent was too small for Dalin to pack his gear with another person inside, she crawled out of it and into the cold.

Only a dusting of snow had fallen within their shield. Outside the perimeter, the white drifts reached Mara's knees. The wind's ferocity had diminished somewhat and, as her travel companion had reported, the clouds were gone, leaving a clear sky for the rising sun.

Walking the few steps to check on the horses, she let her shoulders slump. Even before the dream, the night had been restless and uncomfortable, as though her mind could not find peace or relaxation.

With no choice but to ignore the wooly, not-quite-awake feeling, she poured most of their water reserves into the clear basin near Herald's things. She also laid out grain for both horses. As the animals ate, Mara ran her fingers through her loose hair to comb out the tangles and then began braiding, using touch as a guide. Her cloak slid off her shoulders as she worked, exposing the gap between the bottom of her uniform jacket and top of her pants to the wind. Shivering, she secured her braid and rewrapped the cloak.

"How are the horses?" Dalin called.

"Both seem fine." She watched him continue his work around the camp, envying the warmth and freedom of movement his jacket provided. "Your gear"—she waved a hand to encompass the small campsite—"is it typical of the other...soldiers you fight with?"

"Yes and no," he said. "Depends on the mission and what the weather experts say we might need."

Mara had always been bothered by the requirement to carry all gear for all engagements, no matter what. And without all that stuff, she smiled to herself, taking down camp and packing took a lot less time. In minutes, she'd closed her last saddlebag and put it on top of the pile.

"We're safe to take down the shield now. Ready to help?" He waited until Mara looked at him. "It's essentially the opposite of putting the shield up." He reached out and clasped one of her hands, pulling her into step as he began to walk the other direction around the perimeter.

This time she wasn't as startled by the energy flow through their linked hands, though it still felt strange. She didn't get touched much except for punches and kicks during sparring. Annelise hugged her sometimes, but that was about it.

Back in the center after the third trip backward around the circle, the tall soldier stopped. "We're going to let go of the anchor and the shield just like you would with a personal shield. Ready?"

She nodded.

"One, two, drop."

Mara staggered backward a step as the energy rebounded through her legs and arms. Dalin caught her before she fell.

"I apologize," he said. "A camp shield is a much larger backwash of energy."

With a correctly placed kick to the backs of his legs, Mara could drop him. She imagined herself saying, *Oh my apologies. The energy spilled through my foot.* And, well, she did want to knock him down again, but thinking about it would have to be enough.

An ice-cold wind whirled through the snow and damp leaves making the shield's absence more pronounced.

"I think we should ride through the trees, at least for the first part of the morning. The wind and blowing snow will be less of a factor."

"Ride or lead the horses?" Mara countered, shifting her line of sight south.

"We can ride," he said. "The trees are rarely too close together to impede a horse and rider."

"Slow going if trackers are coming," she said, pressing a hand to her stomach, churning with hunger and worry.

Dalin gave her a handful of dried meat strips, a piece of bread, and a piece of red fruit. "This is for breakfast and possibly lunch as well. We're going to erase all this before we leave." He gestured toward the fire pit and the other evidence of humans and horses.

"Thanks." She tucked the food into her uniform pockets.

Saddling horses and strapping on gear was short work for the two young veterans. Nothing could hide the evidence of the disturbed snow, but the blowing wind had already softened and partially filled the deepest tracks.

"Listen," Dalin began, one hand on Herald, one hand in a pocket. He sighed, gray eyes unsettled. "Where we're going—my, ah, my settlement—is very different from the places you've been in the North."

She shrugged, not wanting to let him know she was worried about any of that, not ready to talk about it either.

"When we stop tonight, I'll try to explain more." His voice trailed off and he dropped his gaze back to the tree line. "The weather experts tell me the snow was lighter about half a day's ride to the south of here. We'll only need to keep to the trees this morning."

From a nearby branch, snow blew onto both soldiers. She pulled up the hood of her cape. Dalin tugged on a small, close-fitting hat. Mara swung herself into the saddle, expecting her travel companion to do the same.

"You go ahead," he said. "I want to go through the campsite one more time, hide the magical traces."

If the Browns were following her or patrolling this far south, leaving any trace or trail was dangerous. "Makes sense," she said, even though she had no idea how to either read or erase magical residue. "Rowan and I can start south on our own."

#

Mara was glad to ride alone. She needed time to think, to develop a strategy for this ride south to Dalin's settlement. She would meet her aunt and maybe work to trade for some Gaishan camp utensils, things small enough to hide. New boots or a jacket like Dalin's would stand out too much once she returned to Protector House.

Now and then she glanced over her shoulder, expecting to see a horse and rider. After a few hours, she was chewing on the strips of dried meat and wondering where they were. As time passed with no sign of the tall Gaishan, Mara began to consider turning back. Even in the protocol for partner recon, Dalin should've checked in by now.

Mara pulled gently on the reins and made a clicking sound. Her horse came to a neat stop.

Dalin? She closed her eyes and called with her mind.

Dry tree branches rattled; snow hit the ground with soft thumps. Rowan shifted her weight and turned slightly. After another breath, Mara was certain they heard hoof beats. She steered her mount under the low hanging branches of an evergreen tree in case it was an enemy approaching. Just as a smile touched her lips at the contradiction in that thought, Dalin and Herald burst through the trees.

The tall soldier saw their tracks and pulled to a stop. "Mara?" he called, looking hard at her hiding place.

She slid from Rowan's back and reached down for a handful of snow. Packing it into a ball, she stepped into the open.

"It's about time you caught up," she said and sent the snowball straight for his face. His personal shield flashed, a tiny hint of response, before he had a face full of snow.

Dalin wiped his face with his sleeve, trying for dignity. "I owe you for that."

At the same time, Mara asked, "You're shielding?"

"Of course you have good aim," he said, wiping away the last of the snow.

She rubbed her cold hands together, trying to hide her glee at hitting him square in the face.

"I have my shields up because I retraced the last segment of your route. I wanted to see the aftermath of the storm and to determine if you'd been followed or not."

Responding to the should-have-done-it-myself expression on her face, Dalin said, "This isn't about oversight. My mission parameters changed when I reported in last night. Otherwise we would've started south together this morning."

"Did you—" But she knew it was something. "What did you find?"

"Someone followed you, a small cluster of soldiers, three, maybe four. But I don't think it was Browns. The formations weren't typical, and I saw some unusual tracks. It might have been another group altogether. Either that or patrol routes are suddenly much longer and much less routine."

"The Browns report to Roland and Garot," Mara said. "That's about all I know about them. I don't know their objectives."

"Ultimately, they report to the Queen. I know some aspects of their mission. Roland comes south on occasion to negotiate." Dalin turned and looked over his shoulder. "We should go." At his rider's signal, Herald pricked up his ears and stepped forward into the trees.

"Wait," Mara called. "How heavy was the snow farther north?"

"About three times as much, plus white-out conditions from high winds," Dalin called back as Mara nudged her horse into motion. "No one's following us now. At least not at the moment. No magical traces and no physical tracks."

"How can you be certain?" Mara asked and then flushed, hearing the challenge and shade of desperation in her voice.

"I was trained by the best," he said. "Your uncle," he added under his breath.

"What?" The horses were moving quickly and it added a buffering layer of sound.

"Let's go, I said." Dalin turned in his saddle. "We have our most difficult ride today. The farther south we can get, the better. Plus, if we reach our goal tonight, then better food." He tapped lightly with his knees and the warhorse picked up the pace.

Pushing her questions aside, she focused on those two tangible facts. *Long way to go. Better food.*

Chapter 12

On through the morning they kept to the Gaishan's relentless pace. As the sun crept overhead, they slowed slightly and turned east. The easterly route took them out of the trees and back onto the narrow plain, where the small stream had widened into a small river. The snow was just a dusting in the shadows beneath low bushes and clumps of grasses.

At the river's edge, Dalin vaulted down from his mount. Mara followed suit. "Ready for a break?" he asked.

"We both are," Mara said, patting her horse's neck.

"Let's get food and water for these horses," he agreed. "And then we can eat."

She led her mare to the sandy bank littered with rocks. Both horses stepped carefully forward and lowered their noses to drink. Mara unhooked her canteen from her belt and was stepping forward herself when Dalin put a hand on her arm.

"Keep your feet dry," he said. "My boots are waterproof and I can get out to those rocks where the water's running clear." He took her canteen and leapt onto a boulder situated deeper in the current. He leaned over and filled Mara's container, capped it, and tossed it to her. "Drink plenty," he said. "I can fill it again before we leave this place."

Mara took a few quick gulps, teeth aching from the icy water, as Dalin filled his metal container and jumped back to the shore.

"I've heard the Browns talk about planets where the water is too dirty to drink." He swallowed and wiped his mouth on his sleeve. "Hard to imagine."

"What's a planet?" Mara gave a half shrug, half headshake.

Dalin took a long swallow, his gray eyes speculative. "A planet is a huge ball of rock and earth where people and animals live. This planet is called Asattha. People from many Origin planets and planets around this system settled here hundreds of years ago. You weren't taught any of that?"

"No. I found pictures scattered in some books in the map room. But if planets are mentioned, it comes across more like a legend than information. Kind of like the story that Gaishan used to be settlers and they broke with all the protocols and became the enemy." She kicked a small stone into the water, unsure how she felt about this new information. It was hard to believe everything Dalin said, but it was also hard to doubt him constantly. Not when she wanted at least some of his words to be true. "When Roland told the Protector assembly about the Queen, it was a shock for most of us."

"Were you shocked?" The tall soldier watched her face very carefully.

"Yes and no." She gulped more water and wiped her chin on her sleeve. "It made sense, what Roland was saying. Before that, I could never figure where any of us came from. But why now? That's the part I just—" She shook her head. "Is it because of this truce Roland started talking about the Queen?"

Instead of answering, Dalin put down his water container and unfastened the feedbag from Herald's saddle. As though they had been traveling together for days, she automatically unfolded an extra blanket and laid it on the ground so he could pour out grain for each horse.

"If we make our goal tonight, will there be food for the horses as well?" Mara asked, eyeing the amount of feed remaining.

"Yes." Dalin patted Rowan's flank. "If we make it, and judging by our location now, I believe we will, everyone will have a warm dinner and shelter tonight."

Her stomach, empty but for cold water, turned over. "Dinner and shelter?"

"Dinner and shelter," he confirmed. "Maybe even a shower." Ignoring Mara's surprised expression, he began rummaging in his pockets. "Do you have any food left from this morning?"

Reaching into her uniform jacket, she produced two strips of dried meat and half the loaf of bread.

"I'm sorry I told you that might be two meals' worth," Dalin said. "I was worried it would be slower going through the trees and that we wouldn't hit this marker until long past noon." He gestured toward a less-than-natural stack of stones under a scrubby bush. "Eat that and I'll see what else we have."

Mara strolled up the river and back as she chewed on her stale bread. Every few bites she did a quick stretch, trying to loosen her stiff muscles.

"This shelter," she asked, "is it different from your tent? Will we need to set a shield?"

Dalin stood still, squinting upwards. The blue sky, with its combination of thin and puffy clouds, gave no indication of worse weather on the way. "Good idea," he said, clearly focused on whatever he was watching. "Under other circumstances, no, but tonight, yes. When we get to the wayhouse, I'll activate the house shield."

She wanted to ask about the wayhouse and clarify what a house shield might be, but Dalin's expression concerned her.

"Are you watching for something? Or did you see something? Report." The command just popped out.

He raised his eyebrows and smiled. "Report?"

"I…I just…" Mara fumbled for words as her cheeks heated.

Dalin stiffened his posture and snapped her a salute. "Ma'am, flying objects or personnel may be tracking us, ma'am."

Consternation shifted to puzzlement. "Flying personnel?" Dalin kept his arms stiffly at his sides, eyes on her ear. She cuffed his shoulder. "At ease. Just tell me."

"Are you in line for promotion?" he asked, slanting her a know-it-all smile.

"No, not really," Mara said. "Just years of habit. Especially with new soldiers, a voice of authority snaps them out of battle confusion… I'm sorry, I have no right to give orders."

Dalin reached over and tugged her braid. "I'm teasing you," he said, backing out of striking range. "We need to keep moving, but I'll brief you while we ride. It would be better if we could both watch for signs of aerial pursuit."

The horses had finished their snack and were munching on grass. Dalin shook out the blanket and deftly repacked it behind the mare's saddle. He turned to his mount, fastening and stowing the food gear and containers. "More water?" he asked holding out his hand for the canteen.

This time she watched his boots as he jumped between rocks. The thick sole material was a lighter color than the boots. Leather? How did Gaishan make leather waterproof? She knew about oiling the seams and such, but if you walked in a river, water still got in.

Stepping back from the riverbank, she shaded her eyes to look at the sky. Nothing. No birds, not even a cloud now.

"Whatever I saw," Dalin said in response to her unspoken question, "is gone. Mount up, soldier, and I'll brief you on the road."

Mara gritted her teeth and flung herself into the saddle. "Teasing," she muttered.

She imagined her partner's reproach. *It's no different than with the Greens. He's just tryin' to be friendly, can't ya see?* Thinking of Annelise softened the tension in her shoulders. This recon was all for the other Greens and the ones too young to fight.

Dalin pulled up to her left side. "Ready?"

"Always," she said.

The horses began with a quick walk and adjusted into a smooth canter. Like Rowan, she was glad to be out of the trees and have running room at last.

Dalin stretched out one arm and made his hand into a flat blade. He sighted along his arm toward invisible landmarks. "We're now traveling due south. Our course is close to the river until nearly the end of today's ride. The wayhouse is tucked back in the woods. It's important to arrive before sundown, if possible."

Many of the trees now had wide trunks and high branches, their silver-green leaves fluttering in the breeze. "We don't have that type of tree in the Protected Territory."

"No," he agreed. "The first stand of *gontra* trees is a visible marker of our borders."

"We're in Gaishan Territory?" she said, trying to suppress a flinch of surprise.

"Gaishan Territory as determined by off-planet mapmakers and politicians," Dalin spat. "Some of us think…" He paused and looked over. "Some of us think what lives here—people, trees, horses, for example—is more important than invisible lines or policies."

Without knowing what a politician was, she understood his point that those in a situation, like soldiers in the field, had a better grasp of necessary action or adjustments than those far back in the command tent or farther back at the compound.

"So what did you see in the sky?"

"Not in the sky, on the ground," Dalin corrected.

"But you were looking up—" she began.

"Because of what I saw on the ground," he continued. "A shadow with nothing to cast it."

Mara shook her head at that impossibility.

"Look," he said. "You like my gear, right? The tent, the cooking tools, my jacket and boots? Just a tiny fraction of developments, of adaptations my people have made. When we get to the city, my settlement, the differences between your boots and mine will seem small compared to the differences in the way our people live."

Dalin wasn't making sense. What did boots have to do with flying people? She'd guessed the Gaishan settlement would be different than those in the North. But the tall soldier seemed normal to her, and her aunt was probably normal. What else mattered?

"What's unseen but casts a shadow? Obviously not boots," Mara said.

"Did you ever fold paper in a special way to get it to fly?"

"Yes, Elias taught us." She'd noticed Dalin's tone changed when he was trying hard to explain things. It wasn't exactly rude, but it reminded her of how an adult might talk to a young child.

"Can you imagine paper so light and yet so strong, it can float on air currents and carry a person?" Dalin asked.

Irritated by the way he asked but intrigued by the question, she thought about a triangle of folded paper as tall as she was. To carry a person, would it have straps? A saddle? She shrugged and nodded.

"So if the paper is"—he searched for a word—"painted on one side to look like the sky, then when someone looks up, it just blends in."

"Camouflage?" she said. "Sky camouflage?"

With visible relief, Dalin said, "Exactly. Sky camouflage. So gliding on this sky…craft is a way to do recon from above. But it still casts a shadow. And I saw two shadows earlier."

"Should we get back to the trees?"

He rubbed a hand along his horse's mane. "We can ride much faster out here. If you see a shadow on the ground, let me know. I'll inform my leadership when I report in tonight and get their take on the situation." He drew a breath as if to say more, but didn't continue. They rode in silence for several long minutes. "I'm supposed to prepare you for how we live, but I truly don't know what to say, what to tell you, what words to use."

A cold sweat crept down her spine. Was it so bad? Were the rumors of people who were half animal true? Rumors of mutations? "Are the other Gaishan like you?"

Dalin stared ahead, jaw tight, eyes narrowed. She checked for shadows on the ground and flying people in the sky. This idea of sky camouflage and flying recon was fascinating. How often had she wished to have a better view, a bird's-eye view, of a battle? Maybe that was one of the mutations? Maybe some of Dalin's people were part bird?

"Are you trying to tell me a group of Gaishan is part bird, with feathers, laying eggs and such, and that's who uses the sky camouflage craft?"

His smile was hard. "Are those mutation rumors still around?"

"Gaishan fight masked," Mara countered. "Everyone speculates on what you might be hiding."

"We're hiding that we look just like you." He paused, running one thumb along his chin. "It's an ancient idea. Masks create fear and anxiety. Also, people who are otherwise peaceful find it easier to fight with masks on or to fight against those who are masked."

"So no Gaishan is part bird or fish. That's what you're saying?"

"Yes."

"The other Gaishan, the other *people* in your settlement"—she corrected herself—"all look like you and me."

"Yes," he agreed after a moment's hesitation. "With all the typical variations in human appearance found among the Origin planets. But appearances don't capture differences the way behavior or preferences might." He looked over. "For example, I'm different from many of the people I know because I chose to specialize in skills like hunting, fighting, camping, tracking, and so on. Most people you'll meet in the South don't have those skills."

"Like settlers?" Mara asked. "Only the ones who used to be Protectors know how to fight."

"Yes, but the lives of the people in the South are much easier than the lives of the settlers you know." He nudged his horse slightly ahead, ending the conversation.

Chapter 13

Mara had a lot to think about as she alternately watched the sky and the ground. What would make a person's life easier besides not being a soldier? The settlers had it pretty easy.

The sound of the river masked too many noises, so she also gave some attention to the tree line. No animals showed themselves. Dalin had promised a good evening meal if they made it to this wayhouse. She tried to ignore the hunger and the accompanying compulsion to stop and hunt.

Though uneasy about what other things might be so different in the Gaishan settlement as to require additional briefing, she was glad she had asked about the mutation stories, and glad he had dismissed the notion. The masks created fear, on and off the battlefield. The worst ones lingered in her dreams, often for months.

But was he saying Gaishan were otherwise peaceful and reluctant to fight? Entirely human, peaceful people who lived easy lives? Good thing the truce had come, then. Maybe the enemy was running out of fighters.

With the sun straight overhead, the air had warmed enough for Mara to shed her cloak. After she tucked it behind her saddle, she took a long drink of water. Dalin slowed slightly to bring their horses side by side.

"Your uniform jacket keeps you warm?" he asked.

"Yes," Mara answered, puzzled.

"The...red," Dalin said. "It's bright for this part of the ride."

"What do you mean?" she said. "We're already in the open."

He grimaced. "There's a skill I've been working on: part shield, part camouflage. I can trick prying eyes, make us blend into the landscape."

"Would I know if this shield-camouflage had been used near me in battle?"

"Were you ever approaching someone who suddenly seemed to disappear?"

Mara gritted her teeth. "Yes, more than once. Which I reported, only to endure fog testing."

Dalin shook his head and blew a breath out through his nose with a low laugh. "I wonder how many reports like yours the

Protectors will collect before making a decision to include the possibility in training." He slowed Herald to a walk, but didn't stop altogether. "It'll be easier if I don't have to hide your red jacket. I can loan you a plain pullover until it's cold enough for both your layers. Or you can wear your cape over your undershirt."

"I'll wear your pullover if we can stop for a moment," she offered after weighing the options against the current weather and time of day.

Mara walked her mare through the tall grass and onto the riverbank. The width of the river and the speed of the water startled her; the sound had changed so gradually as they rode.

"Be careful," Mara warned her horse.

Rowan walked forward until the shallow water just covered her hooves, lowered her nose, and drank. Mara drank from her canteen and then stepped as close as she dared to fill it. The water was fast moving, clear, and ice cold.

Would the wayhouse have a water source? Most small houses in the settlements had an indoor pump in the kitchen and a few pumps to draw a bath. Only the Protector compounds had indoor running water, warm water, for showers. Stretching her arms over her head, she bent forward from the waist to loosen her legs. Small tremors shook her calf muscles but her hips just ached. She straightened when she heard Dalin talking softly to his warhorse, heading toward the water.

"Thanks for suggesting the stop," he said. "Herald had small ice-covered pebbles in two of his hooves. Did Rowan have anything like that?"

She bristled, but more from concern for her horse than irritation. "I wanted Rowan to drink before I checked her." She led the mare back onto the grassy plain and coaxed her to lift each leg. The horseshoes looked fine, no ice chunks or rocks in the grooves.

"We're roughly four hours from the wayhouse. I can see the next few landmarks downriver." He pointed southeast, the sun glinting off his short, light hair.

"You can see something that far away?"

"Not on my own," he said. "I used this." He held out a small black cylinder. She lifted the cylinder from his palm with caution. It was heavier than she expected and made of smooth black metal. At either end of the metal was a circle of glass.

Dalin tapped one end of the cylinder. "You look through here."

Turning toward the trees, she raised the cylinder to her right eye. Tree trunks jumped into her field of view so suddenly Mara took an involuntary step back, bumping into Dalin.

"Try again," he said, reaching around and bringing the distance-viewer back up to her eye. He guided her hand until she was looking south along the edge of the tree line.

She gasped at the clear details revealed by the viewer: the tops of the waving grass, dry yellow seeds at the top of each stalk, a trio of rabbits bounding out of the trees, tiny whiskers quivering. Mara lowered the cylinder. "Amazing," she said, rolling the viewer in her hand and thinking of the battlefield advantages. "Does it work at night?"

"Some do." He replaced the viewer in a pocket. "This one needs light to work."

Although she immediately wanted to talk about tactics, her stomach reminded her of a more important question. "Do we need to hunt before we get to the wayhouse? I saw some rabbits just now."

"That's not a terrible idea," he answered. "Usually the house is stocked, but we can always leave the rabbit behind for the next guests."

"Leave food behind—" Mara began to protest.

"The wayhouse is only a day's ride north of my settlement," Dalin interrupted.

Her stomach turned over, but not from hunger this time. The Gaishan people. A Gaishan settlement. She'd imagined talking to him in the woods, like in her dream, getting all the answers, and then riding back to the compound. Now she was less than two days' ride from a Gaishan settlement, a large one if she understood Dalin's attempts to prepare her.

She swallowed her questions and walked to her horse. She would have Rowan near if she needed to flee. And, she admitted to herself, she trusted this Gaishan to help her, to protect her. "Or at least help me protect myself," Mara muttered. Rowan flicked her ears and lifted her head from the grass.

After slipping into the saddle, Mara unbuttoned the bright uniform jacket and tugged her arms from the sleeves. Shivering in the cold wind, she nudged the mare with her knees until they faced Dalin. "May I please borrow your pullover now?"

He looked up, visibly startled to see Mara in her undershirt. "Of course." Fumbling in one of his bags, he produced a dark gray top. He unrolled it as he hurried over.

"Thank you," she said as he laid the garment over her outstretched arm.

Dalin paused and one corner of his mouth turned up. "It's clean," he said and whisked her uniform jacket from her lap. "I'll stow this for you. My bag's already open."

She opened her mouth to argue and gasped instead at the chill in the next gust of wind. Pulling the finely woven sweater over her head, she inhaled the scent of herbs and trees from the thick, soft material. Although she could still feel the wind, it no longer bothered her. She fastened the shoulder harness for her sword over the sweater and watched Dalin swing into his saddle.

"Are you going to use the camouflage shield now that I'm dressed for it?" She forced a light tone.

He scanned the sky, then the ground. "I haven't seen the shadows since we stopped. But better to be shielded as we cross this final open stretch. I'll need you to keep within a length."

Mara let go of the retort she had ready. Instead she asked, "Do you need help?"

"Not at the moment," Dalin responded. "But this will burn a lot of energy and I'm as low on food as you are."

"I'll take point once we get to the woods," she said. She watched an argument flit across his face and waited.

"You don't know how to get there."

"You can show me, like you did the first part of my travel." Mara held out her palm.

"Right," he agreed, reluctance evident. He inhaled and exhaled, then reached for Mara's hand and closed his eyes. As he began to trace the route, she saw the wayhouse as well as the landmarks that would get them there. She felt relieved the wayhouse looked like a house. After Dalin's cryptic comments about boots and gear, she hadn't known what to expect. *It looks cozy*, she thought, studying the approach, *certainly better than a tent*.

"Glad you approve," Dalin thought back.

Mara's eyes flew open as she yanked back her hand.

"Physical contact makes rapport very easy," he explained, a crooked smile lifting the corner of his mouth. "Now you know the way." He nudged his horse slightly ahead, then turned to look over his shoulder.

Mara cradled her hand as though it had been burned and glared at him.

"The camouflage shield is up," Dalin said. He leaned forward and his horse began to pick up speed.

Mara matched his pace, keeping within a length. Eventually, the pleasure of her running horse and the afternoon sun forced out the surprise and irritation of having Dalin touch her mind in person.

Physical contact wasn't necessary for mental communication, she knew. And soldiers couldn't touch each other in battle anyway. That would be just as awkward as trying to talk and fight at the same time. But to share tactical information, thought-to-thought, would be useful. The rest of the time? Did a casual touch, like brushing past someone in a market, open up that person's thoughts?

The questions heightened Mara's uneasiness. She knew next to nothing about where they were headed, the people, the terrain. The danger in breaking the rule of preparation had never been more evident.

Chapter 14

The sun was much lower when Dalin guided them into the edge of the woods and stopped. He dismounted, clutching his water bottle, and stumbled against the nearest tree. Mara slid out of her saddle as he took several gulping drinks.

"Shielding two people and two horses was more challenging than I thought," Dalin admitted, a slight tremor in his hand as he tried to recap the bottle.

"What's the point of a better shield if using it leaves you like this?" She began rummaging through her largest saddlebag.

"It's new," he said, no trace of a smile, eyes somber and shadowed. "We haven't worked out the best way to source the energy while moving. It's also mental energy that keeps the camouflage in place."

"Mm hmm," Mara said, disapproval in her tone. She turned and thrust a fruit and grain bar at him. "I keep these for emergencies. My partner..." She swallowed. "My partner, Annelise, her family makes them."

The tall soldier shook his head. "Yours," he mumbled.

She waited, hand extended. A Protector would take the offered food, particularly in extreme need. *Sentiment and pride are not relevant factors when it comes to basic needs,* the senior Protectors would say.

"You're offering me the last scrap of food you have," he said, straightening and looking her in the eye.

"You protected us," she countered.

"Split it?" Dalin offered. His voice had returned to normal, though his hands weren't quite steady.

"Fine." Unwrapping the chewy bar, she broke it into halves.

He accepted the larger half with a small smile and a slight bow. "My thanks."

Mara gave him her best flat-eyed stare, the one that made Protectors-in-training shrink into themselves and huddle against the wall in combat class. "Mount up, soldier," she said trying to imitate Twyla's growl. She offered no further assistance but checked Dalin's ability to keep his seat under the pretense of securing her canteen.

And she continued to check back as she led them farther south and west into the woods. The map and the travel view in her mind kept her confidence high that she was leading them to safe shelter. The dusky woods, full of unfamiliar trees, rock formations, and animal sounds, kept her from relaxing out of full vigilance. Twice she saw rabbits and, later a bird with distinct brown, red, and white markings burst from a bush to scold them. The terrain began to rise and fall and the rock formations grew large enough to contain shadowed caves. Caves a full-grown person could use while waiting to ambush travelers.

"Relax," Dalin said. "It's safe enough."

"Get out of my head," she snarled.

"Not in your head, watching your back. You're strung as tight as a violin." His tone was quiet.

"I'm on point because you knew you would have limited capacity. This is unfamiliar territory and—"

The woods had gone suddenly quiet; even the trees stilled in a hush that demanded silence. The leaves of a low-hanging branch brushed her cheek and Mara's sword flashed out.

"We're here," Dalin said.

She scanned the area for a structure but nothing matched the image he'd provided. Squinting into the shadows, she could just make out the bottom of a staircase behind a stand of trees.

Dismounting, Dalin led his horse into the thicket and disappeared. Sword still out, knuckles tight with fatigue and unease, Mara followed, pushing through a double row of underbrush and high branches.

From outside the clearing, the tall trees with green and silver leaves had appeared to be growing in a natural formation. Once in full view of the small stone house and stable, it was clear planning had helped create the living boundary. Mara touched her head to her mare's shoulder in relief, breathing in the familiar smell of sweaty horse. The wayhouse not only looked just like the picture in her mind, it looked similar to a typical house in the Protected Territory. She murmured, "Thank the Light," as she walked toward the stable.

Once inside, Mara closed the large doors behind her and stared around the stable like a child at her first market. Bright lights hung from the ceiling, water poured into a huge trough with its own water source, and sweet, fresh hay partially covered the otherwise-clean stone floor. "Only has four stalls," Dalin said, glancing up from his gear. "Take your pick."

Years of habit turned Mara's attention to caring for her horse. Throwing her cloak over one half wall, she stripped off saddlebags and sleeping blankets first, then removed saddle and bridle.

"You can leave tack on that bench," Dalin said, indicating a low shelf built onto the front of the first stall.

"Do you have stablehands who will clean the leather in your settlement? Otherwise, I can do it." She took a curry brush from one of the hooks on the wall and began brushing away sweat and dirt with short, quick strokes.

"We have a few public stables," he answered from the next stall. "My family also has small barns like this one on each of our properties. The horse staff takes care of everything."

Mara paused with the curry brush in the air. "How many properties does your family have?" she asked.

"Between all of us, four."

Startled, she peered over the wall to check the other soldier's expression for humor.

"What?" he asked.

"Your family owns four barns and enough livestock to fill them?" That sort of wealth would explain his well-made equipment.

Dalin resumed brushing his horse, his face in shadow. "Is that so different from the families of your acquaintance?"

She hung the brush on its hook and wiped her hands on her pants. "Most families don't own horses. Some have goats and chickens; some have cows or sheep." Absently scratching her mare behind the ears, she added, "Horses go to the Protectors and the families who have wealth, I suppose."

"Not many families in the South choose to own horses the way mine does."

Mara leaned against the wall, breathing in the smell of grain and mash mixed with the other smells of a well-kept stable. The choice to commit treason, by meeting up with a Gaishan and leaving the Protected Territory, felt overwhelming again. When she had the answers, could she go back? The loud rattling of feed broke into her thoughts.

"Enjoy your dinner, Herald," Dalin said. "Ready to eat, Rowan?" The mare's ears pricked up, nostrils flaring, as the tall soldier held up the grain bucket. After he emptied the last of the grain into the other trough, he asked, "Ready to eat, Mara?" in the same tone he had used for her horse.

"Nothing left in the bucket," she grumbled.

"True." Dalin opened the interior door, motioning for her to enter. "Let's see what human food might be available. I've got to eat before I do anything else."

Fully aware that she was not only hungry but weary, mentally and physically, Mara shook her head at dark doorway. "After you." She could have been captured at any point up until now, but this was certainly their most secluded stop. Though Dalin had neither poisoned her nor killed her in her sleep, she couldn't unseat the large rock of paranoia that still weighed her down.

He shrugged and walked up the short flight of stairs. Lights flicked on, showing the length of a hallway as Dalin stopped to hang his jacket on a hook and step out of his boots before disappearing into a room on the right. The sounds of doors opening and closing and running water seemed very much like a settler's home.

She touched the wall with the hooks, feeling the impossibly smooth surface. The texture was similar to a very fine whitewash, though less thick and painted a pretty yellow color. Lights were set in rectangles about the size of a hand, roughly knee height from the wooden floor. The soft illumination gave the hallway a warm, cheerful aspect. And the air smelled fresh, as though the house had been recently aired and cleaned. With a sigh, she tugged off her boots as well. Even without his jacket, Dalin no doubt had plenty of weapons, so she kept her sword in place.

"Hey, come in the kitchen and have a snack while we sort out dinner." Dalin led her to one of two wooden chairs at a small table. "How about some fruit and cheese to start?"

"Yes, please." She couldn't stop looking around, soaking in all of the details of her enemy's life. It was a relatively small kitchen, the size of her room and Annelise's combined. Much of the wall space was taken by a shiny stone countertop with wooden cabinets above and below. A large metal sink next to a glass door took up most of the far side of the room opposite the table.

Dalin waved his hand in a downward motion in front of the dark glass door. When the door became transparent and a light flicked on, Mara couldn't suppress a gasp. Inside, on clear shelves and in clear drawers, was an abundance of food, more than any one family would have in a week, if not a month. Opening the transparent door, he lifted out berries and two pieces of the red fruit to place on the table. From an inside drawer he took out a wedge of orange cheese. When the door closed, Dalin waved his hand upward and the transparency vanished. Only then did she notice he was no longer wearing a sword.

The reality of the wayhouse in no way matched Mara's predictions. She'd thought it would be a rustic cabin or shack or lean-to, not a house full of food and conveniences. If all of the Gaishan were as well off as this, why would they bother fighting over land in the North?

After placing plates and a kitchen knife on the table, Dalin offered a small glass. "This will help," he said. He held an identical glass in his other hand.

The deep-amber-colored liquid gave off a warm, spicy smell. "What is it?"

Dropping into the chair across from her, he attempted a weary grin. "Remember the strong stuff from my flask last night at the campfire? Same stuff," he said, "but better." He threw his glass back and drained the contents.

Mara imitated her host. Though she still didn't trust him, at this point poisoning was as unlikely as capture. The drink burned a fiery path down her throat and stoked a hot glow in her stomach. She wiped her mouth on her sleeve, savoring the smooth combination of honey, cinnamon, and nectar.

"Much better than the stuff in your flask." She helped herself to a slice of cheese.

Dalin grinned. "We keep the good liquor at home."

"I thought you said this was—"

"—a wayhouse," he finished. "And it is. But it was built by my father and we use it almost exclusively." As her expression began to cloud, he said, "Snap to, soldier. Need to secure the premises and prepare food."

Tired and vulnerable, she couldn't help but respond to the tone of an officer. "Put me to work." She stood, swaying only a little.

"Do you know your way around a kitchen?" Dalin asked in his normal voice.

"A little. But I've never seen many of the things you have here."
She gestured toward the now-opaque cabinet doors.

"Perimeter detail then." He stretched, reaching his arms up
toward the ceiling. "Go out the front; check the perimeter. If you're
up for it, set some snares. Once you feel confident we're secure,
check the interior. It will help you get familiar with the layout,
facilities, and sleeping options."

"On it." Before she took two steps, Dalin caught her by one side
of the waist and turned her to face him.

"I'm sorry I didn't tell you this wayhouse was mostly my
family's place. And I'm sorry you had to lead us here." It seemed
like the genuine concern of a fellow soldier on his face.

She leaned toward him and stopped herself. Shaking her head
once, she moved into the hall.

"I…it's not important." She put her hand on the doorframe and
looked back at Dalin. His clothes were dirty and wrinkled; his jaw
had several days' worth of stubble. Again the compulsion to lean in,
offer comfort, take comfort, was a strong tightness in her chest. *Face
but not friend,* she reminded herself. "Doesn't matter," she
murmured. "Shelter is the important part."

She didn't wait for Dalin to respond, but headed to her right
down the hall in the opposite direction of the stable. She passed
several more doors and open space on the left and then came to what
could only be the front door.

After undoing several bolts, she tugged on the handle of the
heavy door. It would be cold without boots, but she didn't want to
walk by the kitchen to get them. Trees rustled, a few birds twittered,
and several soft thuds sounded as well.

More alert, Mara walked down the few stone steps to the ground.
Several more quiet thuds caught her attention. She walked across the
front yard toward the sound, whirling with her sword drawn as a
thud sounded right behind her. A large blue seedpod, the size of a
fist, bounced and landed at her feet. The nearest tree had at least
two-dozen seedpods in its lower branches swaying in the light breeze.
Mara gathered the other fallen pods and placed them on the porch.
No animals stirred—no rabbits, more specifically.

She found a break in the front tree line and followed the trees
around to the right of the house and stable, fingers brushing each
trunk as she passed. Underfoot the ground was rough but not sharp

against her socks. Seedpods continued to fall, so Mara picked each one off the ground, tucking them inside the Gaishan's pullover.

Ducking into the stable, she grabbed her snares and quickly set three outside the rear wall, just in case. Along the north side of the house, the ambient light from the front porch allowed her to see fifty paces or so to the north. Two birds flapped from one tree to another. Leaves rustled; branches clicked. Nothing else moved. Finished with her circuit, she deposited all but one seedpod with the others on the porch and opened the front door. The mouth-watering smell of onions and meat cooking in butter greeted her.

"Perimeter appears secure," she said. "The only unusual movement was from these." She held out a blue pod. Dalin's smile wavered for a second as he left the stove to examine Mara's find.

"Did you collect them?"

"I did," she said. "I thought maybe your people ate them or something, like almonds or walnuts…" Dalin shook his head vehemently. "Not to eat, got it," she finished.

He reached into a high cabinet and produced a woven basket. "You can pile the *gontras* into this," he said.

"That might not be big enough."

Pain or maybe just surprise flashed across Dalin's face. "How many did you collect?"

"About ten. What's wrong?"

"Oh…" The other soldier drew out the word into a sigh and reached for a larger basket of woven silver. "The *gontras* don't typically fall this time of year. And…*gontras* are…important to our culture."

Mara took the basket back to the porch. Holding a *gontra* toward the overhead light, she considered it. The seedpod was roughly spherical, but lumpy. Given Dalin's response, she decided not to open this pod, despite her curiosity. She collected the remainder of the fallen *gontras* and counted them: thirteen in all. As she opened the front door, the wind gusted again, its chill reminiscent of the snow in the North. She breathed a prayer that her friends and fellow soldiers also had a warm place to sleep tonight.

Chapter 15

Placing the basket on the kitchen table, Mara said, "Dinner smells good." Good did not begin to cover what she smelled, actually.

Dalin looked up from the mixture of onions and vegetables he was stirring. "Since we're both hungry, I decided we could make do without bread or rice tonight. Takes too long." He shrugged. "This"—he nodded at the skillet— "and the roast"—he pointed at a handle in the wall—"will be finished soon."

"You went outside without taking a snack and I've been eating this whole time. Have something." He nodded toward the cheese slices and berries on the table. Mara slumped in one of the small chairs, eyes glazing as she ate.

He shook the skillet. "Mara," he said, "is the interior secure?"

"Not yet," she answered, recovering some focus.

"We should be fine," her host said. "If someone was here or had been here uninvited, the house would let us know."

She puzzled over that for a moment and bit into more of the sharp orange cheese. "Better to confirm."

"Agreed," said Dalin, tapping the illuminated circles near the pans he was stirring. "Take a look around, check for anything unusual, and while you're at it, choose a place to sleep."

#

As she checked the interior of the wayhouse, Mara muttered to herself, "Roast, lights turning on by themselves, doors that only look like glass some of the time—nothing unusual." Roast was never hungry-traveler food. In the settlements, and even more rarely in the compound, roast was once- or twice-a-year celebration food.

She started her interior check with the large room to the right of the front door. Two overhead lights flicked on. It was a common room with several couches and a handful of chairs. The walls were a warm nutmeg color, the furniture covered in beautiful, multihued patterns. A stone fireplace graced the wall opposite the open doorway. Mara turned slowly, noting none of the couches was large enough for sleeping. As she faced out the doorway, she gaped. Both sides of the entrance were framed by tall, built-in bookshelves. Full bookshelves. She had never seen this many books in one place, not even in the map room in the compound. Running her fingertips along the spines, she admired the colors and brightness of the etched symbols.

Across the hall, she found a sleeping room. Though more luxurious than any Protector quarters, it still had the usual bed, wardrobe, and chair, but no fireplace. Mara continued through an open door into a washroom. The floor was covered in golden, speckled tiles, the walls a light cream color. Two showers and a tub for submersion bathing were across from a bank of mirrors and a counter with three sinks.

She took in a deep breath, closed her eyes, and slowly let it out. One corner of her mouth turned up in wry acknowledgement of her appearance. Over the course of the day, a great deal of dark hair had escaped the confines of the braid. Those strands either hung down or were tucked behind her ears. Her lips were chapped from the wind and her lightly tanned skin was reddened along her cheeks, nose, and forehead. Both the wisps of hair around her head and Dalin's pullover sported bits of leaves.

Mara pulled the leather tie from her hair and shook out the remaining braid. Without a comb, brush, or Annelise, it seemed best to leave it down for the night. Cabinets tucked in one corner of the washroom contained soft white towels and face cloths. She washed her hands and with a damp face cloth wiped the grime from her face and neck, feeling much better for the change.

Across from the kitchen was another common room, this one filled by a large dining table and eight chairs. The rest of the rooms were for sleeping. The one on the right held a large bed with Dalin's bags and sword tossed onto the center. Mara chose the room across from his and slightly closer to the stable, fetched her saddlebags, and set them on the room's only chair. After a moment's consideration, she took off her shoulder harness and laid the sword on the bed. A soft tan rug covered almost the entire floor, the bed was loaded with pillows and linens all dyed in tones of purple and blue, but like the other four sleeping rooms, no fireplace.

"Interior secure," she reported from the door.

"Perfect timing." He gestured for her to sit at the kitchen table.

Mara covered her mouth in surprise. Two plates heaped with roast, vegetables, onions, and potatoes sat next to delicate faceted

glasses and a full pitcher of water. The basket of *gontras* was behind
two lit candles, one yellow, one white. Not only had Mara never
seen so much food on one plate, she could not believe the Gaishan lit
the candles for thanksgiving.

Dalin hesitated behind his chair. "What?"

She sat down and pointed at the candles. "You light the same
candles."

"We light the yellow candle for thanks and the white candle for
purity or healing after a battle or other difficulty. It seemed
appropriate tonight. You, the settlements, have something similar?"

"Exactly the same," Mara murmured. "Some of my teachers and
Elias..."

"What about your fellow Protectors?"

She breathed in the rich scent of her dinner. "Only me, that I
know of."

"Are you ready to eat?" he asked with a grin, obviously proud of
the meal.

She lifted her water glass. "Thank you for cooking."

"You're welcome." Dalin clinked his glass against hers, holding
her gaze until Mara ducked her head and unfettered dark hair swung
a curtain between them. She settled into a comfortable position and
began to eat in earnest. Every few bites, her attention would stray to
the candles and she would add her own silent prayers of gratitude.

The pair ate in comfortable silence. More than halfway through
her portion of roast, Mara stopped herself and said, "This is delicious.
I was stuffing myself and enjoying every bite. I...I didn't mean to be
rude. We never sit down at the same table as the cook..." Her cheeks
warmed.

"Ravenous eating is as good a compliment as any," he replied.
"Are you ready for a second serving?" He stood and loaded both
plates at the stove.

"Yes, please," she said with a sigh. After the varying levels of
hunger she'd experienced since leaving the compound, this meal
seemed beyond decadent. "Do you always eat like this?"

Dalin picked up his fork and tapped it against the water glass. A
single note formed and lingered in the air. "Yes and no," he said.
"Food is plentiful in the South. We believe meals, cooking, can be a
way to express caring, joy, or gratitude. From a cultural perspective,

me throwing everything on one plate like this is nearly as poor of form as eating burned rabbit on flat rocks."

Surprised and skeptical, Mara said, "Every family, every child has enough to eat all the time?"

Dalin took a sip of water. "Yes."

Thinking of Cole and other tax children like him who only received adequate food once they were given to the Protectors, Mara shook her head. What could possibly provoke the Gaishan into attacking people who clearly had so much less?

She was well into her second serving when Dalin stood for thirds. Stomach almost uncomfortably full, she leaned back in her chair and watched him carefully place the heaping plate on the table.

"So you really eat like this all of the time?" she prodded.

He chewed for a moment before answering. "Meals are supposed to be appealing to the eye as well as the stomach. So this meal would have been served in the dining room with fresh bread, the vegetables arranged in side dishes, probably flowers and linen on the table. My parents are good with that stuff."

Mara nodded and frowned at her lap.

"Most families can eat a healthy dinner, with meat, two to three times a week. The other meals are still excellent and filling, but might not include roast, for example."

Her gaze fell to the basket of *gontras* sitting behind the candles. Something familiar tugged at a corner of her mind.

"Hey." Dalin's low, quiet voice broke into her thoughts. "Ask your questions as they come. You're traveling south to learn and I want you to feel comfortable—" He stopped as Mara lifted a *gontra* from the basket and brought it to her nose.

"I knew this smell was familiar." She sniffed her borrowed sweater. "This"—she held out the seedpod—"smells like this"—she plucked at her sleeve. "I noticed it in the tent last night, a spicy tree smell." She sniffed the *gontra* again and returned it to the basket.

Dalin cleared his throat. "I was going to suggest you take the basket to your room tonight. Thirteen *gontras* falling is excellent luck. And according to our traditions, when a *gontra* presents itself to you, as these did"—he gestured to the blue pods—"you become responsible for it or them, until the purpose is revealed."

Mara raised her eyebrows. "That seems a bit foggy."

"How right you are." Dalin inclined his head. "Are you finished eating?"

Had she made light of the *gontras* and offended Dalin? He seemed fine, standing up with his plate, gray eyes calm, lips curved in a slight smile. For an instant, she thought she was seeing just another Gaishan mask, that Dalin's true thoughts and feelings were hidden behind his pleasant expression.

"I'll clean since you cooked." Mara stood and pushed in her chair.

Dalin laid his plate in the large sink. "Thanks for the offer, but cleaning will be like cooking. A lot of the"—he gestured around the room—"workings in this kitchen are unfamiliar to you." He took Mara's plate. "Tomorrow I'll show you." He opened a low cabinet and rolled out a rack containing several plates. Mara stared for a moment, trying to divine the purpose of the rack. "Are you still interested in a shower?"

She ran a hand through her hair. "More than interested."

"Go ahead and do that while I finish in here," Dalin said. "Most of the shower controls are the same as in the Protector compound."

Suddenly, Mara wanted to peel off her dirty travel clothes and step under warm water more than anything else. She hurried through the door, but hesitated, feeling her thanks for the meal and the shelter had been insufficient. Annelise would've offered a quick hug and kiss on the cheek to a friendly, attractive male who cooked for her. But Mara only turned and left, regretting her utter lack of easy ways with people.

#

The sleeping room had its own closet instead of an external wardrobe. Inside she found a soft robe and several sets of tunics and pants made of a light, soft fabric in shades of blue and green. Thinking of her own clothes, Mara dumped everything out of her largest pack. Nothing looked as clean or appealing as the house clothes or robe in the closet. Shedding her travel layers, she hung her uniform pants and donned the tunic, pants, and robe.

The lights in the washroom clicked on as she entered. In bare feet for the first time, Mara noticed the floor was warm. Warm air was also blowing across her toes. Puzzled, Mara bent her good leg and looked for the source of the air current. Under the sinks, a slatted panel in the wall blew warmed air. If every room had a warmed floor and warmed air, no need for a fireplace.

Soap for her body and hair was not sitting on a shelf in either shower, as it would be in the compound. Mara opened the cabinet where she had found towels on her initial investigation. From a lower shelf, she helped herself to a toothbrush. On the other side of the shelf was a row of bottles made from a clear material, lighter than glass. One had a picture of a woman washing her hair. One showed a picture of a woman's leg with soapsuds on it. Several other bottles had markings Mara didn't recognize—instead there were pictures of flowers, pictures of trees, and pictures of clouds. She opened the bottle with flowers on its label and sniffed. The white cream inside smelled like spring flowers.

"Body cream," Mara muttered. She had never used any but knew some of her friends did, especially during white-storm season, when the cold dried everyone's skin.

While she wanted to linger in the warm, steamy shower, she didn't. Dalin hadn't entered and must be waiting for a turn. Males and females shared the main washroom at Protector House, but Mara knew this was not the custom in all settlements. After drying with the towel, she smoothed cream over her arms, legs, and feet, barely pausing at some of the newer bruises and scrapes. Most seemed to be fading. With a start, Mara realized she had not thought about or noticed her leg injury since midday. The pink scar didn't look as bright and the muscles underneath, though still bruised-feeling, were not terribly painful, just stiff.

Less pain, full belly, clean hair and skin—altogether the best shape Mara had been in for some time. Another sleeping room was open, lights glowing from within. Dalin had dumped out several bags worth of gear and appeared to be folding and repacking.

"Washroom is all yours," Mara called.

Her host picked up her uniform jacket and took two steps to the doorway. After handing it over, he leaned one shoulder into the frame and stuck the other hand in the front pocket of his pants. "Good shower?" She nodded happily. He bent forward and sniffed. "You smell nice."

"It's an improvement," Mara agreed. "You must have females come through here sometimes to keep flower-scented body cream in the cabinet."

"The women in my family have all been here at one time or another," Dalin said. "My mother insists we stock some nice things for guests."

"Is your mother also a soldier?"

He laughed. "My mother? No. She comes out here to keep my father company while he hunts. She has good woodcraft skills but has never used a weapon, as far as I know. Soon you can ask her yourself."

Nerves tightened in Mara's chest, the glow and well being she felt from the shower giving way to unease.

"Don't worry about meeting anyone right now. Sorry I mentioned it." He reached forward as though to touch her cheek and patted her shoulder instead. "Before you sleep, tell me: How's the leg? You haven't been limping."

"The new repairs on the inside of the muscle"—she smoothed a hand over the scar—"are just fine. It's still sore, but nowhere near as bad. I think the healers did something to accelerate the process."

"This injury happened while I was supposed to be watching over you. It bothers me—" Dalin began.

"Injury is a natural consequence of battle." Mara's lips quirked. She sounded like a senior Protector.

"Right," he conceded. "Sleep well, Protector."

"And you." *Gaishan,* she added.

#

Though the bed looked tempting, Mara hesitated. The sheets and blankets seemed so fine, she felt as though she didn't belong between them. Did Dalin's mother know he was escorting a Protector home? Fatigue pushed past her reluctance to sully the beautifully made bed. She shoved all but one pillow aside and pulled back the covers but paused to consider the temperature in the room. In the loose-fitting house clothes, she would be warm enough. After hanging the soft robe alongside her travel pants, she crawled into the bed. The overhead light was still on.

She could hear the shower water running and knew it would be impolite to barge in and bother Dalin about the light. Lying back on the pillow, she inhaled the woody smell that permeated her surroundings, even stronger here than it had been in the tent. The steady hum of the shower reminded her of being under the water, surrounded by fragrant steam. Mara closed her eyes and tilted her chin to feel the delicate needles of water on her face...

"Mara?"

Mara's eyes flew open. *"Dalin, what is—? Why are you in my head?"*

"You're in mine, sharing the shower."

Mara could hear the laughter in the thought. And he was right, she realized. She could still feel the water on the side of her/his face and, moreover, she could sense Dalin's astonishment. The overhead light in her room winked out.

"The lights go out without movement in the room," he said.

Mara's breathing was shallow. She lay flat on her back, stiff with shock. *"What is...? Why...? How do I...?"* She tried to form a question.

"I'll close the connection. We can talk face to face in the morning." Behind the thought, surprise had been replaced by calm confidence. *"Sleep well, Mara."* Dalin pulled a curtain between their minds.

At least that was how it felt. She could still sense him, but only his presence, nothing else.

Looking at the now-dark ceiling, she shivered. Sharing Dalin's shower? She'd only thought about popping in to ask a question and suddenly she popped into his mind? Mara curled into a ball and pulled the covers over her head as she had done in her room at the compound not long ago. She forced her breathing to deepen and slow.

In her mind, the Gaishan was staying behind his curtain, but Mara could almost sense other minds, other people, as though Dalin were her neighbor and she could hear his harvest party.

Chapter 16

The next morning, white flakes whirled through dim and watery sunlight. Mara shrugged into the robe and stepped into a soft pair of house shoes. The house was quiet, and even the kitchen and common rooms with their plentiful windows were relatively dark.

She paused to peer through the narrow windowpane next to the front door. Snow blew across the front porch, a strong wind whipping leaves and small branches across the covered surface as well.

Curious to see if the snow was accumulating, she walked out to the edge of the porch, the wind tugging at her thin robe. Thick gray clouds hovered low and falling snow kept visibility down below thirty meters. Along the forest floor, snow as deep as her ankles drifted against the closest row of trees. Mara's hair flew around her head as she turned and hurried back inside. She took a deep breath and lightly stomped her feet to shake off any snowflakes or leaves.

The large common room didn't have overhead lighting. Instead, lamps were placed on tables near the groups of sofas and chairs. Still chilled from the wind, Mara rubbed her arms and moved to have a closer look at the titles on the shelves. Some of the books had symbols printed along the spines; some didn't. She only recognized a few words here and there.

During battle, the Gaishan often shouted incomprehensible words and phrases. Maybe it was common for people in the South to be from other planets and speak other languages.

Since her thoughts were drifting that way, Mara scanned the bookshelves for anything to do with planets or how to travel from one planet to another. On the bottom of one shelf, among the tallest books, she found an atlas and lugged it to a comfortable chair near the unlit fireplace. The wind rattled the flue inside the chimney, but no cold air escaped into the room.

She touched the nearest lamp and it lit, just like the tiny lantern in the tent. Flipping pages, Mara wished she knew more of the words. Relying so heavily on the pictures left her to puzzle out incomplete ideas for each section.

Nearly an hour later, Dalin appeared, rumpled from sleep and not yet fully awake. "First one up is supposed to make breakfast," he said, part joking, part grumpy.

"White storm is here." She gestured toward the windows. "No one's going anywhere."

"What are you reading?" He moved closer and peered at the book.

"An atlas, I think," Mara said. "It has a lot of illustrations of planets, pictures and charts about different types of terrain, stuff like that."

Plucking the heavy volume from her lap, he read aloud, "*The Origin and Its Solar System, Known Solar Systems, and Current Exploration.*"

Mara sighed. "I wish I knew how to read those markings."

Dalin shot her a questioning look. "It's written in one of the common languages of the Origin. It's what we're speaking right now."

She reached out for the book and frowned at the cover, trying to make sense of the groupings of letters and symbols.

Dropping into the chair across from her, he said, "Something that's always puzzled me is how settler children go to school. And if school is a part of Protector life at all."

"A few of the settlements in the north and northwest have schools. Why?"

"In the South, children learn to read, write, and speak at least one, usually two or three languages while attending school."

"All the children?" Mara asked, as skeptical as she had been about plentiful food.

"All the children are required to attend school, no cost to families. Education is a service, or an opportunity, I guess you would say, provided to everyone."

Unfamiliar longing colored with jealousy swept through her. Mara looked down at the book cover again and traced a finger over the unfamiliar word shapes. "I've never been to school," she admitted. "It costs a great deal. Farmers' children can't afford to go, let alone orphans." She forced herself to look up. "In the compound, the Protectors don't read books, but we're taught to read maps. I've learned some words from the maps, from signposts in the settlements. The map room has maps and books, but the books are restricted."

Pressure built in Mara's chest, shame for her powerlessness and ignorance compared to young children in the South. That she hadn't been raised by her parents was the old wound. Fresh on top of that was a new bruise that she, through no direct fault, had missed a chance to learn reading and writing.

"In my settlement is a place you can go to learn," Dalin said, his tone factual, no trace of sympathy or pity. "When new scientists, new workers, come from off-planet, they spend part of each day learning the Origin-standard language we use. It's a class of adults. One of the teachers is your aunt."

Mara let out the breath she didn't realize she had been holding. She scanned the other soldier's face for hints of teasing or scorn but saw nothing beyond his usual open expression. It would be awful for Dalin to think less of her in any way, but especially for something outside of her control.

"Bring the book to breakfast," Dalin suggested. "We can talk through the chapters."

She unfolded herself from the comfortable chair and stood. So many questions. The freedom to ask them was a greater luxury than the food and beautiful furnishings. Pointing toward the fireplace, she asked, "How do you heat this house without using the fireplace?"

Dalin slapped her on the back. "We have a lot to talk about. Good thing you learn quickly."

Feeling certain he was teasing now, Mara stepped on his bootless foot as she walked past.

#

While he cooked, Dalin described the system that blew either warm or cool air through the house. He explained how the energy for the lights and the stove, cold box and heat came from a small generator. "It uses a similar type of energy exchange that the light for my tent uses," he said.

Mara just nodded as she had through most of the explanations. Breakfast was eggs baked into biscuits and a warm porridge with berries and nuts on top. Despite the large dinner, she was ravenous again.

Thinking about the amazing food jogged her memory of the previous night and a flush crept up her neck as she remembered their weird connection through the shower. With some reluctance to broach the subject, she said, "Before I met you in battle, I never had the ability to communicate with thoughts. What exactly did you do to me? Is it permanent?" Worry came through in her face and voice.

Dalin finished chewing and pushed a quiet thought into her mind. *"Permanent."*

Mara closed her eyes, took a breath, opened her eyes. She didn't want to argue, not in this nice house, with this nice food. When they were back on the trail, she could knock him off his horse and beat him with sticks. Which served to remind her, whatever else Dalin had done that night on the battlefield, he had saved her life.

"So, I'll need your help learning control. It must work along the same lines as personal shields, correct?" Mara tried to keep it matter-of-fact. Once she went back north it wouldn't matter anyway—the change wasn't visible, thank the Light.

At first it seemed like he would answer her question about communicating with thoughts. But the explanation quickly became broader as he tried to make a connection to machines and energy use and what she might know from the settlements or the Protector compound. It quickly became evident Mara knew little about how most things worked—both in terms of construction and energy.

"We have two main groups of scientists and researchers in the South," Dalin said. "One group works with the plant biosystems, particularly the trees. And the other works on refining the energy exchange process and products. To that group, what you and I might see as magic is the next level of physics." He shook his head and sighed. "Forgive me. I'm just throwing ideas at you."

Mara brushed her fingers across the cover of the planetary atlas. "No, you're trying to teach me," she said. "I asked questions but I had no idea the answers were so large." She gathered up the juice and water glasses. Dalin followed suit, returning the containers for sugar and nuts to the shelves and the remaining bowl of berries to the cold cabinet.

"I feel"—he paused in the act of wiping down the table— "rushed. We have time but not enough time. I want you to feel comfortable when we get to the city."

"*Thecity*? Is that the name of your settlement?" Mara asked.

Dalin smiled ruefully. "*City* is a word for a large settlement. Something like five hundred thousand people live in my city, which is called Satri." He shook his head and looked away. "You deserve a better teacher. They should have sent someone else."

Outside the kitchen window, the storm swirled around the trees at the perimeter. "What was the mission exactly?"

Holding out his left hand, he ticked off the points with his right. "Observe you and report. Make contact during battle. Establish mental rapport. Intercept you en route. Escort you south. Prep you for a stay in the city. Answer questions as needed."

"You targeted me." It was one of her objectives as a leader—to draw the Gaishan aggression away from the children. "But it was your mission, specifically."

Staring over her head, he crossed his arms. "Yes, I requested the assignment."

His face, golden tan except for the shadow along his jaw, gave nothing away. And his slightly upturned eyes, which had warmed to a deep gray last night, were back to flinty silver. He'd gone from transparent to opaque, just like the cold cabinet.

She had no rules, no recourse, no protocol for consorting with a fighter who was both enemy and ally. She gripped her spoon like a dagger, breakfast quickly forming a cold lump in her stomach.

"I slept later this morning because I was up so late conferring with various people," Dalin said, his tone weary, his expression softening as they faced off across the small kitchen. "Everyone except the weather watchers wants us to head south at first light tomorrow. The weather scientists advise waiting another day, maybe two."

"Do you have orders for us to leave in the morning?"

"Conditional orders to depart, weather permitting." He paused and rubbed a hand over his eyes. "My senior officers won't relax until we're both within the city boundaries, with additional protection from the militia."

Mara bristled. "Why?"

Dalin held his right palm toward her. "Easy," he said. "This isn't about our fighting skills."

Her shoulders were still tight and she had unconsciously dropped her right foot back into a fighting stance. "Then what's the urgency about?"

"The urgency is about who's in pursuit." He took in a long breath and let it out. "And about your potential value to the people in the South."

"Dalin." Mara shook her head, trying to deny his words, even as a sense of dread tingled at the base of her throat. "Who could follow us, let alone find us, in this?" She gestured toward the window.

"We believe the Queen's Soldiers have that capacity."

Mara had to accept this revelation just as she had to accept so many things over the past few days. "Is this location at risk?"

"My officers are concerned about that possibility. But..." He paused. "But we put ourselves in a different type of danger heading out into a storm."

"Does the storm fall as far south as your...city?" Mara asked.

"Yes," Dalin said, a smile ghosting across his lips. "Snow in Satri. My sister will be happy."

"How long is the ride?" Mara asked. "With the snow, two days?"

"It depends on the storm, but it's at least a sixteen-hour ride."

"I think we should go now." Mara looked Dalin in the eye. "If there's a chance this location is compromised, we've been here too long. We should move."

Dalin searched her face. "Did you dream...?"

Mara could tell by the way he shifted his weight to the balls of his feet that the other soldier was also itching to go. She shook her head and glanced around the kitchen, taking in the candles on the table and the snow blowing outside the window.

"No, it's my soldier's instincts, I guess you would call it. The same as I get in battle. We need to leave. The sooner, the better."

"I agree," Dalin said. "But we put ourselves and our horses at risk," he added.

"I accept the conditions," she said, impatience creeping into her voice. She turned toward her room, mentally sorting and organizing her bags.

"Wait," Dalin said. "You need Gaishan gear." Though it was another traitorous assimilation, Mara knew he was right. Over the next half an hour, she received a thin, lightweight undershirt and leggings, gloves, a jacket like Dalin's, a sleep sack, and a bracelet that was somehow for tracking.

She packed her cape and uniform into a tight roll. She also rolled Rowan's blankets and secured both with tight straps. It felt good to be moving out. Dalin's talk about a shadow and danger were getting to her.

"Food packs?" Mara yelled down the hall.

"On it now," Dalin's reply came from the kitchen. "Can you prep the horses?"

"Affirmative." As she entered the stable, both Rowan and Herald looked up and whinnied. "Hey there," Mara said softly. "Ready for a ride?"

She scratched the mare's ears, bent, and tapped one leg. Rowan lifted her foot so her mistress could check the first shoe and hoof. Once satisfied with her horse's condition, Mara repeated the process with the warhorse. After measuring out a small amount of grain, she rummaged through the tack bench until she found four bags that could carry additional feed. Bounding up the steps and into the hall, she barreled right into Dalin.

"Hey!" and "sorry!" came out simultaneously.

"Leaving is the right thing to do," Mara said. "Your wayhouse is nice but— What?" she took in his tense expression.

"The house's outer perimeter alert was just triggered at the northeastern corner. No animals in this area are large enough to trip the sensors. We have about twenty to thirty minutes to get out, depending on how fast the intruder is coming."

The Protector smiled, the thrill of battle anticipation flooding her veins.

"Mara." Dalin's voice was sharp. "We're not going to fight. We're going to run."

He stepped past her into the stable and began to saddle his horse. She did the same with Rowan, adding the blanket rolls. When he was ready, she traded Dalin two bags of grain for three bags of food.

Both soldiers went back through the wayhouse checking for anything out of place. Dalin hit a button that sent metal shutters sliding over all the windows and the front door. "We can pull down the stable shutter behind us," he said. He reached for Mara's wrist and touched the square in the center of the bracelet. "One tap shows your coordinates. Two taps shows your location and your destination on a map." First numbers, then a map floated above her wrist.

"Don't draw energy or try rapport until we're well away," he added. "The tracker will help keep you oriented in the storm. We're heading to a hunting shack my friends sometimes use. It's not much of a shelter compared to here, but we don't have another option. The shack is southwest and not due south, which might shake our pursuers," Dalin continued. "If this is more than a lucky hit in their search and the Browns are specifically hunting for you, they'll expect us to run south. Anyway, we used next to no magic here and the house is shut down, so they may think they missed us. The weather will take care of our tracks."

He shrugged into his jacket and showed Mara how to adjust her hood, tightening it with the drawstring until only her eyes showed. He checked a small panel inside the stable door. "House says seven minutes have elapsed since the sensors tripped. Ready?"

"Ready." Swinging into her saddle, she nudged Rowan out into the blowing storm. The mare danced around, pulling her head back toward the stable.

Mounted on his warhorse, Dalin reached above the doorframe and gave the metal shutter a fierce tug. It came down with a muffled clatter. Sliding from the saddle, he hooked a lock through both a metal loop bolted into the ground and a loop attached to the bottom of the shutter.

"West," he said. "Stay with me."

He vaulted onto Herald's back and urged his mount into a fast trot.

#

They rode through the day, pausing only briefly to care for the horses. It took all of Mara's concentration to keep sight of the Gaishan, especially as daylight began to fade. The snow on the ground and the blowing snow made riding through the forest challenging. Mara glanced behind and listened for pursuit as often as she could, but the conditions demanded attention to the obstacles ahead.

Dalin's left arm went out, bent upward at the elbow, his hand in a fist. Pulling gently on her reins, she stopped alongside him. Both horses were breathing hard, their breath a gray fog in the dim light. "The shack is ahead, but someone's using it," he whispered.

"What?" Mara sputtered. "Who?"

"I have a guess." The other soldier's face was too hidden for Mara to read his expression. "Stay with the horses." Without warning, he dismounted and melted into the trees.

Mara slid to the snow-covered ground, legs quivering with relief. She glanced at the tracker on her wrist. Though no structure was visible, the tracker indicated something was dead ahead. She hesitated to reach out with her mind, assuming that would use magical energy. Unrolling saddle blankets to drape over each horse, she stomped her cold, damp feet. The steady stream of flakes continued, coating bushes and the lower branches of trees.

A blue *gontra* dropped right in front of her, making a small indentation in the snow. Mara looked up but couldn't see any other seedpods in the branches above. She bent down to retrieve the *gontra* and felt a blade press against her throat.

"He shouldn't ha' left you alone, girl," rumbled a deep male voice.

Mara slapped both her gloved hands on top of the blade and yanked, throwing her weight into a half roll. The assailant stumbled and slipped, giving her time to get underneath his reach and draw her sword. Mara pivoted and faced the stranger. The snow on the forest floor made footing uncertain but she didn't care. Lunging forward, she slashed at the side of the man's neck. He blocked the strike and threw a kick at her legs. She jumped back, slipped, and recovered in time to parry a strike to her ribs. Countering with a strike to his face, she managed to catch the edge of the man's hood.

Mara danced to the left to avoid a strike that whistled under her arm. Her injured leg wobbled and the assailant moved in to press the advantage. She pivoted on her good leg, stepping inside his guard and hitting him in the nose with her elbow. As he leaned forward, she slammed her knee into his face, grabbed his coat and heaved him under her other arm, causing him to spin. The man grunted and came up on one knee. Drops of red blood spattered the snow.

Mara took a breath. "Who are you?" she gasped.

The man's free hand whipped out and hooked her behind both legs, pulling her down as he stood. He caught her shoulder with one booted foot and again laid his blade across her throat. The stranger slowly bent down to take her sword.

"Never give up an advantage," the man growled. "Step out of fist-range and use your sword."

"Like this?" came Dalin's voice, directly behind the man.

"Think you have me, boy?" the man spat, not taking his eyes off of Mara. "I could kill this lettle girl right now."

The scowling attacker had fierce blue eyes and a scar cutting through one dark eyebrow. Blood trickled over his upper lip and down his chin. He wasn't wearing a uniform, but dressed like a hunter.

"Mara?" Dalin called.

"Now," she yelled and rolled toward the hand holding the sword, kicking out toward the man's shins. Her weight and momentum caused the attacker to stagger back, giving Mara space to scramble out of sword range. She pulled herself up using a tree trunk and turned, hoping to see Dalin finish the fight.

Instead, he was holding out a hand, helping the man to stand. Mara's hands fumbled over the unfamiliar jacket, searching for her belt knife, getting it ready to throw.

"Wait!" Dalin's voice was in her mind this time. *"Wait—he is a friend."* Out loud he said, "Jameson, meet your niece. Mara, this is your uncle."

Chapter 17

Mara breathed in ragged gasps. In the snowy twilight, she couldn't see much of either the Gaishan or the man with the scar.

"Mara?" Dalin's voice in her head was worried. *"Are you hurt?"*

She swallowed and tried to slow her breathing by inhaling through her nose. *"I'm unharmed,"* she thought. *"But he sliced this jacket."*

Out loud he said, "Now that we've had introductions, let's see the accommodations."

With a crooked grin, Jameson held out his hand to Mara. "Good fight," he said. "Glad those Protectors taught you how ta handle yerself."

Mara shook his hand, trying to manage the shock of meeting her uncle, her *uncle*, in a close fight. "You were going to kill me," she said.

"It always feels like that," Dalin interjected. "Once he punched me in the jaw so hard, my teeth were loose for two weeks."

"Shouldn't ha' let down your guard," the hunter replied. "Let's get inside."

Dalin led them along a broken snow trail. Mara followed and Jameson brought up the rear, leading both horses. *My uncle,* Mara kept saying to herself. *My uncle. Not just an aunt but an uncle.*

Like the wayhouse, the hunting cabin's foundation was stone. It was much smaller, however, more the size of a family home in the northern settlements. The stable in the rear was small, too.

"I'll take care of these fine mounts," Jameson offered, once they'd all clattered inside. "You two grab your gear and get warm."

Rowan butted her nose into her rider's chest, a signal to have her ears scratched. Mara took a moment to check Rowan's legs and feet and scratch the horse's ears before unloading blankets, gear, and bags. Her uncle was checking on his own horse, a dappled brown and white mare with a brown mane.

When Mara began to loosen the saddle, Jameson called, "Leave it, lass. Go on. I'll tend to your girl here."

He patted Rowan's flank and murmured something to her in a different language. The mare twitched one ear and turned her nose slightly to look at him.

"What's the name of this beauty?" he asked.

"Rowan," Mara said, still tense and uncomfortable with this stranger. "And yours?" she asked, nodding toward his horse.

"That fine lady's Gwen. Now off with you." He made a shooing motion with his hands. "Leave Rowan and me to get acquainted."

From the outside, the hunting cabin betrayed no signs of life. Mara stumbled through the soggy underbrush alongside the cabin until she reached the front door.

Dalin opened it and stepped outside to take some of her load. "Jameson has the smaller sleeping room, so you and I have the larger."

She followed him inside, noting the similarity in layout to the wayhouse. Dalin showed her to a room where he'd already dumped his things on the narrow bed nearest the door. The furnishings were dark brown, as was the rug. Nothing looked new, but it appeared mostly clean.

"Are we sure we want to stay here?" Mara asked. She looked down at her gear, then wrapped her arms around her torso and dropped to the other bed. "He doesn't seem interested in visitors." Her chest heaved as she took a deep breath, willing tears not to come. "I guess I can't blame him," she said. "I grew up with the enemy. But, I thought…I imagined…if I had a relative and I finally met that person, he would be glad to see me…" She trailed off, eyes burning with misery.

"Give him a chance," Dalin said. He patted her shoulder and left her alone.

#

Mara had changed into clean, dry clothes and was repacking her things when her uncle appeared in the doorway holding a mug.

"Any damage from our little scuffle?"

She stiffened. "No."

"Well, old Zam did a good job with you," Jameson said. He handed her the tea. "You don't over rely on your weapon, you have good balance, you stay aware and focused on your opponent, and you can improvise when the fight changes."

Jameson's evaluation of her skills slid by in her surprise. "You know Zam?"

"Know him?" he chuckled. "We come from the same place, him and me. Used to fight together. He'll be right proud to hear you spilled my blood." He tapped his nose and winked.

Mara gaped, too surprised to respond.

"Anyway, we may get to stay the night here, but it's good to see you're checkin' through your stuff. Might have to run again. Best to be prepared."

She choked on her tea. How did this man know Zam and the Protector training?

"I can guess what you're wonderin', and it's a good story. Even got some archived images at the house. For now, I've gotta get you and the boy current on the situation."

Jameson paused and wiped a hand over his face. He shoved the other hand in a pocket. "Your aunt," he began, "she's been torn up about losin' you all these years. So I'm eager to get you home to her. When we get to Satri, you can stay with us and go to school. We mean to keep you with us the full season."

Mara swayed, suddenly dizzy.

Reaching out, Jameson took the tea before she could drop it. He narrowed his eyes. "Right, well, that's talk for later. Gotta get out of this first, don't we?" He clapped her on the shoulder. "Come on ta the kitchen when you've finished with your gear." He returned the cup and walked out of the room.

Wrapping her cold hands around the hot cup, she took a deep breath. The man who just tried to kill her used to fight with Zam, was married to her aunt, and invited her to stay at his house.

She was far from home, sipping tea in a so-called shack every bit as nice as many settlers' homes. Instinct told her the Gaishan had brewed the tea and sent Jameson in to talk with her. That small certainty in a world full of puzzles helped Mara pull herself together.

#

In the tiny kitchen, her uncle leaned on the counter while Dalin melted cheese on small piles of meat. He laid one stack of meat and cheese on a thick slice of brown bread on each of three plates.

"Jameson brought cheese," he said. "An excellent contribution for an early evening meal." He handed two plates to Mara and ushered her through the kitchen doorway and down the hall.

The walls of the common room were plain white with exposed stone at the foundation and wood beams running across the ceiling. An unlit hearth dominated the front corner of the room.

Jameson entered carrying three cups and a water pitcher. He set those on a small table and dropped onto a short couch facing the two younger fighters.

"Do you mind catching us up while we eat?" Dalin asked.

"Not a'tall," he replied, pouring water and handing the glasses around. "The Queen's top commander on this planet declared a truce, a ceasing of military action within the Protected Territory, not quite two weeks ago. She sent her people 'round to all five Protector compounds to spread the news." He paused to take a bite.

"For a handful of days now, the Browns in Satri ha' been actin' strange. Irregular patrols, questionin' the scientists, hasslin' your mum and the other city leaders. And there's a rumor of King's Men sneakin' about." Dalin's face tightened, his eyes flinty silver. The hunter took another bite.

"Your mum is fine," he said. "She gave as good as she got, quizzin' them Browns about their bad behavior. Your da is right there at the labs, boy. Nothin' to worry about. I only mention it 'cause these are unusual actions for the Browns. Some of the lads are checkin' on this bit about the King's Men. We'll sort it out."

Rather than worry and wonder about what authority the Browns might have in Satri, Mara set her plate down. "Are we staying here?"

"That one will report in as soon as he's finished," Jameson said, tipping his cup toward Dalin. "And I'm goin' to scout back along your trail. For all that the lad calls this place a shack, it's plenty fine, but not equipped with detection systems like the wayhouse."

"I guess I'll go through the food and supplies in case we need to ride out sooner rather than later." She stood and stacked the plates, not comfortable sitting, not able to relax.

Dalin stretched until his fingers brushed a beam in the ceiling. "Thanks. I'll come get you in a few minutes. You need to learn how to link in distance reporting."

Brushing crumbs from his lap as he stood, Jameson gave his niece an appraising look. "You're learnin' to do the head talk?"

She shrugged. "So far I can only talk with Dalin. I haven't tried with anyone else."

"Still," Jameson said, "that's a marvel." He pulled on a heavy coat. "Don't expect me for a while." He strapped on two knives and a sword, stepped into heavy boots, tugged on a hat and gloves, and walked out the door.

Brow knit with confusion, Mara said, "He...is my uncle?"

Dalin's lips curved as though he were about to make a joke. "Yes and the best soldier I know. Better than both of us." It was a measure of how far they had come and of her earlier experience with Jameson that she accepted this assessment without challenge.

"Once I finish the report to my officers, I'll call you so we can link and check in with the council."

"Your mother is part of the settlement...the city"—she corrected herself—"leadership?" She opened and shut a few doors below and next to the sink.

"No dishwashing machine here," he said. He reached up to an open shelf above the sink and brought down a bottle with a picture of plates and cups in water. "My mother is part of the city leadership and she's looking forward to meeting you." He gave Mara's braid a quick tug and walked out.

She washed and dried the plates, water glasses, and the pan, feeling young again and dismissed from anything important. Wiping her hands on her pants, she turned to emptying and sorting food bags, trying to keep her thoughts firmly in the present. They had a hodgepodge of fresh food and trail food. But not enough for two people on a two-day ride, let alone three.

The cold cabinet yielded a few more options, particularly if they had to leave soon. She didn't take anything out, but grouped items on shelves to make packing flow more quickly.

The last bag contained the thirteen *gontras*. How odd that as they were fleeing, Dalin had packed them. Mara rolled one in her hand, liking the rough texture of the bumpy blue skin and the smell it released with the movement. It reminded her of tree sap, like the scent that clung to Dalin. With regret she realized she'd left the *gontra* thrown by Jameson in the woods.

Hearing someone talking, she leaned into the hall. Jameson hadn't returned. Was the Gaishan speaking aloud?

Mara found the tall soldier sitting on the floor of the sleeping room between the narrow beds. His eyes were closed and though his back was straight, he appeared relaxed. The voices were a bit louder in here. Looking for the source of the sound, her gaze fell on the window. Surely no tracker would stand outside a window and talk? She checked every room and looked out every window but the voices were definitely coming from the sleeping room.

With a sigh, she lowered herself to the floor facing Dalin and assumed a cross-legged position similar to his. Treyton and Jules had talked about a healing link before they'd mended her leg. Maybe linking was just touch. Mara closed her eyes and listened, almost certain now one of the male voices was Dalin's.

Stretching out one booted foot, she touched the tip of his boot. The garbled sound didn't change. It was hard to imagine soldiers holding hands while reporting. What kind of contact would work? She scooted over and sat next to Dalin, her posture mirroring his. She took a deep breath and moved a fraction closer so the far side of her knee touched his.

The sensation was like leaning on a wall and finding only paper. Mara nearly fell over, blinking hard, trying to orient herself. Two men faced them, the younger one appearing surprised while the older remained impassive. The paneled room was empty except for a large table and four chairs.

Dalin gave his head a slight shake of disapproval. "Gentlemen, allow me to introduce Mara de la Luz."

She kept very still except to nod at both officers. Each wore a plain gray uniform with a sequence of colors and symbols on the left chest. Prominent among the symbols and decorations was a large tree and crossed swords.

"Today I planned to teach our guest how to link in and report. She anticipates orders, as you can see," Dalin said.

For a moment, no one spoke. Mara tried unsuccessfully to stop staring at the Gaishan senior officers. They ignored her. Realizing she had intruded on a confidential report, she began to shift away to break the link.

When Dalin touched her wrist and stood, Mara stood with him. He nodded at the older man. "Wing, I'll report in person when we arrive."

The officer's face was grave. "Safe travel."

He nodded at the other officer. "Carter," he said.

"De Forest," the man replied. "Get back to Satri."

"Yes, sir." He wrapped two fingers around Mara's wrist. The world shifted and suddenly they were sitting on the floor again. He immediately rounded on her. "What was that?"

She angled away from his glare, fighting disorientation and nausea from the quick transition. "I heard voices," she said. "I hear voices, Dalin, especially at night. I think I've been hearing your reports."

His look was assessing. "Go on."

"I hear the voices, but not the words. Today, it was clear the sound was coming from this room, somehow from you or near you." Mara frowned down at the worn rug. "I wondered how the link might work. If some kind of physical touch would make a difference in how the voices sounded. My knee brushed yours and I appeared in the room with you. I-I'm sorry for the breach in protocol. Is a formal apology required?"

He waved her offer away, stare softening. "You hear voices at night?"

"Since the first night in the tent."

Dalin's gaze fell on the *gontra* clutched in Mara's hand. "How long were you working in the kitchen?"

"Between half an hour and three-quarters of an hour. Why?"

"We have a second report to make to the city leadership, well, specifically to my mother. And then we'll figure this out."

Dalin rotated so that his back was to the bed and gestured for Mara to do the same. "Do you feel tired or disoriented?"

"Not really." She felt confused and full of questions. Fatigue was a constant, not worth mentioning.

"If you sit next to me like you just did, that will work. Light physical contact allows me to take you with me, mentally." He shifted so, as before, his left knee lightly touched Mara's right.

"Wait." She broke the contact. "Could you brief me on how this needs to go?"

Shifting so he could see her, he said, "We've been honing distance rapport for two generations. Most groups, whether it's the militia or the city council, have a rapport conference space. So the room is a real place, but we no longer have to go there physically to have a meeting. Do you understand?"

She didn't fully understand, but she had a sense of what he meant. A little.

"The room we were just using? None of us was actually there. That's why timing is still very crucial. The minds have to connect first, in rapport, and then each person's image of the agreed-upon place is supported by the others'."

"So the forest clearing...?" Mara began.

"Exactly," he agreed. "I showed you the place in your mind first and then, the next time, called you and connected with you beforehand so that we could both see it."

She rocked back and forth trying to get her thoughts in order. "What should I know about this next report?"

"My mother is the elected head of the Satri Council. She's held the position for five years. I'm reporting in because the council cosponsored my mission north to contact you."

"I don't...what?" Mara interrupted.

"Finding you was a civilian priority first and only became a military operation because of your status as a Protector. A dangerous Protector," he added with a grin.

Mara was struggling. "So if I hadn't been a Protector, if I'd lived somewhere in the northwestern settlements, your mother would have sent civilians to make contact?"

"Good point. Listen: We sit when my mother sits and stand when she stands. When she has her robes on, she is the leader. You won't need to say much. They may not question you directly."

Mara grasped most of what Dalin had told her. It was the years of both hints and direct teaching about the Gaishan that made her stomach twist. This was a clear act of treachery, communicating directly with a Gaishan leader.

"We need to make this contact soon," Dalin said, breaking into her thoughts. "Are you ready?"

Mara met his eyes. "Let's go."

They shifted until they were again sitting side-by-side, knees touching. He closed his eyes and Mara did the same. Almost immediately, she heard voices. Her eyes flew open, taking in a raised platform, desks, and chairs, all fashioned from a golden-hued wood. A magnificent, shimmering tree hung in the air, not real, as far as she could tell, but projected there by magic.

"Greetings, Leader de Forest," Dalin said.

"Greetings, Lieutenant," replied a regal woman whose light hair was pinned and curled around her face. "Greetings, citizen. You're Mara de la Luz?"

"I'm called Mara. Ma'am," she added.

At slightly lower desks, a man and a woman sat on either side of the leader. They stared with frank but friendly appraisal. All three wore long, green, official-looking robes.

"What is your current location?" the leader asked.

"We're at one of Jon Jameson's hunting cabins," Dalin answered. A flash of relief crossed the leader's face. "Jameson has gone to scout back along our trail. If he finds signs of pursuit, we'll continue toward Satri immediately. If not, we'll rest here and ride out at first light."

"And the wayhouse?" the leader asked.

"The outer perimeter alarms were triggered mid-morning. I believe we were out quickly and quietly enough to avoid detection."

The leader turned toward the man on her left. "These soldiers have had pursuers on every stretch of their journey. I need you to reach out to the networks and confirm it's Roland and his people. And if not them, find out who is responsible."

The man stood, nodded at the two guests, and vanished.

Mara startled.

"Remember: None of us is truly here," Dalin whispered as he touched a steadying hand to her shoulder.

To the woman on her right, the leader said, "Please go back to the Tree scholars and get an opinion. We need to know more about this girl's significance if we're to keep her safe."

The woman stood. "Yes, Leader." And then she vanished too.

"Dismissing people mid-meeting can make them suspicious. Dispatching people with work makes sense. Now"—the leader narrowed her eyes at her son—"are you all right?" She stood and began unfastening her green robe. Both soldiers stood also.

The leader stepped out of her robe of office, draped it over the chair, and walked behind the desks. The shimmering layers of her pale blue and purple dress bounced as she hurried down the stairs to Dalin. "Son," she said, reaching up and hugging him.

Mara edged away from the pair, trailing her fingers over the smooth, dark-green audience chairs. To have a caring mother worrying over you must feel…nice. The slightly rounded walls draped in dappled green fabric enclosed a meeting space large enough to hold a group of twenty or more.

With a start, she remembered they were not, in fact, here in the most richly appointed room she had ever seen. And, further, that she and Dalin were no longer touching. "Dalin? Should we…?"

He was pulling away from his mother. "It's just like the clearing. Once you have a sense of the place, you can be here without a link."

Dalin's mother was taller and stronger than she looked, her hair and face so similar to her son's. Reaching out both hands, she clasped Mara's in her own. "It takes me back fifteen years to look at you. My name is Yadira de Forest. But you're family, so please call me Yadira." The woman's blue eyes filled. "It was terrible to lose first you, and then your parents. Jin, Elana, and I grieved for so long. And then when Jameson found you, he was certain you were safer in the North. It wasn't until the Tree—" She broke off and sniffed, brushing her cheek. "Well, we can talk further of such things when you arrive."

Yadira released Mara's hands. "I look forward to seeing you under less pressing circumstances, my dear." She patted the girl's arm. "You're in good hands with Dalin and Jameson. If anyone can get you here safely, it's those two."

Dalin's torso jerked. "Jameson's back," he said to his mother. "You can plan on our arrival between tomorrow and the next day." He grabbed Mara's hand and tugged.

She opened her eyes to see Jameson sitting on the opposite bed next to her gear. "'Bout time you two got back from reporting. How's your mother?" he asked.

"Worried. She sent Marly back to the Tree."

Jameson raised his eyebrows. "Did she now?"

Dalin stood. "What did you find?"

Steadying herself as she stood, Mara locked down her shock and confusion from all that Yadira de Forest had revealed.

"Nothing," her uncle said. "No signs of pursuit. Problem is two horses leave a trail in snowy woods. So I erased signs of your passage for about three kilometers and set a false trail out to the plain. If whoever is following you is neither canny nor diligent, we should be alright this far west." He looked directly at Mara, blue eyes sharp. "Are you up for an evenin' ride, lass?"

"Of course," she said.

"That's what I like to hear." He turned to Dalin. "You've had a meal and a rest and a chat with your mum—"

"Let's go," Dalin interrupted.

"There's my lad." He winked and jerked his thumb. "This wee one may look a bit fragile, but he's all right in a scratch." Dalin feinted at Jameson's head. When one of the man's hands went up to protect his face, the tall soldier pivoted and tagged Jameson in the ribs. "Ooh, that's tricky," he said. "We'll have time to play later. If we leave as soon as possible, with the wind and trees working for us, we should make it to the plains east of Satri roughly ten hours from now, near dawn."

Chapter 18

Rowan, used to multiple weeks at the front, stood calm and steady as Mara tightened her saddle and loaded bags. It felt good to be traveling with two experienced fighters. The continuing evidence of pursuit, combined with Yadira de Forest's obvious concern, put her closer to true fear than she'd been in a long time. She patted her horse and murmured to her as they hurried through their departure routine.

Jameson walked his horse to the center of the stable, facing the other two. "Look, I don't think anyone is on our tail at the moment. I'm goin' to lead us through some back ways. We may go over certain ground more than once." He put his hands on his hips and looked up. "Can't believe I'm about to say this but, for this kind of ride, discipline is key. We must stay together. We must be silent. We only stop when I say so. Understood?"

"Sir," Mara answered, straightening a little.

"Yes, sir," Dalin said and snapped a salute.

Jameson stared hard at them, and then swung into his saddle. "Girl, you'll ride between Dalin and me." She began to protest but her uncle held up his hand. "I promised my wife that I would bring you back in one piece. And," he added, "we know the terrain."

Moving into position behind Jameson, she knew he was right. Yet being protected felt uncomfortable, almost demeaning. She had been on her own and protecting others, leading others, for years now. As the horses stepped out into the night, Mara pulled the hood of her borrowed jacket up and tightened it. Her fingertips brushed the rip in the fabric made by Jameson's sword. Was she really safe with him?

#

The older man set a challenging pace given the snow, wind, cold, and darkness. Fortunately, the trees were never so thick as to prevent passage. Sometimes she could catch a glimpse of clouds. Even with gloves, it was necessary to alternate one hand on the reins and one hand in a pocket for warmth.

To keep her mind off the cold, Mara imagined what Satri might be like. A settlement that large probably needed a massive main square with at least six times as many carts and stalls as where Elias lived. Beautifully dressed men and women like Dalin's mother, strolling, arms linked, baskets of food brimming. Mara pushed herself to consider what "really different" might be. Maybe people flew using paper wings. Maybe it was quiet because everyone talked using mental communication. Doorways, counters, chairs, everything would have to be higher to accommodate tall people—

"*Mara.*" Dalin's voice broke into her musings. "*You awake?*"

"*Of course,*" she thought back.

"*We've been on the move more than five hours, but Jameson will push until the horses need rest.*"

"*Fine with me.*" She pursed her lips. "*Can you read my thoughts? Other people's thoughts?*"

"*No,*" came the reply with a hint of laughter. "*Just what you say. It's still a normal conversation, more or less.*"

The trees were beginning to thin and the wind had increased. "*Jameson says he can't talk with his mind.*"

"*As far as I know, that's true,*" Dalin said. "*It doesn't work for everyone, maybe ten percent of the population. When people relocate to Asattha as adults, gaining the ability for mental rapport is unlikely.*"

People moving between planets—the colorful, round-looking objects in the book at the wayhouse. How was that possible? "*But you were born here, on this planet? You and your parents?*"

"*My mother was born here,*" Dalin said. "*She is fourth generation, which is rare. But my dad was born on one of the Origin planets.*"

The wind had blown the clouds to tatters. Stars gleamed in the black sky. Or maybe planets? A shadowy rock formation emerged on the right side of the trail.

A shout burst across her mind. "*Do you smell that? Jameson is brilliant!*"

"*What? Smell what?*" Mara shot back.

"*The gulf, the ocean. He took us southeast, but all the way to the water. Now we just ride east to Satri. We'll be nearly impossible to track because of the rocks and the water.*"

She wished she could see beyond the rocks to understand what he was excited about. Up ahead, a flickering light showed her uncle had dismounted and was leading his horse into a cave. Mara dismounted and followed, Dalin close behind.

About twenty paces inside the cave entrance, Jameson had begun pulling firewood from under a tarp. "Nice night for a ride, eh?" He assembled his small pile of wood and struck a spark to light it. "Got to protect the wood from the sea air," he said, feeding medium-sized pieces to the blaze. "Never know when ya might need a fire."

Now that they were stopped, fatigue hit her hard and faint tremors ran up the back of her legs. Fighting the temptation to stretch out by the warmth and rest, she turned and fumbled for the bag of feed.

Jameson walked farther into the cave. The ceiling sloped lower but was still well over three meters high. "There's a natural basin here," he called. "I poured water in it for Gwen the last time we passed through. Works like a trough."

Untying her canteen, she led her mare past the fire to where her uncle stood.

"Don't use your water for the horses, lass. I've got water stored." He pulled another tarp and revealed a stack of cubes with slightly rounded corners.

"How did you get these here?" Dalin exclaimed.

Jameson only grunted and lifted the top cube, which sloshed. He carried it to the rock basin, unscrewed a lid and tipped the container on one of its edges. The faces of the cubes were gray and grooved and about as wide as Mara's shoulder to her elbow. She ran a hand over the surface—not metal, not stone, not cloth, not glass, not wood. As Rowan joined the other two horses for a drink, the girl continued to run her fingers over the strange material, her tired mind stuck on this small anomaly.

"We stopping long enough to eat and sleep? Or just eat?" Dalin asked.

"Tired already?" The older man pushed the water cube off to the side and straightened.

"I want to finish this mission, but not at the risk of our horses or our safety."

Mara stood there running her hands over the water jugs until Jameson said, "Right. The horses need saddles off and a quick rub down. Lass, that's you. Boy, if you go back and hide the trail where we came out of the woods, I'll get us a meal."

Dalin checked his pockets and bent to adjust one of his boots. "It's made out of plastic," he said quietly.

"Plastic?"

"We use it for a lot of things. You'll see it all over Satri."

"Seems very useful," Mara said. Giving herself a small shake, she untied the food bags from each saddle and stacked them near the fire.

"None of the food needs to be cooked," Jameson said, looking over his shoulder. "But the heat helps us all, including the horses. Sorry we can't take a proper rest here, but we'll have a right good middle-of-the-night snack."

Surprised by the note of concern in his voice, Mara continued caring for the horses in silence. She didn't know what to say to this man. It was easier to think of him as a senior officer. Jameson certainly looked the part with his worn travel leathers, grim face, and close-cropped hair.

But something about him nudged her memory. She gave the mare a final pat and moved to the fire to rest for a few minutes.

"Clear." Dalin's voice disrupted her thoughts. *"Tell Jameson, all clear."* Mixed with the words was information coming through his senses. The gulf air smelled like brine and damp. He was hungry but not cold.

"Jameson's making something delicious. Can you smell it?" she asked.

"No," came the quick reply. *"Wait. Maybe...through you. Be there in ten."*

"Dalin says to tell you all clear and he'll be back in ten," Mara reported.

"Good." Jameson was pressing layers of sliced potatoes, meat, vegetables, and cheese into a cook pot. The pot hung on the same kind of Gaishan apparatus, but this time instead of a double spit, the extra rods were being used in the frame to hold the weight. "Food'll be ready by then."

Jameson sat back on his haunches. She scooted her soggy boots closer to the fire and put herself sideways to his stare.

"You look like your mother," he said. "And there's some resemblance to Elana as well."

"Did you know my mother?"

"No, and I'm sorry for it." He poked at the cook pot with a metal spoon. "We have your parents' things at the house. Elana never stopped believing you were alive. She kept everythin'." He stirred the food again. "Gonna be a lot of learning comin' at you once we get to Satri." Resting the spoon on a rock, Jameson rubbed a thumb over the scar on his eyebrow.

The gesture connected to a piece of a memory. "You," she began. "We've met before. In Elias's settlement, you were there to buy horses each year. And you would talk to me about the horses, which ones I liked."

His expression was rueful. "At first, it was a present for your aunt. I found you for her. You were a fine little lass. Tall for your age, skinny, good eye for horses, too." Looking down and poking at the fire, he said, "You only came to that horse fair for three years. And that's been nearly ten years ago. Elias convinced me to trust him. Said you were safer with him and his wife watchin' out. Broke your aunt's heart, but he had the right of it."

She couldn't dwell on what this man was revealing. Talking about her parents' things? Talking about her as though she had been lost? Her mind protected itself by filing the information away for future examination.

"Elias called you a name I didn't know. *Eye-resh? Was that it?"

Jameson chuckled. "Irish is right. I come from an Anglo-European Origin planet, Kels. Many an Irishman can be found there."

Dalin appeared in the cave entrance. "Did you pack any whiskey as a testament to your national pride?" he asked.

"No, nor if I had would I be sharin' any with a smooth-faced youngster like yourself," he snorted.

Dropped next to the fire, Dalin grinned. "No pursuit," he said. "I followed our trail back a kilometer or two. Nothing."

"Wind picked up again?" Jameson asked.

"Yes and no. We'll be sheltered by the cliffs for a good distance."

Jameson poked the contents of the cook pot and grunted. "Bowls," he said. Dalin passed him three bowls and gave a spoon to Mara. Jameson frowned as he divided the delicious-smelling mixture into three portions.

"Bothers me. No one chasin' us."

"What do you mean?" Dalin asked.

"Look," said Jameson. "They tracked and chased you on the plain. Tracked you to the wayhouse, flushed you out, and now nothin'?"

Mara tried a mouthful of dinner and burned her tongue. "That doesn't make sense," she agreed.

"Leaving the wayhouse, we only had one place to go," Dalin picked up the thought.

"The city," Jameson said.

"Why track us in the snowy woods when they can just set a picket outside Satri? I would set it on the west side," Dalin added.

"So we'll have to fight our way in," Mara said. "Can we choose the ground?"

Dalin nodded and took a few quick bites of his food.

Jameson ate more slowly, thinking. "They can watch us from the gulf, but won't be able to send reinforcements up the cliffs."

"The Browns want to keep this quiet, like always. I'm thinking they would set a squad or two on picket and gamble that we won't be approaching from the north." Dalin continued to eat but his grin had vanished. "We can choose the ground by choosing a line of entry into Satri."

Jameson perched his bowl on a rock and picked up a stick. He drew a circle and a squiggle inside it. "That's Satri." Next he drew a series of jagged lines and two crossed lines. "Here's the cliffs and here's us. See this area?" He pointed to a smooth expanse between the cliffs and the city. "It levels out here. Open stretch is maybe only two kilometers."

"We hide"—Dalin pointed to the cliffs—"watch for the squad to come by, jump them, and ride through."

"How many?" Mara asked.

"In a squad of Browns?" Jameson took a bite and chewed. "Ten to twelve, shouldn't be more than that. If they send two squads, that's a bit more trouble."

"What about your fighters or a Gaishan patrol? Could we ask them for help?"

The older and younger soldier exchanged a look. "Not everyone realizes the Browns, some of them anyway, are the enemy," Dalin said. "Most of the citizens of Satri consider them ambassadors or advisors from the Queen. Kind of like they are in the Protected Territory." He met Mara's eyes and waited for her to put it together.

"So if the Browns are chasing us, chasing me…" She tucked hair behind her ears and pulled her knees into her chest.

"People will assume we are at fault," he finished the thought.

"They don't want people leaving the boundaries in the North and coming here. And they don't like loose ends, you said. But otherwise the Browns are neutral in the war between the Protectors and the Gaishan? How can that be?" The ideas scarcely made sense laid out next to each other, but she was trying to grasp the larger forces impacting their immediate situation.

"It's simple: Your queen is our queen, and these are her soldiers."

Suddenly the memory of Roland's announcement came back. "This is the emblem of your queen," he had said. *The Queen.* Mara imagined the golden knot with the lioness at the center, threads reaching out to the Gaishan, to the Protectors, to the Browns.

"My senior officers want this mission to happen as quietly as possible," Dalin added. "It's imperative to avoid provoking Roland."

"So we're back to choosing our ground, then fighting our way through the picket, however many men that might be," Jameson said, unconcerned. "You were right the first time, girl."

Dalin stretched out and kicked Jameson's boot. "For all his virtues, this fellow never fought as part of a larger unit," he explained. "Your question was logical. I wish my guys could ride out here and escort us home. But we can't risk more people being involved."

Two parts of Mara's brain were wrestling against each other. The soldier was excited and focused on the coming opportunity to test her skills. The girl wanted a simple ride south to meet her aunt and learn about her parents. Mara flexed her legs against the cold sandy floor of the cave and told the softer side to quit whining.

"Do you have your chrono?" Jameson asked.

Dalin raised an eyebrow. "Can't bring any kind of tech north," he said. "Contaminates the experiment."

"Right." Shaking his head with disgust, Jameson dug into a pocket and pulled out a thumbnail-sized black disc. "Just past midnight," he said. "We want to be crossing the open stretch before dawn. It's about four hours' ride, maybe more if the wind picks up."

A question had been nagging at Mara. "So if a section of the picket, say a team of two Browns, stops patrolling their stretch, won't the rest come to investigate?"

Her uncle shrugged and showed his teeth in a fierce approximation of a smile.

"But, I mean, if the goal is stealth, shouldn't we try to avoid disrupting the picket?" she pressed.

"Yeah, we can watch the timing," he said. "But it's a long open stretch either way."

Dalin scraped one last bite of food from his bowl. "Good cooking. Thanks."

While Jameson studied his map on the cave floor, Mara reviewed the little she knew of the Brown soldiers. They kept to themselves. They were neither cruel nor kind to their horses. Sometimes an exemplary soldier from among the Protectors would be recruited to join the Browns, never to be seen again. Roland had significant magical skill, but Garot—he was the one who scared her.

"Do the regular Brown soldiers have magic like Roland?" she asked. "I've never seen them use any. Not even for shielding."

Jameson glanced up from disassembling the cooking stand. "No, they recruit people without energy potential or skills. They prefer brutes who have no allegiance to a particular group or people, who will conduct themselves as professional soldiers and follow orders without question. At least the grunts. Above them's the analysts and decision-makers, the science people."

"Have you seen them armed with anything besides swords and knives?" Dalin asked.

"Not here. Yet." Jameson shook his head.

Chapter 19

"Stay on the trail," Jameson ordered. "Same formation."

The wind ripped at Mara's hood and chilled her hands on the reins. The moons were low in the sky, partially obscured by fast-moving clouds. As before, her uncle set a fast pace. The sandy trail was so narrow she could almost touch the rocks on either side.

As they passed a medium-sized crevice, nearly big enough to be a cave, Mara sent a thought to Dalin. *"Any chance others are using caves along this stretch?"*

"Don't think so," he answered. *"Jameson seemed confident this path was virtually unknown."*

She felt uneasy about tomorrow, meeting her aunt, and about the more immediate future, riding through a Brown patrol in the small hours of the morning. *"Why do the Browns want me anyway?"* she asked. "Not just because I rode south on leave."

"No one knows for sure."

Dalin hadn't told her nearly enough on most subjects related to the Gaishan. It was like putting together a puzzle with Elias and the other stable children, a frequent pastime in the slow winter months. "Find the common colors and patterns," the stable master would tell them. "Look for the boundaries; look for the center."

Ahead, Jameson's hand went out, his arm bent up at the elbow, palm flat. As she came up on his right side, Dalin and his warhorse blocked them in. "Nearing the end of the cliffs," her uncle said. "Wait here." He slid from his horse and disappeared into the darkness.

"You stopped talking to me," Mara said.

An errant shaft of moonlight lit the frustrated look on Dalin's face. "I've been getting conflicting orders about what you need to know. And I'm certain I'm not getting all the information either."

"We're risking our lives based on an uncertain set of facts?"

"Haven't you been doing that for four years already?" he countered.

Mara tightened her hood and rubbed at one eye to cover her surprise at the sucker punch. "Fine. Good point. Do we know enough to get into your settlement city from here?"

"The old man will get us through. With your hair covered, the Browns won't suspect you're female. But if the fight gets bad, I want you to run."

She flinched, stunned by the affront to her honor. As she drew herself up to demand an apology, the clouds parted again, this time revealing the look of worried determination on Dalin's face. "If I were a person who could run from a fight," she said in an even tone, "where would I run? This is unfamiliar ground. Nor do I know my way in your settlement, should my run take me there."

"I can show you." Dalin reached for her hand.

"No," she said, turning her body to keep out of his reach. "We've come this far together."

She began checking her sword harness, knife belt, boots, and coat fastenings. Once satisfied, she dismounted and checked her horse's saddle, bridle, stirrups, and horseshoes. After a few moments, Dalin started his own check.

Jameson came blasting down the path. "Mount up, now!" He wheeled his horse around and galloped back the way he had come. Mara threw herself onto the mare's back and urged her into a run, Dalin and his warhorse close behind. The last of the rocks rushed by and they were free.

The damp wind blowing in from the gulf pushed at Mara's right side. She leaned forward and squinted, just able to see her uncle and the line of cover due east. Narrowing her focus to Jameson's back, she chased him across the empty plain.

A few lengths from the tree line, a wedge of seven Brown foot soldiers emerged, stopping Jameson. Not seeing any weapons drawn, Mara pulled up several lengths away with Dalin. The exchange appeared calm, Jameson's confidence coming through in his posture and gestures.

Her uncle rode back their way. "I've explained we're scientists returning to the city after setting our equipment to record measurements."

"What are we studying?" Dalin asked.

"Wave patterns and erosion of the cliffs," Jameson grinned. "Don't think it'll work. Worth a try."

Edging closer now, the apparent leader of the Brown group called, "If you're scientists, why are two of you wearing swords?"

"Can't be too careful gathering information for the Queen," Jameson answered. He'd changed his speech pattern and eliminated his accent.

The Brown in charge spoke to his men and the entire group moved forward until they were standing in a loose formation around the three mounted fighters. "Reports indicate rogue Satri militia members may be out this way, as well as Protectors."

"Protectors from the North, here?" Dalin asked.

The leader nodded. "And they may be traveling with an armed woman."

"How odd," said Jameson. "That's not something you see every day."

One of the other Brown soldiers laughed and his leader shot him a glare. "Let's have a look under that hood," the leader said, gesturing to Mara. "Then you scientists can be on your way."

Jameson made eye contact with Mara and winked.

"Ready for a fight?" Mara thought at Dalin.

"On your signal."

Mara reached for the drawstring with exaggerated care. As she loosened the knot and eased the hood back, the wind whipped her long dark hair out like a flag.

"It's them," a Brown soldier shouted, only to fall forward, one of Jameson's knives in his throat.

Planting a boot on the chest of the soldier nearest her, Mara vaulted from her saddle, taking down another Brown with her momentum. She drew her sword and faced her two opponents as they struggled to stand. Stepping in, she stabbed with one smooth motion, kicked the man off her sword, and hit the approaching soldier in the face with her elbow. When he doubled over, she sliced downward, the scent of blood rising in the cold, damp wind. Her heart raced but her head was clearer than it had been in days.

Jameson had also downed two opponents and Dalin was engaged with his second. The remaining soldier held his sword at the ready but was inching backward toward the trees.

Before he could flee, Jameson snagged the man by his sword arm and neatly took the weapon. "Who ordered the surveillance?" he asked, unhurried, friendly.

The man's eyes were wide. "She serves the Tree," he said, pointing a trembling hand.

"What's your home planet, soldier?" When the man didn't answer, Jameson wrenched his elbow behind his back, forcing the Brown soldier forward onto his knees. Peering at the skin behind the man's left ear, her uncle grunted. "Right. He's from Iloel. Not going to get any answers." He hit the man across the back of the head with his sword hilt, sending him unconscious to the ground.

Dalin's low whisper carried just far enough. "At least eighteen, on your right."

Jameson sprinted to his horse and pulled a device from one of his bags. With swift precision, he snagged a quiver of short arrows and swung the contraption to face the oncoming soldiers. He pulled the trigger and swept the device in a half circle, landing arrows in six soldiers' chests, necks, or faces. This brought a shout and a rush from the remaining men. Jameson loaded one more round and downed another four soldiers. He hooked the weapon to his belt and put his sword up.

Mara raised her sword as well. She took a breath and let it out as she checked her position and her shield. She was so close to the edge of the plain a tree branch brushed her face. As one of the Browns shouldered a weapon she had never seen, Dalin stepped in front of her, putting himself in the soldier's sights.

"Down," she shouted with her voice and mind as she pulled a throwing knife with her left hand and let it fly. With the throw, a pressure wave of air and energy swept outward. The ground rippled, the force throwing the charging soldiers from their feet.

Jameson ran forward to stab the nearest one, but Dalin shouted, "Wait." He pointed at the Browns, all of whom had dropped their weapons and were holding their heads. The Gaishan kicked the sword and long knife away from the nearest Brown soldier. *What did you do?"*

Chapter 20

Mara's head ached and her ears rang. She tried to shrug off the dizziness and collect weapons, but it was as though the ground still rolled. Staggering a little, she reached for the unusual weapon that had been aimed at Dalin. Her uncle plucked it from her fingers.

"Not for you, miss," he said.

"But you already have..." she protested.

"Do you know what just happened?"

"No." Mara snatched a sword from a man rocking and moaning on the ground.

Dalin pulled one of the unharmed Browns to his knees. "Who put out the alert? Who ordered this surveillance?"

The man looked around, clearly dazed. He covered his mouth when he saw the fallen men. "Oh no. What happened? Where am I?"

"What is your name?" Dalin asked, his tone less harsh.

The man looked upset. "*No sé.* I don't know," he said. "Paulo or Pablo? I can't— *No puedo...recordar.*" His face sagged in dismay.

"He's fogged. No external symptoms, but more confusion and more amnesia than I've ever seen," Dalin said.

"Scan the area, as far as you can," Jameson said. "We'll stash the weapons." He turned to Mara. "Come now, lass, help me get these out of sight. When the gents don't check in, someone's going to come looking."

Bewildered and nearly numb, she helped gather the remaining arrows, swords, and knives. A part of her knew she had caused what was wrong with the Brown soldiers. Her stomach churned and her sword hand clenched and unclenched as the last of the battle energy pumped tremors through her frame.

A few paces away, Dalin closed his eyes and turned in a slow circle. "No one within a kilometer, maybe farther."

The two men persuaded the remaining ten Brown soldiers, including the partially conscious and now fogged man from Iloel, to help hide the bodies of their fallen comrades in the underbrush and to use branches and leaves to cover the worst of the blood. In a few minutes, the site of the skirmish was nearly indistinguishable from the scrubby plain around it.

"Thoughts about these men? The numbers?" Dalin gave Jameson long look.

"No."

"Recognize any of 'em?"

"No." Jameson drank from his water bottle and spit. "Take them to the relocation center. They're used to fogged folk wandering in. Strip off anything marking them as Browns before you get there."

The group of men huddled close. A few were asking questions of the others. Most were still in shock.

"All right, men," Dalin said, voice full of authority, "You all worked on a collective farm in the North and you journeyed south to start new lives."

"What about the others?" one of the Browns asked, pointing toward the trees where the bodies were concealed.

"Outlaws lie in wait along the main road, preying on innocent travelers like yourselves. Sadly, your group was attacked." Muttering rippled through the group, but they seemed to accept this version of events. "Dawn approaches." Dalin gestured toward the sky. The stars were nearly invisible as pink-gold light shimmered on the trees. "We have a community house where you will all get a warm breakfast. The staff will assist you in finding work and permanent places to stay. Follow me." He leapt onto his horse and disappeared into the forest, the shuffling men trailing behind.

Enveloped in sudden silence, Mara stood alone with her uncle.

"We're headin' home," he said. "Elana and I don't live in the center of the city. Just close enough for her to walk or ride ta work and far enough for me ta come and go without notice." He surveyed the area one more time before swinging himself into the saddle.

Mara went through a swift and nearly automatic check of bags and buckles before pulling herself into the saddle. She'd never fought an unmasked enemy, never had to deal with corpses of fallen men because the Gaishan didn't leave bodies behind.

According to the simple but strict Protector training, she'd just killed potential allies. No mask equaled human. Face equaled friend. Cold sweat prickled across her forehead and her throat tightened before she was forced to lean to one side and vomit up the contents of her stomach.

"You did a good job in the fight," Jameson said, nudging his horse into a walk. "But your sword arm needs some work and your guard is too loose. Going to work on that."

After some time in the thin, scrubby woods, they turned onto a faint path. Jameson didn't coax his horse into a run—the mounts were too tired for that—but he urged them to a fast trot.

They'd almost passed the first house when Mara saw it and jerked the reins in surprise. The red house looked like two houses stacked on top of each other with one roof. She rubbed a hand over her tired eyes, but the construction didn't change.

Gradually, the path became more distinct and covered in gravel. More of the double-stack houses could be seen through the trees, some blue, some green, some brown, and shades in between. All were part stone and part wood. The trees thinned and the path widened. Eventually, Jameson followed a fork to the right and soon they were trotting along a wide lane lined with houses, some doubled, some single.

The lane opened up to the east, the bright rays of the morning sun glistening on its white-pebbled surface. Houses were everywhere now. Not exactly crowded together but close. A few had visible, though dormant, gardens. No Gaishan were about, nor any horses or domestic animals. The only movement came from the chilly breeze ruffling the tree branches.

Her uncle turned to the right again, clearly hurrying. The clopping of the horses' hooves rang loud in the morning stillness. They turned left onto a street that ended at a small circular drive. A tidy, green, double-stack house with white shutters perched at the top of the circle. The next gust of wind carried a tang of salt and reminded Mara of the smell along the cliffs.

"Here we are," Jameson said. "Stable's 'round back." A hint of a proud smile crossed his face before he dismounted to lead his horse toward the south side of the house. Both disappeared behind a thick perimeter of *gontra* trees screening the back walkway from the road.

Energy reserves depleted, Mara took an extra moment to dismount and follow. Her uncle had already started water running in the small but very organized stable and was now scooping from a white bucket into the feeding bins of two stalls. She patted Rowan's flank, removing the saddle and gear. Similar to the stable at the hunting shack, this structure was not connected to the main house, but sat far back on the property, surrounded by lawn and trees. Jameson didn't talk as they worked, only a quiet grunt escaping as he shoveled fresh straw into the stalls. In a very short time both horses were watered, rubbed, brushed, and fed. Without a backward glance, Jameson left the stable, heading for the house.

"Excellent work today, girl," Mara whispered to her mare before she closed the stall door. "We'll begin improving your sword arm and guard tomorrow." She was so tired, she laughed at her own joke. A quick splash of cold water on her face and hands only helped a little. Dirty, sweaty, and uniform showing dark patches of drying blood—she couldn't imagine being more out of place in the pretty open space between the stable and the house. Between the flowerbeds, the lawn, and the large vegetable garden, the back of her aunt and uncle's property was nearly half the size of the courtyard at the compound.

In Mara's childhood dreams, her family was kind and friendly like the best of the families she had observed in the settlements. She hadn't imagined having a family in a long time, but what if her aunt was harsh or cold? She ran a hand over her hair and tucked the loose pieces behind her ears, then ambled over to take a closer look at the vegetable patch. A much greater fear than she'd felt at the sight of the Brown soldiers gripped her now. That, coupled with intense fatigue, made her consider shaking out a saddle blanket and napping in the stable.

"Do you like to garden?" a soft, female voice asked.

Mara whirled and froze, staring at her only living blood relative, the sense of kinship immediate. Pain shot through her forehead as a snippet of memory, of running to this woman and hugging her legs, burst in her mind.

"I'm sorry to startle you," the pretty brunette said. "But it's still a bit chilly out here and I thought you might want to get warm and eat breakfast." She hugged herself and took a deep breath, eyes filling with tears. "I'm sorry," she whispered. "Thirteen years since I've seen you…I hoped not to cry." She sniffed.

"You're Elana?" Mara asked, taking a step closer. Her voice came out low and rougher than she intended.

The woman sniffed again and swiped a hand across her eyes. "I'm your Aunt Elana. Welcome home, Mara." Face suffused with hope and pain, she opened her arms.

Chapter 21

The fear stilling the girl's arms and legs loosened enough for her to step into a long hug, though her chest felt too tight to breathe. All these years alone. She swallowed, her own eyes pricking with tears. Elana's arms tightened and released. She brushed hair from Mara's cheek as though the bloody soldier in front of her was a little girl. Just like in the memory.

"You look like Dhanya," she whispered. "But also like your father. You got this hair from our side, your mother and me." Elana gestured at her own dark hair pulled back in a loose ponytail. "But you have your father's features and his height."

Mara's curiosity sparked past her fear and fatigue. Watching families, particularly those in Elias's settlement, she had often wondered if she looked like her parents. So many children did. "Jameson said you had images?"

"Oh yes, in the house. Everything is in the house. We have a room ready and breakfast." She paused, blinking rapidly. "I'm sorry." She reached for Mara's hand. "Let's get you fed and rested. There's time. We have time now."

At the back door of the house, Elana gestured to a wooden bench. "You can leave your boots here." Once the heavy boots dropped to the ground, she held the door and motioned for her niece to precede her inside. "Jameson tells me neither of you had the opportunity to sleep last night."

Her uncle had already helped himself to eggs, toast, and a mug full of something. He was tucking into his food when the women entered the kitchen.

"Goodness, sit down and I'll bring you a plate." The petite woman frowned at her husband as she bustled around to the other side of the kitchen counter.

Slipping off her sword and her borrowed jacket, Mara hung them on the back of the chair before sitting down at the small, dark-wood table across from Jameson.

The kitchen was two or three times the size of the kitchen at the wayhouse. Cabinets, stove, and sink were on one side; a counter wrapped around and split part of the room. A scattering of colorful paintings covered the walls at irregular intervals. Behind Jameson, sunlight poured through an open archway that led to a room with an entire wall of windows. Mara pinched the bridge of her nose and closed her eyes. The details and her feelings were overwhelming.

"There you go." Elana placed a glass of water and a heaping plate of eggs and toast in front of Mara. "Do you eat meat?" she asked, twisting her hands together. "I wasn't sure, so I didn't make any. But I could—"

"No," Mara interrupted. She awkwardly patted her aunt's arm. "I mean, yes, I eat meat, but you don't need to cook anything else. This is perfect."

Elana placed serving platters of eggs and toast on the table, and then perched on the chair between her husband and her niece.

Jameson tugged his wife's ponytail and gave her a peck on the cheek. "Goin' to eat, sweetheart?"

"I ate a little as I was cooking. And I do need to get to work…"

Mara looked up from her eggs. "Work?"

"I'm a teacher," Elana said. "But I don't work with children. I work with adults who are new to this planet." At her niece's puzzled expression, she continued, "Most of the Origin cultures are represented in the Commonwealth and that means many languages are spoken. I help with new-language acquisition and give guidance about the cultures of Asattha. Most of the adults in my classes have come here to work in the labs. But occasionally I also get people from the North who have found their way here." She blinked and made a shooing gesture with her hands. "Go on and eat. Please."

Taking another bite of her eggs, Mara paused to be thankful for the pleasure of eating, especially something so delicious. Dalin had told her about her aunt teaching adults but not the specifics. It was good to know her aunt helped people, good to know they had at least that in common.

Elana stepped out and returned to the kitchen a moment later wearing a long coat and carrying two bags over her shoulder. Jameson stood and met her on the counter side of the table. He whispered in her ear, leaned in to kiss her.

"Rest well, both of you," she said. "Jameson, will my niece be here when I return?" She opened a door and pulled out a small box with a handle, stern tone offset by a slight tremor.

"That's the plan," he said. "Best not to mention her to your friends, though. Folk may be out lookin' for a tall Protector female the next few days."

Elana's expression shifted. "Mara, did you bring other clothes with you besides, ah, military?"

She took a drink of water to wash down a huge mouthful of toast. "No."

"Hmm." Her aunt's delicate brows knit together. "Maybe I—"

"She won't be going anywhere today, sweetheart," Jameson said. "Try not to worry." Together they walked down the hall, their conversation muffled by footsteps and doors opening.

The more Mara ate, the more inclined she became to lay her head on the table and sleep right there. But she helped herself to more of everything, mind wandering as she chewed.

Jameson returned to his chair and paused, fork mid-air. "It's killin' her to leave right now. But I told her we had to act normal, just in case. Too many people know Dalin is involved. Don't trust that council, too many people wantin' more power for themselves—"

"How does Dalin being involved connect back to you and Elana?" Mara asked.

"Our families are close, d'ya see?" He took a huge bite and chewed. "When you were taken, Elana was only fourteen. She was your mama's baby sister. Lived with your parents, helped care for you while they worked in the labs. They got to know Jin, that's Dalin's dad, when they were promoted to the main lab. The families lived near each other then. Yadira and your mum became close friends, you and Dalin being so similar in age and all."

This simple story was a corner piece in the confusing puzzle of her history. Mara nodded, hoping he would continue.

"So when you were taken, the de Forest family gave your parents the money to go searching for you. Yadira and Jin took Elana into their home and raised her with their two, once word came of your parents' deaths."

Mara stared down at her empty plate as cold distress settled at the base of her throat. All this time she'd been told her parents abandoned her. She'd made up many stories to soften the impact: Her parents had been young, had been poor or sick, in some way unable to care for a child. To hear Jameson repeat, "When you were taken," didn't fit with her carefully constructed truth. She'd been taken from this life, this place—and two people had loved her enough to die trying to get her back.

"Don't know why I told you all that now," Jameson said. He tapped Mara's plate with his forefinger until she looked up. "I'll clear these dishes," he said. "Let's get you to your room."

He pushed back his chair and stood, stacking Mara's plate on top of his own. She stood as well, head hurting from this latest scrap of history. Jameson left the dishes on the counter and walked past his niece through the open archway.

She followed a few steps and then stopped, mouth open in surprise. The wall of windows gave a spectacular view of the largest body of water Mara had ever seen. Down below the house, blue-gray water churned and splashed against the rocky cliffs, making a faint roaring, crashing sound.

"The cliffs here are quite a bit closer to the water than where we were earlier. The land flattens out into a basin as you go east," Jameson said. "That's called the Gulf of Almac," he added, "and beyond is the Southern Sea."

"How far...how far does the water go?" Mara asked, mesmerized by the movement of the waves.

Jameson scratched his nose. "The gulf goes about twice as far as you've traveled since leaving Protector House. And the sea goes about ten times farther than that."

It was a magnitude too large to comprehend. Her uncle put a firm hand on her back and propelled Mara through the next archway and up the stairs. Though she'd never been in a house with a floor above, she didn't question it now.

At the top of the stairs, Jameson stopped. "That's the washroom." He indicated the second door. "And that's your room." He pointed to the first door on the left. "Need to wash up before you sleep?"

Shaking her head, she pushed open the sleeping room's door. Curtains darkened the windows, making the space invitingly dim. All she could see was the bed she needed so desperately.

Jameson clapped her on the shoulder and she stumbled forward. "See you when you wake," he said and ambled down the hall.

Eyes adjusting quickly, she perched on a wooden chair to slip out of her dirty uniform pants, filthy socks, and overtunic. She stumbled to the bed, not seeing any other details of the room, crawled under the covers, and was asleep in two breaths.

#

Mara dreamed of a giant tree. She stood under its branches, one hand on the trunk, and looked up. The bright sun sparkled on the silvery topside of the leaves and the blue seedpods swayed in an imperceptible breeze.

"Friend," said a light voice.

Leaning against the massive trunk, Mara looked around. She was alone.

"Friend, welcome," came the voice again.

In her dream state, she realized the voice was inside her mind, like thought speech. She closed her eyes and leaned back against the warm tree.

"Hello?" she called.

"Here, Mara," came the voice. *"Open your eyes."*

Mara opened her eyes and took in the vast empty white space around her. As her shocked senses tried to comprehend the emptiness, something rustled nearby and she whirled around. A barefoot young woman wearing a simple silver tunic with dark-green leggings stood to one side, head cocked in curiosity.

Reaching for both Mara's hands, she said, *"The Light welcomes you."*

Mara peered into the woman's face, resisting the urge to pull away. *"Do I know you?"*

"We were childhood friends, here in Satri." The woman laughed, a whispery, musical sound.

But nothing about the woman's eerie dark eyes, luminous brown skin, or long curling dark hair triggered a sense of recognition, nothing like she'd felt with her aunt. The space near their feet was no longer white, but a grassy field. Mara dropped her right hand to twist and look around as the world colored itself in. Her left hand remained in the woman's gentle, papery grasp.

"This is dream speech then?" Mara asked, feeling that was not quite accurate. *"And since we have not been friends for many years, it took the dream a moment to find a common environment?"*

The woman watched with Mara as the white space transformed into a small park with trees, slides, swings, and climbing towers. A stone wall laced with green vines formed the boundary on two sides. *"Have I been to this place?"* she murmured as now recognition sparked.

"When you were very small, your parents would bring you here to play. We would play together. Sometimes your aunt would join us. But only you could see me. That is how I became aware of your gifts."

Mara freed her hand with a gentle tug and walked to sit on the bottom step of a climbing tower, the leather of her uniform creaking as she shifted. The breeze lifted tendrils of her hair while the branches and leaves whispered overhead. *"I'm sorry I don't truly remember you or this lovely place,"* she said. *"I'm tired from...traveling."*

"And fleeing and fighting," the woman said. *"I know what you have been through."*

Mara tried to pull her thoughts together. *"Are you—?"* She had been about to say Dalin's sister, but given this person claimed to be invisible to all but her, that seemed unlikely. *"Who are you?"*

The woman sat next to Mara on the wide bottom step. She stretched out her legs and wiggled her toes in the grass. Fine, intricate markings ran along most of her visible skin. She sighed. *"When you were small, it was enough to say I was a friend who lived nearby. Older humans"*—she paused, considering—*"are often less open to possibility."*

A part of Mara's mind knew she was asleep at Jameson and Elana's house and yet she sensed this dream visitor held another crucial piece to her puzzle.

The woman smiled. *"You seek knowledge. Yes, this was true of you from the very beginning of our acquaintance. But now you have this."* She pointed at the stone fence, the silvery-green vines wrapping around the rocks. *"The time of our acquaintance and much more is hidden from you."*

Mara stared at the woman, who was twitching her feet up and down and leaning back against the play equipment. *"I didn't know people could read minds in dream speech."*

"Generally, people can't," the woman agreed. *"Dalin and a few others of his generation can lift images and feelings, but not full thoughts."*

"But you—" Mara started to interrupt.

"Ah, that is the heart of the matter." The woman smiled, showing straight white teeth. *"I'm not a person. I'm a tree. I'm the Tree."*

Not dream speech. Just a dream. She reached to close the curtain in her mind. If her dream was going this foggy, she didn't want Dalin sensing any of it.

"Wait," the woman said, her voice deeper now, laced with authority. *"I'll show you."* She stood and tugged Mara's hand, leading her back to the largest tree in the park. *"This is how I look on the outside, like a plant, you might say. But I'm alive and aware, more than a rabbit or a horse. I think. I dream."* Her beautiful face was serious, her entirely black eyes locked on Mara's. *"And I'm connected to every tree of my kind on this planet. My roots weave us into one being. Let me show you."*

She placed the girl's hand on the trunk of the tree and covered it with her own. Mara's head and stomach lurched at the sudden sensation of diving into the ground. Then she was running along endless kilometers of root systems, her consciousness tugged up through trunks and branches out to leaves. She felt the joy of wind and sun. All around, other living beings, little lives rushed past. Through it all, surrounding it all, was a pulsing brightness. *"The Light?"* Mara asked.

"Very good." The response chimed through the network of trees. *"The Light is the living energy of All That We Know."*

Energy hummed along Mara's body, nourishing her as it nourished the trees. Then the woman's hand was gone and she was leaning against the tree in the park, alone. *"I have more to show you, little Protector,"* said the Tree's lilting voice. *"For now you must rest. Be welcome and be healed."*

Chapter 22

Hours later, Mara flinched awake reaching for her sword but finding only soft blanket.

"Jameson's house," she said aloud. "My aunt's house," she spoke more quietly.

When she stood, overhead lamps didn't turn on as they had at the wayhouse. She opened the door a crack and peered out to find a pile of clothes just outside the doorway. Leaning down to scoop up the pile, her hand touched a plate in the wall and the overhead light blinked on.

The sleeping room had things stacked in every corner, as though it was used for storage more often than sleeping. Under the windows, a small desk and chair were also full of stacked items, mostly books and papers. The walls were white, the rug a soft cream color, and the bed linens were a mix of whites, yellows, and oranges. She smoothed the covers back into place and laid out the clothes.

Her aunt had loaned her a light-blue dress with a fitted top and narrow sleeves. A short undertunic made of stretchy material, undershorts made of the same material, and blue shoes completed the outfit. As Mara finished laying out the last piece, she heard steps on the stair, followed by a light knock at the door.

"Mara?" Elana scanned her the way a partner would do a visual check for injuries. She smiled a tentative smile. "Do you feel rested?"

"Yes, thank you," Mara said, staring back at her aunt. Thick and dark hair, like her own, lay smoothly across Elana's shoulders. Her eyes were nearly identical in shape to Mara's and also fringed by dark lashes, but the color was more green than blue. Elana's build was more petite, more delicate, especially the bones of her face and hands.

"Jameson has been through the shower already. We thought you might wish to rinse before the evening meal." Elana's gaze fell on the clothing on the bed. "Some of the women I've met from the North have told me dresses are not commonly worn by most, but saved for special occasions like dances and festivals." She smoothed her hands over her lavender tunic and dark-blue skirt. "Here, women generally wear dresses or skirts, so I thought, since we are hiding your"—she struggled for a word—"your affiliation, I thought we would try you in my clothes first and then purchase new clothes once we find what suits you."

Mara had no idea how to respond to the startling idea of wearing a dress every day. Why would women of the South choose such impractical clothing? How could they be ready to ride or fight?

"I'm sorry. Here you're just awake and I'm rattling on about dresses. Let me show you the washroom." Mara followed her aunt down the hall and into the long, narrow room. "Your uncle doesn't like most of the automated options," Elana said with a touch of wistfulness. Sliding back a panel to reveal a tiled shower, she said, "But we do have auto soap and auto steam." A low cabinet yielded a stack of fluffy, white towels. She clicked her tongue. "I don't have a robe for you. So for now, you can use an extra towel." Wrapping her arms around herself, she hunched her slim shoulders. "I should start a list of all the things you might need."

Wanting to be polite, better than polite, the tall girl forced a smile that probably looked more like a grimace. "Thank you. I'll shower, dress, and come to the kitchen as quickly as I can."

Politeness, kindness, respect—those were good. But it was clear her aunt wanted warmth and hugs, things Mara had little experience with.

Inside the shower, several buttons were grouped together along the back wall. Although each button had markings underneath, it was impossible to guess what they indicated. She found auto soap and auto steam through trial and error and successfully washed away the grime from the last leg traveling and the lingering scent of blood from the fight.

Back in the sleeping room, she found a piece of white paper atop the pile of clothes. It was a hand-drawn female figure wearing the short undertunic and undershorts. Arrows and other markings ranged around the picture. Lifting the small, stretchy tunic from the pile, Mara peered at the picture and then pulled the half tunic over her head, wrestling it into place. The rest of the clothes were much easier to manage. The blue shoes were a decent fit, slightly short but not uncomfortable. After hastily toweling her hair dry, she used the mirror in the washroom to make sure it went smoothly into a braid.

At the top of the steps, Mara paused and looked down. Setting one floor of a house on top of another seemed an obvious innovation now that she was experiencing it. Why hadn't the wealthier families in the North expanded their homes this way? At the bottom of the stairs, she turned right and saw a common room with shelves and shelves of books, even more than in the wayhouse. Mara stared at the books, forgetting one hunger for another. But voices and delicious smells wafted from the kitchen, so she walked around the other way through the room with the now-darkened view of the water.

Dalin was at the stove cooking alongside another tall man and Elana. Jameson sat on a stool at the counter talking with a fair-haired woman. As she turned, Mara recognized Dalin's mother.

"Hey," Dalin said, looking up from the pan he was stirring.

"Hey," she replied, stepping into the room. In her mind she added, *"You could've let me know you were here."*

"You've met my mother, Yadira de Forest. This is my father, Jin Tek."

The man at the stove gave a slight half bow and grinned. "Pleased to meet you." His hair was light brown and very short, his eyes a warm amber. Though not quite as tall as his son, he had a similar build and similar posture.

"I'm glad to meet you," she said, returning the bow. "Thank you for the hospitality of your wayhouse," she said to Jin and Yadira, hoping it was the correct thing to say. "It was a fine place to stay after many nights camping."

Yadira shuddered. "I don't know how you people sleep outside for weeks at a time. It must be dreadful."

Raising her eyebrows in surprise, Mara said, "We don't sleep outside; we have tents."

Both Dalin and Jin smiled the same smile at her response, eyes going narrow and crinkling at the corners.

"But now that you're here," Yadira continued, "you won't have to worry about any of that."

Her uncle gave Mara a tiny wink before resuming the conversation with Yadira.

"Anything I can do to help?" she asked.

"Not at the moment, dear." Elana was scraping rice into a serving bowl with a flat wooden paddle. "Dalin and Jin are in charge of the difficult work."

Dalin was rapidly stirring a large metal bowl of colorful vegetables over a low flame. His father was turning a pan full of…she wasn't sure.

"My dad comes from a Chinese Origin planet," Dalin said, glancing up and catching her puzzled expression. "We're making his famous stir-fry shrimp and scallops."

"Stir-fry is the way we are cooking. Shrimp and scallops come from the sea. Fishermen get them from the sea," he clarified through rapport.

"Here, Mara," Elana said. "You can help me prepare the serving dishes."

In a few short minutes, father and son had everything ready. And while they arranged the shrimp, scallops, and vegetables to their satisfaction, Elana removed a dish of peeled red fruit from the cold storage cabinet.

"We're going to have baked apples for dessert," she explained to her niece. "They'll cook while we eat." After tapping a few buttons near the oven, she slid the baking dish inside.

Conversation flowed between the four old friends while the two younger soldiers concentrated on eating. Mara learned both Jin and Jameson had been off-planet during the past summer season. Nuwa, Dalin's younger sister, was currently working in the gulf on a marine biology and marine energy project. The Satri Council only met three times a season unless an issue arose, such as too many Browns in the city. And since the council had allocated additional funding for Elana's school last year, she was due to give a report at the final session of the winter season.

Much of the talk was challenging to understand. They discussed aspects of life in Satri and in the Commonwealth that, while she recognized the individual words, made little sense together. The food, however, was absolutely delicious and Mara kept herself busy enjoying the new textures and flavors. The table was covered in a beautifully patterned cloth and each person had a cloth napkin. A small grouping of low candles sat on a silver plate in the center of the rectangle. She paid compliments to all three cooks as she spooned a third helping onto her plate.

"We have been told the Protectors are fed well and have good accommodations," Elana said. "Is that true?"

Mara chewed her bite, considering her aunt's strained expression. It was more than a simple question, she realized. Elana was asking about a long-held fear.

"Yes, that's true," she said. "Even the children who stay and work at Protector compounds are fed much better than many children in the settlements."

"It's gone too far," Yadira said, her voice angry. "All children should have plenty to eat."

"Think about the restrictions on trade, limitations to funding," Jin interjected. He placed his hand on his wife's shoulder.

"I know about the rules," she said, eyes flashing with frustration, "but we have abundant resources in the South. The whole continent could be fed—"

Jin kissed his wife's cheek and patted her hand. "Later, *qingren*. Our guest was just about to tell us a little about her life."

Taking a slow breath, Mara assured herself she wasn't revealing Protector secrets. Of this group, only Dalin had ever been a part of the regular fighting. But his father's request was still somehow surprising. "What did you want to know?"

Jin tilted his head to the side and rested his chin on one hand. "Could you describe a typical day? Your typical day?"

"During a fighting season?" she asked before spearing one of the white shrimps—or scallops, she wasn't sure—and swishing it around in the delicious sauce.

"No, when you're at the compound, at the Northwest Protector House."

"Well," Mara said. "When the white storms come, the Gaishan don't fight." She took a breath, trying to decide if this was more like giving a report or more like conversation. It felt a little like a spontaneous report, so she sat up straighter in her chair. "During that time, we train and also work around Protector House, repairing the walls or doing other maintenance activities. So on a typical winter day, if I were home right now"—she caught a slight flinch from Elana—"I would get up and wake up my partner, Annelise. We would shower, put on house uniforms, and go to breakfast. At breakfast, one of the senior Protectors would hand out assignments to fighting pairs for the day. Sometimes it's just a pair working together on a small task, like to inventory all the cooking pans in the kitchen. I had to do that once. Sometimes a job is really big so a whole cohort will work on it. Last year the Green cohort got assigned the main courtyard. We had to sweep away all the snow and then find all the loose stones that needed repair or replacing."

"About one hundred fifty in a cohort?" Jin asked.

"Usually," she agreed.

Dalin nodded as well. "Let me see if I can get the cohort details right. You finish eating." Mara raised her eyebrows. *"Jin is asking partly for Elana and partly because he's curious. You know scientists."*

"No?"

"Tell you later," Dalin thought. "So each cohort has about 75 fighting pairs," he said. "The cohorts are organized by color: red, blue, green, and yellow. Each cohort has at least one senior Protector as a leader, each lives in a color-coded section of the compound, and each draws different assignments in a given battle. Am I right so far?"

It was hard not to be startled by how accurate his information was. "So far," she said.

"Within each cohort, the pairs are assigned a Greek letter and a number—"

"What's a Greek letter?" Mara interrupted.

"Like alpha, beta, delta, gamma..."

"Oh those," she said. "That's how they design battle plans within the cohort. The individuals are clustered by their...Greek letters. The senior Protectors draw the symbols on the map in the color of our cohort so we can see what our formations are supposed to look like."

"We thought maybe you went to school in the winter," Elana said.

The girl shrugged. "We have weapons class and different kinds of fighting classes, sometimes map class, sometimes strategy class, but that's all. Nothing like the schools in the settlements."

"No school," Jin said. "That's a new variable."

"I can't stand it." Yadira slammed her hand on the table. "This is inexcusable. They have materials, books, trained teachers. To not educate...so many..." But everyone was looking at Elana, who was growing pale, her eyes watery.

"Protectors used to have school, maybe right up until you moved into the ranks," Dalin said.

"Does everyone in Satri have books in their homes?" Mara asked.

Her aunt looked even more strained. "You haven't had books?"

She wanted to find a way to keep Elana from becoming more distraught, but couldn't think of anything but the truth. "No, the books in Protector House are kept in a library next to the map room. Only senior Protectors and Browns are allowed access."

"What about in the settlements?" Jin asked.

Feeling the childhood longing return, she sighed. "A family might have one book, maybe two, that's passed down. Once I heard a trader's daughter say her family had ten books. But we thought she was lying."

In the kitchen, a small series of beeps sounded. Elana startled and pushed back her chair. "The apples are ready. Jameson, will you help me?" As they walked into the kitchen, Jameson took his wife's hand.

Dalin also stood and began stacking plates and utensils. Mara pushed back her own chair but he stopped her with a hand on her shoulder. "It's fine. You can get the dessert dishes." He took everything to the sink and began talking quietly with Elana and Jameson.

Yadira leaned across the table and smiled. "How was traveling with my son?"

"Yadira," Jin said.

Mara responded with the first thing that came to mind. "He is a good soldier."

"You played together when you were both small. Did you know that?" the older woman said. "Dhanya and I often joked about what a fine match you made."

Jin made a sympathetic face, rolled his eyes, and shook his head.

Tense and confused by both of them, Mara said, "It's important to make a good match with fighting pairs, so they can support each other during training and especially during the swing."

"The swing?" Jin asked, interested despite his obvious disapproval of his wife's choice of conversation topics.

"Well, a soldier is only on the front for three weeks at a time," Mara explained. She began to relax a tiny bit. "The swing is the length of time between when one half of a pair gets back to the compound and the other half, the other person," she corrected herself, "departs for the front. Sometimes it's an hour. Sometimes the swing can be a day or two depending on the battle and battle plans."

Dalin began filling water glasses while Jameson scooped something white onto each clean plate and Elana added a baked apple and a sprinkle of cinnamon.

"What does the swing have to do with fighting pairs? Is that what you're wondering, *Fushin*?"

Jin nodded sheepishly at his son.

"Can I give the answer a try? This is something I've been studying."

She shrugged, distracted by her first bite of the incredible dessert. The baked red fruit, the apple, was soft and coated lightly with cinnamon. The white mound next to the apple was cold, sweet, and creamy. Taking another bite, she closed her eyes to fully enjoy the sensation. Jameson discreetly tapped her plate and showed her his spoon had both a piece of baked apple and some of the white stuff. She smiled and copied him.

"This is the best part of the experiment," Dalin was saying. "You know how we lose soldiers because of stress or a lack of connection to the unit?"

Jameson and Jin nodded.

"Well, the Protector Project keeps each soldier affiliated as part of the cohort and as part of a pair. So in the swing, as Mara was saying"—he glanced over—"a soldier gets cared for, attended to, by one significant person, a partner who is trained to check in on mental health, physical health, provide a debrief, and so on. They are trained to be honest. It is expected between partners. So the bravado, the machismo, that sometimes prevents soldiers from sharing concerns with each other or with an officer and ultimately can set up dangerous situations in our system doesn't exist for the Protectors."

"Partners or, ah, fighting pairs only see each other in the swing?" his mother asked.

"During battle seasons," Mara said. "When everyone's back, we do pair training and pair competitions, sometimes cohort competitions. The young ones especially like those." She looked down at her plate and smiled, thinking of the contests she and Dalin could win.

Chapter 23

Jameson cleared his throat. "Gentlemen, that was a fine feast you put together and I thank you for it." He leaned over and kissed his wife's cheek. "And you as well, my beauty. Thank you for a sweet finish."

"Does anyone want tea or coffee?" Elana asked.

"Yes, please," said Jin.

Mara stood and stacked the dessert plates. Her full stomach reminded her she hadn't checked on Rowan and there was no stable master here. When her aunt began preparing tea, she quietly asked, "Do you mind if I check on my horse? I slept all day and—"

"Jameson was in the stable at least twice today, so I know she's been cared for," she replied. "But of course you can slip out and see your horse. I'm sure all the questions get difficult."

Keeping her hands busy with the dishes, Mara thought for a moment. "Yes. There's so much I don't know."

"I can help with some of that," her aunt murmured. "Tomorrow isn't a school day, so we'll have some time to relax and figure out what you do know and where you need support."

After placing the last plate in the washer, Mara brushed her fingers over the soft fabric of the borrowed blue dress. "Thank you," she said and reached out to squeeze Elana's hand. Looking away, she grabbed an apple from the fruit bowl and slipped out the back door, the cold air a shock after the warmth of the house.

The mare whuffed at her stall door. She leaned out and sniffed the object in her rider's hand before taking it with her teeth. In the dim light from the workbench, Mara could see Gwen in her stall. "Sorry, girl," she apologized. "I didn't think to bring a treat for you."

When the stable door opened behind her, Mara automatically reached for her sword and touched only empty air. She closed her right hand into a fist, stepped her right foot back, and flexed her knees.

Dalin held out both palms as he ducked into the doorway. A pointless gesture, really—she knew he was carrying at least one weapon.

"Ready to punch me again so soon?" he joked. The faint light left his face in shadow.

Mara relaxed her fist. "You promised me sparring, Gaishan. Here is as good as anywhere."

Dalin appraised her attire. "While I'm sure you're ready, even in a dress, I came out here to say good night. Sparring is in the near future though, I promise. My dad wants to work with you, too."

Suddenly it occurred to Mara that people in Satri lived far from each other, not within easy reach like at Protector House. "You didn't ride Herald," she said. "Is your home close to here?"

"Yes and no. Sometimes I just like to walk." He moved closer. "What is it?"

Throat tight, she couldn't find the words to explain about every last thing seeming new, about meeting the Tree in her dream, about him living far away. He was a stranger and technically an enemy, but at least he was a soldier too.

"Look, I know I said you would be safer in the South. And you are, despite the fight outside the city this morning," he said.

"How are those men?" she asked, flushing with fresh guilt.

"Oh, settling in," Dalin said. "Looking forward to finding work and a place to live. Did you figure out what you did?"

Mara closed her eyes and swallowed hard. "I don't know."

Dalin slid his thumb and forefinger along a loose strand of her hair. "Whatever you did, it probably saved my life. Thank you." He wrapped one arm around Mara and pulled her sideways into his chest.

"Of course," she said, inhaling his now-familiar smell. "You'd have done the same for me." Standing so close, she could hear his heart beat.

Dalin stroked down the length of her braid. "Does Elana have plans for you tomorrow?"

With a sigh, Mara said, "She says we need to go shopping for non-military clothes. The Browns will be looking for a Protector female so I should try to blend in."

"She's right: Civilian clothes will help." His arm tightened a fraction. "But I'll get you a practice uniform from Nuwa so you won't have to fight our dad in a dress."

Mara smiled at the image he sent of her and Jin, both wearing dresses, circling and throwing kicks.

He took her hand and spun her out and then back against him. "Have fun shopping," he said. He gave Mara one more squeeze and stepped away. "Ask Jameson to get you a leg sheath for a throwing knife." He tapped his temple, walked to the stable door. "You know how to reach me if you need me. Rest well."

"Rest well," she responded as the door swung shut.

She turned and kissed her mare on the nose. "I'll take you out soon," she promised.

#

Entering the kitchen through the sliding glass door, she tried not to disturb the four adults deep in conversation.

"Did Dalin find you before he left?" Elana asked.

"Yes, he did," Mara answered. "I'm heading to my room now."

Searching her niece's face, she sighed. "Of course. Take your tea with you."

Mara accepted the hot cup and nodded first at Jin, then at Yadira. "Thank you for such a fine meal," she said to Dalin's father.

He smiled at her. "You're most welcome."

"Good to see you again, ma'am," she said to his mother.

She snorted. "Please, we think of you as family. Call me Yadira."

"Good to see you again, Yadira," Mara said.

"That's better." The imperious blonde smiled.

Turning to her uncle, she said, "Jameson, thank you for looking after Rowan this afternoon." He nodded.

Mara held her tea carefully as she made her way up the stairs to her room. She leaned against the doorframe and awkwardly fumbled for the light panel. With a sigh, she sank to the floor and leaned against the bed. The tightness in her chest redoubled as she looked at her strange surroundings.

"I'm in the swing with no partner," she said out loud. Giving herself a mental shake, she said, "I can call Dalin if I need him. Elana and Jameson would help if I asked."

But her brisk tone and attempt to convince herself only made the tight, unhappy feelings worse. Sipping the tea, she recognized it was the same kind as in the wayhouse. She took a deep breath, then another sip, then another deep breath, then another sip, trying to keep the tears from coming. Finally, the pressure in her chest began to ease. Footsteps and voices echoed up from the bottom of the stairs. The front door opened and closed.

Mara stood and began poking through her gear bags looking for something remotely clean to sleep in, but all of her clothes were gone. The tracker she'd worn on her wrist was gone as well.

Elana knocked on the door and stuck her head through. "Are you all right?"

Reminded of Annelise by the action, she said, "Yes, but I miss my partner."

"I thought Dalin was your partner now." Her aunt perched on the side of the bed.

"He—" Mara began. "No, we…no. That would be good, I think, but…"

"You haven't talked about it," Elana finished the sentence. Mara huffed out a breath and sat on the opposite edge of the bed, facing her aunt. "Jameson says you're able to stay through the northern storm season. Maybe longer. You should have time to figure things out."

"Do you have my clothes?" she asked, not wanting to talk about partners.

Her aunt laughed. "I do. I mean, everything has been washed. Jameson is going to stash your uniform somewhere safe. And he returned the tracker to Dalin." She looked around the room, noting the mess of stacked papers, books, and boxes of odds and ends. "I'll get this room cleared out, so you have places to put your clean clothes as well as your new clothes."

"You don't need to buy new clothes." Buying was something only wealthy families did.

Elana's gaze shifted to the windows before she spoke. "I've been waiting to buy things for you, to spoil my niece, for many years." Shifting her focus back, she said, "I hope you'll indulge me."

"Is that what aunts do in Satri? Spoil their nieces and nephews?" It was hard to resist the pretty woman with her wistful green eyes.

"Yes," said Elana. "It's required. Oh, and speaking of required, one of my colleagues told me the Queen's Soldiers were out checking ladies' hands in Market Square this afternoon. It happens now and again. They may be out there again tomorrow. Can I see a hand please?"

Mara scooted a little closer and placed her left hand, palm down, on Elana's right. Elana reached for her other hand and examined the back, nails, and cuticles, then the palm. "How did you get these scars?"

Mara frowned at her right hand. "I got pretty scraped up repairing fences a few years ago. And"—she paused to think—"the rest are either from combat classes, learning to use different weapons, or from actual battle."

"You would've had such a different life here," Elana whispered.

"Do you think the Browns will know I'm a Protector just by looking at my hands?" She didn't want to talk about what could have been.

"Anything is possible with that lot," said Jameson from the doorway.

"I have an idea that might help," her aunt said, standing up. "But we can talk about it in the morning. Let's get your things."

"These things?" said Jameson, holding up a stack of clothes.

"Yes, thank you." She kissed her husband on the cheek. He handed the clothes to Mara and pulled his wife out into the hall to kiss her more thoroughly.

Turning her back to give them privacy, Mara began sorting clean things into categories. Regretfully, the gear bags weren't particularly clean, but good enough for now. The important thing was to be prepared.

Elana peeked back through the doorway, the color returned to her face. "Need anything else before you sleep?"

"No, all set. Thank you for washing my clothes," Mara said.

Her uncle tugged Elana's hand, pulling her toward the other end of the hall. "Our room is just down here if you need anything," she said, trailing after her husband.

After a quick trip to the washroom, Mara resumed organizing and packing her clothes until every item was put away except for a house tunic. Face washed and teeth brushed, she looked around for candles and briefly considered borrowing a few from the kitchen. It felt foolish to want comfort, especially as she was with real family. Shaking her head at the strange feelings, she changed into the tunic, turned out the overhead light, and crawled into bed.

Not truly tired yet, she relaxed onto the soft bed as she shuffled and reviewed events in her head. So much had happened in the space of so little time.

"Mara?"

"Hey, Dalin," she replied, surprised and pleased to hear his voice.

"Where do you want to talk?"

"Forest clearing," she said.

He laughed. *"Sure."*

Suddenly, the guest room was replaced with the sunny forest clearing she remembered. Instead of lying on the guest bed, she was lying on a soft wool blanket. Relieved to see she was wearing a full house uniform, not just a tunic and undershorts, she quickly sat up as Dalin appeared across from her.

"Are you at your house?" Mara asked.

"I am," he said. "You'll have to come visit soon so we'll have the option of using rapport here. You're too strong now for me to bring you into an unfamiliar place like I did when I brought you to this clearing."

Mara thought about that. "How do people visit in Satri?"

"Just walk over and knock on the door usually," he said. "Or you can contact someone by having your house system talk to their house system. At least that's how it was for my grandparents' generation. Only some of them had strong mental rapport abilities. About a quarter of us who are third or fourth generation on Asattha can use mental communication well. Military use is growing. But rapport can get tiring so most prefer talking in person when possible."

He shifted on the blanket, stretching out his long legs. "Look, when you're out with Elana tomorrow, follow her lead. Women here are far less likely to be soldiers, so even the way you carry yourself, the way you walk, might attract unwanted attention."

"What? How can I walk differently?"

"We have women in our government, women who are scientists and teachers, but for some reason, fighting women can be seen as"—he shrugged—"unnatural."

Mara bristled. "How are they trained, your women? How are they prepared to fight?"

"We've never had fighting here in Satri or even near Satri. The fight is always far away to the north. A regular citizen is scarcely aware of the military, even the local militia." He rubbed a hand across his hair.

"In the settlements, everyone has some training, in case the Gaishan stage a raid, correct?" He waited for her nod. "Here, it's the opposite. Only people who actively seek to learn are taught any kind of combat or weapons skills. Does that help you understand why you might stand out in the markets tomorrow?"

Mara was struggling with a mental image of women from Satri, in their beautiful clothes, trying to fend off a horde of Gaishan. "Will I have to wear dresses and skirts the whole time I'm here?"

Dalin didn't laugh. "I'm trying to picture the women I see in my neighborhood. Most wear skirts, but some are in pants, the flowing kind of pants, like my sister wears."

Flowing pants sounded like a decent compromise. "Nuwa? That's your sister's name?"

"Yes. She was sorry work kept her from dinner tonight." He looked up at the blue sky. "I think you two will get along. Nuwa is smart and fierce."

That description made Mara think of Jahella, ironically wearing a dress the last time Mara saw her. She leaned back on her elbows, not wanting to argue. He was trying to help.

"It's really quiet. Never thought I would miss the noise and the people all around but…" She shrugged, worried her words might catch in her throat. Out of the corner of her eye, she saw Dalin watching her with his intense gray gaze. A thought occurred to her. "Are you trying to help me in the swing?"

One side of his generous mouth curved up. "Maybe," he said.

Mara narrowed her eyes, but forced herself to stay in a relaxed position.

"Look, we should at least try to figure out what happened with those Brown soldiers this morning," Dalin added.

"I don't know," she said. "It didn't exactly come from me and…I've never had anything like that happen before."

Wind blew through the clearing, rustling tree leaves and stirring the carpet of pine needles. Chilled despite the canvas sleeves, she rubbed her arms.

Dalin reached behind his back and produced a sweater similar to the one she'd borrowed on their journey. "I think it has something to do with the *gontra*..."

Mara shook her head.

"Listen," he insisted. "I think it has something to do with the *gontra* because those men are what appears to be permanently fogged. They haven't remembered anything about who they are or their mission. We make the blowing powders from *gontras*. But the typical reaction to the powder, the one you've witnessed on the battlefield, is nowhere near as strong."

The wind blew again, hard enough to lift a side of the blanket. Dalin looked around, frowning. "Are you doing that?" he asked.

"Making the wind blow? No."

He closed his eyes for a moment, a line of concentration creasing his forehead. The sun's rays shone more brightly through the trees and a bird called. Opening his eyes, he asked, "What were your impressions of the fight?"

Mara crossed her legs and sat up straighter so that she could breathe more deeply. She pictured the short fight in her mind, slowed down the action. "Not only did they know we were coming," she began, "someone prepared them for a bigger engagement than just with three people."

He nodded. "What else?"

"They had kill orders, I think," she said. "Although kill orders makes the number of soldiers sent even more strange."

"I didn't find restraints or anything else that would have indicated an intent to capture us," Dalin agreed. "What else?"

"The second wave had a scout or mental communication or some other way of knowing the status of our fight with the first wave. The second group wasn't on a picket route—they were coming for us," she said. Thinking through the next steps after the swing, Mara asked, "Will I need to give a report to...to your senior officers?"

"My team wasn't informed about where I've been or that you, the Protector I've been monitoring, have been brought here. I reported in to the officers who sent me, the two you met. Orders are to hide you as a civilian."

"And the fogging?"

"Well," Dalin hedged, "ah, that's, um, not entirely in my report." He folded his arms across his chest.

"Jameson?" she asked.

"Only that you're staying with him," he replied, then grinned. "What's the next step in the protocol?"

She twitched her foot back and forth, torn between annoyance and relief that the Gaishan was trying this with her. "I thought you had studied the swing," she muttered. "Physical health usually comes first, then debrief, then mental health." She hugged herself in the warm sweater.

Dalin's grin faded. "Were you hurt?"

"No," she said. "No, I mean, bruises, scrapes, exhaustion— nothing…requiring healers."

Relief passed over his face. "Good. Okay, mental health?"

Drawing her knees up to her chest, she rested her chin on them. "I slept all day, but in the middle I had a strange dream." Silver flickered in Dalin's gray eyes as his gaze sharpened. "A person, female, just a little older than me…she took me to a park. Well, first it was this strange white space and then the park filled in." Having committed to telling about the dream, she wanted to get the details right. "When I was little, she said, we were all playmates in that same park. But I was the only child who could see her. She had long, curly brown hair and silvery brown skin." Mara closed her eyes to clarify the image of the Tree in her mind. "She had black eyes, all the way black, no white around the outside, no colored circle. And…she called me by name. She said her name was…she said she was the Tree."

Dalin jerked upright. "Repeat that last part?"

Mara kept her voice steady, knowing it sounded like a fog hallucination. "She said she was the Tree."

"Was there more?"

"A little," she said.

Dalin visibly calmed himself, crossed his long legs and rested a palm on each knee. "Please tell me."

"She knew you, knew about our travels, the fight. She put my hand on the bark of a huge tree and told me it was *her*—on the outside. She tried to show me how her mind, her thinking, works. She is connected and aware of everything through roots, through branches and leaves." Dalin nodded, but Mara could sense his grin lurking just below the surface. "What?" she said.

"The Tree almost never talks to anyone. But she chose you."
Dalin looked both excited and proud.

Mara hunched her shoulders. "So it wasn't just a strange
dream." She made the statement flat, not a question.

"Is that the end?" Dalin asked.

Mara shrugged, "More or less."

"If you see the Tree again, ask her about the thirteen *gontras*.
Ask about what happened with the Browns," Dalin said.

Mara nodded, keeping her legs pulled into her chest. She felt
relaxed surprisingly with all of that out, even if he wasn't exactly her
partner. She tapped her feet and rocked on her tailbone. "What about
you?"

He raised his eyebrows. "What do you mean?"

"Are you hurt? Did you sustain any injury*?*" she asked,
beginning the swing questions for Dalin.

Chapter 24

Dropping her right knee onto the deep cushioned window seat of the guest room, Mara shifted the curtain to one side, letting in the early morning light. Today would be her first trip into the center of Satri, the heart of Gaishan Territory. Houses filled her western view along with lots of trees, but to the south she could see a sideways sliver of the gulf. Below her window was a small front yard and front walk flanked by two trees serving as natural gateposts. The glass surface of the window was cold, but nothing like the deep frost in the North.

By the time Mara finished a quick shower, she could smell breakfast cooking downstairs. She hurried to her room, intending to wear the same blue dress she had borrowed the night before. Instead, on her bed she found a long, evergreen skirt and a coordinating shirt in a lighter shade of green. The top fit fine, but the skirt was narrow and forced her to shorten her normally long stride. Mara ran her fingers through her hair and resolved to braid it before she and Elana left.

Downstairs at the kitchen table, her aunt was arranging plates of oatcakes and berries. "Good morning." she said.

"Good morning," Mara answered.

Elana indicated the place across from her own. "Please join me. Tea?"

"Yes please," Mara said, unnerved by the formality and the quiet. "Where is Jameson?"

Elana smiled and looked down as she returned Mara's full teacup and filled her own. "Oh, he's around somewhere. I've learned not to ask. Did you need him?"

Mara poured a thin stream of syrup over her oatcakes. "No," she said. "I guess not."

The warm breakfast was as delicious as dinner had been and, as Dalin had told her, served in a beautiful way. Not only were the dishes gleaming white on the polished table, but her aunt had added a vase of fresh flowers and used bright orange and pink flower buds to garnish the oatcake serving plate.

It was hard not to relax given the open feeling of the space and the sun shining in through the sliding glass doors. As she chewed and swallowed, she wondered what Dalin's kitchen looked like.

"The markets open in about half an hour," Elana said. "If we want to see the latest styles from around the Commonwealth, we need to be there near to the opening time. Sought-after items tend to sell out."

"We want to see the clothes that are popular on other planets?"

"Jameson's family is from a planet called Kels. It's an English Origin planet where a larger proportion of the citizens live as you've been living in the North: horses for transportation, subsistence agriculture, lots of skirmishes and fights between different groups. The story we intend to use is that you're the daughter of one of Jameson's brothers. You were serving in the militia on Kels, but you've come here to get an education and to look for work. With the outside possibility that you will return to Kels for a military career."

Her aunt's expression revealed no levity or sign that this was not entirely serious or necessary. "Jameson has been here for ten years. He keeps to himself most of the time. But when he is chatting with our neighbors or Dalin and the militia guys, he always mentions his brothers and his large family. More oatcakes?"

"Yes, thank you." Mara held out her plate. "I'm already Jameson's niece. Why would I need to say more than that?"

"Most of the time, you won't." She filled the plate and passed it back. "But the Browns are looking for you and we need a story to explain why you, a person who fits the description of the young woman they claim is a fugitive, is living in our home.

"You're going to make mistakes in Satri," Elana added, "because you weren't raised here. The story about you coming from a different planet covers that, too."

"Kels is the name of my home?" Mara asked.

"Kels is your home planet," she corrected. "I brought some books from my school's library for you to study. And, of course, your uncle will help you with specific details about the area where his family lives, the closest city, the alliances, and so forth."

So much she had not known to consider before following Dalin south. She had two families now: her fellow soldiers, but also her aunt and uncle. Fortunately, at the moment her need to gather information served both. "Thank you," she said, hoping the books had lots of pictures and maps.

#

Tapping a sequence of numbers into a panel near the door, Elana said, "This is how we secure the house. When we get back this afternoon, I'll teach you the codes." She ushered her niece out and pulled the door closed. A series of soft clicks followed. "Do you mind if we walk to the markets?" she asked with a bright smile.

"No, not at all," Mara said. A walk might work out the kinks in her back and hips. "I'd like to ride Rowan later though, if that's possible."

"One of the guys can take you, I'm sure."

Elana led the way down the short front walk and out into the small circle. In another minute, they were out on a pretty lane lined with small white pebbles.

"We live on Ansel Street," she said. "South Ansel Street." She indicated a post with writing on it. If you go any farther south than our house, you run into the gulf."

At the corner, her aunt looked both left and right before turning east onto a larger thoroughfare. "Divis Street will take us almost to Market Square." Elana glanced over as they walked. "I don't want to take a chance on you getting lost if we're separated for any reason."

"Divis Street to South Ansel Street," Mara said. "And the door panel sequence is 402-890." She looked up sharply, hearing a strange sound, like a humming whine.

"Step to your right, smile, and nod," Elana whispered.

A woman on a moving, wheeled platform approached at a swift pace. As she got closer, the noise grew louder. The basic shape of the conveyance was a podium with one handgrip on each side. Golden mirrors ran down both sides of the podium or driver's box, which balanced on two shiny gray wheels about the size of dinner plates. Both women nodded as the driver zoomed by.

"Do you know her?" Mara asked.

"No," Elana said, starting to walk again. "Satri is too big to know everyone. We'll see a lot more autos today. They're used on many worlds, including Kels, so try not to stare."

"How does it...how does the auto move?"

"Most of the Commonwealth-standard tech doesn't work on our planet. The scientists say the trees have something to do with that." Elana paused, looked down Divis Street again. "The autos had to be modified before we could use them. On Asattha, autos use a tiny battery fed by solar collectors. The handgrips tap into the driver's energy field. Those combined energy sources feed a motor that turns the wheels.

"We have an auto at home I use to go back and forth to school when the weather gets really warm. I can show you how to drive it if you like," she offered.

"If a distance is too far to walk, I think I would prefer to ride Rowan," Mara said.

"I don't ride much," Elana said. "But Jameson or Dalin can show you the horse paths around the city." She hesitated. "We all agree you shouldn't go anywhere on your own. At least not for a while."

The closer they got to Market Square, the more houses began to appear closer to the street and closer together. In that, at least, Satri was similar to the northern settlements. What was quite different was the abundance of color on the homes. The farther east they walked, the more the colors of the structures ranged in brightness and variety. Not only were walls, doors, and shutters adorned in every shade imaginable, but large urns in many patterns and sizes appeared to be popular lawn ornaments.

Despite a cold, damp breeze kicking up from the south, Mara paused to admire a house painted summer-grass green on two sides and yellow on the third visible side, sporting sky-blue shutters and a deeper-blue front door.

"Your house is green and white on the outside," she said. "Did you ever wish for something more...vivid?"

Elana laughed. "The green was Jameson's concession to fitting in. I told him in this city, a plain house stands out and is more memorable than a house with color. Especially with so many people coming from other planets to work in the labs and study at the universities. Everyone brings his or her own sense of home."

Divis came to a dead end at the next cross street. Most of the people flowed north, but some turned south.

"This part of Satri is a series of squares. The first one"—Elana pointed ahead and to the right—"is called Artist's Square. We are going to Market Square, the farthest southeast. The markets grew up near the spaceport so that goods could be unloaded and sold immediately."

"Spaceport?" Mara kept her voice quiet, aware they were in a steadily increasing throng of people.

"People travel between planets on starships. As you did from Kels, remember?" Her aunt's tone was quiet, but her expression was playful. "When you landed here, we picked you up at the spaceport. I have the papers in my bag to show you arrived on the ship from Kels three days ago, if anyone asks."

She confidently steered Mara through a series of left and right turns, smiling and nodding at some of the passersby. "Here we are, Market Square," Elana announced. "It's expanded quite a bit since you were little. Let me know if anything seems familiar."

Nothing looked familiar as Mara trailed along a few steps behind her aunt, who aimed for a stall full of women's apparel. Dropping onto a bench in plain view of the stall, she took a deep breath. It was hard not to be overwhelmed by the sheer size of the market, the length of twenty houses along each side.

Some of the stalls had permanent-looking walls or roofs; other vendors were selling items from carts. Shopkeepers bustled around, stacking and arranging their wares. The square was not yet crowded and already, between the buyers and the sellers, she could count as many people as lived in her Protector compound.

Elana turned and looked around, panic flashing across her face. Mara rose and took two running steps toward the stall. Immediately, the smaller woman relaxed and unfolded a pair of pants from the middle of a pile.

"Have a look," she said. "These are women's trousers from Tian. Feel the material."

The legs were wide, the fabric soft and smooth, nothing to restrict movement. "Are these like Dalin's sister wears?"

"Yes," she said. "This style is very popular with the young researchers, especially the botanists and dendrologists."

The pants were the plainest item in the stall, otherwise crowded with dozens of skirts, brightly patterned vests, and long gauze scarves.

"I think we should start you with two pairs if this is a style you like. Would you mind trying them on for length?"

Her aunt said something to the vendor in another language. The vendor pointed to a curtain stretched across the back corner of the canvas stall.

Mara took the pants behind the curtain into a dusty space just large enough to step out of her skirt and into the black trousers. The waist was a piece of stretchy material that could be folded under the belly button or unfolded to encircle the lower ribs. It was comfortable, but almost too loose. The pants seemed in some danger of falling down around her ankles. But when she held them in place, the hem just touched the tops of her feet.

When she stepped out to show the fit, her aunt and the vendor nodded at the length. But when the vendor bent to look more closely at the waist, she made a clicking sound and said something.

"She says you're too thin," Elana translated.

She asked the woman a question. The woman clicked again, answered in her own language, and gave a slight nod. Elana spoke a few more sentences.

"She's going to look for a few pairs with a smaller waist. I told her we'd be back in a while."

Once Mara changed back into the skirt, Elana ushered her out of the stall. "Next stop is shoes. Jameson says you can keep using your boots for riding, but you need shoes for school and social occasions."

Across the corner of the square was a storefront adorned with pictures of shoes. Inside, an older couple and their two daughters were dusting and stocking racks and racks of shoes. One of the girls was about Mara's age. While the mother began coaxing Elana into trying on a few pairs of fancy shoes, the daughter asked Mara what she was looking for.

"Mostly I wear boots," she said.

"What do you need today?" the shop girl asked.

"My aunt says I need shoes for school. Shoes that will go with skirts or long pants."

The girl brought out a wooden platform with outlines of feet drawn on it. "Step up here please."

After placing her feet in the two outlines, Mara rose to her full height. The additional lift of the platform provided an excellent view of the square through the shop window. In the midst of the growing crush of shoppers and carts, a soldier in a Brown uniform talked to a family group. He looked at the hands of the mother and three older girls, front and back, then tapped a silver rectangle.

The shop girl said, "You can step down now. I'm going to get a few things for you to try."

"Thank you," Mara said, her eyes following the Brown soldier as he approached another group of women and asked to see their hands. "Elana, look." She moved so her aunt could step onto the measuring platform.

They both watched as the lone man stopped two individual girls and then another family group. He checked fronts and backs of the females' hands, touched the silver rectangle again, and moved on.

The shop girl returned with prospective shoes for Mara and tapped her on the shoulder.

"It's been a while since this happened. Any idea why they're doing hand checks?" Elana asked, pointing out the window.

"Not really," the girl replied. "They came in here yesterday and looked at our hands." She lowered her voice and moved closer. "But last night one of my friends told me she heard from her brother that they're looking for a Protector."

Mara froze, but her aunt laughed. "What would a Protector be doing in Market Square?" she asked.

The girl shrugged. "Not buying shoes, I can tell you. We've had nothing but regular folk pass through the last few days." She gestured for Mara to sit down.

Elana sat in the next chair and took over the proceedings. Mara flexed her feet, pointed her toes, stood and sat on command. Her mind was preoccupied with the Browns in the square and the shop girl's casual comment about Protectors not being "regular folk."

Finally, they settled on a pair of cushioned black shoes molded to follow the natural curves of the foot. The shoes had a single strap running across the top and a nubby tread on the bottom. Although they would look nice with a skirt, Mara knew she could also run or fight in them.

As they left the store, both women scanned for soldiers in the swirling crowd. Elana tugged on her niece's arm, pulling her along the outer ring of stores. She stopped in front of a plain white building with pictures of hands and feet on its sign.

Just inside the door, a woman with upswept hair smiled at them. "How can we help you today?"

"My niece went camping last week and just wrecked her hands. Can you do a skin polish as well as her nails?" Elana asked. Her voice held just the right mix of affection and exasperation.

"Of course," said the woman. "And for you?"

"Hands and feet, please," Elana said.

Two rows of small tables and chairs ran the length of the room. Ten women dressed in white tunics and black pants sat at various tables, some holding hands with women dressed in regular clothes. Aunt and niece were led to adjacent tables facing the windows. In a matter of moments, Mara, too, was holding hands with a woman in a white tunic.

The woman examined her nails, cuticles, knuckles, wrists, and palms. She ran her thumb over Mara's sword calluses, frowned, and looked up. "Are you from one of those families that keeps horses?"

She glanced away. "Um—"

"It's her uncle," Elana said, and rolled her eyes. "He's a bit eccentric."

The woman smiled. "Satri gets all kinds. But"—she turned her attention back to Mara—"horses, camping—it all takes a toll on your skin, especially your hands. We can polish down the scars and calluses, but they won't be completely gone."

"That's just wonderful," chirped Elana. "With the Winter Festival coming up, my girl needs to look her best."

"You don't want a young man to take your hand for a dance and think he's picked a farmer by mistake," said the woman working on her aunt's nails. Mara flinched, but the other three women laughed.

"It's all right," Elana spoke in her mind. *"Laugh along with the joke."*

"Elana?" She tried to hide her surprise. *"You can...? Why didn't you...?"*

"It's hard for me," she admitted. *"So I don't use mental rapport much."* Out loud she said, "Relax, dear, these ladies will think you've never had your hands polished before."

The ladies chuckled. Mara smiled a sheepish smile at the woman rubbing cream into her scars.

"Don't worry, sweetie," the woman said. She had friendly brown eyes and black hair with silver at the temples. "We'll have you fixed up in no time."

"Good for business, those Browns," said the woman working on Elana's hands. "Everyone feels self-conscious after being inspected and runs right in here. I mind it but I don't, if you know what I mean."

Her remark launched a conversation about nails and grooming and how fashions on Satri were beginning to change. Mara slumped in her chair and let the chatter flow around her, surprised and relieved her aunt was such a good liar. She would have to learn to tell the false story about herself with the same smooth confidence.

"What color?" the woman tapped Mara's arm.

She shrugged. "I don't—"

"Natural," Elana interrupted. "This one keeps everything natural. Next time I'll talk her into a color before we come in."

Chapter 25

Emerging from the nail shop into mid-morning sunshine, Mara wore her new shoes, happy her toes had more room, and carried the bag with the borrowed flats. Market Square brimmed nearly full with hundreds of people walking, standing, or involved in some kind of transaction.

"Can you handle one more stop before we eat?"

"Sure," Mara said mentally. *"You wouldn't get tired doing this if you practiced."*

"You're probably right," Elana agreed out loud. "And it could prove useful when you and I are at school together."

At first Mara felt closed in by the crowd, bumping into people and muttering, "Pardon, pardon." She was only taller than about half the men and women she passed. Another quarter of the people were very near her height and about a quarter were taller.

"I'm not the tallest person here," she sent. *"In the North I can see over most crowds. That's got to be why the market feels so full to me."*

"That and this is a thick crowd," Elana sent back. She froze in place for a moment. *"Browns ahead. Don't talk unless you have to."*

Two soldiers were stopping women as they walked, repeating the same inspection and notation process. They had added a stamp at the end for each woman, on the inside of the wrist.

"Let's get this over with." Elana stepped up to one of the men and waited.

"Names?" he asked, tone flat.

"Tikva and Danitova Crowell," she said.

The silver rectangle was thin as paper, held in place to a larger plastic holder with clips at the corners. When the soldier tapped inside faint shimmering squares, symbols flashed across the upper part of the paper, not much larger than a slice of bread.

"Hands please," he said.

Elana held her hands out, palms facing down. The gold paint on her nails sparkled in the intermittent sunshine. The soldier looked, flipped Elana's hands over, glanced at her palms, and stamped a small black emblem onto her left wrist. It was the lioness in the knot.

The soldier carried no visible weapons, and although his uniform was crisp, he had rings of sweat under his arms. He stood back to back with another soldier, but that one didn't have any weapons either.

"Hands," the soldier said to Mara.

She put her hands out as her aunt had done. Only one serious scar remained and even that looked faded and old. "How did you get the scar?" the soldier asked.

"Fighting with her brother," Elana said. "Those two were always wrestling around when they were small."

The soldier made a note. He motioned for Mara to show her palms, nodded, stamped her wrist, and said, "Thank you."

As she moved to her aunt's side, an older woman with long white hair tapped the soldier's arm. "We haven't had hand checks in an age. What are you looking for? You've upset a lot of ladies this morning!"

"Just procedure, ma'am," he said.

"Since when?" the older woman pressed. "Why, I've lived in Satri for over thirty years and this is not..."

The soldier began to walk away, beads of sweat appearing on his brow and upper lip. "Not at liberty to say," he replied, voice frayed.

Mara and her aunt didn't speak again until they were deep in the crowd. "Whose names...who are the people whose names we just used?"

"Neighbors traveling off-planet for the rest of the season," Elana said. "If they come back before the searching concludes, though I think that's unlikely, I'll let Tikva know."

As they walked, the sea of faces began to blur. Mara played a game to keep her focus by choosing an individual and thinking about whom in the Protector compound that person looked like. She also tried to guess some shoppers' occupations by their attire. But that proved impossible because everyone looked like a merchant.

"Last stop," Elana announced. She'd brought them to a stall piled high with ladies' tops. Shirts and sweaters hung from hooks all along the front awning. "You should choose at least four things."

"No," Mara started to protest. "You purchased these shoes." She picked up her right foot. "And promised for two pairs of pants. I can share clothes with you for the rest. At least until I can—"

Elana hugged her close and whispered, "How do we explain that you came all the way from Kels with no clothes of your own? When we're at school, people might recognize my clothing on you." More loudly she said, "Only four shirts today. Don't press for more."

The stall keeper hustled over at that and offered her help. Soon Mara was in another curtained corner trying on a selection of shirts, jackets, and sweaters. She emerged at last with a gray jacket, two pullovers with hoods and pockets, three long sleeved fitted tops like Dalin wore and three stretchy undertunics. The stall keeper was so pleased with all of their purchases, she gave them a fabric bag for carrying the clothing at no charge.

Every time she looked at her aunt, Elana smiled or squeezed her hand. She had also hugged Mara several times over the course of the morning. It wasn't the same as having a mother, but it was hopeful, comforting.

Suddenly shoving Mara to the left, she said, "Let's try in here," her cheery tone not matching her sudden actions.

They stumbled over the doorframe and into a tiny shop filled with silver items. "Elana, what…?"

"Brown soldiers and senior officers," she said, her mental voice nearly a shout. "We need a new fruit tray," she chirped. "And I've been meaning to shop for Yadira's birthday. It's coming up soon."

Two other customers were conversing with the shopkeeper. Setting her clothes bag on the floor, Mara moved a hanging string of silver cups to peer out the window. A group of almost three-dozen Brown soldiers walked in formation, heading east.

"To the spaceport?"

"Could be," was Elana's response. *"Please get away from the window."*

Mara let the cups fall gently back into place and took a few steps deeper in the shop. When she looked out again, she was screened by two large urns. As the last soldier passed, he turned and glared at the crowd of shoppers behind him. Mara inhaled sharply and held perfectly still, not even breathing.

"What?" Elana asked.

"Garot. He reports to Roland. I met him at the compound. We spoke just before I left—"

Elana hefted the clothes bag and handed over the shoe bag. "Let's go."

"Wait," Mara said. "Those silver hair ties…" She gestured to a basket on the counter. *"I need to tell Dalin."*

Her aunt nodded. "Perhaps a bowl for Yadira. I'll look for a few more minutes."

Mara lifted a braided leather headband threaded with silver buttons, then put it back in the basket and let her fingers roam over the textures.

"Dalin," she called. *"Garot is here."*

No response came.

"Dalin, at least one Brown soldier is here who will recognize me." She lifted another hair tie from the basket and admired the silver feather design.

Suddenly, her mind was flooded with the impression that Dalin was fighting. *"Busy,"* he managed, ducking a punch and kicking someone else.

"Do you need help?" she asked. She felt Dalin's next punch land on the side of an opponent's head.

"No. Training." He kicked out. She felt the aim and the swing as he missed.

"A Brown who knows me is here. In Market Square," she repeated.

She felt Dalin still. *"Did he see you?"*

She considered as she dug down to the bottom of the basket. *"No, I don't think so."*

"Is your hair down?"

Mara threw part of the dark mass of loose waves over one shoulder. *"Yes, I forgot to braid it."*

"Good, keep it down. Tell Elana it's time to pierce your ears and get some cosmetics."

"What? What are…?"

"Just tell her," he insisted. *"Confirm what a female raised on Kels would do and do it. Also, carry as many shopping bags as you can. The unbalanced load and the weight will help hide your posture."*

"Elana wants to leave the market," Mara said.

"No, keep doing what you had planned. Is Jameson around?"

"Not that I know," she said.

"Right. I'll meet you within the hour." He broke the connection before she could say they were fine, that she was just passing along the information.

After neatly rearranging the hair ties, she called to her aunt, "Find something for Yadira?"

"Not quite. Ready to go now?" Elana responded.

"Yes, thanks."

Outside, the wind had picked up. Clouds were rolling in from the south, partially covering the sun. Reached for the full bag of clothes, she said, "Dalin suggested I carry all the bags to disguise my posture."

Elana pressed her lips together. "Did he have any other ideas?"

Reaching up to touch her earlobe, she said, "Pierce my ears and get cosmetics? Whatever a girl from Kels would do to her appearance, that's what I'm supposed to do."

"We don't get a lot of scientists or students from Kels, so I'm not completely sure." Her aunt continued walking in the general direction of the pants stall. "I don't like having you in the open like this."

"It won't be any safer at the house," Mara began. "If they know who I am and are already looking specifically…" She stopped. "Elana, wait." The smaller woman turned, eyes overly bright and cheeks flushed. She dropped the heavy bag and patted her aunt's shoulder. "We aren't helpless. Your words and the smooth way you tell stories are…are good tools."

Elana swiped a hand over her face and took a deep breath. "I know, it's…" She sighed. "I knew it wouldn't be easy when you finally came home. But I wanted to believe you would be safe with Jameson and me…" She trailed off and raised a trembling hand to her mouth. People walked around them, giving Mara the sense of being a small island in a flowing stream.

"Did Dalin say anything else?" Elana cleared her throat.

"He said to keep doing what you had planned. He'll find us in the next hour or sooner."

"The stall with the pants is just over there. And piercing can be done at many of the jewelry shops."

"Lunch?" Mara asked.

Elana managed a weak smile. "We'll need to pack snacks for you to make it through afternoon classes." She turned in a half circle, considering the options. "There's a jewelry shop next to a food stall I particularly like. Let's grab your new pants and try there."

#

Thirty minutes later, Mara wore a blue hooded sweater and gray pants, had tiny hoops in each ear, and was sitting in a tall chair with three bags at her feet. She bit into a thick slice of bread and watched the crowd. The sun was completely behind the clouds now and the wind continued in small gusts.

A fence made from a white and yellow patterned banner surrounded the food stall. The tables and chairs were high, made of something that looked like wood but wasn't. Each table had a white cloth cover and a vase of flowers, both cleverly anchored to the table. Roughly half the tables were occupied.

Elana tugged a shawl from her bag and wrapped it around her shoulders. Leaning forward, she said, "This soup is a specialty here. It's made from lentils, vegetables, and sausage."

Mara smiled, always genuinely happy about good food. "It smells wonderful." She picked up her spoon and stirred, inhaling the fragrant steam.

"Any chance of getting a third bowl and another piece of bread?" a familiar voice asked. Mara looked up as Dalin approached their table. "Ladies, may I join you?"

He wore the gray uniform she'd seen in rapport. But even as accustomed as she was to being around people in uniform, she couldn't help but appreciate how the lines of the jacket skimmed his torso and how the color of the material looked against his tan skin.

Catching her gaze, he smiled slowly, eyes warm with appreciation. "It took me an extra minute to find you," he said. "You look like you've been in Satri all your life."

"I think so too," Elana agreed.

As Dalin sat down at their table, he alternately took in the other details of Mara's changed appearance and observed the crowd. "You went to a nail shop?"

Elana gave a quick explanation of the hand checks in the square. His bowl of soup arrived as she finished.

"I can see why they thought hand checks might catch out a Protector female, but these actions overstep the legal limits for the

Queen's Soldiers, especially in Satri. The council ended that practice by ordinance at least two years ago." He lifted Mara's left hand and examined first the back, then her palm. "Skin polishing?" he asked.

"Amazing, isn't it?" Elana's smile was pleased.

The lunch crowd dwindled, leaving more empty tables around them. Dalin tapped Mara's manicured hand. "Good thing you were with your aunt today. No one else would have thought of nail and skin polishing to trick the soldiers doing hand inspections." He grinned.

"You suggested the pierced ears," she replied. "We thought to start with one hole on each side until I check with Jameson about customs on Kels."

Dalin's expression stayed calm and interested, but his eyes moved across the square with regular sweeps. He leaned in and quietly asked, "Tell me again, which Brown did you see? I wasn't able to focus on the name earlier."

"Did you win the training fight?"

"Of course." He stirred his bowl of soup.

It took a moment to sense the humor underneath the arrogance. Dalin made a "go ahead" motion with his hand and kept eating.

"The name on his uniform was Garot. When the Browns were in the compound, he appeared to have nearly as high a rank as Roland, but I didn't witness him using any magic. He knew about me, he had talked to Twyla about me. It was...uncomfortable."

"Could you describe him?" Dalin asked.

"Dark hair, light eyes, medium build, about the same age as Roland. The texture of his face, it's yellowish and pitted." Mara brought a picture of the man into her mind and pushed the image to Dalin. "There, that's him."

He smiled at Elana. "Your niece learns quickly."

"Of course," she said.

"I want to get this sorted out so you can enjoy being with your family."

That piece had been nagging Mara since she arrived. "Why haven't the Browns come looking for me at Elana and Jameson's place?"

Her two lunch companions exchanged looks.

"Go ahead," Elana said.

"When you were taken, your parents caused an uproar with the tale of your kidnapping by a Protector. The truth is, they were ready to ride north, ruin the experiment...the project"—Dalin corrected himself—"if they had to. Nothing was more important than finding you. Right so far?"

Elana nodded, face set in tight lines.

"By the time they finally got clearance, obtained horses, disguised their appearances, and headed north, three days had passed. About five days later, your father, Esteban, got a lead in the settlement of Tamoh. Heard of it?" he asked Mara.

"Yes," she said, trying to process the story he was telling. "It's the settlement next to Arlis, where Elias and his wife live."

"Two more weeks went by"—he touched Elana lightly on the arm—"Elana, Yadira, and Jin learned of your parents' deaths when one of the sanctioned traders brought their bodies back to Satri."

Elana's eyes were reddening. Mara's own throat felt dry and her eyes stung.

"Your parents were liked and respected in the scientific community. Despite their deaths, inquiries into your whereabouts continued for nearly a year. The conclusion was whoever kidnapped you may not have been a Protector or even connected to the Protector Project. Only the uniform worn by the kidnapper had pointed people in that direction to begin with. By the time that conclusion was reached, unfortunately, the trail was cold." Dalin spooned a chunk of sausage out of his bowl and chewed it.

"We are fairly certain the Browns haven't connected you with the story of the girl who was kidnapped thirteen years ago. Hence, they haven't come knocking on Elana and Jameson's door."

Mara folded her newly polished hands under her chin and leaned her elbows on the table. Though the tale fit with the dream, it seemed more like a sad story from someone else's family, not a piece of her history. She tried to remember back before she was with Elias, but there was nothing. The lack of memories had never bothered her before. It hadn't seemed like being abandoned was a memory worth keeping. But the Tree had showed her the wall in her mind. A few memories had come through: one of Jameson trading horses and one of hugging Elana. So there was more in her mind to know, she just couldn't see it yet.

Dalin chewed his last bite of bread and looked around. "Best to be moving on. It'll be too easy to spot you without the big crowds, and rain is coming." He stood and went to pay their bill.

Both women stood as well. Mara hugged herself and rolled her shoulders. She felt stiff all over. The clouds overhead continued to blow across the sky, but no longer just wisps. Now they traveled as dark gray masses and the wind carried a hint of rain.

"Are you going to escort us back?" Elana asked.

Before he could reply, Mara said, "Thank you for lunch. We don't need an escort."

She expected a teasing reply but instead Dalin's face was grave as he motioned for them to begin walking to the edge of the square. "I had hoped to take you and Rowan out this afternoon. But right now I need to follow up on this Garot. If the weather holds, we can get a short ride in at the end of the day. But since these clouds look like they're going to dump rain, how about planning to work out in one of the militia training rooms instead? Those are usually empty by late afternoon."

Mara's eyes lit up and energy surged through her arms and legs. "Fighting?" she asked.

Dalin's lips twitched. "In a way," he said. "I want to assess your skills in a few areas before we set your new training regimen."

She bared her teeth and sent an image of him flat on his back, with her standing over him, a staff against his chin.

With a laugh, Dalin said, "You can try."

On the western side of Market Square, Dalin bowed to Elana, winked at Mara, and headed off. Realizing she was staring after him, she flushed and adjusted one of the shopping bags on her shoulder.

"My original idea was to stop by my school and show you around," Elana said. "Would you like to see it?"

"Yes, I would," Mara said, and then hesitated. "Are students there today?"

"Most of my students are adults who work in the labs. It's a part of the compensation offered when the labs recruit on other planets. Language—reading and writing instruction—as well as cultural support."

"What are labs?" She kept hearing that word and really wanted to know how *labs* related to her parents.

Her aunt took a deep breath. "I'll try to explain as we walk."

Chapter 26

The school was north of Divis Street and west of the squares in a neighborhood full of brightly colored homes. Though the dwellings were relatively small, they were well spaced and screened by stands of trees. Painted a soft shade of orange and highlighted with bright pink shutters and a sunny yellow front door, the school was in a slightly larger house on a corner lot.

After Elana had given Mara a quick tour of the four classrooms, the entrance area that doubled as common room, and the office, she said, "Will you be all right on your own for a few minutes? I just realized I didn't finish the last set of files for the incoming class." At Mara's puzzled expression, she clarified, "A new class will be starting in two days."

"And they will learn reading and writing in this…this Origin language that we speak?" she asked, a wistful note in her voice.

"Yes," Elana said. "My job is to bring them up to proficiency in Origin English."

"So they can read and write reports and communicate better with the other"—Mara searched her memory—"scientists?"

"Exactly." As Elana walked into the main office, the overhead light flickered on. From a shelf, she pulled a large book held together by metal rings and handed it to her niece. "Why don't you look through the first three sections in this binder? I'll check on you in a little bit."

The lights in the nearest classroom blinked on when Mara was five steps into the room. Six medium tables, each with two or three chairs, occupied the center of the room. Two of the walls had shelves running floor to ceiling. Some held books; others held a variety of objects like a bird's nest; a plate, cup, bowl, and utensils; and soft stuffed animal toys. On the back wall were large maps depicting wholly unfamiliar terrain.

She left the binder on a table and moved on to explore the other classrooms. The school's interior walls were light, neutral colors, and the floors were either bare wood or covered in area rugs. Weak sunlight trickled through the hallway windows. In the next room, she found similar furniture but different materials on the walls and different objects on the shelves. Mara checked out the third and fourth classrooms as well. In the fourth, she found a wall-size image of a *gontra* tree. Each individual part—leaves, seedpods, branches, trunk, and roots—had a line of printed symbols next to it.

She peered out the classroom window into a small courtyard. Stone benches were scattered across the grass and flowerbeds graced much of the perimeter. A loud clap of thunder echoed from the sky. Mara jumped back from the window and caught her breath as fat raindrops began splashing down.

"Mara?" Elana called.

"In the classroom with the tree picture."

"Do you mind staying here until the rain subsides?" her aunt asked, appearing in the doorway. "I didn't think to check the weather projections or to bring umbrellas this morning. I was too excited to take you to the market." She made a rueful face. Lightning flashed and thunder clapped again. "Dalin told me you didn't attend school in the settlement or in the compound. You spoke a little about that at dinner, too."

Mara gazed out the window at a *gontra* tree very similar to the picture on the wall. The branches shook under the onslaught of rain. "That's correct," she acknowledged. She didn't look at her aunt, couldn't bear to see pity on her face.

"I would be more than pleased to teach you," Elana said quietly. "If you feel ready, you can join the class that's about to start."

Mara nodded, still watching the rain. "I'm ready," she said, almost reflexively. Then she caught herself and looked at her aunt. "In the North we are taught to honor our instructors." She bowed from the waist. "Thank you for offering to teach me to read and write. I'll show you my best effort."

Elana's restless hands stilled and she returned her niece's bow. "My pleasure," she murmured.

"Once I can read, I'll learn from all of these books," Mara vowed, glaring at a bookshelf as though it were an armed opponent.

"Yes," Elana agreed, placing a gentle hand on her niece's shoulder. "You will."

For the next hour, Elana administered a series of interesting but tiring tests to determine Mara's literacy level. And though she wanted to please her new teacher by demonstrating skill and knowledge, Mara forced herself to be honest about her low level of ability.

Elana had retrieved the binder from the first classroom and was using it to make notes as they progressed through the assessments. "You'll have some advantage being a native Origin English speaker. But most of your new classmates will have been exposed to at least some Origin English as well. When the other students are working on speaking and pronunciation, you will work on building your vocabulary."

She flipped to the back of the binder and carefully removed a piece of shiny silver paper from a clear sleeve, lifting it by one corner and laying it on the table. "This is your vocabulary guide."

Tapping twice on the right hand corner of the page caused an image to pop up.

"A," a female voice said. "This is the letter A." The three-dimensional red and white A hung over the paper.

Mara cautiously tried to poke the A, but her finger passed through. Elana lightly brushed the left side of the silver paper.

"Index," said the voice and a word appeared where the A had been.

Elana said, "Scientist." The suspended image changed again, this time displaying first a group of letters and then a woman wearing a white jacket and eye coverings, looking between several glass jars and the notes she was making on a clipboard. The voice gave a full definition of the word *scientist*, showed three alternate images, and then returned to the initial image and group of letters.

It was like Roland's magic from the Great Hall, but tiny. Mara leaned forward to peer at the silver paper.

"If you hear a word in conversation and you want to know more, open the index and speak the word. If you see a new word when you're looking through a book, use the index to type in the letters." Elana tapped the lower left hand corner of the shiny paper. Squiggles of light appeared and merged to form a grid. Each space on the grid had a letter inside. "For example, you mentioned looking at maps and charts as part of planning for battle."

"Yes, all the time," Mara said.

"A word you might see on a map is *elevation*." Elana wrote out the word *elevation* on one of the binder pages. She touched each letter she had written on the grid, in the same order.

"Elevation," the voice said. A map appeared.

Her aunt said, "Stop," and the moving image froze. "See how that works?"

Mara swallowed. "Yes, ma'am." Her voice was hushed with awe. "This is wonderful magic."

Elana patted her niece's hand. "What seems like magic is usually some form of energy manipulation. Please choose a book from the shelf."

Quickly navigating the tables, Mara crouched down to get a better look at a medium-sized tome with green binding and shiny gold letters. The cover didn't have any pictures, but when Mara flipped through the pages, she found pictures of Satri and lots of pictures of *gontra* trees.

Stretching out her hand for the book, her aunt asked, "May I see?" She scanned the title and turned a few pages. "*The Great Tree of Satri,*" she said. "This is about our most famous resident."

Mara opened her mouth to say, "I've met her," but decided against it.

Her aunt turned to a section of pages filled with pictures. "Try using the index to read the words under the pictures. I'm going to check on the rain and then I'll be in my office getting organized."

It was still darker outside than it should have been, but rain wasn't falling any longer. Mara took the book over to the table where the silver paper and binder lay and sat in the closest chair. She brushed her finger along the left side of the paper as she had seen Elana do.

"Mara," she said.

"Mara," the voice repeated and a word with four letters appeared in the air. She memorized the shape of her name, savoring it.

#

Some time later, when Elana returned to the classroom, Mara was tapping one hand on the letter grid and holding open the front of her book with the other. "How's it going?" Elana asked.

Mara stopped tapping. "I'm learning. I…thank you."

Elana looked over her shoulder. "You're working on chapter one?"

"Yes, I finished the pictures and now I'm…reading about the farmer and the Tree." She smiled, pleased and proud. "May I take this back to your house?"

Elana slid the silver paper into its protective cover and tucked it into the green book. "Of course, but I'll put it in my school bag. You have clothes to carry."

"Yes, ma'am," Mara said as she stood and pushed in her chair.

Along the walk home, she felt a bubble of happiness from the learning accomplished at her aunt's school. Protector House was set up for people to navigate without reading, as was most of life in the settlements. But it wasn't right that only a few were given formal instruction.

Mara continued thinking about access to learning as she hung her new clothes in the guest room closet. She straightened and tightened the bed covers and opened a window to let in the smell of rain and trees. The room looked larger now that many of the boxes and stacks of miscellaneous things were gone. The one remaining box contained the mementos of her parents, but she hadn't opened it yet.

After refolding the borrowed clothes, Mara carried them down the hall to her aunt's door. "Brought back your clothes," she called.

Elana motioned her inside so she could put the clothes down on the corner of the large bed, next to a pile of clean clothes.

"I have a question," Mara said.

"Just one?" Her aunt's tone was light and teasing

"For now." Mara shifted to a comfortable stance, feet slightly apart, hands behind her back. "Only certain people can read in Protector House and the settlements, and only certain information or learning is available. So here in Satri and in other places, if everyone can read, everyone can get books and indexes"—she made an encompassing gesture—"does everyone know everything?"

Mara had been hoping to catch up to Dalin and others her age. But as she began to comprehend all the information that must be available, the idea of catching up seemed far less possible.

Her aunt picked up a pair of socks and began twisting them together. "When is Dalin coming by to get you for sparring practice?"

"He hasn't contacted me yet." She'd completely forgotten about their tentative plans.

"Well," Elana said. "This is a big question. We can talk about it over a cup of tea—how does that sound?"

Once settled at the kitchen table with cups of tea, a plate of apple slices, and ginger cookies, Elana took a deep breath and folded her hands on the table. "We, the residents of this planet, are part of a seven-planet system. All one commonwealth under a queen." She paused and looked at her niece. "Each of the planets has a roughly similar education system that is available to most of the population. In general, children begin reading instruction in the main Origin language of their planet around age three. Remind me and I'll take you to see a play center.

"Formal school on Satri begins around age five. At that time, children learn first to speak and later to read and write at least two other Origin languages." Elana paused to take a bite of ginger cookie and a sip of tea. "With me so far?" she asked.

"Seven planets. Part of a commonwealth. One queen. School starts at three, other languages at five." Mara took a bite of apple. "So then, why do some adult scientists need your school?"

"This is an English Origin planet. Most of the seminal work on the Great Tree was recorded in Origin English. But across the Commonwealth, six Origin languages are represented heavily and at least fifty others with countless dialects are spoken in communities spread across our worlds."

Mara ate a few more apple slices. "So a child might know three languages, but it's entirely possible that none of those is Origin English?"

"Yes, exactly." Her aunt stood and opened the windows facing the gulf. The sound of the waves hitting the rocks drifted in.

"In school," Mara began, "do the children get to learn whatever they want? How many years do they get to stay?"

"By age fourteen, give or take, children begin to have more and more choices about what they want to spend time learning. Dalin, for example"—Elana paused—"still haven't heard from him?"

"No." She touched the tiny hoop in her ear.

"More tea?" Elana asked, rising with her cup.

Mara was about to repeat, "Dalin, for example," when she noticed her aunt's lips curved in a teasing smile. Elias used to do the same thing when it was nearly the season to travel to the horse fair.

He would torture the young stablehands by mentioning only small bits of information at a time.

Mara crossed her arms and took three slow breaths, putting effort into keeping her expression smoothly neutral. Feelings belonged on the inside.

Sitting down with her tea, Elana smiled more broadly, like a proud older sister. "Dalin showed early promise in both intellectual pursuits and fighting skills. At thirteen, he began spending part of his days at the militia headquarters and part of his days at Satri University studying history. At first he was trying to get a grasp of the Commonwealth: how it works, how it was established. Yadira thought he might follow her into political leadership. The rest of us thought he would join the Queen's War Projects and Military Strategy Council." Elana shook her head and shrugged. "But recently, he extended his decision to stay here, as part of Satri's militia."

Dalin had attended at least ten years of basic school and another six of advanced school. And she had exactly two hours of learning so far. The disparity hurt like a punch to the kidney. Partners had to be evenly matched or the support was lopsided and the pairing grew to be a burden for the stronger half.

Pushing back her chair, Mara stood, the need to distract herself too great. "I might never have seen this." She gestured at the water. "Might never have met you and Jameson if Dalin hadn't found me on the battlefield." Words failed as she contemplated the enormity of his actions. Not only were they unequally matched; she also owed the Gaishan a bigger debt than was possible to repay.

Eventually, she came back to her original question. "What is so different about the compounds and the settlements? Why don't we get to learn and have choices?"

Joining her at the window, Elana said, "Jameson did something to the sensors in the house to prevent our conversations being monitored. He set it up so that it seems like natural interference from the wind, water, and trees.

"Most people know at least a little about the war experiments, but nobody talks about them. It's considered treason." Her aunt looked sideways at her. "And what I'm about to tell you isn't in any index or book, so don't go looking."

Elana gazed at the gulf and fussed with the sleeves of her shirt for a moment, brushing away imaginary crumbs. "War historians, as far back as the Origin times and certainly those on the Queen's strategy council, agree that wars can be won or lost for a variety of reasons. It was the intent of the Queen's great-great grandfather, the first king of the Commonwealth, to study war in his own territory, perfect a certain number of techniques, and then wage war on the neighboring planets and planetary groups. He fancied himself a scientist and believed that if he got the variables just right, he, or rather, his forces could not lose.

"His son, the next king, and the king after that altered the rationale. Rather than prepare the Commonwealth to wage war, the second and third kings decreed the purpose of the war experiments was to prepare us to fend off any kind of attack. By then planetary geologists had discovered valuable mineral and ore resources on Laska and Iloel, and xenobiologists on Satri found the Tree."

Elana sighed. "Each of the seven planets in this commonwealth has a different type of war experiment going on. On Asattha, our project is the Gaishan versus the settlers and Protectors."

Cold washed through Mara, stiffening her limbs. She turned from the window. "The war in the North has lasted more than three generations. People have died. My partners..." Her voice caught.

Expression tight with pain, her aunt whispered, "I know. Every day I knew the next death could be yours."

"A 'project' is building a new fence or installing shelves in the kitchen. How can a war, a real war, be called a project? Why would a leader approve of people, of children, losing their lives for nothing?"

"Mara?" Dalin's voice in her head. *"I'm on my way so we can get some sparring in before dinner. Your mind...what's going on? Are you all right?"*

She suddenly remembered something he had said about the Gaishan: "We wear masks to hide we look just like you." Dalin knew all about this. Her hand curled into a fist.

"Fine," she sent. *"See you soon."* And she pulled a thick, dark curtain around her mind.

A few minutes later they heard Dalin let himself in through the sliding glass door in the back. Mara remained on the couch next to her aunt.

Hurrying over, Dalin knelt, taking the smaller woman's hands. "Elana? What's happened? Where's Jameson?"

She looked up at him and shook her head. "You have to tell her the rest."

He glanced at Mara. "The rest of what?"

"After lunch we went to Elana's school. When we got back to the house, I asked about the differences between the settlements and Satri, specifically why so few settlers and Protectors have access to school," Mara said.

Dalin remained perfectly still, his handsome face neutral and composed.

"Elana started to explain about the war experiments," she continued in her reporting voice. "When you were talking at lunch about my parents riding north and ruining the experiment, I thought you meant an experiment they had going in their lab. But you meant…" Mara's jaw clenched. "You meant ruin the war experiment by revealing the Gaishan as human and the existence of Satri. And last night at dinner when you knew about partners, how we're supposed to work together, I thought it was because you studied us, as the enemy. But if the Protector Corps is part of an experiment, then everyone studies us." Mara could keep her face empty and her eyes flat, but her chest rose and fell with quick, shallow breaths.

Dalin rocked backward onto his feet and stood in one smooth motion. "Do you still want to train today?"

"Yes," Mara said. Anything to replace the sickening horror of her aunt's words. She needed to fight something, someone, right now.

"Go and try to forget the war," Elana said. "I'm sorry I couldn't answer your questions without making us both upset."

Mara watched as Dalin pulled her aunt into a quick hug. "Can I eat with you tonight? By the time we finish, it might be too late to eat at HQ."

Elana ran a finger under first one eye and then the other. "You're always welcome, D," she said and hurried toward the stairs.

Chapter 27

Dalin set a brisk pace, striding through the neighborhood to the north. The streets and walkways had absorbed the water, but the air felt like more rain was coming.

After a few minutes of fast walking, he said, "I was under orders not to tell you the true situation between the Protectors and the Gaishan."

"But—"

Holding up a hand, he said, "Be fair to both of us. My priority was to get you here in one piece. I knew once you were in Satri the truth would come out. And before you got here, would you have believed me?"

Mara jammed her hands in her pockets. She still felt tricked, but he was right. She wouldn't have believed anyone who told her the war wasn't real. Where was the logic in forbidding the sharing of direct information yet ordering Dalin to bring her to the one place she could find the truth herself?

"They kept me, they keep us, from the truth, and even the...the ability to understand." Her anger expanded to include the monarchs responsible for so much ignorance, pain, and death.

After several twists and turns through a neighborhood of large houses and tall trees, they approached the front door of a house painted purple with red trim. The building was set far enough from the main road that the third level was nearly obscured by trees.

Dalin tapped a sequence of numbers onto the door panel and the door opened with an internal clunking sound. She let out a silent breath. Without her uniform, nothing obvious gave away her identity as a Protector. Still, the fingers of her sword hand flexed as she suppressed the urge to reach for a sword that wasn't there.

A man with dark-red hair wearing the Satri militia uniform walked by. "Sir," he said, nodding at Dalin.

"Fiorelli," Dalin replied, nodding back.

"Do they...?" she began.

In her mind, he answered, *"No one here knows who you are. I got clearance to bring a family friend from Kels who serves in the militia through the facility. Since some people who know that story also know you're Jameson's niece, they won't bother you."*

He led them past several empty offices, a small kitchen, and around a corner to the top of a staircase. The walls were a plain gray, the floor polished wood. Everything was clean and sleek.

"Are your senior officers here?" Mara asked. The lights snapped on as they descended the stairs.

"No, they're at our main facility. It's southeast of the square where we ate lunch." Out loud he continued, "But I did ask a couple of my guys to join us this afternoon." They entered a room lined with tiny doors. In the center were three benches spaced evenly apart.

A well-built man with brown skin smiled from the closest bench. He was wrapping a long strip of fabric around each hand.

"Hey, I'm Gruffald," he said, extending the hand that was already wrapped.

Mara smiled back, liking his twinkling green eyes and his deep voice. "Mara," she said, shaking his hand.

"Lieutenant here says you're thinking of going career, out on Kels, is it?"

"Yes," she said.

"They have more women in the ranks?" he asked, resuming his wrapping.

"They do," Dalin said before she could answer. "More than here, not as many as the Commonwealth military has overall." He opened one of the little doors and pulled out a tunic and pants. "Gruffald is the best hand-to-hand guy in our unit," he said. "You're going to start with him and then move on to weapons." He pointed down a narrow hall. "You can change in one of the washrooms through there."

As she took the tunic and pants and began to make her way around the benches, she heard Gruffald ask, "Who's coming in for weapons?"

"Puente," Dalin answered. Their voices faded almost immediately as she entered the hallway.

Opening the first door, she found an equipment closet full of padded helmets, padded chest shields, and gloves. The next door was ajar and music drifted out. Mara peered in and saw rows of machines. One machine was in use by a man with dark blond hair. He looked slightly older than the other soldiers she had seen and was working on lifting his legs one at a time.

The man waved. "Hey, you the lieutenant's family friend?"

She nodded.

"I'm Puente," he said. "We're going to do some weapons work later on." He nodded at the clothes she held. "Looking for a place to change?"

"Dalin said down this hall?"

"Yeah, one more door," he said, pointing. "Hey, you're starting with Gruffald, right?"

Mara shrugged. "That's what he said his name was."

Puente grinned and leaned forward, his tone conspiratorial. "He likes to go inside. He throws a lot of fakes so keep up your center guard. And he can lead with either hand, so don't get confused by that."

"I appreciate the advice," she said.

"Later," Puente said and began lifting his legs again.

As she changed clothes in the small washroom, Mara smiled to herself. Though she was still frustrated with Dalin, for the first time that day she felt almost comfortable. A tiny part of her mind worried that her skills wouldn't measure up. No better way to improve at fighting than fighting. Mara put the revelations about the war away in her mind, even though the boxes in there were getting very full. Distraction was an enemy of preparation, but she'd have time to sort things out later when she was alone.

The sleeves of the practice tunic were a tad short, as were the legs of the loose-fitting pants. Mara folded her new clothes, stacked them on her shoes, and carried them with her, padding barefoot back down the hall. A few steps past the room with the benches brought her into a different room with a padded floor and mirrors on one side. The two men stood in the center talking, one tall and slender, the other broad and heavily muscled.

"Do you want gloves?" Dalin asked her.

"Do you bruise easily?" she asked Gruffald, tone sincere. She placed her stack of clothes in the corner.

Dalin laughed and Gruffald joined in. "I like this girl," he said.

"Gruffald is going to take you through a series of moves. We're looking for your ability not only to strike and block, but also to counter."

It was hard to keep her expression neutral because she was lighting up with happiness and relief inside. Finally something that made sense. "Right," she said.

"This is a training fight," Dalin continued. "Hits are light. The goal is to make contact, not break a rib. And since I don't know the exact nature of the training you've completed on Kels, this piece will help us determine next steps for you. Also," he added, "try to focus on using your upper body. We'll add kicks later."

Gruffald moved to the exact center of the floor and motioned for her to join him. His tunic was sleeveless, the same color gray as his pants. His arms were almost bulky, but not overly long. Different bodies fight differently, she reminded herself.

"Guard," Dalin said.

Gruffald pulled his hands up near his face. Mara did the same. "Begin."

Her opponent opened with a wide punch to the head. She ducked under his arm and tagged him in the ribs. Darting outside his reach, she shifted her weight to the balls of her feet. When he threw two fast jabs, she parried the second jab with an open palm and followed through with a straight punch to his ear. Mara backed away again and saw Gruffald looking at Dalin. She had a split second to wonder if they were using rapport and then he closed the distance and began throwing punches in a much faster rhythm.

Thought narrowed to reinforcing her blocks even as she countered and threw her own jabs, crosses, hooks, and elbow strikes. Just as she pivoted to throw a spinning backfist into her opponent's nose, Dalin called, "Time." With some satisfaction, she noted they were both breathing hard. The mat wasn't slick, but it emitted a faint and familiar smell of sweat.

"You're definitely related to Jameson," Gruffald said, respect in his voice. "Even when you didn't counter like I thought you would, you kept outside my range, didn't drop your guard, and didn't lose a beat when I changed up sides."

"Thanks, Gruffald," Dalin said.

"Thank you," she echoed.

While the other fighter ambled out toward the benches, Dalin motioned her over and handed her a tall cup of water.

"Well?"

"You're pretty good without your sword," he said. "And you won't always have it, so it's important to keep honing your hand-to-hand skills. I can see a few blocks and counters we need to add to your repertoire, *and I can see why you earned your sword,"* he added in her mind.

"Best day of my life," she said, her lips curving as she remembered the sword ceremony.

Gruffald had reappeared in the doorway with a towel around his neck, holding a water bottle. Dalin asked, "Would you be willing to train with her?"

He took a pull of water from his bottle. "Sure. Too bad we don't have any females for her to match up with." He looked at the ceiling, expression thoughtful. "I don't envy those Protectors much, but they do have a lot of females in the ranks. Makes a difference."

When Mara stiffened, Dalin touched her mind. *"Calm."* Inclining his head toward Mara, he prompted the other man. "Makes a difference because the females are so fierce?"

Gruffald took the hint. "Yeah, fierce and fast. Some of those little ones are really quick. They hit the lines so young up North." He shook his head.

"We'll find you as many different sparring match-ups as we can," Dalin said. "Jameson used to say, 'Work your technique *and* the guy you're fighting.' Speaking of," he continued, "ready for weapons?"

Mara bowed to her opponent. "I would appreciate the opportunity to learn from you, especially more counters."

Gruffald's eyes went to Dalin. Again she had the sense they were talking mentally. "Whatever you want," he said with a smile. "We don't have much action right now. Plus, all of us need practice fighting females, so you're doin' us a favor, too."

"Mornings? I think I'm to be working with my aunt in the afternoons."

"Sure," Gruffald said. "Lieutenant keeps the schedule so…" He started loosening the wrapping on his left hand. Then his head came up, remembering something. "Listen, with Puente, his strength is his footwork. Don't let his motion distract you, and when you need to, get out of the way fast. Even in practice fights he hits hard."

Dalin had disappeared down the hall and now reappeared in the doorway. "Do you want to start with sticks or staffs?" he asked.

"Sticks," she answered without hesitating.

Dalin opened the door to the equipment room. Gruffald had finished unwrapping both hands and was taking clothes out of one of the narrow cabinets lining the wall.

"Thank you," she repeated.

"See you soon," he said with a wink.

Happy and relaxed, Mara helped herself to a pair of sticks from the equipment room. Each stick was made from a light-brown, speckled wood and was nearly the length of a sword. These were a bit heavier than the sticks she'd used in Zam's class, but still lighter than a real sword. She ran her palm over the smooth, rounded surface, checking for any damage. The relatively small width of the sticks, roughly double the diameter of a wooden spoon handle, felt good in her palm.

Soon, she and Puente were facing each other on the padded floor. His build was lighter than Gruffald's, and judging by the lines on his face and the silver hair at his temples, she guessed Puente to be closer in age to Zam. All told, just the particulars of an opponent who would choose the finesse of a sword/stick over the brutality of hand-to-hand.

Mara was already so focused on her opponent when Dalin called, "Guard," she startled.

Puente opened with a fast strike at her knees. She jumped back and followed the swing with her own stick looking for an opening. Her first strike caught only his tunic sleeve. Faking an overhead strike, she went for Puente's solar plexus, but he blocked her and aimed a strike at her ribs. The pace of their fight was a steady exchange of strikes and blocks at first. At a signal from Dalin, Puente intensified his attack, raining blows down on her head and neck. Mara shifted her grip, gritted her teeth, and responded as quickly as she could. She got a few lucky shots at Puente's midsection, but too soon found herself in a corner, Puente's stick to her throat.

"You weren't taught on Kels," Puente rasped, his dark eyes intense on her face. "I fed you three different patterns from their training repertoire and you didn't respond with any of the set moves."

"Hold, Chris," Dalin said.

"What's going on de Forest?"

"Chris," Dalin said, steel in his quiet tone. "Let her go."

Puente stepped back and dropped his sticks to his sides. "She fights like Twyla," he said.

Mara's eyes flashed over her opponent. Similar height and weight. Same nose, eyes, jaw, same blond-gray hair... Her lips parted in astonishment.

"Wait," Dalin said. *"I'll talk with him."*

"Twyla's brother?"

"Twin" was his soft reply.

"Mara, you're dismissed." Dalin kept his focus on Puente. "Get changed and I'll meet you at the main door."

Tucking her sticks under one arm, she bowed to Puente to show respect for his skill. "Thank you."

He inclined his head in return.

As she changed back into her new clothes and shoes, Mara's mind was whirling. *Puente is Twyla's twin brother?* The connections between her world and Satri were baffling. By the time she returned down the corridor and headed up the stairs, the lower level of the militia facility was silent.

She chose a chair in the kitchen and angled it so she could see the main entrance of the building. Lingering but not unpleasant smells told her food was prepared here, at least some of the time. As she waited for Dalin, her eyes were drawn to a map on the wall showing a view of the main continent of Asattha.

A dark, crosshatched line cut across the middle, running along a natural ridge. She stood to take a closer look. Markings she couldn't decipher ran along the boundary, but it was familiar terrain. Inside the line were all five Protector compounds marked with red squares. The settlements were labeled with black circles. Along the white border of the map, in small print, were words Mara had just learned: *War Project 7.* Here was the confirmation, the plain fact of a boundary separating the war territory from the prosperous and peaceful South.

"I should have known who you were just by the way you carry yourself." Puente spoke from the doorway. He was still wearing his gray training uniform. "Been in enough skirmishes to recognize a Protector from a kilometer away."

Just as he appeared behind Puente, Dalin said, *"Mara, you can trust him."*

How could she trust anyone who participated in this insanity? Dalin included. Mouth gone dry, she asked, "You know my teachers?"

"Just like Jameson, I fought with Zam long ago. Twyla and I both did." He paused and gave her a measuring stare. "De Forest tell you Twyla is my sister?"

"Just now," Mara said. "You look so much like her and you sound like her, too—"

"You fight with her?" Puente interrupted.

"Speak freely. We're nearly alone and I've already begun erasing these conversations from the building system." Dalin turned and vanished from view.

Pulling out another chair, Puente flipped it around to straddle it and lean forward. Although his seated position was casual, his lips turned down and his eyes narrowed.

"Twyla is my senior Protector. She leads the Green cohort, my cohort," Mara said. "I've trained under her and fought by her side for four years now."

He nodded. "I tried a move on you that she and I put together. When you knew it…"

It was Mara's turn to nod. Otherwise she stood very still, watching Puente and wondering where Dalin had gone.

"De Forest says you just heard about the war experiments. That you've only been in Satri a couple of days."

"Yes," she said, eyes going to the map. "When I was trying to learn more about the labs and the scientists earlier today, I looked up the word *experiment*. And…I'm not sure how that applies to a war. The people in the North are fighting—the Protectors are fighting for their land, their food, their children."

Puente shook his head and sighed. "What if I told you the only true danger to the people of the North is ignorance?"

"I don't understand." Brow furrowed, she tried to decipher the older man's bitter expression.

"Exactly my point," he said, slamming his hand on the chair.

"System is resetting, so we need to take this outside," Dalin said, reappearing in the doorway.

"Jameson should call a meeting," Puente growled. "We need to end this before any more turn out like her."

Mara's chin went up. "You dishonor your sister, sir. She has made me a fine soldier."

The older fighter shoved back his chair and stood, leaning in until his face was close. "Twyla serves with the Protectors because she has to. Of course she made you a fine *soldier*." He emphasized the word. "But what else are you?"

Mara stared at him. She didn't have an answer. It hurt worse than the stick slashing across the backs of her legs, to have this stranger toss her deepest fear in her face, especially in front of Dalin.

Chapter 28

Out on the street, Mara looked left and right, recommitting the location of the militia's facility to memory. Puente's last question ricocheted around in her mind. *What else are you? What else are you?* She tried to lock down the confusion and frustration, but her whole being felt tight, sore, and unsettled.

Despite her anger with him earlier and the nagging worry about what else he had orders not to talk about, she appreciated Dalin's steady, silent presence as they walked. If she asked, he would help her talk through Puente's revelations about Twyla and the Gaishan/Protector conflict. But she wouldn't ask.

More people were out now, some with children, some carrying market bags. The soft whining purr of the autos hung in the air as dozens of the upright vehicles traveled the roads. Dalin turned down a street she hadn't seen on their initial route and led her up the pebbled walk of the house on the far corner. The wooden trim, shutters, and door were painted scarlet. The rest of the structure was gray stone. When Dalin began tapping a sequence of numbers into the door panel, she realized this must be his house.

Pushing open the door, he reached back for her hand and gave it a quick squeeze. "Just a quick stop," he said. "I want to change out of uniform and also check messages."

"That's fine," she said, too busy looking around to say anything else.

The entrance opened into a large common room. Like at the wayhouse, several tall, full bookcases graced the walls. But what was drawing Mara across the room, over soft gray rugs and around comfortable-looking chairs, were two square paintings hung on either side of the fireplace. From a distance, the bright range of colors was most compelling. Up close she studied the subjects. On the left was a portrait of the Great Tree on a sunny summer day. On the right was the Great Tree at night, the radiance of two moons sparkling on its leaves.

As Dalin ran lightly up the stairs, she continued to study the two paintings. Painted art was rare in the settlements and completely absent in Northwest Protector House. Some of her friends could draw well with colored pencils—faces, animals, maps—but none had ever done a larger drawing like these or used paint.

"Did you make these?" Mara asked.

She caught amusement before he answered. *"No, but the artist lives in Satri."*

"Artist," she murmured, stepping back to the center of the room to appreciate the interplay of colors in each piece. And then she saw the key connection in the pair of paintings. "It's the Light, isn't it?" Her heart sped up, awed by the power of this artist to capture something so important.

Dalin interrupted her thoughts. *"Elana says dinner is in forty minutes. She doesn't need us to bring anything. I've got fruit and bread in the kitchen if you need a snack now."*

The house felt warm after walking in the chill of the evening air. She pushed up the sleeves of her sweater and walked to the doorway on the far side of the common room. Beyond was his kitchen, nearly twice the size of the kitchen in the wayhouse. Both the window over the sink and a connected set of three windows surrounding a small table looked out over the back yard. On the facing wall, she recognized the design of the cold box and waved her hand to see if the door would become transparent. To her delight, it did.

Surveying the contents, her stomach suddenly became interested. She'd been too upset to eat much earlier. Given the limited choices, she selected two apples and then waved her hand to banish the transparency. A loaf of bread in a clear bag sat on the counter top. She brought the food to the square wooden table and sat down, contemplating the overgrown collection of dormant vegetation out back.

At the far end of the yard, Mara noticed a structure nearly hidden by bushes and other growth. By its location and size, Mara guessed it was a personal stable like the one at her aunt's house. *"Is Herald here?"* she sent.

"No, he's at my parents' stable. He has lots of friends there."

"Will your parents be at dinner tonight?" she asked.

"No, not tonight," Dalin replied. *"My mom has council business and my dad...I think something is going on at his lab."*

Mara bit into one of the apples and gazed at the dark cloudy sky visible above the stable's roofline. More rain was likely. In the North it was probably snowing, maybe even a full white storm. As she opened the clear bag and tore off a small piece of bread, Puente's parting question bubbled up in her mind. *What else are you?*

Mara still wasn't sure she could answer the question. She only knew what she was not. Not a scientist or an artist or a teacher, and at the moment, not even an assistant combat instructor. Which surfaced the next question: *Do I really want to be something else?* Dalin and Jameson, as far as she could tell, were only soldiers. Why did Puente, who was a soldier himself, make it sound like something was wrong with her?

When Dalin entered the kitchen, his brows knit together at Mara's expression. "What?" he said.

She shook her head and swallowed, forcing herself to meet Dalin's bright silver gaze. He'd changed into relatively snug dark pants and wore a blue shirt under a light-gray pullover. Hair slightly mussed and out of uniform, he looked closer to his nineteen years.

He picked up the other apple and took a bite before sitting in the chair facing her. "Forget Puente," he said. "I never would've let him near you if I'd known he was so"—Dalin searched for a description—"bitter. Never seen darkness in him like that before."

"He said the only true danger to the settlers and Protectors in the North is ignorance." She was incredibly conscious of her own sweaty state, despite her relatively clean, new clothes.

He tore off a piece of bread, turning it over in his hands, one foot tapping at the side of the table.

"How long have you lived here alone?" Mara asked.

"Almost two years. When I finished the last round of training, I was able to request where I would be stationed. I chose Satri."

"Because of your family?"

Dalin took a last bite of his apple and set the core aside. "In part," he said. "This house belonged to my grandparents. But when my gran died, she left the house to me. It helped to know I would have my own place to live." He looked directly at her. "And in part because, as a professional soldier, the war experiment here is the only one in which I'm willing to participate."

She could almost sense something underneath his words, another layer of meaning. "But do you get lonely? Living by yourself?"

"Are you thinking of the compound? The noise of so many people under the same roof? I had plenty of that when I was away studying," he replied. "The quiet, after all the planning, fighting, and debriefing, it's relaxing. Your room must be like that for you, right?"

One corner of Mara's mouth turned up. "Not since Annelise was assigned as my partner." Her smile faded. "Have you heard anything about the storms in the North? Is…is everyone safe?"

"Last I heard," he said, "Protectors were all out on leave and expected to stay out until thawing clears the roads—"

"That's what you said last—" Mara interrupted.

He reached across the table and touched Mara's arm, the heat of his palm warming her bare skin and multiplying their connection. Eyes locked, they took a breath as one. Without his uniform, his rules for himself were stronger…and something else. She almost had the full thought.

Dalin broke the contact by casually reaching for the bread again. "And conditions haven't changed, though I hear more storms are expected. We have a few months before you'll need to report in."

A few months. How much, how fast could she learn in that time?

"You fought well today," he said into the silence. "I let both matches run twice as long as normal practice sparring, but you were fine."

"I look forward to learning from Gruffald," Mara said, waving off his you-were-fine remark. Then she grinned. "I'll learn more when he doesn't feel constrained by your presence. Lieutenant."

"I told them to take you through sequences of moves from beginning to advanced. Neither was meant to be an all-out fight."

Mara started a retort and then snapped her fingers. "*That's* what's been bothering me for over a year. It's never meant to be an all-out fight, is it? You, the Gaishan, are practicing on us, to get better at that kind of warfare. And we, the Protectors, improve also. Both sides adapt to the practice technique and then one side changes tactics…"

She stared at him as the revelation unfolded. "It's all training. That's why the territorial lines never really change." She gripped the sides of the table, thinking of Annelise now, and of others who were so vulnerable in this deadly game. "People died, Dalin."

"A few died, yes. Most who have been presumed dead were fogged enough to wander south from the battlefield. Those Protectors were gathered up and brought here."

Reeling from this new blow, she asked, "How many dead, truly dead?"

"How many bodies have you seen?" Dalin responded. "Not on the battlefield, but back at the compound?"

She shook her head, thinking back. "Two, maybe three this year. For everyone else, we had memorial services. Nothing to bury. The Gaishan take all their fallen—we thought you took ours, too." The next revelation burst through her mind. "My first partner, Enriet? I never saw her body. Could she…?"

"Be here? Or somewhere else, happy and alive? Yes."

Covering her mouth to hide her trembling lips, Mara tried to breathe through the shock. The patterns in the dark-wood tabletop swam and blurred.

"Listen, Jameson and I are part of a network across the Commonwealth that works to prevent casualties in the war experiments." He leaned forward, the words rushing out. "On this planet, we specifically watch for Protectors who might tip the balance or change the experiment. Those leaders become the targets of heavy fogging, battle after battle, until we are able to secure them. Your reconfiguring of battle plans and constant questions drew unwanted attention, for example."

Mara rubbed a hand across her forehead. She closed her eyes and let out a breath. "But what about the other contagions? The sores, the sickness?"

"As far as we know, those were weapons tests." Dalin shook his head with disgust. "They're blind tests too. The guys don't know what they're carrying because the tools of the Gaishan arrive preloaded. The uniforms were designed to mask any differences in physique and prevent any contagion from penetrating through our skin."

She'd asked for answers, but this was more terrible than she'd imagined. "Who else knows this?"

"In our network?"

"If that's what you call it, yes." Frustration broke through in her voice.

"Zam and Twyla. Elias. Two or three in each of the other color cohorts, and a few of your healers. But all of the senior Protectors know the parameters of the experiment. Know which variables are important to the Queen in a given season." He rubbed a hand over his short hair. "All the Gaishan, well, the Satri militiamen know their assignment. Know it's not a real war, I mean. Only a few are connected to Jameson the way Puente is."

"I don't understand," Mara said.

"For most of the men I serve with, going north—putting on the masks and fencing with Protectors—is just an assignment. They don't care if some of the Protectors die from the poisons or violence, don't care if some wander off. They're fighting because they're paid to do it. We have other jobs as the local militia, but it's one of the duty rotations—"

"The Queen pays you to scare settlers and practice fighting techniques against my people, against children?" Her voice rose in pitch and volume. "Sure you don't get extra for the kills?" Bile rose and burned her throat. She wanted to hit something, do something.

He abruptly pushed back his chair, the legs scraping loudly against the tile floor. In a few swift motions, he cleared the apple cores and the remainder of the bread into the composting recycler.

"When I learned what I just told you, I was fifteen. That afternoon, I ran away into the woods. I just couldn't believe people I admired, good people, were involved, contributing to something so stupid. And the worst part, worst by far, was *you* were there in the North being raised as a Protector. And due to begin fighting soon."

Even without physical contact, she felt the anger in his mind burning as strongly as her own.

"Jameson found me after a day. I think he could have found me sooner, but he left me alone to cool down. That's when he told me about the network of people committed to ending the war experiments. I joined on the spot. Now for every fighting mission, I help run at least one rescue mission, moving potential targets out of the project and into hiding. We're the reason you've had so few bodies to bury. And that's why we know how unusual it is for you to be pursued like this."

As she stood, Dalin braced his shoulders, ready for the punch she was thinking about throwing. But when her hand snapped out, she grasped his wrist in the customary clasp of fellow soldiers. "I wish to add my commitment to yours," she said, "I can do more than fight."

Dalin grasped her wrist and shook. "Done."

Chapter 29

The next morning began what was to become routine. Dalin woke Mara just before dawn with a mental call. They ran through Satri on a winding and varied route and ended at one of the militia station houses for stretching, sparring, and weight training. But they weren't partners. She wasn't sure they were even really friends. Mara had decided to ask as few questions as possible to avoid Dalin lying to her. And Dalin seemed perfectly at ease with the near-absence of conversation.

In the afternoons, she studied her index and the Origin English tutorials. On a handful of occasions, Jin came by to tutor her in mental rapport and shielding. Other times, Mara rode Rowan around the perimeter of the city, enjoying the variety of people and scenery. Wherever she went, in the markets and the parks, she looked for her former partner, but had yet to see the girl's face anywhere.

At regular intervals, Mara traveled with Jameson on short missions to the nearest settlements. Disguised as traders, they brought supplies and gathered information. On two separate occasions they smuggled individuals back to Satri. The settlements looked so much worse, partly in contrast to the comforts of the city, partly because things were getting worse.

Materials to repair structures were scarce, as were medicines for winter sicknesses. Her dreams were often filled with the sounds of ragged, coughing children. Each trip, Mara listened far more than she talked. Never once did she hear anything but tales of record snowfall at the North and Northwest compounds. The truce story seemed to be holding as well.

Though it continued to rain on a regular basis and occasionally grew cold enough for heavy jackets, no snow fell in Satri. Signs of Brown interest in the "escaped Protector" dwindled. Jameson cautioned that the Browns, or whoever was behind the pursuit, had not given up the hunt but were biding their time.

With Elana's gentle help and her daily practice, Mara was learning to read Origin English. In the course of her first month in Satri, she decoded all the picture captions and even the first several chapters in another book on the Great Tree.

She borrowed a third book from the school library, this one about the planets in the Commonwealth. The chapter on Kels was disappointingly shorter than the others, containing only a few pretty images of fields with livestock grazing. Though she'd hoped for more information about the people of Kels and how they lived, at least what was there confirmed Jameson's stories.

Soon after, her aunt invited her to begin participating in class in the afternoons. "These are brilliant people," Elana told her, "in their own labs on their own planets. Here they feel at a disadvantage until they get comfortable in the primary language of Satri." When Mara didn't respond, she added, "I think your classmates will understand the frustrating challenge of being new at something. They are all, like you, experts in their focus area. Just not in Origin English."

The night before her first class, Mara went to visit the Great Tree in her physical home. Since their first introduction, the Tree had not appeared again, but Mara had learned quite a bit from her schoolbooks and was more curious than ever. Since the Tree and the *gontras* were part of Satri's culture, she knew her aunt would be teaching about them during class, but she wanted to learn for herself as well. The Tree had requested this much of her.

When Mara entered the central square where the Great Tree stood, it was nearly dark outside and a light breeze rustled the branches above her head. Miniature lights sparkled on the surrounding structures and a few discreetly placed spotlights partially illuminated the underside of the huge, arching branches. A handful of people walked nearby, gazing upward or laying hands on the bark of the massive tree trunk. The base of the trunk was about as wide as the main floor of Elana's school. Walking the perimeter, Mara counted 110 steps before she arrived back at her starting place.

She leaned her cheek against the massive trunk and rested her palm on the rough, silvery bark. The rough surface carried a trace of smell: hints of citrus, sandalwood, and musk. Closing her eyes, she reached out with her mind as Jin had taught her. *"Hello, Tree,"* she thought. From her reading she knew only one person had truly ever spoken with the Tree. That same, skeptical part of her questioned the dream conversation with the girl in the park, the girl who claimed to be the Tree in human form.

"I understand a little more about the gift of thirteen gontras. *I wish to thank you."* She'd learned *gontras* only dropped once a year

in early autumn. Other instances of *gontras* falling were considered special blessings, even if only caused by wind. If any member of an Asatthan family didn't have at least one *gontra* of his or her own, it was permitted to collect one during the drop period in autumn. Otherwise, by special decree, the blue seedpods were to be left where they fell to grow into new trees. Except for those that landed on stone walkways, rooftops, or any place that might prevent a seed from taking root. These were collected and redistributed north, on the northern edges of the city.

"I thank you for your generosity." She turned and pressed her back against the trunk. The night air carried a damp chill, but the bark wasn't cold to the touch.

Her thoughts drifted toward the apprehension she felt about meeting new people the next day. Thus far her time in Satri had been filled with very few people. And most of those knew her true identity. Mara pictured the bright network of roots and branches connecting all the *gontra* trees on the planet as she had witnessed in her dream. She imagined sinking into the bark and finding the strange girl inside, as though the Great Tree were a well-lit home one could visit.

"I've never been to school," Mara said to her imaginary hostess. *"I'm just learning to read and only in this one language. I've never traveled between planets—"*

"Mara?"

She whirled to her right, expecting to see the embodiment of the Tree. Instead she saw a girl with dark straight hair, nearly her own height and age.

The girl put up both hands, palms out. "Hello, I'm Nuwa. Dalin's sister?"

In the soft light surrounding the Tree, Mara could see the girl had Yadira's delicate features and Jin's slightly upturned eyes. "Hello," she said, voice rough. "How...?"

"Dalin thought you might be here so he suggested I pick you up on my way to Elana and Jameson's. I've been wanting to meet you, but I couldn't get away from my lab for most of the month."

Nodding, Mara fell into step alongside Nuwa. The girl's slender frame was reminiscent of Yadira as well. And though Dalin's sister seemed content to walk in silence, Mara wondered if she should say something.

"I've been hoping to meet you as well," Mara said.

"Did my dad explain I was out on the gulf?" Nuwa asked.

"Someone in your family did." She searched her memory for the words she needed. "Is your lab on a boat? Or a floating platform?"

"Both. And part of our work is underwater, so we have a submersible habitat and use submersible gear."

Mara was reminded of how little she knew about the labs or the scientists' work on Satri. If only she could read faster. "Doesn't much of the...research center around the Great Tree?"

She and Nuwa paused for a family group crossing Divis Street from the other direction. All the children were bundled into several layers of clothing. Mara tugged the hood of her sweater over her head and pulled her sleeves down over her hands.

Dalin's sister was zipped into a warm-looking jacket and didn't react to the cold breeze gusting in from the south. "Most of the research *is* about the Tree," she agreed as they began walking again. "My team, though, is doing species cataloging and ecosystem mapping. It's a partnership with five of the other planets in the Commonwealth. We all have significant aquatic environments with uncharted resources. Hold on." She stopped and bent to examine her shoe. Mara had started across the next intersection but paused to wait.

The girl shook her head as she straightened. "This strap is nearly torn through but I haven't made time to shop for a new p—"

A man barreled into Nuwa and grabbed her wrist. "You're coming with me," he rasped.

Mara sprinted back, but Dalin's sister had already snapped her hand down against her attacker's thumb, kicked him in the shin, and chopped him in the throat. The man dropped to one knee, gagging and clutching his neck. Grabbing one of his wrists, Mara bent his arm behind his back, wrenching it into a painful position near his shoulder blade.

"What do you want?" Nuwa asked. She drew a shaky breath and glared at her assailant.

The man shook his head back and forth. "Gonna be sick," he said, his voice a scratchy whisper. Everything about the man was unremarkable, from his plain, dark clothes to his dark eyes and brown hair.

Mara torqued the man's arm higher, forcing him to bend forward. "What do you want? Why were you attacking her?"

"Mara?" Dalin's voice in her head. *"Nuwa called for help. Is she…?"*

"She's good with her hands," Mara sent. *"We're safe."*

Less than two minutes later Dalin appeared, running flat out. He slowed as he reached the corner and nodded at Mara, visibly approving of the painful hold she was using on the attacker. He hugged his sister hard.

"Some of the guys are on their way to talk with this gentleman," he said, giving Nuwa one more squeeze. With no warning, he punched the man in the stomach. The attacker doubled over, making retching sounds.

Mara released the man's wrist and he fell forward onto both hands with a groan.

"Take Nuwa to your aunt's house. Everyone is waiting there. Please." Dalin tugged her hood back over her hair. "Be alert. On the double, okay?" He winked at his sister, though a smile only ghosted across his mouth. "Nice work, ladies. Let me know when you get there."

Nuwa started down the street and Mara jogged a few steps to catch up. The girl increased her pace until she was nearly running.

"Nuwa?"

"I'm fine," she answered, not sounding fine.

"You seem…upset." Mara wasn't sure what to say.

"I'm not like my brother," she said. "I always complained when he and Dad made me practice defending myself. So many years practicing and I always felt safe."

"But I wasn't," she said.

"It worked," Mara said at the same time. Fighting, being attacked, was part of her life on such a deep level that she wasn't sure how to relate to the girl's shock.

As they turned onto Ansel Street, Nuwa said, "Thank you."

"For what?" Mara asked, truly surprised. "I'm a soldier and I didn't get a hand on the guy before you dropped him." Her tone made it sound as though she'd been deprived of a terrifically fun opportunity.

When the girl laughed, it was wobbly, but as she spoke again her voice was stronger. "No wonder my brother likes you. You two are just the same. Oh and I just told him we got here without any other surprises." She pushed open the door and walked inside.

In the settlements, when a girl said, "My brother likes you," she meant it in a way specific to teasing, courting, and, sometimes, kissing. Given that Mara had literally nothing to bring to a match, she decided Dalin's sister had misspoken. She must have meant something more like, "My brother doesn't mind you being around even though his mission is technically over."

During their brief time at the wayhouse, Dalin had been considerate and open. Mara had trusted him with her questions. And even her first few days in Satri, he'd been kind, helping her through the swing, checking in through rapport. But just now, the moment when he'd touched her hair, clarified how little they'd connected beyond occupying the same physical space for weeks.

Mara bit her lip hard. It wasn't that she liked Dalin or expected anything from him. Losing the tiny, tangible connection they had just reminded her how much she missed the comfort of being around people she'd known since she could remember. He was good to look at and smart and an excellent fighter. But even if she wanted something different, took Nuwa's offhand remark more literally, it wouldn't matter. Because to him she was an assignment that had been completed, nothing more.

"…something is happening within the laboratory system," Nuwa was saying as Mara entered the kitchen.

"You're a scientist," Jin interjected, his tone that of a chiding father. "What evidence do you have?"

"Dad, you're a scientist." She put her hands on her hips, imitating his tone. "But you're so involved in your work with the Tree, you're missing important data points and other trend indicators."

Yadira was helping Elana at the stove, but Jameson wasn't in the room. To avoid walking through the father-daughter argument, Mara leaned on the doorframe and waited.

"Dad, all but Central Lab is down to a tiny staff. Two-thirds of existing teams have either been reassigned or sent to fieldwork, like I was. Or have gone back to their home planets," she added.

Both fell silent.

Jin said, "I'll look into it tomorrow. Especially if you think tonight's attack was related to your work."

She took a breath to answer, her eyes lost focus, and she nodded. "Dalin says to eat without him. And he says it's possible the attacker mistook me for Mara. He and Jameson are following up about the king's something. That part was fuzzy. Anyway, they have the guy locked up, but he's not talking so far."

Chapter 30

Back at her aunt's house after her run and hand-to-hand practice with Gruffald the next morning, Mara indulged in an extra long shower. Drying off, she stood and contemplated her clothing choices. The attack the night before had reinforced her compulsion to carry at least one weapon so, prior to dressing, she strapped a knife sheath around her right forearm and another on the inside of her left lower leg. Her favorite blue sweater and gray pants combination would cover both with room to spare.

Once dressed, she checked her reflection in the washroom mirror. Although she had not needed additional ear piercings to appear as a girl from Kels would, Elana had learned that the most common hairstyles involved small braids around the face. Sighing, she reached for the comb.

Downstairs, she found her aunt on the couch staring at the gulf, her normally serene expression troubled. Mara began to walk through, intending to leave her aunt to her private thoughts, but Elana stopped her with a hand.

"I received disturbing information just now." She patted the space next to her, indicating her niece should sit. Yet even when Mara came closer, Elana avoided eye contact and continued to stare at the rolling water.

"Because I'm married to Jameson, I've known for a long time of…of the network of people working to reduce casualties and ultimately to end the Crown's war experiments."

Mara tilted her head to one side, considering. She hadn't heard the explanation put in such plain terms but it went along with the things Dalin had said.

"Jin spent most of last night investigating Nuwa's concerns about transfers of people in and out of labs and back to their home planets." Her aunt's hands fluttered over her skirt, smoothing the fabric, straightening the hem. "She was right." Elana clasped her hands together. "He now has reason to believe members of the scientific community have been quietly forming similar alliances to end their part—the data analysis and experimental design part—of the war projects.

"When we are in class today, we need to listen for what the newly arrived scientists know about this. Their files indicate your classmates are higher ranking than the individuals I've taught over the past few years."

"The person who attacked Nuwa thought she had something to do with this alliance? With the scientists organizing themselves?" It was hard to imagine what threat civilians could be against the Queen and her multi-planet army.

"Maybe," said Elana. "If the attacker admitted who his target was, no one's told me."

#

As they entered the school, Mara's feelings of excitement and dread churned in her stomach. Elana, lost in her own thoughts, had not spoken much on the walk over.

"I need to do a few things in my office," her aunt said quietly. "Would you mind working on your own for a while?"

"That's fine," Mara said.

"Thanks." The small woman's eyes were heavy and shadowed. "I feel like I should review your classmates' information one more time. We'll be working in Classroom Four, so you can settle in there."

Mara adjusted the bag on her shoulder and headed to Classroom Four. Two steps inside and the lights came on. Heavy, oppressive clouds had filled the skies of Satri for multiple days, causing her to be very glad about the overhead lights in so many of the city's structures.

From the desks arranged in a semicircle, Mara chose one closest to the wall with the mural of the Great Tree. Even though her dream of the Tree seemed more fog than reality, she often revisited the memory. No one had mentioned the mass fogging of the Brown soldiers in a while, but Mara had a hunch it was connected with the Tree, that some momentary power had come through the root network to her.

The wind rattled branches along the classroom windows, startling Mara out of her thoughts. She lifted her bag onto the desk and carefully removed a notebook, pen, and the binder of reading practice lessons. On one of their runs last week, Dalin had explained that Satri had far less active tech than the other planets in the Commonwealth, primarily because of the Tree species. As a result, a secondary line of study into passive tech and low-energy-use tech was also in progress. Dalin had continued with enthusiasm about low-energy exports, which she'd assumed was like trade, but she'd quickly lost the thread of the conversation.

Mara still didn't understand why Dalin had broken weeks of silence on their runs to talk about the tech on Satri and trade, but things had just gotten worse when he noticed her attention wandering. "You have to understand the bigger picture, Mara," he'd said, as exasperated as if she'd botched a simple counterstrike. "Just because you didn't, I mean, because you haven't…"

"Because I haven't what?" she'd demanded. He didn't respond and they hadn't talked since.

The silvery paper of her index only needed a bit of sunlight every few days to keep working, meaning it was probably passive tech. She turned to lesson ten in her binder and opened the corresponding section in her index. Like the previous lessons, the content Mara attempted to read was part history of the Commonwealth and part culture lesson. Despite Dalin's accusation, she was doing what she could to understand the bigger picture.

"King Chandragupta died in 2683. Though his daughter, Princess Inrian, and her husband, Charles, were both alive and able to ascend to the throne, Chandragupta's express desire, recorded in his will and stated in open council, was for Princess Vanora to begin a new era. Queen Vanora was crowned at a grand ceremony attended by ambassadors from all seven planets." Mara stopped reading. "Index, show me a picture of Queen Vanora."

The picture developed slowly, the suspended image as large as half the desk, showing the young Queen at her coronation. Mara tapped the silvery page to isolate the Queen from the background and increase the detail. Her dark eyes were nearly a solid, glittering black. Long, ebony hair wound in a tall, woven design on top of her head. And though glossy and red, the Queen's mouth was thin. Her nose was also thin and long for her face.

In the years since Vanora had taken the throne, the brutality of the war experiments had intensified. Without the considerable efforts of Jameson's group, casualties would have increased significantly as well. Mara took in the proud tilt of the Queen's chin, her glowing golden-brown skin, and the intricately embroidered bronze dress. *This is the face of my enemy.*

In Elias's settlement, the wealthiest of the merchant families had three daughters. The oldest had some of the same cold beauty as the Queen. She was proud, spoiled, and known to purposefully ride her horse toward and sometimes over other children. Both Elias and his wife had given strict instructions to stay away from the entire family. When Mara protested, asked why the girl would behave in such a way, Elias's wife would say, "Because she can, child, and no one taught her it was wrong."

Footsteps at the classroom entrance caused Mara to look up and hastily eliminate the image.

"Mara, your first classmate is here," Elana said. "This is Apurna." Her aunt ushered forward a girl about Mara's age carrying an armload of books.

Mara stood to help but when her eyes met the other girl's, she hesitated. With her petite build, warm bronze skin, and long dark hair, the female student looked very much like the Queen. Then Apurna smiled and the resemblance disappeared as her eyes crinkled at the corners and a dimple flashed in her cheek.

"Hello. Where to sit?" Apurna asked, her speech giving a musical cadence to the words.

"Anywhere you like," Elana said. "Class will start in half an hour or once everyone is here." She headed back out the door as Apurna dumped her things on the nearest desk.

"This world uses more paper than come before my eyes," the girl said, rubbing her arms. Mara wasn't sure how to respond, but Apurna continued talking. "Books, good for learning"—she searched for words—"but heavy."

Mara nodded sympathetically. She put her right palm flat against her chest. "I'm Mara."

"Apurna," said the other young woman, mirroring the gesture. They both smiled awkwardly. "What planet you're from?"

"Kels," said Mara.

Apurna looked puzzled. "Kels is English Origin, yes?"

Mara nodded, "Yes."

"Why in class, you?" asked Apurna.

Today would be a major test of her false autobiography. She'd been studying Kels and getting details from Jameson to prepare.

"I grew up in horse country, far from the main cities," Mara said. "The people my family worked for had a little school on the estate. But my father needed me to work, so I didn't go to the school very often." Mara's cheeks heated as she spoke the true part of her tale. "Even though I speak it, I never learned to read or write in Origin English. I have an uncle who lives here in Satri. He's married to Elana, our teacher." She gestured toward the classroom door, conscious of Apurna's intense gaze. "My parents sent me to live with them just a few weeks ago. I've been a part of the militia, but everyone says I'll get better work, maybe get promoted, if I can read and write." She shrugged, trying to breathe evenly and keep her mental shields smooth.

Apurna's dimple deepened as she smiled. "Good luck, uncle married to teacher."

"Yes," Mara agreed. "Good luck." She craned her neck for a moment, thinking she heard voices in the hall.

The new student's books thumped as she put everything but her reading binder under the desk.

"Sounds like you ladies are settling in," said Elana, leading in a group of adults. "We're waiting for two more," she added. "And then we will begin."

The group of newcomers contained four men and one woman. Trying not to stare, Mara paged through her binder. While the newcomers dropped their books and moved the chairs, they spoke softly to each other in a language she'd never heard. All but one of the formally dressed men had heavy beards, thick mats of hair puffing out more than three centimeters from cheeks and chins. The woman wore a flowing tunic and pants made from an iridescent orange fabric with a coordinating scarf loosely wrapped around her head and neck, while the men wore untucked shirts and trousers. Though all five had dark hair, their skin tones ranged from light to deeply tanned.

Just as the five finally settled into their seats and their conversation died down, Elana entered with an older woman and a young man in his late teens. As the two were getting seated, she focused on the group murmuring among themselves and spoke quietly in the same language they were speaking. The five nodded, though one man scowled when she looked away.

Sitting in the desk at the top of the semicircle, she said, "I asked that while in this building and especially in this classroom, all students focus on speaking Origin English." Elana scanned the nine faces. "My goal is to help you learn not only to speak Origin English, but to think in it as well. Many of you speak two or more languages already." Several people nodded. "You can confirm for the rest of us that thinking in a new language, instead of translating in your head, is the best way to become smooth in your speech and, eventually, fluent." More heads nodded.

"Most of our activities will be in pairs or groups to insure everyone has plenty of opportunities to speak." She stood and began pairing people off. When she came to Mara, she said, "Ladies, may Elsebet join you?" She gestured toward the older woman.

"Of course," said Apurna. She circled her right hand, palm open, and then pressed it flat to her chest and gave a small bow. "Welcome."

Elsebet brought her hands together in front of her chest, pressed them together, and returned the bow, then bowed to Mara, who nodded her head and bowed back. The newcomer shifted her chair slightly to face them and settled into her seat, giving Mara a moment to admire the woman's elegant lavender trousers and long jacket. Elsebet had rings on every finger and large sparkling hoops in each ear. Her silver and black hair was gathered back from her dark, angular face in dozens of braids joined by a silver hair tie into one long ponytail.

"Please introduce yourselves to your partners," Elana said. "Be sure to include your name, the planet you're from, and your work specialty. If it was not work which brought you to Asattha, please share the reason."

Apurna smiled and introduced herself as Apurna Parasarathy. "I'm from the Crown world, Laska, and I speak Origin Hindi and Origin Arabic, some dialects also. I'm here to study the Tree, dendrology. I come here to do cross-comparisons with what may or may not be new species of Tree on my planet."

Mara and Elsebet both nodded. Impressed, Mara asked, "How long have you been a dendrologist?"

"Three years," Apurna said.

Elsebet gestured for Mara to go next, so she took a breath and repeated the story she had told Apurna.

"Just Mara? Your name?" Elsebet asked, her voice low and resonant. "Family name?"

"It's the Jameson clan," Elana said as she paused to observe their trio.

"Jameson," Mara said. "I'm part of the Jameson clan."

"Clan name," the older woman nodded. She sat up and folded her hands together, looking first at Apurna and then at Mara. "My name is Dr. Elsebet Iskindar and my specialty is war." Mara's eyes darted to Elsebet's hands. She hadn't noticed many scars or sword calluses. "I speak Origin Arabic also." She nodded to Apurna. "But I, to study oldest records, I learn oldest languages like Swahili and Urdu and Farsi. Also Aramaic and Greek."

"What planet?" asked Apurna.

"Iloel is my home, but I study on every planet in the Commonwealth except Asattha. War history from the Origin, it come from different places and times, hm, different cultural views, yes? At last, I come here."

Their teacher stood, signaling for attention. "Asattha and its culture are also a part of this class." Her eyes scanned the group and a slight smile hovered around her mouth. "As the farthest planet from the Crown world, Asattha was the last of our Commonwealth to be settled. We have the smallest and least dense population among the seven planets.

"The first scientists and settlers here felt very free, especially so far from any true royal control. Early on, it became clear normal communication tech and transport tech wouldn't work on this planet. And that, in many ways, cut Asattha off from the capital far more effectively than distance. Out of an emerging sense of freedom, and certainly due in large part to the original hundred fifty people who settled here, Asatthans created a new naming tradition."

The students, including Mara, were staring with a range of puzzled expressions. "Some of you carry names from your mother's family, father's family, or spouse's family. Some carry clan, tribe, or region-based names. But how many of you chose your own names?"

Understanding dawned on both of her partners' faces, but Mara still felt confused.

"A cultural as well as legal part of Asatthan life, particularly here in the capital, is that individuals may choose their own names. Or may choose a translation of their name which reflects its meaning more closely than a transliterated or literal translation. As you work alongside those scientists and experts who are native to Asattha or have permanently relocated to this planet, keep this in mind," she concluded.

With an assessing look, she said, "Take a moment and write your names for me, first in your native tongue. Next to that, write your full name in Origin English."

Noise erupted as the nine students reached under their desks for paper and pencils. Mara hastily scrawled *MARA* on her paper, hesitated, and attempted her uncle's clan name, *JAMSON*.

"Good," said Elana. She scanned the students' faces again. "How many of you know the story of the farmer and the Tree?" Most of the class nodded or raised a hand. "Well, the farmer had a sister who was much more interested in the forests around Satri than in the plans or places to cultivate crops. She was not a farmer." Elana smiled.

"The story goes that after living among the trees for several years, she declared her name, going forward would be de Forest or *of the forest*. Have any of you encountered the leader of our council, Yadira de Forest?"

Mara's mouth opened, but her aunt sent, *"Wait."*

A bearded man raised his hand. "In main lab is marriage partner of leader. Not de Forest, how he calls himself."

"Where you come from, families all have the same name?" Elana asked.

He nodded. "Yes, it is so."

"How big is a family?"

The man blew out his breath and rubbed his beard with his right hand. He made an expansive gesture with his left arm. "Four times ten to five times ten individuals."

Mara watched her classmates to see if they were as surprised as she. Elsebet and the boy who came with her both looked relaxed and a bit bored with the exchange. Apurna and the others looked interested.

"Each individual born into subsequent generations of the de Forest family eventually decided whether she or he shared the connection to the trees. In this current generation, the leader's husband comes from a Chinese Origin planet. Though he is one of the head scientists studying the Great Tree, he has not chosen to change his name as would be acceptable under Asatthan law and tradition."

"But what about their children?" Mara blurted.

Her aunt looked down and cleared her throat. "One child carries the leader's family name, de Forest, and the other carries the father's family name, Tek. It is a choice all children here have at age fifteen. Some also take or create entirely new names."

The boy who came with Elsebet grinned. Apurna and the other female scientist both wore thoughtful expressions.

In the Protector compound, each soldier had only one name. Sometimes people used family names in the settlements, but it wasn't consistent. Mara shifted in her chair, mulling it over.

Elana surveyed the group. "Two tasks right now. First, decide what your new name might be if you were to adopt Asatthan cultural norms. Second, turn to lesson twelve in your binders. The text reviews what I just told you about naming conventions. Read through it and note your questions. We will come back together as a whole group in fifteen minutes."

The remainder of class followed a similar pattern. Elana would ask them to talk about an idea in Origin English. Then she would touch on the connection to local history or culture. Most of the time, the key concepts of the topic were in the class binder. The class flowed so smoothly Mara was startled when her aunt ended the afternoon session. Her mind was still buzzing with new information as she bowed and said good-bye to Apurna and Elsebet.

In the entry hall, cloudy light coming through the windows made the hour seem later than it was. When the door closed behind the group of five, Elana sighed and went to her office. She motioned for her niece to sit in the chair opposite the desk.

"Impressions?" asked Elana.

"You're a good teacher," Mara said.

Her aunt snorted, but her lips curved in a pleased smile. "No, not about me. Though I thank you for the compliment. I meant impressions about your classmates."

With Mara's mind still working on the new information from class, it was hard to shift focus to the other students. "They must all be very intelligent to have jobs and specialties, to know other languages and now be learning Origin English."

"You get the impression your classmates are smart?"

Mara leaned back in the chair and looked at the ceiling. "Everyone seemed able to learn quickly. You didn't have to slow down or repeat much. Apurna is from the Crown world, so I think she knows more about the Queen. Elsebet is fierce." She grinned as she pictured the woman's dark face, braided hair, and tawny eyes. Elsebet was big, too. When she stood to leave, they were eye to eye. "Did you hear her say her specialty is war? I bet she knows about the Protector Proj—"

Elana held up a hand to stop the words. "Elsebet Iskindar is the most prominent person in your class."

Raising her eyebrows, Mara asked, "In what way?"

"She is one of the Commonwealth's foremost experts on the Origin wars."

"Wars about the Origin or wars on the Origin?"

"Both, I suppose," her aunt answered with a frown. "Dalin has read all her books. You'll have to ask him." She sighed and dropped the pencil she'd been toying with. "Her presence here is significant. It's no secret Dr. Iskindar was part of the royal inner circle for at least a decade."

"Who's the boy traveling with her?" Mara asked.

"Papers say her nephew, but I'm thinking bodyguard. He's almost exactly your age, by the way."

"I don't think Elsebet needs a bodyguard. And..." Mara paused and brought an image of the tall, strong woman to her mind's eye. "And I think she was armed."

Elana grimaced and jotted a note. "Anything else?"

"I'm relieved no one challenged my story about being from Kels."

#

At dinner that night, Elana related the details of her new students to her husband. He continued eating as he listened intently to her summary.

"Nothin's come in from the labs so far that would raise suspicion, but they're all uneasy, and that means somethin' to me." He nodded at his niece. "This Elsebet Iskindar, my first source says she's on the outs with Vanora. A few more sources are working to verify that. She mention the Queen?"

"Our teacher only lets us talk about certain topics," she said, trying to make a joke.

Elana threw her a mock glare. "Your teacher has a curriculum to follow."

"I noticed the royal family is mentioned in our materials later on. Don't they all know about the Queen and the history of the Commonwealth already? Why is that a part of the class?" Mara asked.

"Two reasons," said Elana. "One, it's required by the Commonwealth. Two, the purpose of the material in your binder is to have conversation topics and highlight key vocabulary in Origin English. The only new content is what everyone is learning about Satri and Asattha."

With a stern look at his niece, Jameson said, "You think Dr. Iskindar was carrying a weapon in class today?"

Mara automatically drew herself up in the chair. Her uncle hadn't used the tone of a commanding officer in a while. "Elsebet is tall and fit-looking. So she is already a weapon in the sense of appearing ready to fight. But the way she held her arms slightly bent, her hands open and loose, it made me think she had something strapped to her forearm or possibly inside her tunic. She looked like we're trained to look."

Jameson stared hard for a moment longer. "I know what y'mean. I'll pass along an inquiry into Dr. Iskindar's training and weapons of choice to the people already working on her situation with the Queen." He turned to his wife. "Anythin' you need delivered to school tomorrow, my dear? I'd like to see this famous warrior author for myself."

Chapter 31

Dalin and Mara took their horses for a run the next morning. She wanted to practice shielding herself and her horse as Dalin had done when they fled across the open plain so many weeks ago.

He led them north through the city and then out east along a coastal plateau. The rising sun cast dazzling red-orange rays across the rocks and churning water. Squinting toward the horizon, she caught a flash of something.

"What's that?"

"Still shielding?"

"Yes," she said, irritated. "Is the land moving?"

A low rumble began vibrating through the earth beneath Rowan's hooves. She leaned over the mare's neck, patting and reassuring her. Looking up, she gasped, watching an impossibly huge shape emerge from behind a ridge.

"Starship," Dalin said. "The really big ones break the planet's atmosphere southeast of the city."

It was nearly impossible to comprehend the enormous metal shape—three times, four times, maybe five times as large as Market Square—rapidly approaching. The rumble and the wind intensified for a full minute as the starship passed directly overhead. Though her horse danced and flattened her ears, Dalin's mount was steady as always.

"The people in my class came to Satri in one of those?" she breathed.

"Yes, you did, too, remember?" Dalin sounded like he was talking to a child.

Mara kept her face turned away, one shoulder hitching up to ward off his condescending stare. It was a starship, built to travel between planets, and humans had made it. She had every right to be amazed.

"Speaking of your class," he said, tugging on the saddle horn to get Mara's attention. "I heard you're working with Elsebet Iskindar?"

Dropping her shields, she exhaled with a sigh, still staring toward Satri, where the starship had gone. "Are they all like that?"

"No, that one is probably for a large order of trade goods or military personnel. Starships can be much smaller." It was useful and interesting information to have, even delivered in that brusque, impatient tone.

Mara jumped from the saddle and poured water into a temporary trough for her horse. Rubbing her hands against the morning chill, she thought about traveling from one planet to the next.

"What's she like? Dr. Iskindar?" Dalin prompted as he too dismounted and put out water for his horse.

"Elsebet?" She absently stroked the mare's flank, wanting to ask a dozen questions about starships of anyone but Dalin. "She's my height, very dark skin, and braided black hair with a little silver at each temple. She moves like she can handle herself in a fight." Mara smiled. "I heard you've read all her books."

"Well, the three that are in wide circulation I've read, as well as all of her published articles. But her first two books are almost impossible to find—" He broke off and narrowed his eyes. "What?"

"If you drop by school to meet her, maybe you'll be able to determine what weapon she's carrying. And then the two of you can have a long chat about Admiral Nelson. Perhaps she admires him as much as you do."

He looked down, cheeks flushed a slight pink. "Hey, I wrote that paper when I was fourteen."

"Oh, I know. Elana told me she helped you with it." Mara laughed. "I now also admire Lord Nelson. Those Britains were lucky to have him in command."

"British, yes," he said, a strange expression on his face. "Did she give you any of my other academic work?"

"Not yet." She grinned as she collapsed the clear plastic water trough and stowed it away. He'd been so serious and remote lately, it was fun having something small to tease him about. "Jameson's going to pretend to deliver a large package to school this afternoon. Maybe you should come, too. Maybe Elsebet will want you for a bodyguard instead of her current companion." And then they could be smart together every minute of every day.

His face tightened, gray eyes flinty as he stowed his horse's trough and checked the straps. "Are you in danger?"

She bit back a scornful response, forcing herself to stop and think. "It's not a battlefield; it's a school. So while I don't think I'm in danger, the truth is I don't know that for certain. Especially after only one day. But I'm armed," she added.

As they both mounted up, Dalin said, "Don't worry about shielding on the way back. You're fighting Jin this morning at his house, I mean, my parents' house."

"Fight your dad? Really?" Her expression lit with interest and delight. Jin had grown up training in an entirely different fighting system on his native planet, but all his lessons thus far had been about mental rapport, control, and shielding.

"Gruffald thinks you're making good progress in hand-to-hand. What Jin can teach you, in terms of fluidity and speed, will provide you additional...options in a close fight."

Mara dismissed the image of the giant starship and concerns about her classmates in the face of this excellent news. "I'm learning so much," she said. "I knew I could. I felt possibilities in the compound library, in the map room. But here"—she flung her arms wide—"I learn hundreds of things every day. Thank you." Leaning over, she laid her hand on one of his. No matter how things were between them now, Dalin was responsible for bringing her to Satri and reuniting her with her aunt.

Through Dalin's skin she could feel his heartbeat, his sore elbow from an incorrect fall, and his feelings in that moment, sharing her happiness and—

Mara gasped and yanked her hand away as though burned. For a split second longer she stared, her own heart pounding. Wheeling her horse around, she urged the mare into an all-out run.

Horse and rider raced toward the city, sun at their backs. Mara only slowed when the first houses appeared, and she realized she didn't know the way to Yadira and Jin's home.

"Dalin?" she called.

Though he didn't answer, she could sense him nearby. How was that possible? Jumping from her horse's back, she looked around, out of breath and feeling foolish.

The homes in this area were small and not in good repair. For Satri. They were fine by settlement standards. The air split in a sudden roar, followed by a loud rumble. Rowan skittered sideways, but Mara managed to keep a calm hand on the bridle.

"The spaceport," Dalin said, riding out from the trees. *"Most of the people who live on this side of Satri work at the spaceport."* He

dismounted when his horse was standing next to them once again. "What frightened you?"

Opening her mouth to automatically deny fear, she stumbled mentally, thoughts breaking rank and scattering. "When I touched your hand," she began, "I could sense you, inside your skin. I could...I could feel your hurt elbow as though it were my own, your pulse, your—"

"So, rather than shield yourself from the excess information, you ran?" he asked with a half smile.

"Oh." She shook her head, embarrassed. "I didn't think...we'd just dropped shields from the external practice..." What she'd seen had been too overwhelming to trigger a logical response.

"Only a few of us can do what you did just now," Dalin said. "Don't worry," he hastened to add. "The skin contact only works if a prior connection has been established. I mean, occasionally I get an impression through a handshake, but nothing specific." Another loud rumble disturbed the little neighborhood. "Let's go," he said. "Jin is probably waiting."

Mara hesitated. "Will it...will I connect like that when I'm fighting Jin? Because I know him?"

"No, Jin is always shielded. May only work with me anyway." Dalin shrugged. "We can test it later."

"No." She bit her lower lip, heart still racing.

Dalin leaned closer, his expression that of a concerned partner. She held her breath, helpless to do anything but stare back. Though he was close to perfect on the outside, she'd seen the roiling mix of darkness and light churning through his thoughts and feelings.

Without another word, he broke the connection and mounted his horse, leading them through a series of back streets. As they rode, the houses and the land around each house gradually increased in size. They cut away from a wide street onto a riding path, and a few minutes later, turned onto a small circular drive.

A groom emerged to take their horses. As she dismounted, Mara studied the graceful white building at the top of the drive. "Is this where you grew up?" she asked.

Dalin exchanged a grin with the groom, an older man with a close-cropped gray beard. "In a sense, yes," he replied. "Calvin here certainly had a hand in my upbringing. Calvin, please meet Mara."

"Hello," the groom said with a slight nod. He reached for Rowan's reins.

"Hello," she replied, soothed as a horse might be by the groom's calm demeanor, despite the changes in Dalin's behavior.

Gently turning her away from the white building, Dalin pointed across the expansive manicured lawn. "My parents' house is over there," he explained. "This is the stable."

At first all she saw was rolling lawn, artfully grouped stands of trees, and a small structure with open sides and a curved roof. A few steps forward and the roofline of a massive house appeared, nestled just below the rise. The structure was easily five or six times larger than Elana and Jameson's house.

"The de Forests were one of the founding families of Satri. They bought this land and built the original house. Each generation added on more rooms..."

His voice was uncharacteristically nervous-sounding as they crossed the lawn, but she was busy admiring the dozens of sparkling windows and the wide, wraparound porch. She tried to picture Dalin, Nuwa, and Elana playing here. Had she herself visited this place as a child?

"My mom and dad didn't want to build another addition. Instead, my dad transformed the level below ground into lab rooms and training space."

Dalin led them along the porch to a single wooden door. He gripped the knob and waited. After a fraction of a second, the lock clicked. "Codes are too easy to hack," he said. "My dad engineered our doors and windows to read energy signatures."

"You don't have that at your house," Mara said.

"Not yet."

Crossing the threshold into the de Forest house, she felt a prick of unease. "Do a lot of people live here?" she asked in a low voice. Though the back hall and every visible space were spotlessly gleaming and fresh-scented, the house felt empty.

"No one else lives here except my parents now. But my mother often hosts important guests, diplomats and those sorts of people. The staff may all be working in the visitors' wing."

Something in his tone caused Mara to turn. "What is it?"

Dalin leaned his shoulder against the wall, mouth turned down, eyes flat. "I don't invite a lot of people here," he said. "It, this place, can be overwhelming." Exhaling heavily, he shoved his hands into his pockets.

She nodded, not sure why he wasn't proud to have such a large, beautiful home.

"Let me show you my favorite part. Jin is probably waiting for us in the arboretum anyway."

Mara wanted to look around, but the brisk pace and circuitous route through a series of small hallways left her little choice but to follow.

In a few minutes, they emerged into a vast space with a high, glass ceiling. Lips parting in a soft *oh* of wonder, she gaped at the groves of trees, mostly *gontra* trees, growing indoors. Dalin steadied her arm as she stepped down from the hallway onto a gravel path.

The damp air in the arboretum was filled with the spicy scent of *gontras*. Mara could hear the sound of running water and moved toward it, curious about the source. Following the pretty, meandering path behind her host, she instinctively knew this was a place of refuge for him. When she spoke, her voice was hushed. "How many trees are in here?"

"Used to be around a hundred," Dalin said. "My dad has been collecting species of trees that are compatible with the *gontras* and adding them in. I'm not sure how many now."

"One hundred forty-two." Jin's voice preceded him before he appeared on the next bend of the path. He gave a slight bow. "Welcome, Mara. Son." They both returned the older man's bow.

"This place is wonderful." Mara stepped forward, smiling.

Jin smiled in response and gestured for her to follow. "Come. We can sit and talk a moment before beginning your practice."

"Enjoy," Dalin said.

She turned to thank him, but he'd already vanished into the trees. Shaking her head, she put her hands on her hips and sighed.

"My son is sometimes hasty," Jin said.

Mara nodded, looking at the trees for a moment more. "There's a question I should have asked earlier: Do you...do you shield all the time?"

He didn't answer, walking farther into the arboretum until they reached a paved stone circle near the center of the enormous room. The narrow path wound around a pond with a small waterfall. A weathered stone sculpture of a seated person graced one side of the pond and several stone benches ringed the perimeter of the peaceful space.

The rustling of the leaves and the chattering of the water crashing across the stones created a soothing backdrop of sound as she moved closer to study the carved figure. The stone person's eyes were closed, his legs crossed in a comfortable sitting pose, palms facing up on each knee. Mara wished she could assume the same position and feel the tranquility carved into the sculpture's face. Instead she let the sights, sounds, and smells of the arboretum wash through her senses, reviving a longing for the wild places of the North.

Jin patted a bench next to him, indicating she should sit. "To answer your question, no, I do not shield all the time, at least not in my home."

"I think I'm beginning to understand why you built the wayhouse."

He inclined his head. "You're a daughter of the Tree. Nature is your home as much as any specific place or dwelling."

Having worked with Jin on many occasions, she knew he didn't necessarily expect a reply. The student's job was to think. She listened to the water and took several deep breaths. "Dalin said I'll be working on speed and fluidity today."

"He said that to me as well," Jin agreed.

She took another deep breath. Reaching back, she undid her ponytail and shook it out. Smoothing both hands through her long hair, she recaptured the strands in a tight bunch, securing them with the hair tie. "I'm ready when you are." In her mind she added the *sir* that was expected in the Protector compound and therefore prone to slip out when speaking to adults in Satri.

Suddenly, stiff as a flat blade, Jin's hand snapped toward her neck. She blocked it with her forearm, leaping back to her feet. "What?" she began, but he shifted onto his back foot and kicked toward her knee. Mara shuffled back in a quick motion, shifted to the balls of her feet, and put her hands up, close to her cheekbones, fingers in loose fists.

Jin angled his body sideways to hers, his right hand up, elbow locked against his ribs, left hand out at an angle in a low fist. "Shield."

As her shield formed with her next breath, she felt something else in the energy of the shield, something new. She watched her teacher's hips, hands, and feet, but she was distracted by the change in the feel of her shield. Jin sprang forward and threw a back fist at her nose. Mara parried the strike and aimed a scoop kick at his shin. Power flowed through her leg with a strength she didn't recognize. Pulling the kick at the last minute, she let Jin dance away. For the first time, she feared harming her teacher.

Jin leapt onto one of the stone benches. Mara followed onto the adjacent bench, narrowly avoiding a roundhouse kick to her face.

"You don't always get to choose your ground," he said. He spun in place and whipped a spinning kick toward her ribs. She knew the counter but couldn't get close enough without risking her balance.

Mara's mind worked furiously on a strategy for the small area. What weapons were available? Water? Sticks? She feinted toward Jin's ear with a hook punch and then slammed a cross punch toward his solar plexus. Again the force behind the move felt powerful, far beyond her natural strength. She managed to soften the punch to a hard tap and then called, "Hold!"

Jin froze. "What is it?"

"When I pulled the energy to source my shield something else came too. I'm afraid I'm going to hurt you." And yet, it was hard to stop. She felt incredibly powerful and energized, ready to take on a whole battlefield.

Jin, ever the scientist, asked, "Can you test it? Hit something." He lowered his hands and jumped from the bench, landing gracefully.

"I don't want to break anything." She looked around.

"Nonsense." He dragged one of the heavy benches to the center of the semicircle. "Try an axe kick."

With misgiving, Mara centered her stance in front of the bench, weight on her left foot.

"Shield."

The energy came with a light tug, but in addition to encasing her, it ran through her, as fast and as powerful as a river current.

Jin barked a command in a language she didn't recognize. Nonetheless the meaning was a clear: "Go!"

Jumping off her left foot, she swung her right leg in a high arc and drove her right heel down through the bench, breaking it into two pieces. She felt the impact with her heel, but the discomfort was not worse than kicking a practice board or pad. Stone. No one broke stone with a kick. She pushed the shield away, mouth dry with fear.

The older man examined the bench. "Have you been shielding in practice every day?" he asked.

"No. A shield changes the nature of the hand-to-hand and stick practice. Have to take the hits to learn." The older man's calm acceptance helped, but she couldn't take her eyes from the broken seat.

He nodded once. "How does Zam handle this challenge?"

"In the training room, we don't shield. In the outdoor practice ring, we wear full uniforms, including helmets, and use both real weapons and shields."

"Battle simulation?" he asked.

"Early winter and late spring we do cohort competitions." Mara couldn't suppress a small grin. "Everyone fights." Her grin faded. "I could hurt my friends now," she murmured.

"You could have hurt them before," Jin reminded her, his voice less patient. "This gift"—he gestured at the bench—"is new strength to learn to balance and control, just as you did with each emerging skill during Protector training."

Mara swallowed and nodded. She felt alien and freshly isolated, as though the weeks of time with her family and Dalin's family had not happened, as though she were alone again, too different to fit in anywhere.

"We can follow Zam's protocol and spar without shields. Inside we have plenty of pads and gloves."

Feeling miserable, she bowed in acknowledgment, trying to swallow past the lump in her throat.

"Dalin has some of the same power," Jin said quietly. "Has he told you that?"

When she finally looked at him, his face was grave, no hint of humor in his dark eyes. "No," she said. "He won't fight me, doesn't say why."

Jin narrowed his eyes, coming to a decision. "Follow me to the training room. I have a great deal to teach you."

Chapter 32

When her afternoon class was dismissed, Mara kissed her aunt on the cheek and headed for the house. She kept vigilant as she walked and forced her mind to stay focused on the present. The door code took a few tries, but she finally got it unlocked and hurried up the stairs to her warm, quiet room.

When she spoke the word to light her yellow and white candle stubs, Mara felt the deep reservoir of power connected to her energy manipulation abilities, the same place from which she drew her shields. Rather than sit in the straight-backed meditation posture taught by Zam, she curled up in a ball on the floor. Closing her eyes, she let herself sink into the soft rug.

The revelations of the morning were foremost in her mind. Thoughts of Dalin, as always, wound through it all.

At first, Mara tried to put her new strength in the same category as her other abilities. "I am a good fighter," she told herself. "I am learning to be a leader. I protect my people." The list didn't work. Instead it reminded her of why she already felt separate from her cohort mates. For years she'd pretended that her sense of difference stemmed from being an orphan, a tax child.

Today, in her family's home, she admitted the differences were greater, ran far deeper than that. She'd fogged a group of Brown soldiers and she could break stone as easily as wood. Only Dalin, maybe, understood what it felt like. And he... Mara wasn't sure how to articulate the distance Dalin was keeping. He just wasn't acting like a partner, if he ever had. The realization named the sadness she was feeling and with it came tears.

#

When Mara opened her eyes much later, the first thing she saw was a slender foot covered with dark, lacy loops and swirling lines. Quickly, she rolled to her knees and stood. The Tree remained sitting in the window seat. She smiled, the blackness of her eyes more pronounced in the candlelight.

"Hello, Daughter."

Mara bobbed her head, heart racing. "Hello."

The Tree flicked long, dark curls over one shoulder, her expression concerned. "You are afraid?"

Beginning to shake her head in denial, Mara stopped. "Yes."

"Do you know how plants grow, child? You had seen roots before I showed you mine?" The Tree's gaze was steady. She didn't blink.

"Yes," Mara said.

"The power you touched today is the result of a well-grown root system. The roots of your ancestors are so deep that you can touch the Light connecting us all and draw from it to nourish yourself and protect others. I felt your touch and came to share my joy."

Mara took a step backward and sat heavily on her bed. She tried to think of what she needed to know, but just like their first conversation, she felt slightly fogged in the Tree's presence. "Have you ever hurt…caused harm with your power? Even though it is otherwise, ah, joyful?"

The Tree tipped her head to one side and drummed the fingers of her right hand on her knee. The movement called attention to the script-like designs tracing her wrist, hand, and fingers. "Yes," the Tree said at last.

Mara let out a shaky breath. "I'm afraid I will cause harm. I always wanted to be strong, but…" Unbidden, the dream image of the Protector kicking down the door of her parents' house rose in her mind's eye.

"Daughter." The Tree's voice was a soft whisper of leaves. "Do you wield your strength, your power, to help others?"

She looked into the Tree's strange and beautiful face. "I try to, yes."

"Is there any other reason to draw on your deep strength?" Her bottomless dark eyes narrowed.

"To protect," Mara said, thinking of Dalin and the Brown soldiers outside of Satri.

The Tree nodded in satisfaction. "Yes, your branches will be strong and you will shelter many."

Thinking this must be a compliment, she said, "Thank you. And you as well."

Mouth curving in a warm, approving smile, the Tree sat up straighter on the window seat. "Listen carefully. My sisters are at risk on the other planets."

Mara was too weary, too raw, to hide her surprise.

"Perhaps another time I can explain further. Suffice to say, Asattha feeds and supports me. I have all I need here and more. The scientists are good stewards and ask for so little in return.

"But my sisters, some of their planets have dirty air, foul water; the soil grows ever more tainted. And the humans who could provide care are taken up with deadly fighting amongst themselves."

Staring openly, Mara just managed to keep her mouth from dropping open. "How do you...?" She was just learning of the other planets and this Tree, this being, was somehow both aware and communicating with her Sister Trees across the Commonwealth?

"It's the Light, little sapling," the Tree said. "We connect through the Light."

The impression of bright, warm sunlight filled her mind, as it had during her journey into the consciousness of the Tree. For a brief instant, a sense of wonder chased away her questions and worries.

"I am young," the Tree said quietly. "On Asattha, I will live a long, fruitful life, as my Mother Tree did. I want the same for my sisters."

"Does Jin know about your sisters? May I speak to him about your concerns?"

"Yes, in a way," the Tree replied. "But he is not the one to solve this problem." The Tree stood and stretched, graceful and balanced as a swordmaster. "Jin Tek is a wise caretaker."

She took a few steps closer, reached out a delicate hand, and squeezed Mara's shoulder. With the contact came the image of the stone wall in the park. "You must take down this wall." Nodding to the untouched box full of things from Mara's childhood, she added, "Have courage, my daughter. The Light will guide you." And then she was gone.

#

Eventually, her aunt knocked on the door and peered in. "Mara? You all right?"

"Yes," she said. It was essentially true.

Elana sat next to her on the floor, facing the candles also. With a sideways look, she asked, "Were you crying?"

Mara gazed at the two small flames. "It's just, today was a hard day. I miss Annelise."

"Want to tell me about it?"

She wasn't sure. When she glimpsed her aunt's now-familiar profile, Elana was watching the candles, her face composed.

"This morning I saw a starship," Mara began. She poured out her hurt feelings and her worries while Elana listened, occasionally asking questions.

It was a relief to talk, partly because she'd been trained not to carry concerns alone and partly because her aunt was an excellent listener. But she hesitated when she got to the part about being in her room. The Tree had only given consent for her to talk with Jin about the Light and her sisters.

"Is that why you were crying?" Elana asked. "Your new strength?"

Having shared so much, Mara felt lighter, more like herself. "No, I cried because Dalin is the one other person who has…who might understand. At first he helped me. We talked about a lot of things. But the past few weeks he's been"—she reached for the right word—"more like a guide or a supervisor at best."

Elana's brows shot up. "Dalin made you cry?"

With a tiny grimace, she said, "No, he didn't make me cry. He is…usually courteous."

Frowning, Elana motioned for her niece to continue.

Mara struggled to find the words. "When I first met Dalin, he smiled a lot and he teased me. He seemed relaxed around me. But lately, he's removed himself. He keeps our routines but he doesn't talk to me." She tapped her temple. "Not much anyway."

"What would you say to Dalin if he were here?"

Hunching her shoulders, she sighed. "I'm not sure. Maybe he just wants me to be someone else's responsibility. Sometimes pairs don't work, especially when the partnership isn't balanced, and the senior Protectors have to reassign them. Maybe Dalin wants to be reassigned." The pain of speaking such a deep worry out loud cut across Mara's heart and her eyes stung. She'd never cared about a boy, never had feelings like that until now.

"You come from circumstances with very little free choice," Elana said carefully. "It must be strange to watch us in Satri and wonder if a person feels compelled to do something or is choosing it."

Mara agreed with the way Elana rephrased her thoughts. As far as she could tell, Dalin only spent time with her now because he was obligated to do so. And the obligation clearly bothered him. "You do have so much, so many choices, I mean."

Her aunt reached out and put one arm around Mara's shoulders. "I don't know about fighting pairs. But I do know about friends. Dalin is downstairs right now, talking to Jameson. I think he's truly here because he's concerned about you. Do you want me to send him up?"

Mara took a deep breath. She felt vulnerable and weak, like she might cry again. It would make the imbalance worse if she spoke to Dalin with her emotions on the outside, instead of on the inside where they belonged.

"No, but thank you. Is he staying for dinner? I think if I eat something I would feel much better."

Elana gave her a bemused look.

"What?" Mara said.

"I had forgotten what it was like at your age."

"And now you remember?"

"I do." Sighing, she stood and turned toward the door. "I'll tell them you'll be down in a few minutes."

#

Dinner was simple and delicious, as always. Jameson kept them laughing with stories about his brothers. When it was time to clear the table, Jameson stood and reached for Elana's hand.

"My dear," he said, "would ya do me the great honor of accompanyin' me to the *dulcería* on the square?"

Elana blushed as she took her husband's hand. "It would be my pleasure, kind sir," she said and dropped a curtsey.

"You youngsters won't mind clearin' away the dishes?"

"No, of course not," Mara replied, standing and pushing in her chair.

Jameson whisked Elana into her coat and out the door in a matter of moments, leaving the pair alone in the kitchen.

Mara avoided Dalin's eyes and started cleaning. They worked side by side in silence. All too soon the dishes were done, counters and table spotless. Mara put her palms on the counter facing into the next room and leaned forward. She racked her brain for a polite way to dismiss him, so he would just leave without making anything worse.

"*Mara.*" Dalin's voice in her mind. At the same time, his hands landed lightly on her shoulders and began to rub away the sore spots. "*I've done that workout with Jin and I know it hurts.*"

She stood frozen with relief and then sagged against the counter as his long fingers found knots around her shoulder blades and in the center of her back. "*I've missed talking with you,*" she admitted.

"*What do you mean?*" he asked. "*We talk all the time.*" His hands stilled for a moment and then resumed their work.

"*Like this,*" Mara sent on a sigh. "*You haven't talked with me in rapport for more than three weeks. At least for longer than a minute or two.*"

Dalin ran one hand down the length of her spine and then pulled her back into his chest, wrapping his arms around her shoulders. His breath tickled her ear as he also sighed. "*I apologize,*" he said. "*I've been distracted.*"

Even through clothes the amount of physical contact was overwhelming. Before she lost her resolve, Mara pulled away and turned to face him. "Do you want to be reassigned?" As soon as the words were out, her breath caught in her throat.

The intensity of his gaze sharpened, the way it did before he made a particularly difficult knife throw. "No," he said. "Not exactly." He cupped her cheek with one callused hand, bent down, and kissed her.

Mara knew lips were sensitive, bruised easily, but the soft brush of his mouth lit up her nerves in a completely new way. Heat coursed through her face, down her arms and legs. The entire kitchen went soft and out of focus; she could only hear Dalin's breathing, only feel his body. He raised his head and she leaned into his shoulder, inhaling the clean scent of trees.

Against his shirt, she murmured, "You don't want to be reassigned—you want to kiss me?"

He leaned down again, this time deepening the kiss and weaving one hand into her hair. *"Wanted to kiss you since the first night on the battlefield."*

Mara felt his fierce joy through the touch. And though surprised, her joy matched his. Never in her life had she felt such a powerful sense of rightness. She wound her arms around his neck and pulled him closer.

When they separated, both were breathing raggedly. "Soldiers who kiss each other get reassigned," she managed to say.

"Not in Satri," Dalin said, his grin resurfacing.

She leaned back against the counter, enjoying, for once, the feeling of being fogged. "How do you know?"

"We've had couples in our station. It wasn't an issue because missions weren't impacted." Dalin lifted his arm and twirled her under it. "The Winter Festival starts tomorrow," he said. "May I escort you?"

"Is an escort required?"

He twirled her again, then pulled her against him for a slow, swaying move. "No," he said. "No escort required. It's just tradition. And you're supposed to reserve most of the dances for the one you're escorting or the one being your escort. I think." His voice trailed off into a mumble and he cleared his throat. "I've never asked to escort someone before, so I don't know for certain."

"As long as you're talking to me again, I would be happy to go to the festival with you."

Dalin's smile faltered. "I…" He dropped his gaze to her lips. "I was also distracted by the information coming through our network." He tugged Mara's hand. "Walk with me? Jameson has the house system rigged for interference, but I need the fresh air."

In a few moments, they both had added the necessary coats, hats, and gloves. Dalin led her onto the path that ran along the south side of Jameson and Elana's house. Fast-moving clouds hid the stars and the night air was sharp, but Mara still felt warm all over, cocooned in the fog of the kiss.

Dalin gazed past her, not really taking in the view of the gulf. "Another reason I haven't been communicating much is because Brown activity is escalating. I didn't want to worry you."

Without conscious thought, she reached toward Dalin's mind with her own.

"Don't," Dalin said, just as her mental touch skimmed his smooth, seamless shields. "Trust me to tell you."

Mara dropped her eyes, stung by the swift change. "I apologize," she said. "It was—"

"—unintentional. I know," Dalin finished her thought. "One of the many reasons why we must continue your training." He continued walking along the gravel path.

That hurt. Just a few moments before, he'd convinced her he didn't want to be reassigned. Now he was putting down her ability. "Only you make me forget my training," she grumbled, matching his long strides.

"It's mutual. I break protocol because of you. Ignore orders more often than not, and here I am doing it again." He grabbed Mara's upper arms and leaned in. "The Browns and at least one other military group know you are in Satri. No one has pinpointed your location, but they're close."

"My aunt and uncle?" Her own welfare mattered far less.

"Are safe for now. Jameson is giving Elana specifics tonight."

"I don't understand. How can the Queen's Soldiers know I'm in Satri and not be able to find me? I'm not hiding."

Dalin ran his palm over his hat as though running it over his hair. Recognizing the gesture as one of deep worry, she felt an icy finger of dread run down her spine.

"You know about the Prophesy of the Tree, right?"

The question took her by surprise. "Not really," Mara admitted. "My book mentions prophesies exist, but not what they say."

Clearly wrestling with his thoughts, Dalin stopped walking and tipped his face to the clouds. "When the Tree first began communicating, confusion was high, both for her and for the people she chose to talk with. Thought speech, or mental rapport, helped. Often the scientists just wrote down what the Tree said and left the analysis for subsequent generations.

"The group that preceded my father's current team made an important discovery using the texts of those early conversations. They became convinced the Tree doesn't experience temporal events as we do. She experiences many possibilities in a simultaneous way, as far as they can tell."

"The Tree," Mara began. "I am always interested in her." A fierce gust of wind buffeted her into a cluster of bare, scrubby bushes. "But I don't see the connection to the Browns. Or to me."

By unspoken consent, they left the gulf path and turned north, walked a few blocks into the neighborhood.

"This briefing is going to take some time and it's too cold out here for that long of a talk. Let's head to my place," Dalin said. "Won't have to worry about surveillance there if we use rapport."

"Forest clearing?"

"Right," he agreed.

#

When they arrived at Dalin's house, he sent a message to Jameson while she shed her outer layers and returned to the common room to look at the paintings of the Tree again.

"I let them know where to find us." He frowned. "Are you warm enough?"

When Mara turned and smiled, his hands fell empty at his sides. For a long moment, he looked at her with only a hint of a smile. "Are you thirsty?" he finally said.

"If you're getting a drink for yourself, otherwise I'm fine."

Clearing his throat, he glanced around the living room. "The best place is probably the couch. For rapport," he added quickly. He sat on the soft, stone-colored cushions and held out his right hand. She took it and sat next to him.

Mara grinned widely as she opened her eyes in the forest clearing. She felt as proud as she had when she'd knocked Gruffald off his feet with a staff.

Dalin grinned back at her. "Well done," he said. "Shall we sit?" He gestured toward a blanket laid across the carpet of leaves and needles. "I don't usually wear my uniform here," he said. "You always wear yours, though. So this is how you see us?"

She dropped to the blanket and shrugged. "Briefing?" she prompted. "The Tree Prophesies? The Browns?"

"Right," Dalin said. He settled himself across from her, too far to touch. "When we were small, sometimes our parents would watch us playing and whisper. About the Tree, I mean."

"She was my friend," Mara said. "Even though the rest of you couldn't see her."

"That was part of it," he agreed. "But in the prophecies, the Tree talks about a champion. A champion who carries the Light... What?" he asked.

"She called me her daughter. So did your dad," Mara said.

A muscle in Dalin's jaw twitched. "In some of the writings, it sounds like the champion fights alone. In most, the champion is half of a pair."

As she frowned, ready to shake her head in denial, Dalin held her gaze. "I've often wondered if the kernel of the idea for the Protector Project, soldiers fighting in pairs, came from the Tree Prophesies."

"So our mothers thought we had something to do with what the Tree said generations ago? A prophesy?" Mara pressed.

Shifting his position, he stretched his legs out in front and leaned back on his hands. "Well, around that time, a series of the Tree's predictions had just come true, specific predictions about the crown skipping a generation and going straight to Vanora," Dalin said. "People in Satri were in the mood to believe. Your parents worked with the Tree—Elana told you that, right? They had access to all the original scribing of the Tree's words."

"I wish I could remember them," Mara said.

"Your parents," he said, "even though I was only three years older than you, they both talked to me like I was an intelligent, thinking person. 'Dalin, you watch over Mara. Keep her safe,' they would say. So then, when you were taken, it was as though I had personally failed." He glanced sideways at her, face full of uncertainty and guilt.

"Why?" she began. "Why haven't you told me this?" Just like the weapons he seemed to produce from thin air, the information that he withheld was sharp and dangerous in the open.

He sat up straight and scrubbed a hand over his face. "For the first several generations, the Tree Prophecies were out for anyone to study. The dominant thinking was, 'Hey, we're a community of scientists and educated people. Let's bend our collective minds to solving our planet's greatest mystery.' But then you were taken and all of that changed."

The breeze had died down, but she felt chilled.

"It was thought that an agent of the new Queen or an independent operative looking to change the course of events was responsible for taking you."

"Because of something the Tree said?" Mara asked.

"The writings contained many descriptions of the champion or pair of champions, details of birth, parentage, skills. Mostly vague, like the ancient prophesies from the Origin, but in some areas, unusually specific."

Dalin shifted again. He couldn't seem to contain the restlessness in his body.

She leaned forward and brushed her fingers along his rough cheek, unable to ignore his distress, offering comfort. "And now?"

Capturing her fingers, he said, "Now it's clear someone with a copy of that text is sending operatives after you again. We thought you would be safe in Satri, away from the fighting, blending with the crowd." He looked down and took a deep breath. "But we were wrong."

She squeezed her eyes closed for a moment, the full impact of his words as dizzying as a punch to the temple. "My family's safety is critical. More important than anything else."

"White-storm season is about to hit a lull between the winter snow and the spring snow. There's a source, a person in one of the northwest settlements who knows more about the Tree Prophesies—"

"I want to go. A longer mission will take me away, help Elana be safe." Mara hugged her knees to her chest and rested her chin on them. The rapport space responded to her emotions, the sun dimming and the birds going entirely quiet.

"I'll find a way to accompany you," Dalin said into the silence.

#

They stayed in the clearing for a long time. Mara occasionally asked a question. Dalin answered.

Much later when he tugged her hand, she opened her eyes, unsurprised to be snuggled on his couch, head on his shoulder. "I fell asleep," she murmured.

Dalin dropped a kiss on the top of her head before standing slowly, releasing her fingers to stretch toward the ceiling. He caught her sleepy gaze and smiled.

"It's late and your aunt and uncle are very likely asleep. I'm going to send a message to their house, confirming you're staying with me."

"Confirming?"

"I said it was a possibility on my first message, depending on how long we talked."

Mara yawned. She felt wrung out, the happiness of kissing Dalin twisting against the fear and frustration of being hunted by the Queen's Soldiers.

As he started toward the stairs, Dalin said, "C'mon, I always keep a room ready for Nuwa. You'll like it."

Chapter 33

Mara found Elana sitting at her kitchen table, staring out the back window at the cold grey morning.

"Jameson says you have to go North again, close to your old compound." Her eyes filled. "It's going to be dangerous." She stood and put her arms around her niece, hugging her hard.

Mara didn't know what to say. It hurt to see her aunt cry. It hurt to think about leaving. Awkwardly, she smoothed her aunt's hair.

"Will you come back?" Elana asked, her voice thin.

"Of course. You are my family." She patted the top of her aunt's arm and helped her sit back down.

Glancing toward the stove, she was reminded of the kiss she shared with Dalin in that exact spot the night before. Her lips tingled and her fingers brushed the note in her pocket that he'd left on her pillow. It was hard not to reach out and call him, send him an image of the kiss.

"I'm going to make us both breakfast and then we'll figure it out."

Mara kept an eye on her aunt, sitting slumped at the table, as she took ingredients from the cold storage unit and readied a pan for scrambled eggs—one of the few things she'd learned how to cook since arriving in Satri.

Growing up in the compound, she'd found it much easier to give comfort for a physical injury. She'd always avoided those suffering from emotional injuries, letting the soldiers with strengths in empathy handle it.

Finally, Elana stood and refilled her cup with hot tea. "I was horrible to Jameson when he told me," she said with remorse. "I told him he shouldn't have made a promise about your safety. I told him it was the same as lying."

"Where is he now?" Mara asked.

"I'm not sure." Elana sighed. "Last night when we picked up Dalin's message from the house, he...he got an idea about something." She took a sip of her tea. "He's been gone a long while this morning."

As she mixed eggs and cheese together, then toasted bread and sliced fruit, Mara considered this. "There's no class today?" she asked, ready to change the subject.

Her aunt looked up. "Our closure runs a little longer than the usual break this time of year. The labs are running maintenance shifts only. Even the spaceport closes for the Winter Festival."

Mara brought over their plates and joined her aunt at the table. "I read a little about the Satri Winter Festival in our textbook. But I didn't realize everything stops."

"Well, almost everything. The market stays open for the first day." Tasting her eggs, Elana exclaimed, "This is good! Thank you." She reached over and laid a hand on her niece's hand. "And thank you for saying you want to come back when all of this is over. I know you have friends in the North." Her blue-green eyes clouded again.

"I have friends here now, too," Mara said, trying for a lighter tone. "But you're here. That's priority. How could I stay away now that I know where my home is?"

"You could attend one of the universities." Elana crunched a bite of fruit. "You could live with us, unless you wanted a place of your own. Nearby, of course."

#

After breakfast, Mara went to her room, intending to begin packing. The room felt like her own, a place she had made. The window seat, the desk with her schoolbooks and binder, clothes hung neatly in the closet. Bed made, rug clean and uncluttered. For contrast, she called up a mental image of her room in Protector House. Stone walls and floors, a tiny bed under a tiny window, fireplace, wardrobe—in her memory it seemed sparse and cold. Empty. The best part was the connecting door to Annelise.

She went once through the pants, shirts, training uniforms, and shoes before calling, "What do people wear to the festival?"

Elana appeared in the doorway. "I usually wear a dress or a skirt that's good for dancing." Her gaze went to the open closet. "You can wear your flowing pants if you want. The variety of clothing at the festival will be as wide as a typical day in Market Square. But"—she tilted her head to one side, considering her niece's options—

"whatever people choose, it's generally considered finery, rather than everyday wear."

"I have three dresses in my wardrobe at Protector House," Mara said.

"I always pictured you in uniform," her aunt said. "You don't have to wear it all the time?"

"No," Mara smiled. "We have regular clothes to wear into the settlements on trade days and to wear for memorial services." Elana's face fell.

"And…and for celebrations and harvest days," she hurried on. "Dalin asked to be my escort, so I should wear something fine, right? Do we have time to go to Market Square?"

"Why didn't you tell me sooner?" her aunt exclaimed. "We should leave this minute."

#

Despite the underlying sadness of imminent separation, aunt and niece were determined to enjoy their outing. Elana talked openly about her sister and their early life on Satri, recalling all the young men who'd asked to escort the lovely Dhanya to the Winter Festival.

At several points, Mara felt someone watching them, but she kept dismissing the worry because she didn't want to upset her aunt. By late morning, they both had acquired new dresses. When they paused to determine what else was needed, Mara remembered the pretty leather and silver embellished hair ties from the silver shop.

"I know what I want," she said. "Will you hold my dress bag while I run to the silver smith? Or do you want to come, too?"

"I'll come," Elana replied.

The shop was tucked along the southern edge of the square. As they approached, Mara slowed down to look at a window display of cups, bowls, and plates. In the reflection, she saw a man emerge from the crowd, stop, and then melt back into a large group of shoppers. Something about his short hair and plain, dark clothing wasn't right.

"Did you see him?" she asked, craning her neck to look through the heavy flow of people.

"What? Who?" said her aunt, turning and looking in the same direction.

"I guess…nothing." Mara couldn't shake her uneasy feelings, the instincts that had kept her alive on the battlefield. "That man, I saw a man, not in uniform but definitely a soldier."

"We should leave now." Elana's tone was urgent.

"I can protect us both," Mara said. She checked her wrist and leg sheaths under the pretense of straightening her clothes. "Please, let's make this last stop and get some soup to take back to your house."

Elana nodded her assent as she cast a wary eye over the crowd.

Once inside the store, her aunt relaxed somewhat. While Mara looked through the basket of hair ties, Elana examined leather headbands. She held out one made of dark-gray leather, braided nearly three fingers wide and decorated with tiny silver pearls.

"Mara," she said, "this will match your dress. Try it on." She caught the end of her niece's braid and undid it. With a few quick strokes, she loosened the hair until it flowed in long waves.

Using both hands, Mara slid the braided leather to just behind her hairline and turned to face her aunt. "Well?"

Elana's eyes went wide and shiny. "Dhanya wore her hair just like that. You truly look like her right now."

Mara hugged her aunt. "Thank you."

Holding her niece for an extra moment, Elana swiped at one of her eyes and sighed. With effort, the petite woman gathered herself and purchased both the leather headband and the hair tie. After a quick stop to buy a container of hot bean soup and a loaf of fresh bread, they were on their way home.

As they turned onto Divis Street, Mara caught a glimpse of dark clothing out of the corner of her eye. She slowed. "I need to check in with Dalin."

"What's wrong?" Elana asked.

"That person from earlier? I've seen someone in the crowd at least two, maybe three times, maybe that same soldier. And I feel as though we're under observation. It's very possible Dalin tasked one of his guys to be our security detail." Mara kept her tone light. "So I'm going to check in."

Elana nodded, her expressive face full of misgiving. "Good idea." She looked over her shoulder.

"Dalin," Mara sent. *"Dalin, someone is following Elana and me. One of your men?"*

"How did you catch him?" The response held laughter.

She let out the breath she had been holding. *"He sticks out in the crowd with his militia-short haircut and plain dark clothes."*

"Can you show me?" he asked, laughter gone.

Concentrating on the moment when she'd seen the man emerge from the market crowd, Mara brought the image into focus for Dalin as best she could.

"That's not my guy," he said, the response slow to come. *"I sent Fiorino. We had a bet whether or not you would spot him."*

"I didn't see Fiorino, so he wins."

"I'm sending him to pick up this guy," Dalin said.

"We've already left Market Square, but I don't think we should go back to the house."

Dalin's mental voice was insistent. *"Don't head home, absolutely not. Make a stop or two. As soon as it's clear, I'll let you know."*

While the pair conferred, Elana walked along in silence. Mara turned to face her aunt. "Dalin suggests we stop and have a picnic lunch."

Glancing up at the scudding clouds, she asked, "Picnic lunch?"

"Well, we shouldn't go to your house until Dalin gives the all clear."

"Of course." Her aunt hesitated. "There's, ah, there's an outdoor eating area in the park just down the next street."

"Perfect," Mara said. Even thought she was ready for a fight, she kept that instinct in check. Engaging with an enemy would leave her unarmed, untrained aunt vulnerable. Scanning for pursuers as they walked down the residential street, Mara kept her shoulders loose, head up.

When Elana began to lead them across the grass to an outdoor table, the Protector allowed herself a slow spin. It had rained in the night and the turf squished underfoot, but no footprints or breaks in the green indicated the presence of other people. No sign of the man from the crowd. No sign of Fiorino.

"Hey," she said. "Have we been to this park before?"

"Does it look familiar to you?"

"Yes," she said. And then it hit her. The first dream of the Tree, the park from her early childhood. "My mother," Mara rasped. "My mother and you, Yadira and Dalin, we played here."

"You remember," Elana breathed.

Seeing the hope and wonder in her aunt's face, she couldn't contradict her. "Not exactly," Mara hedged. "I'd been told about this park and now that I'm here, it does seem familiar. Especially the slide."

"The slide is one of the few pieces of playground equipment remaining from when you were small," Elana said. "Most of it has been replaced." She slid onto a stone stool adjacent to a stone table and shivered. "Let's eat before the soup gets cold."

Mara swung her leg over and straddled a stool. Her instincts insisted that danger was near, objected to sitting out in the open. She ground her teeth and held her position. Dalin had to believe she was capable of following orders.

Chapter 34

A shout echoed across the park. A lone man ran toward them from the street. Mara jumped to her feet, knife in hand.

"Behind you," the man yelled. In the split second before she turned, Mara recognized Fiorino's dark, reddish curls and short beard.

Two enemies sprinted in from the opposite direction. One ran with empty hands and the other held something circular that reflected the light with a dull metal sheen.

Mara seized the energy source and cast a shield around herself and Elana. She tested the weight of her knife and shifted to the balls of her feet. In three more strides, the attackers would be in throwing range.

"Drop it," Fiorino yelled at the attackers.

Light flashed from the circular weapon. Fiorino flinched and staggered back, clutching his arm.

Whipping her knife end over end, she hit the man with the weapon in the cleft between his neck and his collarbone. He grunted and staggered but kept coming.

She pulled her second knife from the leg sheath, ready to throw. Light flashed to her left. The second attacker's head snapped back and he fell. Light flashed again and the armed attacker dropped to the grass, holding his thigh.

As she started forward, weapon ready, Fiorino croaked, "Hold." He was bleeding from a shoulder wound but he kept moving until he was standing between Mara and the two men, something round and dark gray in his palm. "Throw your weapon to the side," he ordered the man on the grass.

Mara's knife had bitten deep, ripped through the assailant's jacket and drawn blood. The man tossed his circle toward Fiorino's feet and rolled to his side, clutching his leg and coughing.

Fiorino leaned over him. "Nice throw," he said.

She narrowed her eyes and glared at the man on the ground, wanting to kick him in the ribs. "Why were you following me?"

The man shook his head.

"Who do you work for?" Fiorino asked, grabbing the attacker's shirtfront and slamming him against the ground.

The man shrugged, dark eyes going to the still form of his unconscious companion.

"Ma'am?" Fiorino said to Elana, his tone gentle. "Could you please check the pockets of this sleeping beauty?"

When Elana moved, the shield shifted with her. Mara kept her covered, letting the energy continue to flow. Her aunt patted the man's pockets before tugging him onto his back to check inside his jacket. "A key," she said, holding up a small brass object. "And a card with an address on it."

"Idiot," the other man muttered with a grimace.

"Check behind his ear for the Iloel tattoo," Mara sent.

Her aunt peered closely at both sides of the man's head. *"Nothing I can see,"* she replied as she stood and hurried back toward the stone table.

Without warning, light flashed from the sky and struck Elana, knocking her onto the grass. With a shriek, Mara reinforced the protection over her aunt and raised her palm to the sky, willing the energy to destroy the attacker. A shockwave hit the dark clouds with a thunderclap. A shape materialized, a lighter shade of gray, a hint of large wings. Another flash sizzled the air.

Fiorino turned and slipped, firing toward the craft as he landed on his backside in the damp grass.

Puente and two additional uniformed men from the Satri militia ran into the park shouting, "Get down!"

Dropping to her belly, Mara crawled to her aunt. Elana's eyelids fluttered as she drew near. "What happened?"

Mara could scarcely hear over the roaring in her ears. Elana injured, the possibility of losing her only family… She stretched shaking fingertips toward the black scorch mark on the fabric covering the small woman's upper left hip.

"Hit by a falling rock, feels like," Elana mumbled.

"Shh, just keep still," Mara said as she held her breath and carefully lifted the hem of her aunt's tunic. An ugly red burn, the size of a saucer, marred the pale skin. The wound had blackened edges and was bleeding, but didn't appear to go deeper than the top layers of skin. A separate part of her mind catalogued the wound as non-life-threatening but in need of treatment. If Elana were a Protector, it would be enough to take her off the lines temporarily.

Fiorino bent down and whispered, "You can drop the shield. They're gone."

Nauseated with guilt, Mara could not reply. She knelt over her aunt's prone form, head bowed, letting the energy drain into the ground.

"That blast could have killed her. Those weapons get through most shields, but whatever you had, it kept the worst of the energy out. You probably saved her life," he continued quietly.

The other two soldiers held the conscious man while Puente searched him. "No labels in the clothes, nothing in the pockets," he reported. "What's a thug like you doing ruining these ladies' lunch?" he asked. "Who's shooting at us from the sky?"

The captive shrugged. Puente jabbed two fingers into the man's throat hard enough to make him gag. "Don't like your attitude." He bent down and slung the other, unconscious attacker over his shoulder, leading his team and their captive away from the park.

Gathering the women's market bags, Fiorino asked, "Do you need medical assistance to make it home?"

With a groan, Elana pushed herself to a kneeling position. "Jameson?" she asked.

"Lieutenant's going to find him and meet us at your house. If you can walk?"

She frowned at the spreading patch of blood on Fiorino's arm. "You're injured, too. Mara?"

"Shh, I'm fine," Mara said, patting her aunt's arm. "Can you stand?"

The two soldiers helped Elana to stand. Though her face was very pale, she gathered herself and stepped out on her own, chin high and shoulders back.

Fighting the impulse to throw another shield over the smaller woman, Mara returned the knife to her leg sheath and followed close behind. She stopped to retrieve her first knife, wiping it on the grass and her pants before sheathing it.

Once they were out on the street, Mara asked, "What was that weapon? You had something similar?"

"Lieutenant give you tech-clearance? There's nothing like this on Kels, far as we know." Fiorino looked sideways at her.

Mara narrowed her eyes and glared. "I have no idea. But someone was aiming at me and nearly took down my aunt. It looked like you were throwing energy, but it was sharp enough, directed enough, to draw blood."

Fiorino nodded as they turned onto the right street. "That's the basics of it. The..." He hesitated. "The weapon shapes the energy into a tight beam and fires it in pulses. Like arrows or spears of energy."

Immediately grasping the concept, she said, "It's a big advantage to attack from a distance like that, but what about wind?"

Fiorino shook his head. "Weather conditions have no impact."

Glancing up at her aunt and uncle's house, she asked, "What about structures?"

He followed her gaze. "Larger weapons of a similar type can be used to destroy structures. Listen, you better ask the lieutenant. He knows what your clearance is."

Nothing would be safe against a weapon like that. Not Elana in her house, not Protectors in the compound.

Elana had begun coding into the house when the militiaman stopped her. "I'm supposed to sweep the premises before you enter, ma'am." She stared pointedly at his shoulder wound. "I won't drip blood on the floor," he added. "It's really a minor injury...looks worse than it is."

A hysterical laugh bubbled up as her small aunt frowned imperiously at their would-be savior. Mara stepped off the front walk. "I'll take the perimeter."

#

"I wish we hadn't committed to the festival," Jameson growled. "Can't believe that healer cleared you to go."

Mara was in the common room reading, but her uncle's voice carried from the kitchen. Elana's reply was too soft to make out the words.

Moving soundlessly to the partially open connecting door, she could see Jameson holding her aunt in a gentle hug, his eyes squeezed shut.

"I canna believe they shot at you," he said, fingers tracing the outline of her bandage. "Bastards violated more codes and agreements..."

Elana shook off part of his hold. "You might have done the same, to get what you wanted." He made a sound of disagreement and smoothed a hand over her hair. "Jameson, I'm fine. Those men were shooting at our niece." The last two words came out in a higher, tremulous tone.

He looked up and caught Mara's eyes. "I worked out a plan today. Come on in, lass," he said. "Might as well hear the first telling."

She slid the door a little wider and slipped through.

"Tomorrow, I will receive word that your mother on Kels, my dear sister-in-law, has taken ill and asked for her daughter to come home. We're working on the papers to document your departure. Yadira has announced to the council that she is extending the festival recess and taking a week with her family at their wayhouse. Dalin is getting new orders and Puente will run the militia station in his absence."

Mara looked between the two adults. Her aunt's expression was also confused. "If Dalin is getting new orders, are you going north with me?"

"No," Jameson said. "His new orders are to escort you to Tamoh, gather information from the resource, and return with you."

"Dalin is going with her?" Elana's voice was full of hope.

Wrapping her arms around her torso, Mara let out a breath. "So how exactly will we—?"

Her uncle stopped her with a hand. "Dunno yet. A related detail is that when you leave Satri, you'll ride out with the de Forest-Tek family, disguised as Nuwa."

He turned back to his wife. "Better?"

Nodding, she leaned into his shoulder. "Better."

Mara slipped back into the common room to give her aunt and uncle some privacy. Jameson was so gruff and secretive and…fierce, yet somehow, he and Elana fit with each other. And the enemy today could have ended that perfect pairing. Like they did with her parents.

Chapter 35

"The first night of the Satri Winter Festival is also called Candle's Promise," Elana said.

"'Candle's Promise has developed multiple meanings over the decades' is what our class text said," Mara muttered, trying to keep still. "But it didn't really say what those meanings are."

When her aunt put down the comb and began braiding the next section of hair, Mara tried to relax into the gentle tug-and-pull rhythm against her scalp.

"Candle's first promise is the return of light and warmth for the spring growing season. On the Origin, seasons would come and go, just like here. But in the heart of the winter, many cultures celebrated with light." Elana tied off the braid and picked up the comb again.

"Candles, bonfires, artificial colored lights on trees and houses, lanterns—these celebrations of Light got people together, out of huddling in the dark, alone. So another meaning of Candle's Promise is the promise of fellowship, of community. We'll watch tonight, and when the people carrying lit candles start passing down our street, we'll join our neighbors walking to the festival."

Elana fastened the last braid and walked in front of her seated niece to survey the finished work. "Have a look."

Mara padded to the washroom and peered into the mirror. The hair around her face had a delicate, woven appearance. Along the sides and back of the crown of her head, thin braids alternated with thicker braids. The longest, underneath layer of her hair streamed free. Mara smiled at her reflection and gave her head an experimental shake to see if any hair would come loose.

"Well?"

"Thank you," she said, turning and catching her aunt in a light hug, painfully aware of the large bandage on Elana's lower back. "What else do we do to get ready for Candle's Promise?"

The smaller woman smiled. "That depends. If a young lady is hoping to impress a young gentleman, she might also apply enhancements to her face, perfume herself, polish hands and nails..." She paused when Mara made an expression of dismay.

"When we had our hands polished, the lady said my hands were rough, like a farmer's." She turned her hands over, palms up, and frowned at the callused skin.

"You spend hours every day swinging a sword, staff, stick, and Light knows what else." The bright smile wavered for a moment. "You have a soldier's hands, just like your escort."

Mara nodded, eyes on her hands. "What are the face enhancements?" she asked.

"Oh, well, that's just fun," Elana replied.

#

As the last reds and golds of the winter sunset faded into the horizon, Mara checked her clothes as carefully as she would a new uniform before a battle. The dress was made from a lightweight but warm fabric dyed a rich purple-blue. The neckline dropped below her collarbone, the bodice fitting snugly against her ribs. Just below her waist, the fabric gathered to make a full skirt. The neckline, sleeves, and bottom half of the skirt were embroidered with silver thread in a pattern of branches and leaves. Mara quickly strapped on her leg sheath and checked the draw on the knife.

Leaning closer to the mirror, she examined the face enhancements. In her entire life, not a single aspect of preparation been designated as "for fun" until now. Her aunt had used a tiny brush to darken the lines of her eyelashes and a slightly larger brush to dust a silver shimmer across her eyelids. Her lips and cheeks appeared slightly softer, rosier. The final touch was some sort of liquid brushed through her eyelashes. Mara blinked, intrigued by the effect. Scooping up the borrowed gloves and long coat, she all but skipped down the stairs.

Her aunt was waiting in the common room. "Dalin's here," she said. "In the kitchen with Jameson. I think he's nervous." As she spoke, she delicately tugged her niece's skirt into place and ran light fingers over her braids.

"He said he'd never escorted someone to the Winter Festival before."

"I think you're right. At least the past few years, if he's gone, he's been on his own." Elana grinned broadly. "And after escorting you, I can't imagine anyone else would compare."

Mara dipped her head. "Thank you."

"I love this dress. I love to go to the festival. Jameson has learned to have fun there, but it's not his first choice for a night out." Elana spun slowly. "Does the bandage show?"

"Not unless I'm looking for it." The terrible guilt from her failure as a protector rolled back in.

Elana narrowed her eyes and folded her arms. "Mara, you and my husband have sustained far worse injuries, correct?" She didn't wait for her niece to respond. "So you, better than most, know that if I don't want this to ruin my enjoyment of the festival, it won't. Besides, the salve Jameson used on this made it almost numb. If the bandage weren't rubbing against my dress, I would probably forget it was there. You'd better forget all of this and have fun with your escort," Elana ordered. "Because that is what I intend to do."

"Yes, ma'am," Mara replied with a reluctant smile.

"Still armed?" Dalin asked from the doorway.

Jameson hit him on the shoulder. "I may have only brothers, but I know you need to do better than that."

Elana put her hands on her hips and gave her near brother a frosty glare.

Taking in the tableau of disapproval, Dalin stepped forward to sweep a deep bow. "Beautiful lady, it would do me great honor to escort you this Candle's Promise night."

Mara bent her knees and kept her back straight in a fair imitation of the curtseys she'd seen settler girls do. "Thank you, sir. The honor is mine."

They stood for a moment grinning at each other. Dalin wore a crisp white shirt and dark pants. He'd shaved and attempted to subdue his spiky hair. Both of them were startled when Elana took the coat and handed it to Dalin.

"Help her with her coat," she directed.

Dalin stepped closer and held the coat for Mara to put her arms in, one sleeve at a time. When he bent to fasten the buttons, Mara parried his hand as she would a punch. "I've got this." She glanced at her aunt and uncle and added, "Thank you kindly, sir."

"Off you go then," Elana said, herding them toward the front door.

"We'll see you there," Jameson added.

Dalin offered his arm. "Shall we?"

All along Divis Street, people carrying candles walked in pairs and small groups. Mara drank in the sight, charmed by the soft, magical glow drifting down the broad boulevard.

She held out her own candle and whispered the word to light it. Dalin stopped walking to lean in and light his candle from hers, pausing to brush a light kiss on her cheek. He pulled Mara into his side and held his now-burning candle next to hers. "Another meaning of Candle's Promise is that we will only share fire with each other," he said, bending close to her ear.

She shivered, perceiving the words meant something more than candle fire.

Dalin's expression changed from playful to concerned. "Cold?" he asked.

"No..." she began. Her eyes moved to a couple up ahead, holding hands and talking.

"Relax—there's no set protocol." He tucked her left arm under his right and started walking. As they strolled, more people with candles joined the growing throng. Here and there, Mara caught snippets of singing.

At the turn for the first public square, they found themselves in a crowd more than ten people deep in any direction. Candles flickered; people laughed, most wearing much fancier clothes than on a regular day. Also, not everyone was in pairs, as she and Dalin were. Many were in family groups or groups of friends.

When Tree Square came into view, she involuntarily stopped and stared. Dalin moved behind her as a buffer from the crowd, close enough that she could feel the heat from his body. "What do you see?"

"The Tree," Mara said, her tone hushed. "Lights, people—it's beautiful."

High above them, tiny lights flickered in the branches of the Great Tree. The larger spotlights had been changed to softer blues and greens. On the open grassy space around the Tree, people holding musical instruments sat or stood near several rows of chairs. The paved area of the square had been swept clean and overlaid with smooth panels for dancing. The citizens of Satri strolled in bright clothes, some with open coats like Mara, some without coats entirely, laughing, talking, gestures sending flickers of candlelight across the scene.

Taking a deep breath and another, she willed herself to remember, to mentally imprint every detail of the celebration. On her next breath, she caught the scent of something delicious. "Do you smell that?"

Dalin inclined his head, lips curving. "Hungry?"

She nodded, feeling as though she could have any wish come true.

"This way." He threaded them through the clusters of people and stopped in front of a food stall. "Here we have bean soup, buttered rolls, or sausages. A little farther down, meat or vegetable pies."

"Pies," Mara decided, her mouth already watering.

In a short span of time, Dalin procured four pies, found them a place to stand closer to the Tree, and extinguished their candles.

As she looked up into the branches of the Tree, she wondered aloud, "Do you think she likes this?" The light and shadows played across the immense trunk and the vast network of limbs rising into the sky.

"The festival is carefully planned and monitored to prevent negative environmental impact. The Tree has always made it known when she doesn't like something."

Mara raised her eyebrows and took a tiny nibble of her first pie. It smelled incredible, but was too hot yet for a full bite.

"Like how only autos work here," he said.

"I heard a little about that," she said. "But not how it relates to the Tree."

"It's nothing the dendrologists can prove conclusively," Dalin began. He also took a small bite. "But the scientists who study the writings and the Tree herself think she likes humans, but not the way we"—he paused and took another small bite—"spread. It's too fast and it hurts the plants and animals. The scientists believe no form of rapid transit works on Satri, because without the means to spread quickly, human settlements tend to be more contained. The autos are the fastest things we have, besides horses."

Taking a large bite of pie, she was rewarded with ground chicken, cabbage, pepper, and onion, among other ingredients. "Delicious," she said through her mouthful of food. "Thank you."

"Glad you like it. As your escort, it is my duty and my pleasure to feed you." His gray eyes crinkled at the corners as he smiled.

Mara had just taken another large bite when a group of girls approached.

"Dalin de Forest, is that you?" one of the girls shrieked. "Where have you been hiding?"

A tiny wince flitted across Dalin's face as he turned to face the newcomers.

Three girls stood together, all attired in expensive-looking dresses, none wearing coats. Mara guessed them to be more or less her same age. The apparent leader had luminous brown skin, blue eyes, and hair arranged in an elaborate configuration of braids and curls. "My mother was on the council with Dalin's mother." This remark was directed at Mara as well as her two friends. She stepped closer with a flirtatious smile. "I heard you were off-planet doing work for the Queen."

"No, I'm with the militia here on Satri," he replied, expression closed.

"Fighting those ignorant savages in the North?" the girl said. She made a face at her companions, who giggled. "How boring."

"Everything we learn from the war projects contributes to the security of the Commonwealth, Adiel; you know that." Dalin's tone bordered on rude. "Funny, I thought your family's finances were tied directly to security." He made an exaggerated glance around the square. "Hate for you to get caught breaking the law with the same surveillance tools that pay for your clothing allowance."

Adiel stiffened and then rolled her eyes at her friends. "I'm leaving this backward little planet as soon as I can. Until then, when you figure out how dull Satri is"—she paused to assess Mara from head to toe—"my family has my contact codes."

With that, she blew Dalin a kiss and swished away, the two other girls trailing giggles as they went.

Dalin heaved a sigh. "Sorry about that," he said, his face equal parts irritation and embarrassment. "People don't...it's not..."

Mara finished the last bite of her meat pie and turned her attention to the vegetable pie. "Ignorant savages?" she said, keeping her eyes on her food. The remark had stung. Every settlement had at least one girl like Adiel. And girls like Adiel had a magical talent for targeting insults to their victims' weaknesses. "We didn't choose to be ignorant."

"That girl is so *ignorant*"—Dalin stressed the word—"she hasn't bothered to learn about a key military engagement on her own planet. And," he continued, "I know she's never had a combat lesson in her life. You could drop her with ten different techniques before she could spit out another insult."

It was exactly the right thing to say. "Palm strike to the nose?"

"An excellent opening move," he agreed. "One of my favorites."

Mara conjured the image in her mind, grinned, and then shrugged off Adiel altogether. The crowd was steadily increasing. Little snatches of music drifted from the musicians.

Dalin tugged her hand. "Let's go," he said. "Dancing won't start for a while and there's more to see."

She let him pull her into the flow of people meandering around the square. Some carried lit candles; others did not. "Do we need to relight our candles?"

"If you like." He squeezed her hand lightly. "The candles are a fun part of the tradition."

He drew the tapers from his coat pocket and lit them, handing one to Mara. She took her candle and peeked through enhanced lashes at her escort. One corner of his mouth turned up in a tiny smile. Her lips twitched up in response. And for a long moment, they both simply stared. Two breaths, three breaths, and then someone jostled her from behind, breaking the spell.

Dalin pulled her close for a quick hug. "Happy?"

"Yes," she answered, although happy did not encompass what she was feeling. She felt connected, at home, and at peace.

On the south side of the square, a group performed acrobatics, another group was juggling, and a third was doing something with ribbons and flowers that Mara couldn't fully see. As she had the first time she went to Market Square, she noticed the adults in the crowd were much taller than in the North.

She turned to ask Dalin about it, the question half-formed, when he said, "Watch out," and pulled her to the side. She looked up and up, mouth dropping open at a pair of people, impossibly tall, striding through the crowd. "Stilts," he whispered.

"I was just going to ask about people being tall in Satri and then..." She laughed, gesturing at the pair, whose knees appeared about head high on the tallest adults in the crowd.

"Stilts are poles of metal or wood on which the wearer learns to balance and walk. For festivals, they wear specially made long pants to create the illusion of immense height." Dalin's eyes swept the crowd. "However, to your other question, each generation, children grow taller than their parents, regardless of their genetic background from the Origin. Height is one way to estimate how many generations a person's family has been on Satri."

"But why does that happen? And why not in the North? That's still Asattha." Mara also faced into the crowd, now wondering about the tallest people in a different way.

"Some call it the Gift of the Tree," Dalin replied.

She shook her head. "I don't understand."

"The Tree only has saplings and smaller trees up to a certain distance away from herself, and then other species fill in, gradually taking over. No *gontras* in the North."

She recalled the moment during their ride south when Dalin had been looking at trees and mentioned some kind of boundary.

"De Forest."

A man in a militia uniform jogged up to them. The soldier, just older than Dalin and attractive in a polished way, took in Mara's presence and the candles both held. He punched Dalin on the arm. "Got yourself *env peng yu*. Not bad."

"Sal, this is Mara," Dalin said. In her mind he added, *"Friend."*

"Salvatore Liu, at your service." He had black eyes and short black hair, tan skin, and an open smile.

"Pleased to meet you," she said.

"The guys at the station said you were here," Sal began. "Sorry to interrupt," he said to Mara, "but I need a word with the big guy here."

"Of course." She turned her back slightly and directed her attention to the jugglers. The air seemed warmer with so many people crowded into the square. She inhaled, catching the smell of something sweet. When Mara glanced back over her shoulder, the two men stood side by side, not speaking. Rapport, she realized.

Sal was broad shouldered and tall. His features, eyes in particular, resembled Nuwa's. Although her first impression had been of a uniform, he wore a loose gray tunic and black trousers under an open wool coat. It was more his bearing and manner that said *soldier*.

Distracted by the sweet smell and still hungry, she continued to scan the area. When she looked again, Sal was leaning to speak in Dalin's ear and clap him on the shoulder. The soldier made his way back to Mara and reached for her hand. "I told him if you are the one he's been waiting for, maybe he's smarter than I thought."

"And I told Sal you could knock him off his feet and punch his teeth down his throat," Dalin said, wrapping a possessive arm around her waist.

Sal winked. "Some guys have all the luck." He touched two fingers to his temple in a half salute. "Lieutenant." And strode away.

Mara watched him disappear into the crowd, distracted by the sensation of being pressed against Dalin's side.

"Has something happened?" she asked.

"No, just an...interesting report. Doesn't change our plans." He released his hold so they could continue walking.

She doubted Sal had gone to the trouble of tracking Dalin down just to share interesting information. But she wanted to believe he'd tell her if she needed to know.

Chapter 36

The wind stirred her braids and nearly guttered the candle. She caught the smell of the ocean. "What happens to Candle's Promise if it's too windy?"

"People carry their candles in lanterns," Dalin replied. "A city on the coast will always have wind, so people here adapted to make sure the tradition could continue and grow." They turned the corner and saw the main dance area and the groups of musicians. "Let's warm up our hands around some hot drinks and find a place to watch."

The crowd still continued to increase, which blocked the wind but delayed the acquisition of hot drinks. Eventually, they found a place to sit and rest near an exposed Tree root. Mara had been inhaling the fragrant steam and now judged it cool enough to taste. The hot liquid was sweet and heavily spiced. She frowned into her cup, trying to sort out the tastes.

"Honey wine, apple cider, *terche* peel, cloves, not sure what else. My dad and I have tried to make this at home and we can't quite get all the flavors," Dalin said.

Leaning against the Tree root, she took another careful sip. Around them people were finding places to sit facing the musicians. Anticipation was building in the air. "How many instruments are there?" she asked.

Dalin chuckled. "I have no idea. Every year they play a combination of songs everyone knows and songs from different planets in the Commonwealth. Usually, musical groups from various Origin cultures also perform music specific to their own winter celebrations."

A swell of sound caused the talking to hush. The sound resolved itself into a merry tune featuring different instruments as it went along. When the last note faded, applause exploded throughout the square. Mara looked at Dalin, who grinned back at her. He pulled a folded square out of one of his pockets and shook it out into blanket size. "Ground gets cold," he said and tugged the light blanket over their legs.

As the songs progressed one to the other, she stopped trying to puzzle out the instruments and just enjoyed each musical piece.

"What do you think?" Dalin whispered.

"I don't know how to explain it," Mara said. "The settlements have hand drums, pipes, flutes, and guitars. All together, even as a large group, they can't do this." She swept her arm to include the musicians and the sound in the air.

"Elana and I, we sometimes used to talk about all the things you missed growing up in the North. We talked about what we would show you, if we could. It was one of our ways of keeping the faith that you were alive."

Rather than see the sympathy on his face, Mara gazed out at the crowd and sipped her drink. They didn't know how lucky they were.

"Even after all this time, we still have no idea who took you or a definitive reason why. When Jameson found you..." The next song started. Out of the corner of her eye, she saw Dalin shake his head.

The music crashed through the square, too loud for talking. She turned over her memories of meeting Jameson at the horse fair.

"I wish he could have told me I had family somewhere."

The next song, a quieter, more somber tune, evoked memories of the loneliness and fear of being so young and having to depend on the kindness of adults. "I don't remember much before I was four. I know I was almost always in a group of children," she said during the applause. "I had clothes, food, and a place to sleep. Most of the time, I was content. Especially once I was placed with Elias and his family." She reached up and touched his shoulder. "I'm sorry you and Elana worried for so long."

Dalin looked sideways at her and smiled ruefully. "You were safe, and in the end, we had to be content as well." He glanced around at the people, who were beginning to stir. "Looks like it's almost time for dancing." Dalin repacked the blanket and stood, holding out a hand as she rose to her feet.

Tree Square was smaller than Market Square and much more crowed tonight than any place she'd ever seen. Although the cold wind continued to gust from the south, few seemed to mind. Mara rubbed her hands together and turned back to Dalin.

He was gone.

Heart sinking, she scanned the surrounding crowd. Surely he wouldn't just leave?

"I'm still here," he said. Suddenly, he was standing exactly where he'd been the moment before.

Mara jumped back, fear shifting to anger in a blink. "What was…? How…?"

"It's a new way to shield," Dalin said, not quite able to contain his grin. "My dad figured it out."

Mara put her hands on her hips. "How does it work?"

"Same as a regular shield, except you also picture the landscape surrounding yourself instead of just energy. Working well, it would look like an empty space on the battlefield." He disappeared again.

Reaching forward, she felt the unpleasant tingle of a shield. "You're going to teach me this, right?"

Dalin grabbed her hand and reappeared. "We're crossing the Northern Plateau in a few days. I'll teach you before we get there."

She imagined the long open stretch and the risks of exposure, her relaxed mood gone.

"Hey, don't stop smiling," Dalin protested. "I just wanted to try that shield variation in a crowd." Both of them looked at the milling people for a moment. No one appeared to be looking in their direction. "I could have waited, or warned you," he murmured. "I'm sorry."

Mara dug her hands in her coat pockets and shrugged. "Don't apologize. I made a promise to myself not to think about leaving during the festival. That's all."

Dalin put his hands in his pockets too and looked at the ground. The only hint of his frustration with himself was the tightness around his jaw.

"Can you tell me what news brought Sal out here to find you?" Mara asked.

"Not if you don't want to think about the North." Despite their respective shields, she sensed him cursing mentally.

She took a deep breath. "Then would you tell me what he meant…that you were waiting for m-…a girl…someone?"

Dalin glanced up, a hesitant grin curving his lips. "I've known Sal a long time. And he loves, um, spending time with females, escorting them around."

Mara nodded. She knew Protectors like that.

"But, I'm not, I don't, I've always been busy. And my family…" He shrugged.

Mara was fascinated. Dalin so rarely appeared uncertain.

"When Sal would give me a bad time about my choices, about how I spent my free time, I would tell him I was waiting for you." He reached for Mara's right hand, tugging it out of her pocket. Gently, he turned her hand over and ran his thumb across the raised calluses. "'She's a soldier, not assigned here,' I used to tell him." Dalin locked his gaze, now a smoky gray, on her face and brushed her palm with a light kiss. Energy tingled from her palm up her arm.

He turned her hand over. "'She's as good as you, Sal,' I would tell him." Dalin kissed her knuckles. "'And tall.'" He feathered kisses over the scars on the back of Mara's hand, tugging her toward him until they were almost touching. She swallowed. Too captivated to look away, she was only dimly aware of the throng of people and the brisk night air.

"'The one for me has blue eyes and long dark hair,' I told him. 'She's beautiful.'" Dalin cupped her face with reverence and kissed her. She leaned into the kiss, heart pounding, feeling dizzy and light.

When he broke the contact and drew a shallow breath, she used her free hand to tug on the collar of his coat. "I must have been waiting for you, too," she whispered.

Dalin's full smile bloomed and his eyes sparkled silver once more. "I promised you dancing, my beautiful soldier. Are you ready?"

Through the beginning dances and well into the second set, Mara experienced all the classic symptoms of fogging: dizziness, inability to track time, disorientation, and shortness of breath. At the end of a rousing tune featuring guitar and drums, she finally asked for a break.

"Is it your leg?" Dalin asked.

She jabbed an elbow at his ribs. "No, I just…I'm thirsty." She wanted to slow down, watch the dancing, take it all in.

He searched her face. "What?"

Laughing, she said, "I feel like I'm fogged. Should I report myself?"

An odd expression crossed his face. But before she could ask, he turned and began leading them off the dance floor toward the drink carts.

As they watched the dancing and rested on a bench, Dalin shared memories of previous Winter Festivals, including the year Jameson escorted Elana for the first time. "She wasn't living with us any longer," he said. "But my parents insisted on meeting Jameson before they went."

Mara liked the idea of Jin and Yadira being protective of her aunt. "What happened? Were you there?"

Dalin shook his head. "No, not for that part. I was fourteen, so it was the end of my first semester at the university and I was studying for exams. But I met them here later that night. Nuwa had been"—he paused to think—"following them is not exactly, well, she was following them. Elana was like our older sister. And she was with a man." He made an exaggerated dreamy face and fluttered his eyelashes.

Mara laughed. She'd seen that kind of face on her friends. "So you met Jameson here at the festival five years ago?"

Dalin took a sip of his drink. His lips quirked when he glanced up. "Elana and Jameson were talking and it was"—he gestured between them—"kind of like this. Even back then I knew we shouldn't interrupt. But…" He sighed. "Nuwa grabbed my hand and pulled me over. Elana didn't mind, I think. But what I really remember is Jameson standing and looking me in the eye. He said, 'So you're Dalin, the smart one Elana's been tellin' me about.'" Dalin did a good imitation of Jameson's rough baritone. "I blurted out that I wanted to be a soldier. He didn't respond, just gave me that stare, taking my measure. In that moment, I knew Elana would be more than fine with this man and…and I knew I wanted to be just like him."

She bumped his shoulder with her own. "Thanks for telling me that story."

"Jameson's been my mentor ever since. Any credit for my success, for earning such a high rank so young, goes to him. He's helped me every step of the way."

"Twyla's been like that for me," Mara offered. "She asks questions, helps guide my thinking about leadership." Her sharp eyes picked out a familiar figure dancing near the Tree. "Do you see her?"

"Twyla?"

"The Tree. She's near that couple on the left. See? Behind the bright orange sweater?"

The Tree, clad in her usual tunic and leggings, skipped and pranced around the other dancers. Her dark curls bounced around her bobbing head. As Mara watched, the Tree paused and looked up. She grinned and waved.

Suddenly, the Tree stood right next to her. Mara inhaled sharply and pressed back against the bench. Dalin mastered his surprise and quickly stood to bow. "Lady," he said. "You do us great honor." Mara stood as well.

The Tree smiled and her eerie all-black eyes turned up at the corners. "These are my favorite nights of the turning," she said. Her bare feet continued to tap and she swayed along with the tune. "My sisters and I did not know music until humans appeared. But once we heard it, we knew it had to be a gift of the Light."

Her young-yet-old face grew serious. "I do not have sisters where you must travel, but my roots run far and deep." She tilted her head up and to the side, appraising Dalin. "You remind me of my farmer." The Tree narrowed her gaze, staring hard without blinking. "You must nurture this sapling, farmer. She is new yet."

The tall soldier nodded once, twice, and then bowed once more. "My lady."

The Tree stood on tiptoe and brushed his face with her long, dry fingers. "My thanks," she said and vanished.

Dalin rubbed a hand over his eyes and forehead. "Ouch. Does she do that to you?"

"Do what?" Mara bit her lip trying to suppress the worry she felt.

"Touch your mind? Surround it?" Dalin shook his head as though trying to clear it, lost his balance, and took a long staggering step to the side.

Mara grabbed his elbow and dragged him back to the bench, forcing him to sit. Dalin's eyes squeezed shut and he put his head in his hands with a groan.

The endlessly moving, noisy crowd, reminded her of a battlefield. She tried to manage her fear by taking in a deep, calming breath, then another. "Dalin, I'm going to get help."

"Wait." Dalin grabbed her wrist and tugged her down next to him. "I'll be fine."

Mara balled her hands into fists and took another breath. *Jameson and Elana are here somewhere*, she thought. *And Yadira and Jin—maybe I could call Jin.* Mara brought a picture of Jin to her mind. A mental scream for help would be too much. Dalin wasn't dying.

"Don't call my dad."

Mara looked at him and raised one eyebrow.

"You get upset, forget about your shields, and you're a loud thinker."

"Maybe your dad can—"

Dalin smiled and it was almost full strength. "The Tree took me by surprise, but I'm fine now." He leaned closer. "Nice to have a partner who cares."

Mara searched his familiar face. She brushed her fingertips across Dalin's forehead. His shields were smooth stone under her mental touch. "I didn't think the Tree would...I should have protected you."

Dalin pulled Mara to her feet as he stood. "From what? From Satri's greatest treasure? I'm fine. Really."

The last high notes faded away, light as wind. Throughout the square, candles flickered to life. The bright lights trained on the Tree dimmed, making the constellations of sparkling flames all the more magical.

Dalin held out a fresh candle.

"What do we do?" she asked.

"Light it together. Ready?" Dalin appeared completely himself once more. A haunting melody began to flit from one instrument to the next.

"Ready."

"One, two, light," he said, and the tiny wick brightened with flame.

Chapter 37

When Mara woke the next morning, she rolled onto her back and looked at the ceiling.

"Last day in Satri for a while," she said aloud.

The sun was just rising, but she wouldn't be going for a run or joining a fighting session today. Gruffald and all the other militiamen except Puente thought she was prepping for her departure on a space transport bound for Kels. When she'd told the part of the story about helping out with the family horse business, Gruffald had muttered, "Waste a lot of fighting talent mucking out stalls."

Sitting up, she wrapped her arms around her knees. She didn't ever want to go back to her old life. She wanted to live with Elana and Jameson and really begin to learn. The only way to be something more than a soldier was to know other things, experience a life outside of fighting. That's why tracking down this next source was important. The more they knew about the Tree and the Tree Prophesies, the closer they would get to discovering the true nature of the enemy.

Always before, she planned to continue as a Protector, working her way to a senior position. Now she saw how small, how false, that life had been. Anger at the entire war project mess bubbled up again.

The Protector Project had to end; no other outcome was acceptable.

Elana tapped on the door, opened it, and peeked in. "How do you want to spend your last day?"

#

Despite trying to savor every moment with her aunt, the hours flew. All too soon the shadows lengthened and Mara was standing in the stable with Jameson checking over her horse's tack.

"Maybe the information we think this source has will help, maybe not. We aren't certain that heading up to the northern settlements will hide you from whoever's lookin'," he said. "So you keep at least two knives on your person at all times."

Mara smiled at him. "What if I get a chance to shower?"

"I been attacked in the latrine, washroom too." Scowling, he took a few steps toward the workbench and turned back. "By most folks thinkin', it'll keep you safe, this mission, whatever's to be learned." He gave his head a sharp shake and grimaced like he had a bad taste in his mouth.

"Jameson, what?"

"Somethin's not right. We've gotten some odd reports from up there and my gut says at least one asset is compromised."

Mara remembered Liu's urgent but only "interesting" report from the night before. "Is the truce still in effect?"

"Yeah, but roads are near passable. Your people are all headin' in." Jameson walked over and clapped her hard on the shoulder. "Just promise me you'll look sharp. Elana she...she can't lose you again. Understood?"

"Sir," Mara said.

Jameson glowered and stomped to the workbench. He lifted a long sack of rough cloth. "Here." He thrust the sack at Mara. "Got ya a new sword. Looks like your old beater, from a distance anyway."

Reaching inside the bag, she felt a sword wrapped in flannel. As she withdrew it, the fabric shifted to reveal a glittering blade. Mara sucked in her breath as she drew the weapon free. Yes, the sword was the same style, in terms of blade shape and hilt design. But this weapon was superior in every way that mattered.

She dropped the flannel bag to the floor and tried a practice swing. "So light," she breathed. She laid the hilt across her left palm, the blade horizontal. "Perfect balance."

Jameson's eyes glinted with pride. "The metal ore was mined on Iloel, but the forging, the craft, that's my people. This blade can withstand more force from a heavier weapon than any sword the Protectors or Gaishan use. Hell, it's a top notch weapon on any planet, not just Asattha."

"Thank you," she whispered. She hugged her uncle with her left arm, keeping the sword flat against her right leg.

Jameson gave her a squeeze and pulled out of the embrace. "Listen, this blade, they gave it an extra feature." He held out his hand and she laid the pommel in it. As the veteran took a few swings, he said, "The master who forged this blade, she also works with energy." His hard blue eyes burned into Mara's. "This sword can hold some of your energy in a fight, she told me. And pierce another's shield like it wasn't even there. You won't get the slow down or the drag."

Mara's mouth dropped open. "How…?"

"I told the sword master I didna want to know the how's and why's of it. Better for everyone that way." He returned the sword and walked back to the workbench. "I know you favor the harness on your back, but ya might need to wear this at your hip. Here's a sword belt and scabbard." Deftly, he reached around Mara and fastened a black leather belt across her hips, positioning the scabbard to lie against her right thigh.

She held the scabbard steady and slid the sword home. "How can I repay you?"

"You can stay alive, that's how."

#

After an early good-bye the next morning, Jameson and Elana took Nuwa to the spaceport. The young scientist wore Mara's favorite blue sweater with the hood pulled up to cover her hair and hide her face. Later that night, Jameson would take Nuwa first to his hunting cabin and then on to the wayhouse so she could meet up with her parents.

Mara rode out with the remainder of the de Forest-Tek family wearing Nuwa's work coat and a scarf around her head and neck. Part of the reason for departing as a family was to afford quick movement through Satri. No one would stop the leader from taking her well-deserved and much-publicized rest.

The group traveled due north, in the open much of the time. Everyone kept a lookout for mysterious shadows on the ground or figures in the sky. The weather was cold, but not unbearable, and Mara was glad to have the scarf around her face. Looking with fresh eyes, she not only noticed, but felt comforted by the significant number of *gontra* trees visible along their route.

The first night they camped just inside the tree line. Clouds obscured the moons, creating a thick darkness under the canopy of trees. The soldiers set up camp with quick efficiency while Jin cooked and Yadira tended the fire.

During her months in Satri, Mara had spent far less time with Dalin's mother than with Jin. She admired the older woman and her family history, especially after reading stories of the de Forests' early pioneer days.

Camping with Yadira didn't exactly diminish the admiration, but it showed another side of the leader. She fussed over her muddy boots, the burned food, and sitting on the cold ground. Even when the group split into two tents for the night, Mara caught a bit of Yadira grumping about the cramped space.

Dalin had just flicked on the tiny overhead light and was arranging his gear. As his mother's voice drifted through the tent walls, Mara glanced over and was hit by a powerful sense of déjà vu.

"We haven't camped since that night in the storm," she said.

His eyes crinkled with a smile as he continued rolling out his sleeping sack. "True."

She'd had so many assumptions about Dalin and about the Gaishan but had known, literally, nothing. Nothing of the Commonwealth, nothing of Satri or Asattha, nothing of her own family. Leaning forward to unlace her boots, she remembered the numbing cold, how ice had caked in the laces, and she shivered.

"Cold?" he asked.

"No, not really," Mara said. "Just thinking about that first night in a tent with you." Then she had stayed as far away as possible, but now, Dalin was the one keeping his distance.

"Oh?" He shifted on his back, putting his hands under his head.

"I didn't know anything then."

"Sure you did. Then and now, you know more about fighting, leading, and certainly more about horses than most of my men."

Tucking her chin to her chest, she pulled off her boots. "I couldn't even read," she mumbled.

"And now that you can, you have another difference to hide from the settlers and any Protectors we might encounter."

With a quiet sigh, she shucked off her outer layers and scooted inside Nuwa's sleeping sack without looking across the tent.

"It's only for a few weeks." He stretched out and tapped the light, plunging the tent into darkness.

"I wasn't thinking about reading," she said. Sensing his amusement, she muttered, "Get out of my head," not able to muster actual anger.

"Your shields are up," Dalin said. "But I can guess you're worried about running into any of your friends."

The centimeters between them in the small tent might as well have been meters. Mara hadn't thought much about sleeping in the same tent with Dalin again, except that it might be nice. She'd heard some spicy stories from other Protectors about those sorts of opportunities.

Rolling on her side to face him in the dark, she made a made a sound of agreement.

Something had changed or reverted since the Tree talked to him. The closeness, the kissing, the story of waiting for her—it was as if those things hadn't happened. Mara had no words, no sense of how to express her confusion. She couldn't plan for or consult about the uncertainty she felt.

Never in her life had she made the first move in anything except a fight. So instead, she imagined reaching out across the small space of the tent and tracing the planes of Dalin's face. Closing her eyes, she brushed her imaginary fingers across his forehead, his nose, and cheekbone. Her lips parted as she imagined drawing one finger across his lips, so soft compared to the roughness of his cheek.

Dalin cleared his throat. "Rest well."

She flinched and squeezed her eyes shut. Did he know what she was imagining? "Good night," she managed.

#

The ride to the wayhouse was easy and uneventful. The soft snow splashed the horses' legs, and the sun broke through the clouds to bring hints of warmth to the cold day. Mara wanted to prolong the hours of freedom with Dalin and his parents, but holding onto the relaxed moments of light laughter and thoughtful conversation was like holding onto water.

After a time inside the forest, Jin announced they were two kilometers out and called a halt. "No one has been here since you two left in a hurry. You did not determine who or what triggered the sensors, correct?"

Dalin looked at his father, then back at her. *"Stay calm about what Jin's going to say."*

She maintained eye contact with him as his father said, "Mara, please stay here with Yadira while we run a sweep."

"Of course," she replied.

"He trusts very few to protect my mother. It's a request made with respect," Dalin sent.

"Understood. Thanks," she added as father and son rode out.

As she dismounted, Yadira said, "Forgive my husband. He sees you as a female first and a soldier second."

Startled, Mara swung around to look at the older woman. "Jin is a good teacher. I respect his orders."

Yadira patted the mare's nose and began a brisk and efficient check of her mount. "Inside the experiment, no one gives you easier or safer duties because you're female."

Not sure where the conversation was headed, Mara agreed. "That's true. I'm a veteran. Dangerous and challenging tasks are my responsibility."

Under the tree canopy as they were, the night shadows had already begun to lengthen. Mara laid Rowan's blanket across the mare's back.

"I know this part of the forest," Yadira said, unrolling a blanket to cover her mount as well. "A storm is coming. The animals are taking shelter."

"Snow?" Mara asked.

"Sometime overnight," Yadira confirmed. She inclined her head. "Can you sense it? Through the trees?"

Placing a steadying hand on a nearby *gontra* tree, Mara reached for the energy source. For a moment, she was completely blinded by the sensations of cold wind and cold earth. But above the trees, the air… She looked at Dalin's mother. "The pressure in the air, that's the storm?"

"Yes," Yadira smiled. "When you're back in Satri for good, perhaps I can teach you a portion of the family lore. Some think my forbearers chose the name de Forest either by simple location or to profit by association with Satri's Great Tree." She gazed in the direction Dalin and Jin had gone. "The truth is, my ancestors forged a connection with the *gontra* trees and the name gave meaning to the connection." She smiled. "Jin says to tell you 'all clear' and that your shields are working better than ever."

Given the murky twilight of the winter afternoon, the two women decided to travel the last distance on foot. Yadira took the lead, and Mara, thinking most threats would come from behind, not from deeper within the woods, took the rear position without argument.

"Could you not reach me?" she sent to Dalin.

"I could, but my dad couldn't. Jin is better at blocking than sending. Plus, he and my mom like to practice." His mental voice was apologetic.

"Got it," she acknowledged.

"See you in a few."

The wind picked up as they walked, rattling the dry branches around them like swords. Mara felt chilled and uneasy for the first time all day.

"After your parents died, we kept looking for you." Yadira's voice carried over the sounds of the forest. "I reached out to every contact I had in the political world. Jin did the same in the scientific community."

Mara's breath caught but she kept silent, wanting to hear more.

"We didn't find much. But each of us found pieces we were certain fit in the larger puzzle. Your parents were our closest friends. It is unthinkable that their deaths should go unresolved." Yadira paused and turned to look her. The dusk left much of her face shadowed, but the anger underneath the leader's words was strong.

"I will discover what happened to my parents, why I was taken." Mara said, her tone firm.

"I'll take your promise on that. Good." Yadira gave one sharp nod. "Your mother had the strongest will of anyone I've met before or since. I see that in you."

Mara felt a surge of pride. From Elana, she knew of Dhanya's intellect and beauty, but no one had spoken of her mother's strength.

Dalin appeared and motioned to them from the rear of the wayhouse. Once inside the small, tidy stable, he took over the care of the horses, shooing Mara into the house behind his mother.

Pausing at the doorway to the sleeping room she had used on her previous stay at the wayhouse, Mara asked, *"Which room, Dalin?"*

"Oh, the same one is fine. Look, once the horses are settled, I'm going to check the sensor that sent us running. I'll be back soon."

"Be safe," she sent as she placed her saddlebags on the floor and ran her hand over the covers of the bed. Such rich colors and fine fabric for a house rarely used. Someone, Dalin she guessed, had

laid the planetary atlas on the pillow. Mara traced the lettering on the cover she could now read: *The Seven Planets of the Laskan Commonwealth.*

She couldn't keep herself from opening the book. And there in the table of contents was a listing for each planet. Mara looked at the names with hunger, the cold and fatigue of the day's ride forgotten. So much to learn. Already a lifetime behind Dalin and now she'd have to endure at least an additional few weeks of enforced ignorance. Her finger landed on the entry for Iloel, page 151. Mara turned to the page and gazed at the colors swirling on the planet's surface.

"'Iloel is the closest planet to the sun in the Laskan system. Heat is one of its defining features and the key challenge for settlers...'" she read.

#

She was sitting on the rug, nose deep in the planetary atlas and still wearing her travel clothes when Dalin returned.

"Mara?"

She looked up, eyes alight with excitement. "Did you know Iloel was the first planet settled? They've found artifacts from previous explorers, maybe as old as the time of the Origin."

"I'm glad you're enjoying the book." Dalin leaned on the doorframe, squeezed his eyes closed, and rubbed his forehead. "I wanted to include you when I show my parents the damage to the perimeter sensor."

Inhaling sharply, she took stock of herself and her surroundings. "How long were you...? I just..." She stood and laid the book and index on the bed. With a glance at his feet, she quickly exchanged her boots for house shoes.

They met Yadira coming out of the kitchen carrying a steaming mug. "Just on my way to tell you tea's on, if you want some," she offered. "Jin says you have news?" She walked back into the kitchen and settled herself at the small table. Mara hesitated near the one remaining chair as Dalin took out two mugs and filled them from a kettle.

The leader made a "sit" motion, indicating Mara should take the other chair.

At the stove, Jin had several pans going. He laid down a large spoon and said, "Well?"

Passing one mug to Mara, Dalin leaned against the wall with his own. He fished in his front pocket and handed a small object to his father.

Jin opened his hand and peered at the fragment, expression darkening. "Energy weapon," he pronounced.

Yadira's mug clattered to the table, "What?"

"Last year, we replaced the standard sensors with these." He held up the twisted brown lump. "These are very sensitive but also the lowest input sensors available. Made in Satri. Nearly impossible to detect."

"This was done with specific intent, using an illegal weapon," Dalin added.

"Someone was trying to flush you out," Yadira said, her voice and eyes hard. "I don't like this, Jin. I want these children with us. We could hide them."

Her husband stopped her with a look. "Even Jameson couldn't keep them safe in Satri. You know hiding isn't a life."

The mood of the foursome was somber well into the evening meal, even though they sat in the beautiful dining room with a fully decorated table. Mara glanced up and caught Dalin looking at her as she pushed the vegetables around on her plate.

"You all right?" he asked.

"Yes. You?"

He shrugged and rubbed at a spot on his temple. His plate wasn't empty either. "Do you mind if we clear the table and then do some planning?" Dalin asked his parents.

His mother's tone was resigned. "Of course, but don't worry about the dishes. We'll take care of the washing."

When he bent down to kiss his mother's cheek, she closed her eyes and gripped his hand before letting go. Both soldiers quickly cleared their plates as well as most of the serving dishes before heading into the common room.

With a sigh, Dalin slouched on the long couch and patted the spot next to him.

Tempted, but uncertain about the parameters of their relationship, Mara chose the chair at the closest angle and curled herself into it. "Have I been declared missing? Do you know?"

"In case you were overdue and the snow was otherwise clear for you to return, Elias was instructed to share a story that his wife located distant relatives of yours at the very southern edge of the settled territory."

It wasn't completely untrue.

"Tomorrow morning we head out early and travel north inside the tree line. When the militia travels north as Gaishan, we generally stick to the open, but not knowing…" His eyes went to the beams in the ceiling.

"Do you have a place in mind to make camp?" Mara filled her mind with the image of the forest clearing they now used as a safe place to talk. "It's only a day's ride from here," she said.

"Technically two days," he clarified. "We don't want to push the horses. But the clearing is on the way, so we could camp there the second night—"

"Four nights camping all together?" Mara interrupted.

"That's why my parents were carrying so much food. It's for us to take." He sat up and absently scratched the stubble along his jaw.

For once, Mara wasn't worried about food as much as the cold and the horses. "We have enough blankets?"

"We do."

As she went through a mental checklist of the gear needed for this length of winter excursion, her mind felt rusty. Who knew such a short time in her new life would alter her level of preparation so drastically? "Can we use your cooking kit?"

"Command only approved my boots. Everything else from Satri has to be hidden or ditched before we get to Tamoh."

She uncurled her legs and winced at the stiffness.

Concern flared in Dalin's eyes. "What was that soldier? I thought you were healed." He leaned forward, reaching out for her leg.

"Easy, Lieutenant, just a little sore from today's ride." Before he could touch her, Mara stood and made a drawn-out stretch for the ceiling. "I'm going to check my bags and then take a last shower if you don't mind."

"Not at all." He stood and stretched also. "I'll grab a shower in the morning."

Chapter 38

"Look after each other," Yadira said as she relinquished her son from a final hug in the early morning light.

"Of course," Dalin said.

"We will," Mara replied at the same time.

"Plant the *gontras* as you go," Jin reminded Mara. "Those thirteen seeds will make a difference one day."

She kissed him on the cheek. "Thank you for training with me."

The older man grinned. "Use your shields, control the energy, and no one will be able to stop you." He clasped hands with Dalin and pulled him in close. It was impossible to hear what father murmured to son.

Dalin led his horse first; Mara followed with her mare. They mounted in near unison. Jin stood in the stable door, Yadira tucked under one arm.

"Thank you," Mara sent to both of them and raised her right hand in salute. Maybe this was what it felt like when the volunteer Protectors left home to join up, this ripping of the fabric of a family. The separation might be temporary, but the risk of permanence was real. How could—more importantly, why would—Dalin choose this life when he had so much to lose?

#

Clouds obscured the sun all day, keeping the forest as full of shadows as Mara's mind. Occasionally, snow made it through the trees, but nothing new accumulated on top of the wisps from the night before. The constant wind made her appreciate her borrowed coat and hat.

At their last stop before making camp, she voiced a question that had been nagging at her most of the afternoon. "Will the Tree be able to reach me?"

"That's unknown," Dalin said. "She's only appeared around Satri, at least appearances that are part of the public record."

Noting the tension in his voice, she swung around to face him.

"Just another hour or two," Dalin said, outwardly calm as always. "No sense making camp in the dark." He vaulted into his saddle and resumed the moderate pace they'd kept all day.

That night, too tired to light a fire, they ate a cold dinner. The horses were fed and watered, brushed and blanketed. Working together, the tent went up and the gear was stowed in short order. A smattering of snow fell, but the wind had finally died down.

Inside the tent, Mara was checking the handle of her new sword when she felt Dalin looking at her.

"What is it?" she asked.

He took a breath to answer and paused.

"Dalin?"

He turned and began unrolling his sleeping sack. "If we use your blankets on top of the tent pad, it will be warmer and softer for sleeping."

"Yes," Mara said with some hesitation. "I'm going to use Nuwa's—"

"And if we fasten our bags together, it will more than double our body heat," he blurted.

Mara's eyes widened for a fraction of a second before she slowly nodded.

"You said I would have to fog you, but that wouldn't work now," Dalin said.

Exhaling, she brushed at a snag on one of her sleeves. "You were the enemy," she reminded him, voice quiet. "And now...now you are a friend and my partner," she finished. The moment held as blue eyes locked with gray.

A twig snapped in the clearing. Dalin opened the tent flap and looked toward the source of the sound. "Just the horses settling in," he reported.

Without further conversation, they arranged the blankets on top of the tent pad and zipped the two sleeping sacks together, creating one large pocket. She shed her outer layers and slipped inside wearing her light tunic and leggings, shivering as she did so. Dalin tapped the tiny cube light dangling from a center strut and did the same.

She had curled herself against one side of the joined sleeping sacks when Dalin tugged on a handful of her unbound hair.

"Hey," Mara protested.

"Come a little closer," he coaxed. "I'm warm."

She scooted half the distance between them and stopped. Dalin reached out and pulled her closer until her head was pillowed on his arm, her right hip almost touching his left side.

"You are warm," she said with a yawn.

Safe and more comfortable than the first night, Mara drifted into sleep, catching images from Dalin about the Tree and why they could never be anything more than a fighting pair.

#

The first thing to penetrate Mara's consciousness was the smell of *gontra*. She was warm and the sheets smelled so delicious that when she opened her eyes, she expected to see her room at the wayhouse. Seeing the roof of the tent, she gasped.

Dalin threw one arm in front of her as he sat up, knife drawn. "What is it?" he demanded, voice rough with sleep.

"Uh, I was so warm and cozy waking up that I thought I was still in the wayhouse but then I saw the tent." Mara's cheeks flamed.

"The tent startled you," he said. His hair stood up in irregular spikes, blonde stubble covered his cheeks, but his eyes were sharp and alert.

Mara covered her face. "I'm sorry," she muttered. "Never thought I would get soft living in a settlement, but…" She shook her head, thrilled and mortified to be this close to Dalin.

Lying back and stretching, he declared, "Best night of sleep I've had in a tent."

She couldn't stop her smile. "How nice for you."

"You fell asleep before I did and woke up thinking you were in a bed."

"True," Mara acknowledged. She did feel rested. But it was hard to relax with Dalin grinning at her. She threw on a jacket and stuck her head out into the cold morning. A dusting of white flakes covered the ground and the horses were huddled together.

Pulling herself back inside, she said, "Colder than yesterday out there. I think a fire and a hot breakfast are in order."

#

As the sun crested the horizon, the pair mounted their horses and continued northward. At times during the morning, the wind would pick up the accumulated snow and blow it in chaotic swirls. Other intervals the wind died down and the sun would break through the clouds.

During their midday stop, Dalin pulled up his camouflage shield and left the cover of the trees to measure their progress along the river.

She waited, having not yet mastered the camouflage technique. Learning to regulate the power flow had taken priority.

A few minutes later, he sent one word, *"Tracks."*

Regular shield snapping into place, she ran to join him. In the hazy light, Dalin's shield didn't camouflage completely, but he did appear nearly translucent. The rough ground and damp grasses were more distinct than he was.

"Look," he said, pointing to a series of human and horse tracks. "I can make out at least three different types of shoe or boot impressions. By the size and depth, I would guess the prints were made by men."

"Traders?" she asked.

Dalin shook his head. "There's a road much farther east. It runs straight north and comes out just east of the settlements. Any sanctioned trader is required to use the road and submit to inspections along the way." He stood up, wiped his muddy hands on his pants, and put his gloves back on. "We can track this group."

"Are the prints fresh enough to be helpful?" The clouds were massing overhead and fresh snow blew sideways with the gusty wind.

Following her gaze up to the sky, he said, "My guess is they're a half a day ahead of us."

"If it's the same unknown group sending men—" Mara paused and pushed down the sudden flare of panic she felt. "If it's the same group, they're heading to Elias's settlement and possibly Northwest Protector house looking for me. Energy weapons could do a lot of damage with the advantage of surprise and distance." She swallowed and pressed hard on her empty stomach.

The grim concern on Dalin's face mirrored her own.

#

The two soldiers urged the horses as fast as they dared, knowing they still had significant distance to cover. Between the fear for her friends, the biting cold, and the frequent stops to look for new tracks, Mara was as exhausted as Rowan when they finally reached the forest clearing near dusk.

Though the light was fading quickly, recognition flared as she looked around. The high tree branches were covered in soft white, as was the open floor of the clearing.

"You must have been here in the warm part of the year. Your version has sunshine," she said.

"This is where Jameson always stopped. No farther north—he was very strict about it." Dalin dismounted and with a few kicks, uncovered a ring of fire rocks.

Without further conversation, he started a fire and began preparing food. Mara removed the remainder of the saddlebags and saddles from both horses and went to work on their shoes and coats. She wished they'd arrived earlier so she could explore the clearing.

Dalin's hat was pulled low, the hollows of his cheeks shadowed and his jaw tight, when Mara sat down near the fire. Though he turned the strips of meat on a thin, flat rock, his eyes were slightly unfocused, mind clearly working through their situation. And though Mara was equally concerned, the smell of the sizzling fat made her mouth water.

"I thought we might catch them. At least find fresher tracks."

"Me too," Mara said. "I'm worried about the settlers and the Protectors. They don't have any way to defend against—"

"Maybe if you were there," Dalin interjected. With precise movements, he slid meat and bread onto each plate. He added a small handful of berries and nuts to the first plate before presenting it. "Ma'am," he said.

"What do you mean, if I was there?" Mara asked as she accepted her plate.

Dalin raised an eyebrow. Suddenly her mind filled with moving images of the end of the skirmish outside of Satri. She saw herself flinging her arm toward the Brown soldiers and the men dropping like stunned birds.

"That was...I was...protecting you." The words came slowly as she saw Dalin's point. "I don't know how to make that happen at will. I can't practice my aim. It just…happens." Mara stared down at her plate.

"I don't like running blind or fighting blind," he said. "We've captured three of these men and still know nothing." He took a bite and chewed, staring into the distance.

"How about fighting blind for four years?" She couldn't keep the bitterness out of her tone.

"You had information on the Gaishan. Maps, battle plans." Mara shot him an incredulous look.

"It never felt right," Dalin admitted. "Especially once I saw you on the other side of the lines."

They finished eating in silence. He set up the tent and stowed their gear while Mara took care of the dinner cleanup. When she returned from the stream, she could see the tiny light glowing through the tent walls. *"I banked the fire. We're going to want it in the morning. Horses are set,"* she sent.

In the center of the dark clearing, Mara looked up. Nothing in the sky but stars. But according to the planetary atlas, Iloel, Kels, Laska, and other planets were out there. Her breath caught as her mind opened to the distant possibilities twinkling in the darkness.

"All clear?" Dalin asked when she crawled into the tent.

Shrugging, she turned to point her feet toward the entrance. "Cold but no signs of a storm coming. No presence I can detect, people or animal."

"Your patrols don't come this far south; our patrols don't come this far north. It's a perfect spot. Especially since no Protector compounds were ever established along the southern border."

"No threats ever came from the south," she murmured, wrestling off her boots and still thinking about the stars.

"Listen," Dalin said. "I need to report in."

The dim light made it hard to see his face, but the strain in his voice was clear. "How many reports?" Mara asked.

"Two. Shouldn't be long, but make sure your mental shields are up before you fall asleep." He took a breath.

Mara waited.

Dalin shook his head, curved his lips in an approximation of a smile, and slipped into the bedding. He assumed his usual position, flat on his back, hands behind his head and closed his eyes. "Sleep well."

He didn't shift or speak again. Mara brushed her teeth, took a last swallow of water, and slid into the wide sleeping sack, careful not to jostle her bedmate.

As her eyes adjusted to the darkness, she checked her shields. Jin had taught her to imagine running her hands over a smooth, circular wall. Worry conjured pictures of the compound under attack from the men with energy weapons.

Rolling to her side, she scrunched into a ball. "Borrowing trouble," she whispered. She forced herself to see the compound as she had left it, filled with the active hum of working people, Protectors preparing for their truce assignments, busy but not rushed. Her friends eating, talking, and laughing, ignorant of how they were being tricked, believing in a war that was only an experiment.

The last thoughts were of the *gontra* seeds in her saddlebags. She had thirteen to plant between here and the compound. During their final workout, Jin had explained to her that this time between the last storms of winter and the first blooms of spring was perfect for planting *gontras*. The seeds would grow quickly, finding resources and sustenance with ease, one of the key distinctions of the unique species.

Would Annelise be more curious about a talking Tree or a war experiment? The Tree. She could imagine Annelise's laughter. *Of course the Tree.*

#

The next day, they rode north along the forest's edge, taking turns scouting ahead.

"The ground is still hard, except near the water," Dalin said after returning from the stream's bank. "If the group we're following was careful, they could hide more of their tracks than I thought."

"So when they stopped for water…"

"Walking along the rocks and keeping the horses away, it could be done."

Mara considered this. "Why leave all those tracks previously then?"

"Disguise numbers. False trail. Or those tracks were an unrelated circumstance."

"If we pick up the pace," she said, "we could gain ourselves some time to approach with caution tomorrow, late afternoon. At least we'd get to Tamoh before full dark."

#

All morning, Dalin had been silent, none of his usual jokes and smiles. He'd helped choose a place to plant the first *gontra* seed, helped her dig the hole. She cradled the seed and visualized wrapping it in a small energy cocoon as Jin had instructed. Replacing the dirt in the hole, Mara smiled with anticipation, hoping to come back to this place and find a tree with silver leaves and blue pods. She repeated the process each time they stopped, though digging through the near-frozen ground became increasingly difficult as they progressed north.

Looking at Dalin's back, she wondered for the tenth time what had happened when he reported in the night before. She knew they needed to be cautious, but she could not deny the happiness she was feeling, riding into familiar territory and the only home she'd known.

"Remember when Liu brought a report to me at the festival?"

"Yes," Mara said, surprise coming through.

"The message from your Protector House was unusual and indicated substantial changes happening in the compound."

"What do you mean? I thought Jameson or Puente was getting information directly from Twyla."

"That's one of the issues. Shielding has increased significantly, somehow at the structural level. It's possible someone erected a shield large enough to cover the compound or an even larger area. The report from Liu's contact implied the war project parameters have been altered."

Mara nudged her horse to bring her alongside the other mount. "The sun is nearly down."

He didn't respond immediately, staring bleakly at the woods.

"I don't think we'll get enough light from the moons to continue safely," she added.

Dalin sat back in his saddle and signaled his horse to stop. The horses blew and stamped, breath streaming white in the cold.

"Here is good. We should stop and rest." He squinted at the overcast sky.

Despite mutual worry and fatigue, the pair had settled into a rhythm of camp tasks and responsibilities. Dalin stirred the fragrant soup over their small fire and watched Mara lay out food and water for the horses. She turned and met his eyes.

"How long?"

"What?" Dalin said.

"How long until the food is ready?"

He peered into the cooking pot. "Fifteen to twenty minutes."

Pulling her new sword from its sheath, she admired it in the firelight. "I'm stiff and cold. And uneasy. So are you." She took a few steps closer. "How 'bout a couple of rounds to loosen up before we eat?"

Dalin unfolded himself from the ground in one smooth motion. He drew his sword from the scabbard on his hip and turned, right shoulder back, weapon raised in the classic fencing stance. "Points? First to three?" he asked.

"If you like," Mara replied.

He attacked, exploiting his long reach with a vicious thrust. The light danced and reflected along Mara's blade as she parried, narrowly escaping injury.

First point went to Dalin when he used a combination of high strikes, forcing her to block too high so that he could tag her in the ribs.

Mara scored the next point with an upward thrust to his belly, pulling the power of the strike at the last moment.

Dalin's longer legs enabled him to force her backward until her feet touched the fire ring. "Point for trapping you," he said.

She feinted right and when he lunged to block her, planted a boot on his thigh and shoved. Scrambling around him, she held her sword upright, elbow protecting her ribs. "Not trapped," she said.

"Kicking in a sword match?" Dalin said, the first relaxed grin of the day spreading across his face. "Point goes to me anyway."

Mara toed the ground. She rubbed her right hip and raised her eyes to Dalin's face. His grin widened.

Leaping forward, she stabbed straight at Dalin's heart. She spun around his parry and laid her sword along his neck. "Oh there's my point," she purred. "Knew I left it around here somewhere."

With an exaggerated sigh, he lifted her sword with his own and moved it away. "Gruffald teach you to talk like that?"

"'Taunting is a secondary skill,'" she quoted, trying to imitate Gruffald's deep rumble. "'Can make the opponent lose focus, maybe lose his cool.'"

"Figures," Dalin muttered.

"Doesn't work on you, Gruffald said." She stepped away and switched her sword to her left hand, wiping her right palm on her pants. "The guys say you don't lose your cool."

Taking a deep breath, he also dried his sword hand before returning to fighting stance. "I'm younger than all of my men. They have to be able to rely on me." He rolled his neck and shoulders once, smile gone. "Last point?"

She raised her sword in answer.

Both fighters closed the gap with a lunge. The pace increased and steel rang against steel in a bright melody of strikes and blocks.

Mara's skill had increased significantly in the past few months. She could mentally map a sequence of blows and evaluate possible openings. But as her shoulders began to ache, she acknowledged it might be another year or possibly two before they would be evenly matched.

When Dalin risked a glance at the cooking pot, she jumped in a half-turn and just missed his chin with the flat of her sword.

The tip of his blade touched her jacket, precisely over her heart. "Flashy move," he said.

"Thought for sure I had you. Thanks for letting me try out Jameson's gift." With a deep sigh, she slid her sword into her shoulder harness before shrugging out of it.

Dalin sheathed his own sword. "Of course." He knelt down to give the soup a stir. "Would you be disappointed to stop after one round? Dinner's ready."

He spooned chunks of vegetables into a bowl, added a good measure of broth, and passed it to Mara.

Sitting carefully, she stirred her soup and blew on it. "You were holding back." Her tone was factual, not angry.

Focusing on the soup and vegetables he was transferring to his bowl, Dalin said, "I've learned and sparred with everyone who taught you in Satri." He raised his bowl. "A toast to those teachers."

She raised her bowl, her smile wry. For a few moments, they ate in silence.

"You have too much power and speed for me to really hold back," he said. "The points you scored were fair."

Swallowing a mouthful of soup, she said, "Hurray for me."

Dalin sliced the last of their travel bread and handed some to Mara. "In the past year, only Puente managed to score against me. And that was just once."

She raised her eyebrows and nodded, chewing.

"I meant…" He looked at her sideways, chagrin plain on his face.

"You meant I should be happy about my two," she said and then really smiled.

Dalin grinned back. "When we were little, you smiled like that right before doing something dangerous."

"Might be doing something dangerous tomorrow," she said.

Chapter 39

Mara woke from a sound sleep, her back pressed against Dalin's. She moved slowly, trying not to disturb her tentmate.

Rowan raised her head and whickered at her mistress's approach. "Homecoming day. We'll be back in Protector Territory," Mara whispered, reaching up to scratch behind the mare's ears. The warhorse bumped her with his nose, so she obliged and scratched his ears, too. The dawn air was cold, but not as cold as the previous morning and the dusting of white on the ground had not increased.

As the first golden brush of sunrise touched their campsite, Mara thought about having breakfast in the main hall of Protector House. In the early part of spring, breakfast still usually included some kind of hot grain cereal with brown sugar. As she led the horses toward the stream, marks on the ground snapped her attention back to the moment.

Mara released the horses to go the last few lengths to the water on their own and squatted down to look. Fresh tracks. She walked in a large circle to confirm the direction. Fresh tracks, heading north, at least four horses.

"Dalin," she called.

"Here," he answered from just inside the trees.

Mara pointed to the tracks. "They were behind us."

"Or this is reinforcements," her partner suggested, closing the distance in a few strides.

Heart picking up speed, Mara fought the urge to race north and put herself between these riders and her friends.

"Not trying to hide," Dalin mused aloud. "Not chasing us then."

She forced herself to stare at the tracks, find the information they needed. "I think it was closer to eight horses, maybe riding as two lines."

"That's my guess," he agreed. "We'd have heard them if it had been more than that. These happened in the past hour." Bending down, he touched the hoof marks. "The frost isn't completely hard. And these are deep, the horses are running."

"Or carrying heavy gear," Mara said.

"Or both," Dalin finished the thought.

#

They packed camp at high speed. Just when it was time to divide food for breakfast in the saddle, Dalin disappeared into the trees.

"Be right back," he called over his shoulder.

Mara watched him fade out of sight before she resumed checking her horse's one loose shoe. Even after so much time together, Dalin fascinated her. As much as she wanted to be more than a soldier one day, she also wanted more from him. With him. Maybe they weren't equals *yet*. But she was determined they could be.

A Protector emerged from the far side of the campsite, just as she stamped out the last embers of the fire.

"Hail, Protector," Mara said, the routine words pushing past her surprise.

"Hail, settler," the Protector said and lifted off the helmet to reveal Dalin's familiar face grinning at her.

Gaping, she said, "Your uniform...fits." She hurried over to touch the sleeve of the red leather jacket. "How...?"

"You should change, too," he advised. "Protectors are on the move right now. Plus, some of the people in Tamoh are bound to recognize you since it's so close to Arlis, right? Better if you're in uniform." Turning away, he hooked the helmet on the pommel of his saddle and began checking his horse's straps.

Mara nodded, staring just a moment longer. He looked unbelievably good, the crimson leather molding to his legs and torso.

Slipping into her well-worn uniform more than reminded her of the urgency and danger of their mission. The creaking leather was as familiar as breathing as she pulled out her old cloak and put Nuwa's jacket away with tinge of regret.

"If you'd showed yourself to me in a Protector uniform, I never would have doubted you," Mara said.

Dalin unrolled a long wool cloak, wrapped it around his shoulders, and buttoned the short row of buttons running from chin to mid-chest. "Obviously, uniforms can be borrowed or copied. We're not the only ones who might be hiding in the settlements or at Northwest Protector House."

#

Mara pulled her visor down against the wind as the horses ran. It limited her sight lines, but kept her eyes from watering and allowed her numb cheeks to warm up. Their story, if questioned, would be that she encountered Dalin on the road two days ago. He had just been transferred from West Protector House to Northwest House and had gained permission to do a bit of trade in Arlis before starting the new assignment. Elias's wife, Claire, was expecting them and would verify the tale.

She clutched her cloak tighter and wished for gloves. It had been at least two hours since she'd forced down the fruit and cheese, but her stomach, accustomed to being full in Satri, was complaining.

Ahead, Dalin stopped and held up his hand. *"Feel that?"*

As she approached his position, the hair on the back of her neck and along her arms stood up. She could hear and feel a humming in the air. Dismounting, she walked forward, cold fingers outstretched. Three steps past the warhorse, her hand brushed a wall of energy much like the one she and Dalin had created to keep out snow.

When Mara pulled back sharply, he grabbed her hand. "Are you hurt?"

"No. It's a shield, but thick and sharp, like sticking my hand into a stream of falling pebbles."

Dalin reached out to test the shield wall, invisible but for a tiny distortion in the air. He squinted toward the cloudy sky.

"How did you know to stop?" Mara asked.

"Herald slowed down, and then I felt it."

"We can probably lead the horses through," she suggested, patting her mare. "But I wonder how wide this is. I wonder if we can go around."

Both remounted and rode hard for a full minute in opposite directions. The shield still hummed where Mara stopped. Dalin confirmed it from his position also.

When they met back at their starting point, Dalin said, "I'd like to try a different experiment."

Mara shrugged and looked around, feeling watched. "Sure."

"I'm going to step through and try to use rapport with you. I want to know if this"—he gestured outwards and then upwards—"is what's keeping our people from reporting in."

Dalin passed through the energy boundary unscathed. He turned to face her, waited a few moments, hands on hips.

"Anything?" he asked, crossing back to her side. When she shook her head, he said, "You try."

Hunching her shoulders, Mara approached the shield boundary slowly. It felt like passing through a shower of needles. A smile tugged at the corner of her mouth. What to say if Dalin couldn't hear?

"You look great in leather," she sent.

He frowned and motioned her back through. *"Leather?"* he said, expression puzzled. "I only got one word."

"I asked, 'How did you get a leather uniform?'" She looked down to hide her embarrassment.

"Same way you got yours." His attention returned to the barrier. "I don't think this has been here more than a week." Crouching down, he studied where the shield touched the ground. "One more test?" he asked Mara.

"What do you need?"

"Go back through and try to tap the power that connects you to the Tree, to the *gontra* network."

"You're wondering if this shield goes into the ground? Where her roots might be?" The concept was upsetting.

"We need to know," Dalin insisted.

Mara stepped through the nearly invisible barrier once more, gritting her teeth at the sensation. She took a deep breath and blew it out slowly. With her next intake of breath, she reached for the reservoir of power she could touch so easily in Satri. The energy came with Mara's pull and formed into a battle shield. Shielded, she walked through the barrier protected from most of the uncomfortable sensation.

"I can connect. The power is there," she confirmed, relieved to still have her gift, both her gifts, from the Tree. She would need to be at her strongest when facing this unknown enemy.

Once inside the shield together, they confirmed rapport worked as long as the energy barrier wasn't between them. Another relief and a definite advantage as they raced toward the settlement of Tamoh.

Dalin sent, *"We stick to the plan, approach from the southeast, stay within the trees. If the shield is monitored they'll know two humans and two horses crossed through. We may not have much time, so look for any changes, however small, things that don't fit."*

"The snow along the road is well-trampled," Mara said immediately. *"I see horse and human tracks all over the place."*

"That's unusual?"

"This is the split in the road that leads to my...to Northwest Protector House. If the storms and the temperatures have been as severe as we were told, a few might venture out. But only if a real thaw happened. Otherwise, no one would want to provoke the Gaishan." Her last statement carried more than a touch of resentment.

Dalin slowed to dismount and began scanning the ground. *"Come look at this."* Dropping the reins, he walked in a large circle.

Reluctantly, she jumped from Rowan's back and picked her way through the icy mud.

"Check out this boot print," he said. "It's the clearest one, but with all of this it's hard to see which direction the group ultimately chose. Or if they divided up."

The frozen impression was of a large boot with a rounded toe and a distinctive sole pattern of small squares with circles inside. Dalin lifted his boot to show the pattern of tread was waves with intermittent squares and cross-hatching. Protector boots had smooth soles and narrow toes with a slight heel for riding.

"These boots were made off-planet," he said.

"What about the Browns?" Mara asked. "Some of them come from off-planet." She couldn't stop looking at the numerous prints, calculating and recalculating how many enemies might be headed toward her home.

Dalin gave his head a slight shake. "Browns notify the Satri militia when they come through the spaceport, either because they're heading to the project zone or because they have business in Satri. A group of eight or more would have been mentioned by one of my officers."

Biting her lip, Mara gave a tight nod of acknowledgment.

"Every man, woman, and child in that compound has had combat training." He squeezed Mara's hand and gave her an encouraging smile. "Annelise is fine."

"I need to see for myself," she said. "Is this person, the source who might have information about me or about the Tree, is he expecting both of us?"

He plainly did not like the question. "You can't investigate on your own. If you're caught—"

"Dalin, I live he-...I lived there. The Protectors are on the move anyway. If I'm seen, I'm back in. But the risk is worth it, just so I—"

"That massive shield means no calling for support."

Who would they trust to help? The situation made less sense every moment.

"Are you worried about going into the settlement alone?" she asked.

"No." Dalin waved a hand impatiently. "No, but I don't want to separate, not knowing what's waiting in either place."

"What if someone is attacking my friends with those energy weapons? I have to see for myself that everything's fine. And if it's not fine, I need to be there, protect them. You even suggested it."

Dalin kicked at the boot tracks and huffed out a breath. He moved closer, looking down at Mara with a mixture of concern and frustration. "I'd go with you, but I can't neglect this lead. If there's even a tiny bit more information about your kidnapping, or the group responsible for the attacks..."

Stretching up, she kissed Dalin's rough cheek. "I know," she said. "Thank you for understanding."

"I will meet you by the kitchen shed in the back of the compound, no later than an hour past sundown. If you're not there, I'm coming in to find you." He brushed her lips with a brief kiss, and then pulled away with a subtle flinch. "You're my partner now. Don't forget."

Mara swung into the saddle. "See you soon."

Flipping through possibilities in her mind, each one ended with her people injured, sometimes dead. Though the compound had never, to her knowledge, needed to live up to its name, it could. And her friends were trained to fight, as Dalin had pointed out. Yet the flash and the quick damage caused by the energy weapons in the park repeated over and over in her thoughts.

After a while, a new question asserted itself and Mara slowed.

Her mare's sides were heaving. With a twinge of remorse, she dismounted and led Rowan through the gloom to a small stream. She dropped the reins so her horse could drink and began to fumble with the saddlebags, looking for food. Hands trembling, she pulled out a handful of dried meat.

"Rowan, if you were going to capture Northwest Protector House, where would you put scouts?"

So far, she hadn't seen anyone, but that meant little if the scouts were good. About a hundred meters from the back of the compound, Mara stopped walking and looked for a good place to tether her horse.

In a dry space between two trees, she wedged the saddle, saddlebags, and extra gear. She gave Rowan a quick rubdown and draped a dark blanket over her back. After a long drink of water, she left her canteen as well. Mara checked the draw of her sword and added a knife at each hip.

It was only a few minutes' walk before the outer wall of the compound loomed through the trees. Light shone through the ports at the roofline of the main hall. The scent of cooking food drifted in the air. Maybe everything was fine. She could just sneak in after lights out, check on her friends, and leave again. Breathing in the familiar smells, she let her shoulders relax.

A dull boom sounded within the walls, followed quickly by another and then a third boom. Faint human cries rose through the windows.

Mara crouched low and sprinted across the large garden to the rear courtyard. Another boom, perceptibly louder, shook the support walls. Shrieks pierced the air. *"Main hall,"* she sent, broadcasting as loudly and as far as she could. *"Explosions. Are you on your way?"*

Dalin's mental reply was slow and strangely muffled. *"It's a trap. Stay where you are!"*

Chapter 40

At the inner door, Mara paused. She reached with her mind and yanked the power up and through her body. Drawing her sword, she opened the door with her left hand. Another boom sounded, and a moment later, debris and dust puffed down the empty hall. This time the vocal response sounded more like shouts of anger than cries of pain.

Mara trotted down the short corridor to the first wide passage. Dust choked the air and chunks of stone, some as large as fists, littered the floor.

A golden glow was forming far ahead. A figure shaped the glow into a blinding ball of light and flung it at the stout doors of the Great Hall with a gigantic boom. The doors rocked on their massive hinges and more debris showered down.

Mara crept forward. Another figure, this one wearing the distinctive red Protector uniform, joined the first outside the doors. Mara rubbed the dust out of her eyes, trying to recognize either person.

Loud male voices came from inside the hall. One door panel opened just wide enough for a small Protector in house uniform to fall through, landing heavily on hands and knees. She retched and drew a shaking hand across her mouth.

Mara was close enough now to make out Haleen's face and see that the magic wielder also wore a house uniform. Haleen coughed and clutched her rounded belly, and when the person in the red uniform turned to help, Mara recognized Twyla.

"They say this isn't a place for a pregnant woman and to send me away," Haleen choked out the words.

The senior Protector grasped her shoulder and began to hurry her away from the open space. "Watch the door," she ordered the magic user, a Protector Mara did not recognize.

Taking a few quick steps, she dropped her shield and said, "Twyla."

Twyla's scarred face registered a moment of shock. Then she snapped, "You're late, soldier."

Before Mara could respond, Haleen pulled out of the older woman's grasp and grabbed Mara's hand, tears running down her flushed cheeks.

"Nearly all the Blues is in there and a good number from the other cohorts, too." Haleen turned back to their senior Protector. "They got everybody sittin' against the wall and they have…things that make fire, they throw fire, and it kills." Her lip trembled. "They killed Bromcott."

Twyla folded her arms across her chest and closed her eyes for a moment. "Bromcott was a good senior for the Blue cohort. He served well."

Letting out a shaky breath, Haleen said, "The men, they say they want the 'daughter of the tree.' And if we give her over, no one else gets hurt."

It was a trap. A trap for her, one they were willing to bait with children. The guilt of having brought these soldiers to her home was overwhelming. "How many Protectors in the Great Hall?" Mara licked her dry lips and tried to swallow down the nausea.

"Close to two hundred. And they brought some prisoner with 'em, a really tall Protector from another house. Dumped him in the corner like a sack of flour."

Mara tasted bile. Her skin felt hot and tight with contained energy. "Is he…is the prisoner hurt?"

"I dunno. We were about to start the first shift of the evening meal and they busted in, yellin' and knockin' over tables." Haleen rubbed a hand over her belly. "They came in through the kitchen calling for the daughter of the tree to show herself—"

"How many men in the attack force?" Twyla interrupted.

"Eight, maybe ten. But those…things, their weapons? We never saw anything like them before. Cut you down where you stand."

The senior Protector glanced back toward the huge doors. "Take her to the healers." Haleen opened her mouth. "Let them check you," Twyla growled.

"Yes, ma'am."

"Then you get back here double time, Mara." Twyla narrowed her eyes. "That leg mended?"

"Yes, ma'am."

Dalin was alive and out of the action. He would be fine for a few minutes more, wouldn't he?

Wrapping her left arm around Haleen's shoulders, Mara led her friend toward the Blue corridor. "A baby?" she asked, glancing down as they hurried along.

Haleen's breath hitched and Mara froze, worried the girl might vomit again. "The leave before this one, I was home in my settlement visiting my betrothed. He…he has a good stake and a nice house, couple of horses," Haleen scrubbed her face with one hand. "I started two years older than most of you and I'm due to finish my service at mid-summer anyway."

"That's good," Mara said as the blue doors came into view. "We'll end this soon and you can tell me everything else." Gently, she stepped in front and edged into the wide hallway entrance, sword first.

"They're all Twyla's age or older," Haleen whispered. "Black uniforms. They keep those circle weapon things on their belts, at least two on each man. Anyone that tried to disobey or escape is down now. Some's dead I think. Besides Bromcott…" She trailed off in a hitching sob.

Cold sweat trickled down Mara's spine and under her arms. She kept up her slow, careful walk down the otherwise-empty and normal-looking hall and forced out her most urgent question. "Annelise?"

"She was a few days behind me. Her mama needed help getting ready for the first spring market. Not sure when she's s'posed to get here." Haleen sounded uncertain.

Letting out the breath she'd been holding, Mara forced herself to focus. "How many do you think are dead?"

"At least fifteen." Her voice was ragged with stress and grief. "What's this daughter of the tree got to do with us?" she asked. "Do you know?"

As Mara pushed open the door to the healers' waiting room, a man in a black uniform whirled to face them, brandishing an energy weapon. Mara shoved Haleen back into the hallway and launched herself at the intruder, slicing across his wrist.

The dark disc flew from his grasp and landed out of reach, sliding across the floor. She kicked him in the center of his ribs. With a crack, the man's breath whooshed out.

Wrenching the man's bleeding arm behind his back, she pulled higher until he dropped to his knees, face grinding into the stone floor.

"Tell me who and why. Now," she ordered.

"King's Men," the prone soldier choked out. Blood bubbled at the corner of his mouth.

"What do you want?"

"Daughter of the Tree. Someone hid her here in the middle of this experiment. One of the five compounds. All hit today." He coughed and spat a bloody wad on the floor. "We will find her and she will serve...the King's purpose." The man's eyes rolled back in his head, his entire body going slack.

Breathing hard, Mara placed a boot on the back of the man's neck and straightened, finally noticing the handful of people huddled on the benches.

"Mara?" Treyton stood under a sign that said, *Please find a place to wait. A healer will call your name.*

"Do you have something we can use to bind his hands and feet?" she asked.

The healer dropped an armload of supplies as he came around the counter, reaching out to clasp Mara's hand. His sandy hair was mussed, his calm demeanor diminished by strain. "Thank you. That man was threatening my patients."

With a pointed look at the waiting group, Mara said, "I need a few of you to bind this intruder and confine him to one of the rooms."

Two females from Yellow cohort stood up. "We can help," one said.

While the two set to work, Mara turned back to Treyton. "I think I broke at least one of his ribs. He won't be fast, but he'll be angry and in pain when he wakes."

"We're used to that around here," the healer said, a smile ghosting across his face. "But a weapon like his"—his pale brows drew together as he shook his head—"definitely not."

"Do you have someone who can check Haleen? They released her from the Great Hall but she's been vomiting from the stress." She opened the door to the healing area and found her friend slumped in the hall.

Jules appeared next to his partner. He clapped his hands and bounced on his toes. "Mara saved us!" he cheered.

"Not yet." She bent to retrieve the energy weapon and gently helped Haleen stand and walk from the hall to Jules. Meanwhile, the two female soldiers were dragging the unconscious King's Man to the back.

For a single irrational moment, Mara was tempted to ask how much Treyton knew about the Protector Project and why he would choose a Protector compound over a lovely city like Satri.

"Mara!" Dalin's voice was urgent in her head. *"Need you now!"* A huge boom rattled the windows. She heard it both through Dalin's ears and her own.

With a nod to her friend, she threw the healers a salute. "Got to go."

"I knocked out a King's Man in the healing center. Took his energy weapon."

"Good. Bring it."

Through their connection, she could sense Dalin fighting. Thank the Light he was free. She sprinted until she reached the corner of the main hallway intersection and skidded to stop in the dust.

One of the massive doors dangled from broken hinges. King's Men fought in pairs, back to back, using energy weapons for distance shots and short swords against anyone who got close. Protectors were making short dashes through the opening, diving in and joining the fight.

"Cover!" Zam's voice boomed.

Every Protector dropped to the ground, arms over heads. The second door shattered, broken pieces blowing into the Great Hall. Shouts rose from within, but above them, Zam bellowed, "Engage! Theta strategy."

Protectors leapt to their feet and formed groups to surround and subdue the King's Men as best they could among the long tables and scores of chairs. At least three were immediately shot in the torso, flailing and disrupting the formations. At close range the weapons were an even greater advantage. What was the formation name for hunt and surprise? Theta, the group swarm Zam had just ordered, wouldn't work.

Mara edged forward, nearing a pair of Protectors attempting to wrestle away energy weapons from a King's Man. One soldier was shot in the leg as he chopped at the intruder's weapon hand. Another took a shot to the ear.

The shrieks, the fallen dead and wounded in her home—if it was incomprehensible to her, no wonder the fight was such a mess, despite the unbalanced numbers.

And no masks on anyone. The interlopers in black demanding the Daughter of the Tree had regular faces, which meant friend at the most basic level of combat instruction. Nothing in the Protector training covered this scenario. They weren't prepared.

From inside the doorway, she yelled, "Sigma strategy!"

Zam picked up the yell. "Sigma, change from Theta to Sigma. Now!"

The veterans, most sixteen and older, dropped and ran for cover. Had the younger fighters even been exposed to hunt and surprise? The theory behind the strategy—to stay behind the attacker and out of any direct line of engagement from blowing poisons—should work.

Partners helped each other, dodging and weaving to get behind the men in black uniforms, though some were shot trying to drag the injured from the center of the floor. It was impossible to tell in the hazy glow of the remaining overhead lights which Protectors might be shielding. Anything to blunt the direct energy cut was better than nothing.

"Protectors, shields!" she ordered. When Zam didn't repeat the order, her stomach rolled over.

"Mara?"

"Dalin, where are you?" A table nearby burst into flames and a handful of small Protectors ran to the next cluster of furniture. Through the fog of dust and smoke, energy shots fired more wildly.

"We have a standoff. It's their leader."

Strained laughter drifted from one corner as the dodging, weaving Protectors lured one of the black-uniformed men into an ambush by three of their comrades. With a shout, two secured the weapon, one sitting on the man's arm, another on his back.

The momentum was turning in the fight and the few King's Men still standing were too occupied to notice her. Energy weapons flashed and the impacts cracked and crashed against the walls and floors, leaving black scorch marks or setting additional fires.

Mara threw her hands out toward the intruders, calling on the power that had protected Dalin and fogged the Brown soldiers. Nothing happened. She dropped to the floor as an energy shot blasted the spot next to her. No time to think about why the power didn't work.

Dalin, Twyla, and four others had formed a semicircle around two black-uniformed men, one standing, one slumped on the floor. The remaining intruders were nearly contained, either bound or pinned by groups of Protectors.

Edging closer to Dalin, she kept her shield up and her sword out. From her vantage point behind an upended table, she saw Garot standing over the downed man, energy disc raised, tracking the movements of the people in the room. Mara wiped sweat and grit out of her eyes, not believing that this was Garot, now changed to a black uniform.

"Their leader is the man on the ground. Twyla got a lucky slice inside his arm. He's losing a lot of blood," Dalin sent.

"Garot, put your weapon down," Twyla ordered. "Your leader needs a healer."

"Mara, can you hit him with a knife? Not to kill, just to distract?"

"Is he shielding?"

"Yes, but don't fog him. We need answers."

Dalin hadn't seen her failed attempt to fog the room. She imagined energy licking down the sword, coating it in the same green glow as the stripes on her uniform. With a lunge, she threw it, aiming for Garot's neck. The sword spun in a sideways arc and sliced deep across his upper arm as though he had no shield to stop it.

Whip fast, Dalin hit Garot's right forearm with the flat of his sword and knocked the disc-shaped weapon loose. Twyla kicked out his knees and gripped the man in a chokehold.

"Great Hall, clear!" Twyla yelled.

"Entrance, clear!" Zam responded.

Ragged shouts and cheers rang out from around the compound. Dalin shifted his stance, looking ready to give orders.

"Wait, remember you're not senior here."

Nodding, he bent to retrieve her sword from the floor, but not before she saw the red weals down the side of his face and along his neck. Mara picked her way through the debris until she reached the group of Protectors surrounding Garot and the fallen leader. Ignoring Garot for the moment, she knelt in the rubble. "Who is the Daughter of the Tree?" she whispered next to the leader's ear.

The man's shallow breathing hitched as he turned his head to lock eyes with Mara. "You," he whispered.

"What business do the King's Men have with the Daughter of the Tree?"

The man who had caused so much destruction sighed and levered himself to a sitting position with his good arm. His shiny black eyes glittered beneath long dark lashes. Tan, sharply ridged cheekbones stood out above his neatly trimmed black and silver beard.

When Dalin laid a hand on the man with the clear intent to assess injury and heal, Garot struggled against Twyla's tight hold.

"Ponapali," he hissed.

"I'm fine," Ponapali said, his tone weary but dismissive.

Dalin sat back. *He's not fine. He doesn't have much time unless we take him to the healers.*

The leader of the King's Men stared at Mara with a desperate need so tangible it rocked her back. "The Daughter was hidden from us. She is the key to the safety of the Commonwealth. Though our King be dead..." Ponapali coughed.

"We serve in his stead," Garot finished.

"This one to healing," Twyla ordered, stabbing the air near Ponapali's head. "The rest to the pen."

Immediately, a handful of Protectors snapped to attention from their various attempts to right tables and sweep the debris into piles. With a chorus of "ma'am" and "yes, ma'am," the teenage captors took the subdued King's Men and herded them out of the room.

"You two," the senior Protector snapped, "with me."

"Ma'am," Mara replied. She and Dalin trailed behind Twyla as the senior officer stalked out of the Great Hall.

Zam was just past the doorway, supervising the binding of the prisoners. Blood trickled from a cut on his hairline, the eye on that side of his face swollen and entirely red. "Your horse?" he asked Mara.

"Out past the kitchen shed," she said. "I heard...and I ran... Are you...?" she fumbled with where to start, but the combat instructor waved her words away.

"I'll send someone to get your horse and gear. Nice rotation on that sword toss, by the way." He winked his good eye.

Chapter 41

Twyla led the pair to the end of a hallway on the southern edge of the main building. She pushed open a door and stepped back, gesturing for them to go ahead of her. The large room contained a kitchen area in the far corner with a window over the sink, chairs grouped around two battered-looking tables, a long low couch, a shorter couch, and a huge, nearly full bookshelf. On the cabinet next to the sink, a sign read, *Do your own dishes. Your mother isn't stationed here.*

"Officers' mess?" Dalin asked.

With a brief nod, the older woman filled three mugs of water and handed them around. She seated herself at the nearest of the two tables, so Mara and Dalin followed suit.

Twyla took a long drink of her water. "You know about the Protector Project." Her statement was flat.

"Yes, ma'am," Mara said.

"You're in charge here?" Dalin asked.

Twyla wrapped her hands around her mug and regarded him for a long moment. "One of the variables in this experiment is the illusion of only two ranks, soldier and senior. But, yes, I'm in command here. Everyone who knows the true nature of the war project reports to me."

Her dark, intense gaze shifted between the two younger fighters. "Can't send a report or request information about our guests until that shield comes down. I dispatched a team to work on it right before the attack. We've got riders moving out to all the other Protector houses. The King's Men coordinated simultaneous strikes at every compound. They used energy weapons, asked all kinds of questions, generally ruined every variable we had running. Cat's out of the bag any way you look at it. I'm glad to be done with all of this." She grimaced as she made a broad gesture meant to include the whole territory.

"The last communication was about a week ago," Twyla continued. "I was given your approximate arrival time in Tamoh and your updated status, Mara, in terms of the project. Garot must have gotten that report, too." She arched one eyebrow. "I hear you acquired some new skills in Satri."

Mara's pulse jumped.

As she took a breath to respond, Dalin sent, *She doesn't know about the Tree. She means that you can read now and that you did advanced sparring and weapons work with my guys.*

With another breath, she looked her senior officer in the eye. "The war experiments are wrong. Children in the settlements don't have enough to eat, even though there's plenty of food in the South. Only a few are taught to read. Fewer still have access to any real learning."

"You met my brother," Twyla said, her tone dry.

"When he assessed my stick fighting and sword craft, he recognized your teaching."

"Did he tell you it was the public expression of his sentiments that landed us in this miserable experiment in the first place?"

Mara sat back in her chair, wishing to pull away from the darkness in the senior officer's tone.

"We were about to retire and had enough money to grow old slowly—the professional soldier's dream. One night, that dumb bastard spouts off in a pub in Crown City. Next thing we know, we're conscripted and stationed on Satri."

"That's exactly how Puente tells that story," Dalin sent. *"But he never said how Twyla ended up with the Protectors and he ended up on the other side of the experiment."*

Mara dropped her eyes to her senior officer's gnarled, scarred hands wrapped around the mug. She didn't have any idea what to say.

"It's not that I disagree with you, Mara." Twyla's voice was softer. "Learn from my brother's mistakes. Think fully but speak cautiously."

"Someone from the Protector side has been feeding false information to Jameson," Dalin began. "Do you—"

"Hey, speak of the darkness," Twyla interrupted. She frowned and then slapped the table, a rare grin brightening her face. "Your guys are here. They met my team and worked together to deactivate the dome shield. Should all arrive inside two hours."

"Satri militia sent men up North?" Dalin asked.

Twyla raised both eyebrows. "If you don't know, who would?"

Rubbing the back of his neck, he said, "Like you said, the experiment was already compromised by King's Men invading all of the compounds. That's what was happening in Tamoh. The group set to invade Northwest Protector House was in final preparations when I arrived. Ponapali was giving orders via com link to set the timing for the attack."

He gingerly touched the marks on his face. "I was shielding, but the hit from one of those weapons took me off my horse. Between the hit and the fall I was unconscious until I woke up inside the fight."

"Who is the enemy?" Mara said. "The King's Men attacked our home. The Browns have been aggressive; they've lied, taken away food and resources." She forced down a swallow of water and tried to swallow her frustration with it.

"This Garot," Dalin said, "he's the one you saw in Satri?"

"And here," she said.

"Some kind of double agent? Or mole?" Dalin said. "A King's Man hiding inside the Queen's Military Science Corps?"

"Don't be getting all fancy with groups and titles yet," Twyla said. "Captain Garot and I will have a friendly visit. Everyone stays in his or her assigned roles until we hear different. De Forest, you're partnered with Gunder in Green cohort. Mara's still assigned to Zam, and you'll be assigned to me—field tactics, mounted combat, and command."

"We weren't... I wasn't going to stay—"

"You got six months left, Mara." Twyla jabbed her finger at Dalin. "And you're wearing my uniform. So you're under my command as well until I hear different. Besides, you weren't gonna run off and leave me with this mess. It's not your style."

Mara wasn't sure if this was directed at her or Dalin.

A hint of Twyla's smile remained. "Being twins, Chris and I have always been connected. But that *gontra* dust"—she shook her head—"it's like being in the same room." She inclined her head toward Mara. "I heard you hit this one with a couple of good shots of the stuff, de Forest. Did it take?"

Mara froze. When she looked at Dalin, his expression confirmed Twyla's casual revelation. But he only said, "Hard to say. Sometimes the response is delayed."

"Too bad," she said. "Far superior to a com system in the field. One of the few bright spots in this assignment for Chris and me."

"Permission to return to my quarters, ma'am?" Mara asked as she stood.

Twyla blinked and then stood as well. "Standard procedure would be to debrief you before you bunk down for the night. But we're going to hold for further instructions." She patted Mara on the shoulder. "Swing by the kitchen and get some food."

Mara gave a sharp nod. "Ma'am." She hurried from the room, her mental shields as strong and cold as she could make them.

She slowed only to avoid sliding in the gritty dust outside the Great Hall. A left turn, then a right, and the Green corridor stretched before her. The lights in the ceiling hadn't been dimmed for the night. Without the predictable routine of compound life, she had no way of knowing what time it was.

Mara pushed open her door, expecting a cold and empty room. Instead, a fire burned merrily in the grate. Several pillows in bright shades of green decorated the bed. Hesitating, she peered down the hall. Had they reassigned her room?

"Mara?" Annelise's familiar voice called. On the other side of the connecting doorway, her partner lounged on a cluster of pillows with Leann, Jahella, and Haleen. "We're eatin' in here 'cause the hall's a wreck."

Tears burning behind her eyes, Mara licked her dry lips and tried to think of something to say that wasn't a lie.

"Why are you in full combat gear?" Jahella asked.

"How's the leg?" asked Leann.

"Zam said she's had quite a time," Annelise answered for her partner. "You all keep eating while I get this Protector squared away." Walking carefully around the pillows, she pushed Mara through the doorway and hugged her.

Tears leaked down Mara's cheeks. "I missed you. Haleen said you were helping your mother so I didn't..." She swallowed hard.

Annelise pulled out of the hug and looked up. Her eyes welled, too. "Here now, don't do that," she soothed. She tugged Mara toward the chair. "I was with my mother, but I left this morning. Got here right before they put us in lockdown."

Opening her partner's wardrobe, Annelise dug around on the shelves. "Let's get you into some comfortable things. Then tea and food in your belly and you'll be good as new."

Mara scrubbed a hand across her eyes and accepted the clothes Annelise handed her.

"Elias told me you met some relations on your journey," she whispered.

An image of Elana and Jameson standing in their kitchen popped into Mara's mind. Her throat tightened again and her shoulders slumped. "I did."

"Why'd you come back here then?" Annelise asked, her tone still hushed.

Mara tugged off her boots and placed them carefully on the floor. "I'm a Protector."

It did help to settle her raw emotions to sit with her friends and eat. The girls took turns telling stories about what they did during the long leave, in the process revealing that the storms had only relented enough for travel in the past week. Mara listened, eating and sipping tea, occasionally nodding and managing a few smiles.

Suddenly, she felt four sets of eyes. "What?" she asked through a mouthful of bread.

"I said, I heard you already met the Protector transferring from West House," Jahella repeated. "And you're sitting there daydreaming. So tell."

Mara wasn't sure how to respond, especially with the men from the Satri militia on their way. She looked at Annelise, who merely shrugged and smiled. Pulling her knees up under her chin, she wrapped her arms around her legs.

"His name is Dalin. He's very tall. Gray eyes, short blond hair. He's good to his horse."

"Do you like him?" Jahella cut in. "Haleen said he had some looks."

Haleen nodded, her eyes sparkling with mischief. "He's very handsome if you like your men tall and thin." She grinned. "C'mon, Mara. Give us a story."

He fogged me and lied about it. He's a great cook and intelligent and keeps secrets. "I...don't know him that well," Mara hedged, though as she spoke she knew it was the truth. "He's going to be Twyla's assistant in mounted combat and field command. You can decide for yourselves."

#

The next afternoon, Mara went to Zam for their first scheduled meeting. The compound hadn't quite returned to normal, but it was clear everyone was expected to carry on as though it had. While planning for the coming round of combat and weapons classes, Zam mentioned that Browns from a large settlement to the south had come to the compound, stayed the night, and left again, taking all of the King's Men except their wounded leader. Mara wondered if Gruffald or any of the men she'd trained with had been part of the group of "Browns" and felt disappointed not to see the guys.

"Mara, for the love of Pete, that's the third time I've asked you how you want to divide the fourteen-year-olds into groups."

"What? I'm sorry, sir," she bit her lip.

Zam scratched the back of his neck and looked at her with exasperation. "It's hard to come back, eh?"

Mara gave a tiny nod.

"Look"—Zam leaned in, lowering his voice—"the game's not over yet, girl. Only way to play is to stay with it."

"Jameson complimented your teaching," she blurted. "I-I gave him a bloody nose the first time we fought."

A huge grin spread across his face. "Did you now? That bugger had it comin', did he?"

"He attacked me in the middle of the woods." Mara tried the arrogant, of-course-I-won shrug and head tilt that Dalin used sometimes.

The combat instructor clapped her on the shoulder. "Well, that bit of cheer earns you some time to get your head straight. Go on then. Come back tomorrow with some ideas about the beginners' class."

Free, Mara's instincts took her to the healers' area. Treyton led her straight back to Ponapali's room.

"He's a trade for the better," Treyton said quietly. "That other King's Man, or whoever he is, nearly tore the room apart. This one is a model patient." Treyton nodded to the guard outside the door.

Mara recognized her as a three-year veteran of the Blue cohort. "Chikako."

"Mara," the girl responded with a nod.

"Twyla sent me," Mara lied.

"The cut in his arm is a deep one," Treyton said, "but he wasn't as lucky as you. Between that wound and one on his side, he lost a lot of blood. Nothing can replace that but time." The healer's face was grave.

"Thank you," she said. She pushed through the door and pulled it shut behind her with a firm click.

Ponapali didn't react to the sounds or her entry. He lay on his back, eyes closed. In repose, his face looked softer, less menacing.

"I'm here to talk to you about the Daughter of the Tree," Mara said.

"The King's Men don't…" Ponapali paused. "It's you." With visible effort, he sat up and opened his eyes.

"Why do you think you recognize me?" she asked, her tone urgent.

"The Tree described you," Ponapali said. "She has spoken of you many times."

"Why did you and your men come here to take me, to take the Daughter?"

The man frowned. He was still a formidable presence, though pale from blood loss and confined to a bed. "It's not safe," he declared. "This war project is collapsing."

"You said I was taken from the King's Men long ago. Lost, you said."

Ponapali shifted and grimaced in pain. Even his lips were pale, the silver in his beard more pronounced. "The first humans to reach this planet were explorers, surveyors, and scientists. The first king of the Commonwealth believed he would find resources on C-7, as this planet was originally called." Sweat began to bead on his brow. Ponapali rubbed at the bandage on his arm.

"Do you require assistance from a healer?" Mara asked.

"No, no." He gave his head a sharp shake, as though trying to dislodge water from his ears. "So the first humans to C-7 found resources and the Tree found them." He laughed, a wet, painful sound. "As the story goes, she scared the darkness out of them." Ponapali took a deep breath and wiped his forehead.

"Before the Tree Prophesies, there was a simple book, a description of the earliest encounters between the Tree and humans. My group has visual records of many of the pages. The Tree told the humans they would have initial success in this planetary system and then face terrible struggles. She told them not to worry 'for those who are part of the Light, my Daughter will protect them.' It is said she took the recorder into her own hands and created drawings of you." Ponapali's voice softened with wonder.

"The first king and each ruler going forward sought the Daughter of the Tree—in part as a sign that the time of struggle is truly at hand, and also so that she may help us in our time of need."

Mara took a step away from the bed and then another until her back was pressed against the cool, smooth wall. From his face and voice it was clear Ponapali believed what he said.

With a sharp cry, he grabbed his head as though holding his skull together. "Were you followed here?" he snapped.

"No," Mara said with sharpness of her own.

Ponapali grunted and lowered one hand. "Our group has watched for the Daughter, searched for the Daughter, under orders from each successive king. We intended to take you into protective custody when you were small. Someone beat us to it." He took in a labored breath. "That's been the only upside to this project falling apart. It led us to you." He arched his back and slammed his head on the bed with a guttural cry.

Mara rushed to the door. "Chikako, get help!"

Ponapali made a gargling sound and blood flecked his lips. "Shield yourself," he hissed. "Mental attack."

As she reached for the energy source and drew power to her personal shield, Mara drew her sword and turned in a slow circle, trying to sense the attack.

Groaning, Ponapali curled into a ball. Mara cast a shield over him as well.

In the space of two breaths, he lifted his dark head, eyes wild. "What did you do?" he asked, blood dribbling into his beard.

"Shielded you."

Eyes glazed with pain he said, "Shielding both of us."

"Who is attacking you? And why?" Yet another critical fact Dalin had kept from her, the possibility of mental assault.

Ponapali wiped his chin with a shaking hand. "The Queen, she wants the King's Men eliminated. We've been hiding since her ascension to the throne—"

When the guard opened the door, Dalin stood behind her.

"Thank you." Mara nodded at the young soldier and motioned for her to close the door.

"Mental attack?" Dalin asked, striding forward.

Mara narrowed her eyes. How did he know?

The older man sighed and gripped the bed covers. Even under duress, he had the presence of a strong leader. "Not the first time," he said. "The Queen has newer recruits who are mentally very strong. And nasty."

Treyton knocked on the door and then entered. "What's happened?" He rushed to his patient's side, stopped. "Please lower your shield and permit me to examine you."

Mara released Ponapali's shield but held on to her own.

Bending forward, the healer gently placed his long fingers on the man's temples. Ponapali convulsed and Treyton staggered back with a cry. Both soldiers rushed to the bed.

Dalin leaned in. "No breath." He lifted the man's wrist. "No pulse."

The healer recovered enough to check the vital signs himself. With a shake of his head, he confirmed Dalin's assessment. "Gone."

Though unsure of her own feelings, she knew Treyton was upset. As she touched his shoulder, Jules pushed the door open. Healers didn't exactly have partners, but Jules would help Treyton sort through the terrible events of the past day.

Dalin didn't speak until the pair had departed. "You put a shield over Ponapali and then dropped it when the healer arrived.

"Yes."

"Why?"

"He was telling me about the mission of the King's Men."

"How did you accomplish that?"

The intensity of the past few minutes fueled Mara's frustrated response. "I knew *he* would be willing to tell me the truth."

A muscle in Dalin's cheek twitched at the jibe.

Tightening her grip on her sword, she glared at him. She maintained eye contact as she sheathed it with an audible snick.

"And?" Dalin finally prompted.

"What the prisoner chose to share is information I will hold until it is required."

He gave her an incredulous look. "And when will that be?"

"For all I know"—Mara checked her shield and barreled ahead—"you did this."

Undisguised surprise passed over Dalin's face and settled into skepticism. "I killed our only source of information about this attack?"

"Not the only source," Mara spit back. "Your men just collected the rest of Ponapali's troops and Garot." She held out her hand and touched her little finger. "You are the only, or one of the very few people at the compound with the training to do this." She touched the next finger. "When Chikako went for help, you were already nearby." She touched the tip of her third finger. "You haven't been able to get through my shield."

Dalin turned to the dead soldier in the plain bed. Mara counted to five, waiting for him to defend himself, to convince her she was wrong. He didn't move. With a shake of her head, she marched out of the room.

Chapter 42

In the course of the next few weeks, riders coming back from the other Protector Houses reported unprecedented shipments of books, the arrival of non-combat faculty, and Brown soldiers showing up to conduct deep search patrols for Gaishan. This would not impact the truce, but rather help to prolong it, everyone was told.

At Northwest Protector House, combat classes resumed along with new classes in reading, writing, and mathematics. After the evening meal each night, one of the new teachers would tell a story of the beginnings of the Commonwealth or the settling of Asattha, gently introducing history beyond life in the settlements.

Mara ate with her friends, taught combat classes, and almost daily rode out on her horse. Occasionally, she felt Dalin test her shields, hoping to reach her through rapport. Each time her mind remained protected by smooth, cold walls. Most meals she picked at her food and didn't join in the regular conversations happening around her anyway. Only Annelise could coax any kind of response out of her and that was usually when she was forcing food onto Mara's plate.

One restless afternoon, Mara paced around her room. Three steps from the hearth to the shared wall with Annelise. Five steps from the bed to the door. Dalin was the one who fogged her, exposed her to what one of the books referred to as *gontra* pollen. Her abilities developed from there. *Gontra* pollen had a wide range of effects on different people, according to Twyla. But since she hadn't admitted any of those abilities to her senior Protector, the only person she could talk to in rapport was Dalin.

And Dalin, the liar, was busy.

Coordinating the delivery and use of all the new materials arriving, as well as the sequencing of new classes being offered, took most of his time outside of regular cohort duties. Two books on her bed—one used and one new, both about the history of the Commonwealth—were evidence of Dalin's efforts.

A story was circulating that a large settlement to the south, called Satri, was sending most of the books. And while a few dozen of the rarest volumes were on loan, the rest were for the compound to keep. According to the Protectors with friends or family in the other compounds, the same changes were taking place across the entire territory. Better food for affordable trade was the bigger news in the settlements, but they were receiving shipments of books as well.

Crouching down, Mara traced the tally marks on her worn stone floor. How many of the fifty-three had died and how many had been fogged and smuggled away? In a few months, she'd graduate from the Protector Corps. And then she could give orders to herself. Orders to find these people maybe.

Mara taught with Zam and completed her regular shifts on watch, but she had so much time now. She could roam anywhere in the compound, including out to the garden or the practice field. The habit of remaining in quarters was hard to break. The habit of preparation, even harder to shake loose. Every day she checked her gear, checked her horse, adjusted and packed non-perishable supplies. No one was going to call her to the front lines, but she'd be ready anyway.

Before, she'd enjoyed the mostly private space of her small, cold room. She hadn't been content as a Protector, but she had little ambition for herself that wasn't linked directly to ending the war. The few months of freedom had reset her expectations of what life could be.

Though the noise and constant contact with people had never bothered her before, it was easier to think away from all the other soldiers. Unable to stop herself, she went to site of her last fight nearly every day. At least she and Rowan both enjoyed the ride. And her new project needed a lot of attention out there. Pressing her fingers to the tally marks in a silent promise, Mara stood and reached for her jacket.

"I can't believe you threatened him, Annelise!" Gunder's voice was loud and angry enough to carry through the connecting door.

"Someone had to say it. And, anyway, he came to me."

"What? Why would he—"

"He's worried about Mara, same as us. Asked where to find her. So I said we knew he was darkness itself in a fight, but that didn't matter when it was all us Greens against just him." Annelise sounded proud of herself.

"Maybe it wasn't him that upset her—" Gunder tried.

"Don't you take that stranger's side. He said or did something to hurt Mara. It's his problem, I told him, and he has exactly one chance to fix it."

Mara slipped out her door with a near smile on her face. Annelise threatened Dalin? If only she could've seen it.

#

Dismounting from her horse, Mara checked the position of the sun. The two hours before dark should be enough time. She followed the crushed grass marking her usual path until she reached the small sapling.

"Hello," she greeted it, giving the tiny tree a light stroke across the highest of the silvery leaves.

In short order, she covered Rowan with a blanket and connected the picket rope. Mara and the baby tree had been working to grow roots back to its mother. In the rapport space, it was much easier to share energy with the sapling. She also found it much easier there to work on another task the Tree had given her: breaking down the wall in her mind. It was closer to crumbling, memories returning as each stone loosened. In rapport, the memories were easier to deal with. She could watch them at a safe distance and carefully tuck the images away.

With the wall coming down, the loss of her family was finally real, so, if anything, that was probably what made her look sad to her friends. She wasn't sad about Dalin being too busy. Or about Dalin avoiding her all day—only to sit next to her at meals and say absolutely nothing.

She'd been his mission and an old family friend. The intimacy of rapport and the time together had fooled her into thinking they fit together as partners and more. Her instincts for battle, for the rightness of fighting alongside someone, clearly didn't transfer off the battlefield.

Multiple scans of the clearing confirmed she was alone as usual. The ground had been softening as the temperature warmed, but it was cool and damp for prolonged sitting. Using two more blankets, one as a pad and one as a wrap, she readied her mind and entered the rapport space for the clearing. Nearly identical to the real place in every way, except sunnier, the clearing was her favorite spot.

If the formerly Protected Territory was to be connected with the rest of the continent, the Tree should be connected as well. She bore some resemblance to a grove-creating species of tree from the Origin, the dendrology books said. But the creation of a root network so large took hundreds and hundreds of years.

Mara wasn't entirely sure what the Tree meant when she said she was young compared to her sisters. But linking the seeds Mara had planted to each other and ultimately to her seemed like a good way to help along the expansion.

The position of the sun moved slowly, but the warmth didn't change. Tiring from the energy work, Mara snuggled down on the blanket for a short nap.

#

A hard shake of her shoulder woke her.

"Mara? Not like Ponapali, please—"

Dalin's voice sounded frantic, his callused fingers checking the pulse in her wrist and neck.

Grabbing his hand, she opened her eyes. "I'm alive. Just I was…I was sleeping."

With a startled expression, Dalin sat back on his heels. "Your eyes are completely black."

"What? That's not possible." Dread filled her stomach as she sat up abruptly, and her vision blurred. "We were in the root network." She gestured at the sapling with a rueful smile. "But, well, maybe that makes me more fogged than usual."

Guilt clouded Dalin's gray eyes. But before he could speak, she said, "I planted the second-to-last *gontra* seed. I give it energy every day so we can grow roots long enough to reach the other seeds we planted and then the Tree."

Dalin's hand cupped her cheek and tilted her face toward his. "Your eyes are blue again." With his thumb, he traced the skin above her cheekbone. "The energy you're giving is draining you. I've been"—he cleared his throat—"everyone has been worried about you, how thin and tired you look."

Disappointment captured the hope she'd felt at his appearance. With a small shift, she pulled away from his touch. Dalin was the kind of officer who made sure the troops maintained top fighting form. That's what this was about, why he'd asked Annelise about her.

With a frown, Mara touched one of the leaves and said, "Banquet's over for today." She stroked a leaf as she stood, then wrapped her arms around herself. "My memories started coming back," she said.

A chill breeze whipped through the branches around them.

"What memories?" Dalin stood too, and stepped off the blanket. He reached down to shake it out and fold it.

"My childhood in Satri, at least a little from that time anyway. You and me, we were together a lot, with our mothers. And you were there at my house the night I was taken. The vision I had, the dream—it was yours, your memory of the night I was kidnapped. I know now because I can remember that night from my own point of view. I remember running, being traded from one person to the next, and ending up with Elias." She paused and looked down at the little tree. "I lost almost everything."

Taking the folded fabric from him, she pressed it to her chest. "You told me a lot of things at the beginning but you left out a lot, too." Just like their first conversation in this spot, the air felt close and charged around them.

He reached out his hand and she took it, dropping the blanket in favor of the warmth from his body. For the first time in rapport, they wore the same house uniform. Dalin pulled her close for a hug and dropped his shields enough for her to feel his relief at holding her. The messy, turbulent feelings she'd accidentally sensed in Satri were there alongside his current concern for her health.

"I'm sorry for not telling you everything about the *gontra* dust, how it can trigger mental rapport."

"I sort of knew," Mara said. "Not everything, but I had a basic guess. Just hearing Twyla say it..."

Dalin squeezed her hand. "So many people have an interest in you and I received so many conflicting sets of directions and orders. At the time, the best course of action seemed to tell you as little as possible. I was trying to avoid getting the competing interests even more tangled."

"We can't be partners if you don't tell me the truth," Mara said, pulling back to look up at him.

"I know."

"Or anything else."

For the first time since Candle's Promise, Dalin's looked at her with heated intention and interest. A smile ghosted across his mouth as he said, "Oh?"

With a full grin, Mara took them both out of rapport only to nearly fall on her face. Her legs couldn't support her weight and she dropped to one knee, groaning and holding her head.

"Can you ride?" Dalin asked urgently.

She wobbled her way upright, Dalin's steadying hand under her elbow. Taking a hesitant step toward Rowan and then heaving herself upward, she muttered, "I felt fine in the clearing."

The familiar feel of the saddle brought Mara fully awake. She reached back and drew her sword, catching the last bit of sun on the blade. "The shadow you warned me about when we first met, I think it's gone," she said.

"For now." Dalin stood right next to her, as though she might fall.

"The Protector Project is changing," Mara said. "That matters less now because I know who I am, where I come from." She leaned past Rowan's ears and kissed Dalin on the cheek. "Even here I can be more than just a soldier." She straightened and sheathed her sword.

Before Dalin could reach for her, before he could say anything, Mara tapped Rowan's sides and urged the horse into a gallop. Dalin would follow.

The Gaishan weren't real. But the person who created them was. They had a lot of work to do.

ACKNOWLEDGMENTS

My favorite book, the book that started it all for me, is *A Wrinkle in Time* by Madeline L'Engle. It opened my mind to a world of possibilities and the main character is a girl! Unfortunately, not many other science fiction books were being published during that decade for people under eighteen. To fill the void, my father loaned me *Stranger in a Strange Land* by Robert Heinlein. And a few years later, the boy I most admired in all of middle school recommended *Dune* by Frank Herbert, *Foundation* by Isaac Asimov, and *Lord Foul's Bane* by Stephen R. Donaldson. So of course I read those too.

With so much of my reading life steeped in the rich worlds of science fiction and fantasy, it's no wonder the idea for this novel was the synthesis of a dream, an obscure Frank Herbert and Bill Ransom book called *The Ascension Factor*, and the movie *The Village* by M. Knight Shyamalan. As I drafted and revised *The Protector Project*, other favorites came to mind, including *The Blue Sword* by Robin McKinley, *Ender's Game* by Orson Scott Card, and pretty much everything written by Tamora Pierce.

I've been talking about this book for a long time, from way back when it was a few scribbled ideas in a journal. So my first acknowledgment goes to the friends in my graduate program and my teacher friends who heard my early "well I was thinking about writing a novel with a sentient tree and teenage soldiers" ramblings and responded with positive noises. Especially you, Mark O., I think you said something sweet like, "I don't usually like science fiction, but I like *this*."

After two full years of sitting at my kitchen table writing by hand (that's using a pen and paper), the first draft of *The Protector Project* clocked in at 138,000 words. The writing experts say it's helpful to have beta readers. And, well, it takes a very nice person to commit to 138,000 words of raw novel. Some friends just read bits and pieces with their own children or students—thank you to Jan D., Stephanie M., Cathy, Shawn, Roger, and Natasha for that. I want to thank Jonas, Wanda, Stacy, Simone, Dan, Jennifer L., and Jason for taking the plunge with the whole darn thing. I also want to thank Abbey M., my first real student reader. When Abbey said, "It seems like it could be a real book," that was high praise indeed. Special thanks to Kyle Cauthron and Bree Ervin for the critical and yet constructive feedback.

Colorado is home to some wonderful, expert writing communities. From weeks with the Colorado Writing Project and the Denver Writing Project, to conferences through Rocky Mountain Fiction Writers and Pikes Peak Writers, I have grown tremendously. Through my good fortune to participate in these groups, I've also found some terrific friends. My critique group, the Northern Colorado Writer's Workshop, has been around for more than forty years and birthed some of Colorado's most well-known science fiction and fantasy writers. Not only do I learn a lot every meeting, but also I'm incredibly grateful to know the members as writers and people. And though I'm a new member, I also want to thank the Heart of Denver Romance Writers, one of the local Denver RWA chapters, for their kindness and support.

It was through a pitch session at the national Romance Writers of America conference that this book found a home. Thank you so much to the conference organizers for the wonderful experiences and opportunities to pitch my work. Additional thanks goes to the online YARWA (Young Adult RWA) chapter for the Day of YA and in general for creating a home for YA writers within RWA.

As I enter this next phase of my career as a writer, I must thank the entire Boroughs Publishing Group family, including Christine Ashworth and all the other wonderful writers I've met online. Thank you, thank you to editor-in-chief Chris Keeslar for requesting the full manuscript. Triple-scoop-hot-fudge-sundae thanks to Camille Hahn, editor extraordinaire, for loving the book as much as I do. *The Protector Project* is stronger because of your thoughtful questions and attention to detail.

T.S. Eliot wrote, "Home is where one starts from." To me, home means family, and I have a lot of families to thank. First I want to thank my taekwondo families at United Martial Arts and Parker Academy of Martial Arts, specifically Master Theresa Byrne and Master Chris Turnquist. Mara and I are both better fighters because of you. Next, I want to thank my work family: Jann, Julie, Valerie, Barb, Courtney, Denise, Brad, and Ian, as well as the larger community of teachers in gifted education.

Just as Meg, the main character from *A Wrinkle in Time*, gained the courage and knowledge from her home to attempt the impossible, so have I had the love and encouragement from my own home to bring a book into the world. Thank you to my parents, my sister and brother, and my husband for your unwavering confidence. Simone and Phoebe, my gorgeous daughters, thank you for your patience and your inspiration. No matter what happens next, when I look at you, I know I've helped create something special.

ABOUT THE AUTHOR

Jenna Lincoln loves to read, write, and talk about reading and writing. She spent many happy years as a language arts teacher doing just those things.

After dabbling in *X-Files*, *Firefly,* and *Supernatural* fan fiction, Jenna got serious about building her own imaginary world, big enough to get lost in for a long, long time. When she comes back to reality, Jenna enjoys her home in beautiful Colorado with her husband and two daughters.

Did you enjoy this book? Drop us a line and say so! We love to hear from readers, and so do our authors. To connect, visit www.boroughspublishinggroup.com online, send comments directly to info@boroughspublishinggroup.com, or friend us on Facebook and Twitter. And be sure to check back regularly for contests and new releases in your favorite subgenres of romance!

Are you an aspiring writer? Check out www.boroughspublishinggroup.com/submit and see if we can help you make your dreams come true.

CPSIA information can be obtained
at www.ICGtesting.com
Printed in the USA
LVOW10s0109200418
574225LV00010B/286/P